SERIES 1 THE BOOK 6

DARKSLAYER

Chaos
at the Castle

CRAIG HALLORAN

THE DARKSLAYER: Chaos at the Castle
By Craig Halloran

Copyright © 2013 by Craig Halloran
Print Edition
Revised April 2015

TWO-TEN BOOK PRESS
P.O. Box 4215, Charleston, WV 25364

ISBN eBook: 978-0-9896216-3-2
ISBN Paperback: 978-0-9896216-4-9

THE DARKSLAYER is a registered trademark, #77670850
http://www.thedarkslayer.net

Cover Illustration by David Chen
Interior Illustrations by Ernie Chan
Map by Gillis Bjork

Publisher's Note
This book is a work of fiction. Names, characters, places, and incidents either are the product of the author's imagination or are used fictitiously, and any resemblance to actual persons, living or dead, events, or locales is entirely coincidental.

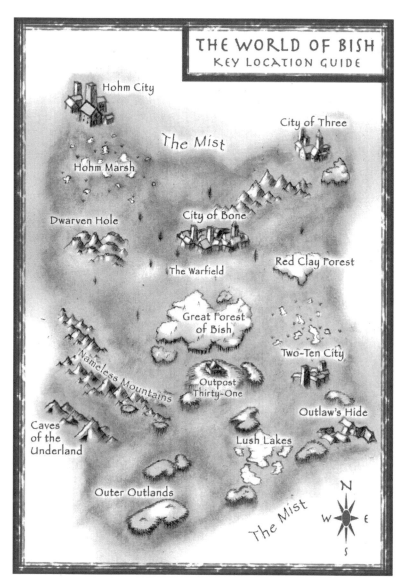

THE WORLD OF BISH
KEY LOCATION GUIDE

Hohm City

City of Three

The Mist

Hohm Marsh

Dwarven Hole

City of Bone

Red Clay Forest

The Warfield

Great Forest
of Bish

Two-Ten City

Nameless Mountains

Outpost
Thirty-One

Outlaw's Hide

Caves
of the
Underland

Lush Lakes

Outer Outlands

The Mist

N
W · E
S

CHAPTER 1

B *LINK.*
Eep looked like he'd been chewed up by a dragon and spit out. He lay quivering on the cave floor. His eye was red. Swollen. The wings on his back were mangled, and many of his teeth were broken. He let out a ragged hiss.

"Massterssss ..."

"I hope you have the Keys, Imp," Verbard said, his eyes glowering with silver fire.

Eep opened his palms. They were empty.

"Vicious!" Verbard snapped.

The hulking figure emerged from the shadows, snatched Eep by the neck and squeezed.

Verbard kept his rage in check as Catten chuckled at his side.

"Brother," Catten began, "we will get the Keys in due time, if need be, but let's find out what happened first before you pull the imp apart, like old times."

Verbard wanted nothing more than to destroy something or someone, but Eep was his most trustworthy servant. Master Kierway wanted his head, but Master Sinway had saved it. Jottenhiem was a loyal soldier and comrade, but even he couldn't be trusted. Now, his brother, Catten, had returned, and that only made him all the more uncomfortable. He should be relieved, but he was far from it.

"What happened, Eep?" he said, looking right into the imp's great eye.

Eep's eye bulged in the socket. He could not speak.

"Ease up!"

Eep gasped.

"Thank you, Mastersss—"

Verbard snatched his snake-like tongue and said, "It's Master."

Eep glanced at Catten, then back at Verbard and nodded.

Verbard released his tongue.

"Pardons, Master Verbard. Ah … the skinny man I found under heavy guard. I had him, but a man, a large man, smote me with white magic. Cracked bones. Eep had no choice. Return or be banished."

"Next time," Verbard said, "I'll have to keep watch on things. Can you find this man again, if you have to?"

"Certainly, Masterss … er … Master."

"You were supposed to bring the Keys or the man, Eep. You have failed," Verbard said, letting a wave of energy course through him. Eep wasn't of any use to him now. The creature was broken and would need time to heal. He couldn't tolerate failure. Not from the imp or any other. He'd make an example of the imp, and he'd do it now.

Save your energy, Brother. Catten had entered his mind. *Banish the imp. Bring him back later. The Keys can wait for now.*

Verbard wanted to smite his brother. Everybody. But, he let his magic ease.

It's time we talked about the Keys.

"Be gone, Imp!" Verbard ordered.

"But Master, I hungers," Eep hissed.

"Be gone!"

Blink.

Catten still sat on his throne, sipping port.

"Up, Brother."

Catten rose, poured another goblet and handed it to Verbard.

Verbard took his seat. Eyeing his brother, he sipped.

"Alright, Brother. Now that we are alone, tell me everything. And don't mince words. I want it all. Your resurrections. Master Sinway's plans. This ludicrous notion that the underlings once lived in this city, and what is so important about these Keys."

Catten's gold eyes brightened. His voice was almost cheerful. He said, "Certainly, Brother. Where would you have me start?"

Verbard patted the Orb of Imbibing that now rested within the folds of his robes. Its presence gave him comfort. An edge he didn't have before with his brother.

"And don't be humble, Catten. It's unlike you. It's difficult to think that you are actually you, seeing how you have changed bodies. It will take some getting used to. Now tell me about your resurrection?"

Catten held his fist to his mouth and coughed.

"Unpleasant. It was bad enough when the Darkslayer ran me through, but merging into another body was far worse than that. The pain was excruciating—"

"I don't care how much it hurt! What happened?"

Catten stiffened, a darkness falling over him as he came closer and said, "I was getting to that, Brother."

That's more like it.

"Good. Continue."

"Master Sinway was alone as he moved me from one body to another. It seemed not all underlings were fit for my powers. Some died and others remained blind in the process."

"I don't care," Verbard said, taking another sip. "What happened?"

"There is a tomb in his Castle filled with many well-preserved underlings. He merged me with one of them."

It was one thing to raise a dead underling, but quite another to raise one without a body. The eyes of the underlings held many powers, and on occasion those eyes, if powerful enough, would be collected and turned over to the master underling. Verbard always suspected he hoarded the magic in them. That they gave him power.

"He merged you with the dead?"

"Yes. The corpse with the best likeness to me. My eyes and essence filled his body." He fanned out his hands. "And now here I am." He coughed. "I lay catatonic at first while Master Sinway let me recover. He told me about your mission and that you would need help. I, like you, Brother, felt him to be insane, but the part about the underlings living above in Bone might be true. He showed me glimpses of his past. He took me across the world. I saw where we underlings finally have men on the run. They are collapsing. Darkslayer or not."

Verbard rubbed his finger under his chin. "There are many humans, Brother. The city above alone holds many more than all of us."

"But, they are not united. They squabble with one another. They fight over power and gold. 'We have corrupted them before, and we can corrupt them again,' Sinway says."

Men could be bought, that much was certain, but Verbard would rather kill them then work with them. After all, the greed of men had led to the fall of Outpost Thirty One and many others. But taking the entire city of Bone still seemed ridiculous.

"Am I to assume that we are to live among them? Make them our slaves?"

"We will use fear against them. Taking one Castle, this Castle Almen, will lead to the capture of others."

"Does this have something to do with the Keys?"

Catten smiled. "'The Keys are only one means to an end,' Master Sinway said. Having them could aid us in the battle, but they are no guarantee of victory. But, he insists that we acquire them, for they are powerful weapons in our enemy's hands."

"Or they are worthless baubles? Hah! Kierway has spent years trying to find them, and now we are being told we don't need them. Tell me more, Catten. Something is not well with Sinway. You know that. I know that. What did you find out?"

"We should not speak of such things, Brother," Catten said. He eyed the Vicious.

"What? Do you think the Vicious can send a message? It can neither write nor talk. They follow orders. They kill. Now out with it, Catten. What did Sinway reveal to you?"

I feel your suspicions are correct, Brother. He's going crazy.

Verbard sank back into his chair. Catten was lying. Or was he? Verbard hoped that he wasn't. If Master Sinway was falling to madness, that thought was comforting. It would lend a greater understanding to it all. Besides, destroying the humans and taking their city wasn't a bad idea. Just a grand one. A grander one than he'd ever imagined before, hence opening the doorway to his doubts.

"Why do you say that, Brother? Is it because of this conquest, or was it something else?"

"Brother, I'm elated with the idea of overtaking the city, if not the entire world. I'm tired of sitting beneath the world of men, and clearly Master Sinway is as well. There is something ancient that he knows, that he remembers, that has come to life and begun to burn. A vengeance hotter than the hottest of fires. An impatience that spreads like a forest fire on a gusty day. He's bringing them out, Brother."

A deep crease formed on Verbard's brow as he sat up and leaned forward.

"The legions."

Verbard nodded.

"How many?"

"All of them."

The Legions consisted of every armed force in the Underland: soldiers, mages, clerics armed with metal and magic from head to toe. They had defended the Underland in centuries long gone, and now they were coming above ground. They would be a black plague on the land. They would destroy everything in their path. If they won, they won everything. If they lost, they lost everything. The Underland would not be defended. It was an insane idea.

Catten shrugged.

Verbard smiled. He loved the idea.

"Well, Brother, let the havoc begin. Jottenhiem!"

CHAPTER 2

"**N**AY, RAYAL! THEY CANNOT ENTER. Your father left the strictest of orders," the sentry said. The tall figure stood, spear at his side, in the entrance of Castle Kling.

It was a spectacular thing. Spires jutting into the moonlit sky, copper tiles twinkling like gold. It was the tallest building in all the City of Bone.

Georgio gawped at its highest point.

"Let me in, Cletus!" Rayal shouted back. "I demand it."

"You can come, and your guards, certainly Rayal, but not the others. Klings and Royal Klings only," the man returned.

The sentry stood firm in his coat of mail and helmet that bore the Royal insignia. A longsword was strapped at his waist. Georgio could see callouses on the insides of his palms as he held them out. This soldier had seen many battles, maybe even been to the Warfield. There was just something about him, but still, he was mindful of the raven-haired woman who seethed with outrage before him.

Her fists were balled up at her sides. She said, "Cletus! My father has his affairs, and I have mine. I owe these two my life." She gestured to Melegal and Haze.

Melegal was draped over Quickster's back. Georgio held him tight. The skinny woman he thought he recognized as Haze. She was one of the women who had rescued him from Tonio and McKnight. She was draped over the shoulder of a large man, called Brak. A girl, Jubilee, hung on to Brak's arm.

Cletus shook his head. "I don't care if they saved your father, you mother, and the grand ones of your family. They are not coming in, Rayal. I'm not losing my head over them, and you might just lose yours as well if you don't get inside these walls now."

"Don't you dare talk to me like that, you oaf. I'll have you quartered."

Cletus tugged at his beard. His face flushed.

"Er, Rayal, you know I am fond of you, but I cannot abandon my duty, no matter how much I'd want to." He bowed. "Forgive my directness, Rayal, but underlings!" He peered over the streets behind them. "They crawl through the city now, leading monsters and horrors that I've not even heard of. I've seen underlings, Rayal. I've seen what they do to people. I cannot bear the thought of them getting hold of you. Please, come in so we can talk about this. We'll find another remedy for those people." He looked Georgio and the rest of them over as if they were little more than urchins. "Perhaps a supply of food and water will help."

"Pig," Rayal said.

Georgio heard the girl, Jubilee, giggle. He turned. Brak's eyes locked on his. There was something there. Something familiar. Something sad in the man's eyes. Blinking, he turned towards Rayal. Everything from her hips to her lips was perfect. The young woman was angry, but poised. She was one of the most gorgeous women he'd ever seen. How the sentry, Cletus, resisted her, he did not know, but he'd dive into a barrel of fire for her if she asked. Wiping his sweaty palms on his clothes, he realized something. *I like brunettes.* He cleared his throat.

"We'll go," Georgio said.

Rayal spun on her heel. "Excuse me?"

"Uh ... I said, 'We'll go.'"

She reached over and twirled Georgio's curly locks in her fingers. "What was your name again?"

He blushed. "Ah ... Georgio. Uh—"

"How well do you know these people, Georgio? Are you their leader?"

"No. I'm no one's leader, but Melegal is my friend." He patted Melegal on the back. "Well, not really a friend so much. More of an acquaintance. But we've been together a long time. I used to live with him and Venir."

Georgio saw that Brak's gaze fell on him and that his eyes narrowed.

"What?" He shrugged. "It's true." He looked back at Rayal, smiling a little. "I don't know those two so well, but the woman over his shoulder saved me once. She saved me from that monster, Tonio."

"What!" Rayal stood up to her full height. Her nostrils flared.

Cletus stepped forward, reaching for her arm.

She jerked away.

"Rayal, Please! You must come inside now. We've word underlings are all over. The menace grows, Rayal!"

"Silence, Cletus." She cusped her hands under Georgio's face and calmly said, "Georgio, tell me more about this Tonio. When did this happen? What does he look like?"

She smells so good. So beautiful.

Rayal pinched his cheeks.

"Tell me!"

Georgio swallowed hard and started blurting words out. "He's a monster! A murderer! Insane. He keeps trying to kill Venir. He's dead, but lives. He tried to kill us days ago in the stables. His face is split. Venir killed him once, but he lives again. No, he killed him twice, actually."

Rayal's eyes were wide as saucers. Her delicate fingers slid from Georgio's face.

"The boy rambles, Rayal. Come in," Cletus said.

She staggered back. Lost and uncertain.

"Did you know him?"

Rayal nodded. "Does Detective Melegal know all this?"

Georgio felt chilly. It seemed he'd already said more than he should have. And this woman was a Royal. No matter how wonderful she seemed, Melegal and Venir both had warned him Royals could not be trusted. *What do I do?* He wasn't a fast talker either. Not like Melegal or Lefty. He wondered how his former halfling friend was doing. He could use his quick wits right now.

"I can't say," Georgio said. "All I think he knows leads me up to the last time I left Bone. And I was getting ready to leave Bone again when I ran across him again."

That part was most of the truth. He'd seen Melegal only once before, this time in Bone, but they hadn't said much, and there'd been no mention of Tonio. Just the Blond-Haired Butcher.

"Sentries!" Cletus said. The soldier grabbed Rayal by the wrist and held her fast.

"Let me go, Cletus!"

"Stop that!" Georgio said. He jumped off Quickster and grabbed at Cletus.

Whop!

Cletus slugged him right across the jaw.

Georgio's knees wobbled. It might have been the hardest he'd ever been hit.

Rayal fought against her bonds.

"Cletus! Unhand me, you pig-headed soldier!"

Half a dozen men in coats of chainmail and brandishing spears stormed out the door. They shoved Georgio, Brak, Haze, and Jubilee back with the tips of their spears.

"That man comes with me, Cletus!" Rayal said. She kicked, thrashed and screamed. "Bring them in the castle with me, or all of your soldiers will suffer the penalty!"

The soldiers paused.

"Get her in there!" Cletus said. "Lord Kling will show no mercy to any who don't follow his direct orders. I won't either! The guillotine is wet enough with blood already."

"Unhand me!"

Catching her eyes, Georgio started to wave. The butt of a spear caught him in the back of his head. When he looked up again, it was pouring rain. The angry wails of the beautiful woman were gone. He rubbed the knot on his head. *I hope I see her again.*

The soldier named Cletus stood at the door with his hands on his hips.

"Get out of here, you over-sized urchins! Hide before the underlings get you. If you stick around any longer, we'll be more than happy to put you out of your misery ourselves."

Wiping the rain from his eyes, Georgio took Quickster by the reins and backed away until he could see the gate of the castle no more.

Brak and Jubilee followed.

"What are we going to do now?" Jubilee asked. Her eyes were bright. Inquisitive.

Georgio didn't know who the big lout Brak and the droopy girl Jubilee were, but he could only assume they were Melegal's friends. If Melegal woke up, maybe he'd know what to do with them.

Something exploded in the air. Everyone flinched. Despite the rain, smoke and fires could be seen lighting up the city in all directions. The City of Bone always had an element of danger, but now it was taken over by something dark and eerie. He wondered if Billip and Mikkel were all right. Perhaps they needed him.

He put his hand on Melegal's back. The thief was so scrawny he could feel his bones. *He's breathing, I think?* He shook him a little, but nothing happened. He knew what a light sleeper Melegal was. A dropped feather would wake him. *I just need to get out of here! That's what Me would do.*

Scratching his head, Georgio looked at Brak. "Don't you have any ideas? You're the oldest who's awake. I just want to get out of here."

Brak leered over at him. Big faced. Unreadable. "I just want to find Venir."

"What? Why would you want to find Venir?"

Jubilee started to chime in. "Because that's his—"

Georgio felt the muscles tighten behind his neck. Something creeped and crawled over the cobblestone road nearby. He ripped out his sword.

"Underlings!"

CHAPTER 3

"WHERE'S MY DAUGHTER, PALOS!"

It was Kam. Half naked. Bleeding. Green eyes blazing with mystic fury unlike anything Lefty had ever seen before. Earlier, she'd been dead; he was certain of it, but now she was alive. Alive as ever. Radiant. Powerful. But, one thing was different: the dark red gemstones glowing through her fist.

Palos chuckled. A bubble of snot formed in his nose and busted. The man's arms were tied behind his back where he sat on a high-backed chair alongside the roaring fire place. His ankles were bound to the chair legs. Sweat dripped down his paunchy face, and his hair was wet and matted on his head. Lefty had never seen the polished man so out of sorts before.

"You won't kill me, Kam." He coughed. "You wouldn't let the halfling kill me, nor would you. You are a good woman, unwilling to cross the line of evil." He eyed her cleavage and licked his lips. "But, you certainly have some very wicked ways. Mmmm. Very wicked indeed."

Kam shoved her fist under his chin. "I'll show you wicked, Palos."

"By all means—"

She slung her arm back and punched him in the nose.

Palos howled. "You broke my nose! You broke my nose, you—"

Smack!

Palos's head rocked back into the chair. He fell silent.

Kam shook her glowing fist in his face. "I'll bust every bone in your face if I have to."

Lefty flinched. Kam was already mad enough at him for getting her into this mess. He'd tried to make it up by saving her daughter, and he'd failed at that. He eased back towards the door.

Without even turning, Kam said, "Don't you move, Lefty. I'm not finished with you either."

A chair slid across the floor and scooped his feet out from under him. "Sit!"

His chin dipped down into his chest. "Y-Yesss, Kam."

Lefty had been nothing short of miserable for days, if not weeks. Palos had ruined his life. Even worse, he'd ruined Kam's.

But at that moment, Lefty felt a little sympathy for the Prince of Thieves. The man was rattled. His bloody nose dripped onto his chest, and his eyes watered in anguish. As much of a demented oddball as Palos had become, it seemed the man's glory days were at end.

Kam was going to find out what she wanted. Lefty was convinced. Even if she had to pull it out of the man one piece at a time. Something bad was going to happen. He sat still, his tiny feet dripping on the floor.

"Kam, you cannot do this to me," Palos said. "My father and your father are allies. Release me, and I'll see no harm comes to you." He shrugged. "Why, I'll even see if we can't somehow locate your daughter, or at least find one that bears a close resemblance to her." He flashed a bloody smile. "Eh?"

Palos was as disgusting a man as there ever was, but he was no fool. No, Kam knew he wouldn't give any information up that might lead to his death. Still, she could feel the fear in the man, actually feel it. And that wasn't all she could feel.

Lefty's heart pounded like a frightened rabbit's where he sat frozen in his chair. And beyond the door she had sealed, a revolution was taking place. Palos's loyalists were at odds with his usurpers. The Prince of Thieves was undone, unless reinforcement of some sort arrived.

She grabbed a log poker and stuck it in the fireplace

"What are you doing, Kam?" Palos said. He eyed her and the poker. "The fire is plenty hot from where I am sitting."

Kill him. I can find your daughter. Kill him. It's time to serve. The gems were speaking to her. The force within had saved her. And now, whatever it was, she owed it service. But at what cost?

Kam's hand drifted to her stomach where the hole that almost took her life had been. It recoiled. Her stomach was in knots. Something bad was happening to her. But the power was so strong! So fulfilling. The gems gave her strength and a confidence that she'd never felt before.

Not looking at him, she twisted the poker in the flames.

"Where is my daughter, Palos? And before you offer a foolish response, I'll remind you that I stuffed Thorn in a fireplace once and I'd have no reservations against doing the same to you."

Palos swallowed.

"Kam, I'm not privy to that information after it reaches a certain point. I merely give the order. Collect the gold. Many other hands work under my directions. Eh, it's a thief's way of avoiding attachment." He blinked the sweat from his eyes. "Ahem. For example, if I were to sell something or someone as precious as you, I wouldn't want to be privy to where you went. I might be tempted to steal you back. And that would not be good for my business."

She jammed the poker deeper into the fire, scattering the coals.

Her voice took a darker tone behind her clenched teeth. "Palos, where is my daughter?"

"Uh … er … Kam, surely even you can sense that my father will not stand for this. I am —"

"A wretch." She jammed the poker into the coals.

"A bastard." Again she did it.

"A swine," she said, pulling it out and eyeing the glow of the red-hot tip.

Kill him! I will find your daughter. Delay me further, and I will not aid. You serve.

The urgings were strong, compelling, even forceful. She tried to open her fist, to release the gems. She didn't need them now. Her fingers were locked around them like a vice. *Blast. What have I done?*

Kill him! I have waited long. It is time to go.

"Agreed, Kam," Palos said. He groaned and shifted in his chair,

"I am all those things and worse. But please consider: you can make plenty more children with those lovely loins of yours. As a matter of fact, I would be a bit surprised if a new seed was not sprouting inside you now."

Kam took the red hot poker and laid it on Palos's seat between his knees and crotch. His eyes widened. His lips trembled.

"And I assure you, Palos: if you don't tell me where my daughter is, you'll have no more seeds to spill."

"I admire your obsession with my nether region, Kam. It's simply thrilling, even in my condition."

Slap!

"Where's my daughter, Palos?"

"Do you ever get tired of repeating yourself, you milk-laden whore? I'll tell you nothing!"

Kam grabbed him by the hair on top of his head.

"We'll see about that."

Twirling her fingers in the air, the leather cords that bound him groaned. His wrists and ankles turned blood red.

"Stop this, you maddened wench! I'll have your head for this!"

"Lefty, find Diller! Bring him here!" she ordered.

Lefty slid from his seat and looked around uncertainly. "But, how can I?"

"How can you not, halfling fool that lost my daughter!"

Quickly, Lefty made his way to the door, but it would not open. "Uh, K—"

With a wave of her hand, the door flew open. "Hurry up, Halfling!"

Lefty dashed out onto the balcony, peeking inside one last time. The door slammed shut.

"As for you, Palos! Your misery has just begun if you don't tell me what I want to know." She stepped behind him and drove her fingers into his temples. She muttered. Incanted. Locked her mind with his. "Where is my daughter, Palos?"

Palos was a silver fox. Quick. Shifty. Darting through a dark forest laughing.

She tracked him down with hounds.

He evaded.

Her hunters shot at him with arrows.

He disappeared. One moment, Palos stood alone on a rocky hilltop, looking down on her, a fox with his eyes in his mouth. In the next moment he was standing behind her with a dagger at her throat.

"Clever, Kam, but like the lactating fool you are, you've done just what I wanted," he said, licking her ear.

Once a woman of power and fury, she found herself under his will. Bound by his vile thoughts. Penetrating her inner weakness. Bringing her to her knees. Once again, she was helpless. His prisoner.

"No, you shall not take me. You shall not take my baby!" she said, trying to yell back, but her voice was weak.

Palos smote her to the ground. "I take whoever and whatever I please." He grabbed her by the head and pulled her down into his suffocating darkness.

CHAPTER 4

"F INALLY!" CASS WAS PANTING.

How long and how far the druid woman had been running after Chongo, she didn't know, but she couldn't have been more grateful that he stopped. Transforming from a large, slender white wolf, she returned back to her lithe form. She rolled from her hands and knees onto her back, still fighting for breath.

Chongo, both tongues hanging out of his big mouths, panted over her.

"I didn't think such a big dog could run so far and so fast before." She reached up and patted on of his cold wet snouts. "You really are a thing of beauty. Like a gallant stallion and mighty lion in one."

He sneezed all over her.

"Uck! Yet lacking in their grace." She giggled. Grabbed him by thick fur under his neck and pulled herself back to her feet. "Now, Chongo, what is it you finally stopped for? I was certain you wouldn't stop unless I died. Maybe not even then."

Chongo moaned a little, noses sniffing in the air, tails stiffly wagging back and forth.

The land had been barren for most of the length of the run, not that it mattered. Cass didn't have the time to stop and smell the flowers, or rather the Thorn Brush Lilies and Bone Trees. At last, the landscape was becoming more accommodating. Tall fields of wheat grass were in the distance, and small trees and shrub groves were scattered over the valley. The brisk wind stirred her long white hair as she followed Chongo up the hill, toward the horizon of the setting suns.

"Where are you taking me?" She looked back over her shoulder. "Lords of Life, how far have I chased you, anyway?"

Nature gave Cass comfort everywhere she went, but there was still much on Bish that she'd yet to see. Behind her was nothing but the hot rugged landscape that was common in the Outlands, harsh and unyielding. Though she loved the warmth, there was little comfort to be found in it. She preferred the forest or the high mountains.

"Not exactly the kind of terrain I'd care to settle in, Chongo. I need more streams, flowers and creatures to feel more comfortable." She grabbed him by one of his tails and followed the big dog up the hill. "You'll just keep on going, won't you? I can barely move my legs. Oosh! I need some rest, Chongo."

One of the giant heads swung back. Drooping eyes gazing at her, tongues hanging from his mouths. Cass swore there was a smile in his big jaws. Chongo was more than a common animal. He had a deeper intelligence in his eyes. He was part of a race of his own.

She gazed up at the hill's peak. "Whew, I see we are almost there, wherever up there is. I must admit it seems strange, you leading me up here like this. Shouldn't we be staying in the valleys?"

Chongo turned away, lion-like feet padding up the steep slope, until they stopped at the crest. He snorted, yawned, and lay down on the ground.

Cass lay on his back and draped her arms around his necks. "This better be spectacular." She gazed over the edge. A stiff wind whipped her white locks of hair into her eyes. Pushing them aside, she held her fingers under her nose. "Such a foul and unnatural odor is about, Chongo. Ugh." She spat. "What is—?"

Her pink eyes widened into circles.

Down in the plains, small black figures moved with purpose through the landscape.

Cass dug her nails into Chongo's furry mane. Underlings. She'd never seen so many before. They were a swarm of black ants moving through their fields. Tending to their macabre garden.

"Are those ..." she muttered.

She cupped her hand behind her ear. What she heard made her stomach cringe.

"Shovels?"

Shovels. Spikes. Screams.

Squinting her eyes, she couldn't hide her disbelief.

The underlings were chopping into bodies. Men, women, and children of all races. The blood watered their twisted version of a garden. They threw the dead bodies head first into their holes. Buried them head first. Legs jutting from the ground. Their tombstones were bloody heads on spikes. Row after row, the field went on and on.

Cass's hands turned clammy. She clutched at her head and squeezed her eyes shut. Nothing rattled her … ever, but this did. This churned inside her core. All of her sympathies and compassion for all things living had changed. It was one thing to fight for your survival, but it was another when you were cruel. A vicious child that pulls the wings from a beautiful butterfly. She'd never dealt with the underlings. She'd always figured they had their reasons to do things, just like any other race. Until now. Maybe men weren't so bad after all.

"Chongo, we must go." She tugged the fur on the back of his neck. She'd been weary before looking down there, but now she was exhausted. "This is too dangerous. We need to go back. We need to be with Fogle."

Fogle Boon. She hadn't given him a single thought since she chased after Chongo. Suddenly, he was all she could think about. She liked him, but now she felt like she needed him. Not that she ever felt she needed anyone for anything, especially a man, but she wouldn't mind having him around now. She felt like a fool. He must be days away now.

"I hope he's looking for me."

Chongo's ears perked up. His necks growled.

The hairs on Cass's neck turned to icicles.

Down the steep slope, a hoard of underlings armed with swords and shovels scurried up the hill. Their chitters meant death.

CHAPTER 5

THE SUNS SET OVER THE southern horizon like two bloodshot eyes before collapsing into the mist. Fogle Boon lay flat on his back, his pillow a pile of dirt and stone.

Barton picked at his skin and complained.

"Barton wants to go find his toys now, Wizard. Why's this take so long? Hmmm. I'm ready. Ready now." He punched his fist into the dirt. "NOW! NOW!"

Fogle coughed. He fanned the dust away from his face.

"Will you stop that, Barton! *You* wouldn't have to wait if *you* hadn't *crushed* my familiar in the first place. And putting him back together is taking longer, no thanks to *you*." He dusted off his hands as he stuffed many of his bottles into his traveling sack and groaned under his breath, "Dolt."

"What did you say?" Barton poked his finger at Fogle's chest. "Dolt? What is *dolt*?"

Fogle took a hard swallow, but he didn't back away. Barton, a deformed monster-child, was one of the scariest things he'd ever seen. Barton had once held Cass in his grasp like a children's doll. Fogle had seen the man smash and eat underlings like bugs. He swallowed again. Barton used to be that scary until they fought Tundoor. That giant was from another world. How they survived that, he'd never know.

Fogle raked his finger over his sleepy eyes and replied in a complimenting manner. "A giant with a man's brain."

Barton rubbed his chin, peering up in the sky. "Hmmm ... Dolt. Like a smart man, right? Like the man who took my toys, right?"

Fogle shrugged. "You could say that."

"But I'm a bigger dolt, right? Stronger dolt than him, right?"

"Oh, absolutely. There's no doubt about that. He is a pretty big dolt, but not nearly as big as you, Barton."

Barton stuck out his chin and grinned.

"Good. Barton is the biggest and strongest dolt of all."

Barton turned, thumped his chest with his fist, and walked away.

Fogle let out a sigh and took a seat by the fire. His grandfather snored on his earthen cot without a care in the world while he stewed with doubt and worry. Cass was long gone. Underlings were cropping up everywhere. He'd almost died a dozen times since he left the City of Three and wasn't so sure he'd live to tell anyone about it. *I must see this through.* He tightened his robes around his shoulders and rubbed his hands over the fire.

"Bish," he muttered, "I feel a hundred years old."

Alongside the fire, a small black figurine sizzled with mystic fire. It was his familiar, Inky, the ebony hawk he had made. Barton had crushed the bird days earlier, losing many of the key components.

"This better work." Fogle reached over and touched the object. The black bird was cold to the touch. "Ah, what am I missing?" He eyed the bird with his green eyes, scanning the ground. "Oh yes." Reaching over, he picked up Venir's hunting knife, and with a small scalpel-like dagger, he shaved off part of the carved horn from the hilt.

"Son of a Bish!" he exclaimed as the knife slipped and he gashed his thumb. The blood dripped freely to the ground. "Just a scratch, Fogle. A tiny wound of the flesh." He pulled the shaving from the hilt and pushed it into the figurine.

He checked his thumb.

"Still bleeding. Ugh. Stop bleeding."

Cass would be laughing at him if she saw the look on his face. He didn't care for the sight of his own blood running down his arm. *She'd probably laugh at me. That two-headed dog would, too. Toughen up, Fogle Boon.* He scooped a pile of dirt up in his good hand.

"I wouldn't do that if I were you," Boon said. The man blinked. Rubbed his eyes and sat up. "You aren't giant flesh, you know."

"Do what?" Fogle said. He dropped the dirt and stuffed his bloody thumb in the folds of his robes. His green robes, once garish in their own way, now looked little better than what a starving nomad would wear.

Boon stood up. His bearded silhouette was formidable against the night sky.

"You know what. You aren't made out of mud, you know." Boon reached over. "Let me take a look at it."

Fogle shifted away.

"I'll be fine, Boon."

"Well, at least wrap it up, will you? We can't have you dripping all over Bish. Underlings can smell the blood of men for miles, don't you know?"

Fogle sighed. It was pretty hard to believe that underlings could smell his blood from miles away. "It's more likely that they'd smell the odor of Barton long before my fragile wound. Besides, I wouldn't be surprised one bit if you were excited that they were right on our trail. Looks like you are plenty rested up for another battle, aren't you?"

Scratching his chest, Boon groaned. "Well... I admit that I wouldn't be against it, but I'd rather have a trap set first. There's nothing quite like seeing a look of surprise on an underling the moment before their face melts away. It tickles my teeth every time."

He's insane. I'm the spawn of a madman.

"Tell you what then, Grandfather. You stay here." Fogle pointed at the ground. "Set a nice magic booby trap while me and Barton go and search for our friends. Does that fit into your plan? Because I'm not sticking around so you can get us all killed. Sure, I realize the underlings are evil, but there is a time and place where you pick your battles."

"NO! You are wrong, Grandson. The time is anytime. The place is anywhere. Every chance you get to kill them, you take it. You don't let evil linger around. You can't let it take root. You must destroy it because if you don't!" Boon seemed as tall as a giant, but his voice was deep and cold. "It will destroy you."

Fogle tucked his chin into his chest and swallowed. He knew the truth when he heard it. Everyone did. The difference in most people was they ignored what they believed, rather than acting on it. He'd been locked inside the mind of one underling already. Even if it had only been a glimpse, an underling's mind was the darkest, most sadistic thing he'd ever seen. The underlings took pleasure in all the vile things they did.

"I understand that. We should kill them. We should kill them all. But right now," Fogle stepped nose to nose with Boon, "I need you to help me find Cass, that dog, and that man. I need your word, Boon. Will you help me find them first?"

Boon rubbed his bearded chin and made some clicking sounds with his mouth.

"Boon?" Fogle said. "I ... well ... hmmm ... well, you really are fond of that gorgeous woman, aren't you? I'd fight a thousand underlings for a woman like that."

"You'd fight a thousand underlings for pleasure."

Boon huffed a laugh.

"You take as much joy in killing them as they take in killing us, don't you?"

"Well, it's not worth doing if you don't enjoy doing it, Grandson. You wouldn't be pursuing the druid if not for her libidinous thighs. Certainly you enjoy them?" He perched his eyebrows up and down. "Hmmm? Hmmm?"

"I pursue her because it's the right thing to do, not because of anything else. Her thighs, her hair—"

"Her bosoms?"

"No—not her bosoms!" Fogle turned away. "And stop changing the subject!"

"I remember the first time I saw your grandmother. She had the most amazing bosoms, like those of three well-formed women in one. She was bathing at the Three Falls. I'd been trying to catch a peek for weeks..."

Fogle stuck his fingers inside his ears. In the process, he ripped his bloody thumb from his robes. "Ow!" *Blood maddened Wizard. He'll get us all killed. I wish Mood were here.* He kicked the dirt. "Bish! Bone! Slat!"

He looked north, where the moons were rising. How long would it take to get back home and sip some wine? *Will I ever see the City of Three again?* And how far was it, anyway? The truth was, he didn't have much of an idea where he was or where Boon had taken him. He paced towards the forest where Barton had trotted off. There was no sign of the giant, but he noticed a track. Mood would be proud. *I can track a giant.* He sniffed. *Humph. I think I can even smell him as well. Pah, why am I looking for the giant, anyway?* He headed back towards camp. For all he knew, he was on the other side of the world.

"Boon, where in Bish are we anyway?"

The old wizard pointed one finger toward the dipping suns and the other at the rising moons and spun around slowly three times. "Let me get my sense of direction. You know, in the Under-Bish, the suns and moons were quite different." He stopped and shrugged. "Well, I don't know where we are, exactly."

"So, maybe we are farther away than we started then? That would be convenient, now wouldn't it? Next time, why don't you send us straight to the Underland? You'd like that, wouldn't you?"

"Why don't you just rest, Grandson? Things will be better when you rise up tomorrow." Boon patted his stomach. "I could use some food about now. Say, where's Barton? I bet he could scare something up."

"Boon!" Fogle grabbed him by the arm and squeezed it. "Get your own food. As soon as my familiar is ready, we are moving in whatever direction it leads us toward Cass. And there's rations in the saddle. I don't think we need to be making too much noise about it. Have you forgotten that giants are still after us too? Not to mention the underlings and Bish knows what else that lies out there. Now, give me your word you will help me find her, or else!"

Boon peeled Fogle's hand off his arm. "Grandson, you have my word, but don't tussle with your elder unless you want to lose that hand."

"And don't tussle with your grandson if you want to keep yours!"

They stood eyeing each other. Unmoving. Unblinking.

Boon's eyes were as hard as diamonds: passionate, powerful and fearless.

Fogle admired them. He wished he had them.

Irritated, Boon said, "Tell me about those golden and silver-eyed underlings, Catten and Verbard. Why did you give those eyes back to them? Did you not realize what you had? Burning them would have dealt a blow to the entire Underland."

"How do you know their names?"

"Never mind that." Boon motioned him over toward the fire and patted the ground. "Just have a seat."

Fogle did so with a sigh. He'd forgotten the conversation they were having earlier when the hoard of underlings attacked. Now it was time for both of them to satisfy each other's questions. As for the golden eyes of the underling he'd given away, he was certain he'd done the right thing, but there was always doubt inside him. He remembered what Mood had said. *You cannot bargain with evil. Evil wins every time.*

With a wave of Fogle's hand, a small book floated out of his sack.

"It was the only way to get the spellbook back. A trade. The eyes for the book." He swallowed. "And the robes too."

"Pah!" Boon spat. "You cannot bargain—"

"I know! With evil! Yes, I know, but you can't sit there and honestly tell me that you wouldn't have done the same." Fogle waggled their spellbook under Boon's nose. "Huh? Wouldn't you?"

Boon took the book from his hand. "Well, I could always make another spellbook." He ran his hands over the leather binding. "And I know it wouldn't be the same, but there is only one golden-eyed underling. And he's one of the most powerful ones. He's the one known as Catten. The other is Verbard, and how did I learn their names? I discovered them when I fought some of their allies. Gold eyes. Silver eyes. The only two of their kind. They were close. So close. I felt them. They felt me. I was young, like you, decades ago." His voice trailed off. "I'd say Catten is fully restored by now."

"What do you mean?"

"Underlings can bring back their dead so long as they have the eyes. That's why people burn them. Why else would his brother, Verbard, have wanted them?"

Fogle shivered. He sprinkled mystic energy from his fingertips on his ebony hawk. It was almost ready. "He was killed once already, you know." He grabbed the knife. "He had this punched through him. Venir did that. And I say if he can be killed once, he can be killed again."

"Give me that." Boon snatched the knife away. "I knew there

was something unique about that blade. I could smell it. I might even be able to track that underling down with it."

"No! You gave your world we'd find Cass! You won't be getting any help from me on that quest!" He grabbed the book and closed it. "And you won't be taking this book."

"Grandson, if we can catch them, surprise them, kill them, and burn their eyes up, then it will be the end of them. The underlings would sink back into their holes and not come out for decades."

"That's never happened, Boon. You're delusional." Fogle scoffed. "You have to quit obsessing over them."

"No." Boon's eyes glazed. Drifted. He ran his fingers over the blade. "They must be destroyed."

"You're mad."

Boon shook his head.

"You're a fool. You don't realize the peril this world is in. I've never felt so many underlings on the surface before. They have invaded. This is not some skirmish. It is full-blown war!"

"Well, if you want to kill them, then I think your best chance is to find Venir. Find The Darkslayer. And if you help me find Cass first, I think I can have a quicker way to find those underlings."

"Oh?" Boon grunted. "Tell me now."

"First, I'm going to prepare some spells for our quest, and when I'm done, you can prepare some as well," Fogle said.

Boon's forehead wrinkled. "Grandson, tell me what you know now."

Fogle tapped his head with the tip of his finger. "I'll keep it safe from you until the time comes." *I'm in control now, you crazy bastard.*

CHAPTER 6

TWO DAYS. LONG, HOT AND miserable. Slim had bitten his nails down to the skin since Venir left. He sat alone, despite being surrounded by a few hundred of the finest horsemen that had ever been. He didn't feel safe. Not because he feared them, but because he'd have felt safer with Venir. Since the warrior left, a feeling of dread had crept into his belly, and it wouldn't go away. *Come on, Venir. Send that flare up.*

The horses nickered. The Royal Riders muttered. The foreboding sense of doom continued to grow. Early in the day a scout had returned, reporting another small army of underlings was leagues away. Bigger than the last one they'd fought. The Royal Riders were bold, brave, fearless as any, but they wouldn't be trapped and slaughtered. They'd fight until they bled their last drop, but it would be on their terms. Given the choice.

"Cleric," said a large man with a long mustache and plate armor, "we can't wait much longer. It's time we go." It was Commander Jans. A good man. A better soldier. His eyes were hard iron. He stared up into the gloom of the forest. "He was a good man, your friend, Venir. A good one."

"Still is a good man, Jans. He's not dead, you know." Slim rose up to his full height and looked down on the weathered soldier. He felt woozy. His blood still felt as thick as mud. Those spiders had taken a toll on him. "You don't know him like I do. He probably hasn't made it inside yet."

Jans stuffed a wad of tobacco into his mouth, sucked on it, then spat.

"Mmmm... now that's worth dying for right there. I should have sent some with your friend." He held his tobacco pouch out, shaking it. "Care for some? It's the best. Dwarven."

Slim held up his hand. "No, I don't think my stomach can handle it. Besides, there are other things I can do to unwind, but now is not the time."

Jans sucked and spit. "Well, so long as I have some chaw in my mouth, I think I'll die a happy man. Of course, I want my horse between my legs and my lance down an underling's throat, too." He made eyes up the hill. "Used to be you could see the flags at the top from here. Seems two lifetimes ago."

Slim nodded. "I remember. The last five years have been long."

And they had been, even for Slim, who had been around longer than most men. Over the decades, he'd seen men, dwarves, orcs and underlings go at it time and time again, but he'd never seen anything like this. It was as if the world was coming to an end. The underlings were creeping up from every corner. In the past, they'd struck terror in the night, keeping the world on edge then moving on. Now, they were getting as thick as a plague of locusts, overtaking and devouring everything in sight.

"Jans, do you think you can hold off another day? There is nowhere for you to run. Our best chance is to see if Venir comes through."

"Another day? Hah! Man, don't you realize that this might just be our last day? All of us." He pointed his mailed hand at Slim. "Now you listen to me, Slim. When the scouts come in with the next reports, if it's not good, we're leaving. And when I say we're leaving, I say we aren't just leaving this spot, but we're leaving our bones to Bish. And we're going to take as many of those dark fiends with us as we can." He patted Slim on the shoulder before he walked off. "I suggest you do the same."

Slim squatted like a vulture by the campfire and scratched his fingers through his hair. He fully expected Venir to come through in his mind, but his gut told him something else. Ever since the rangy warrior dashed up into the forest, Slim couldn't shake the feeling that he'd seen his friend for the last time. Perhaps, it wasn't Venir who wouldn't survive. Maybe it was him. Maybe his time had come to perish battling the underlings.

What was I thinking? I shouldn't have let him go alone! I should have died with him!

He nibbled at his fingernails and took another long look up the hill where Outpost Thirty One sat.

"A thousand underlings against one man," he said. Sadness fell over him. "No one could survive that."

CHAPTER 7

"RUMPH."

Venir's eyes fluttered open, but there was nothing to see. The bag on his head was still in place. His tongue was swollen with thirst, and the stinging sweat that once dripped in his eyes was gone. He groaned.

Every time he dozed off inside the stockade, a biting pain inside his wrists awoke him. The small bones in both wrists ached in a way that such small things had no business aching. His fingers were black and blue, but he could move them. Several hours had been tolerable, but now he'd lost all track of time. He couldn't tell which was worse: being in the Mist, or being shackled and wounded in a fort full of underlings.

Must escape.

Venir had been hopeful at first.

Just wait it out until my enemies reveal themselves.

But the nagging pain in his wrists kept reminding him that he couldn't do anything. He was crippled. Invalid. Diminished. And the Royal Riders who were waiting on him would be slaughtered. He had failed them. He had failed Slim. He'd failed everyone.

His stomach groaned. His tongue was as thick as wool in his mouth.

"Waterrr ..." he moaned.

Venir had never begged for anything before, not even when he was a starving young boy, but his conditions were beyond miserable. He was shackled inside the darkness. Hungering. Thirsting. No chance for escape. He flexed his limbs and fought against the restraints. They didn't groan. Days ago, they would have.

Bish.

Hours ago, it had been *Son of a Bish*, but now his deteriorating thoughts couldn't even muster that. Memories of the Mist sprung forth, worsening his fears. In the Mist, at least he could move; he could walk and talk, and there was water in abundance. In the Mist, there were sounds of life. Here, there was nothing.

Here, it was black. Painful. Agitating. Eroding and sweltering. The minutes felt like hours. His great strength faded. His will was breaking. This wasn't like the dungeons in the City of Bone. This was much worse. A hundred times worse, it seemed.

Fool.

Images were coming and going inside his mind. Friends and foes, distinct and drifting. What had he done in life that had led him here? Into the belly of his very enemy? Georgio and Melegal, what had become of them? And the tiny boy, Lefty? He'd forsaken them so he could pursue his enemy. Perhaps Billip and Mikkel were still looking after them. It seemed like decades since he'd seen them.

His knees trembled. He sagged to the ground. His feet were numb from countless hours of standing. The middle of his back felt like an anvil was stuck inside it. He wanted to sit, rest, but his pinned and swollen wrists wouldn't allow it. He hung. Locked in the stockade. His suffering increasing by the minute.

No. Must fight it. Focus.

It was hard to even think, but the beautiful face of Kam found its way inside his mind. Why would any man leave such a magnificent woman? Only a bull-headed fool would do that. And he had no lust for her now. Only the desire to see her face and to know that she was alright without him.

Many other memories came to mind. The Battle in the Pit with Son of Farc. As devastating as that had been, he'd rather risk another beating than die like this. And the blonde-haired half-orc woman, Dolly, with the snaggled teeth. Why did he wonder about her?

Jarla.

Was that when all the madness started? The day of her betrayal? The day he took the armament from the sack and hewed down the gnolls, Throk and Keel? His swollen fingers twitched in the darkness. His life had been nothing but underlings after that. He'd hated them even before. They'd killed his family when he was a boy. They'd buried him alive. Yet he'd survived somehow.

Mood.

Chongo.

They had saved him before. He lurched inside the stockade. Rocked his bullish shoulders back and forth, on his toes.

"Grrrrr … *umph!*"

Nothing moved but him.

He tried again with the same result.

"Bish!" His voice was more of a croak than a sound.

He'd failed his friends and his dog. He'd failed them all, and they would all die at the hands of the underlings in the end. Now, all he could do was sit in misery and wait for his slow death to come. His thoughts drifted back and forth, between reality and some other world, hour after hour, day after day for all he knew.

His inner fire was dim, but not out. Not as long as the scent of underling skin that he knew so well was about. Hatred kept his heart beating when most men's would fail. Vengeance stoked the coals in his belly. Somehow, if he could get ahold of one more underling, he could die satisfied. If he could even just sink his teeth around one of their throats.

Dead silence. His ragged breathing. His only company until the familiar sound of a key being turned in a lock clicked in his ears. It might as well have been a trumpet blast that jostled Venir from his sleepless slumber. Stiff as a board, every joint in his body ached. He tried to move. The gash in his thigh where the underling stabbed him throbbed with its own life.

"Water," he said. It wasn't audible. The deep recesses of his mind blurted out another warning.

Be quiet, Fool! Shut up! Listen!

A steel door swung open and banged against the wall. A rush of cool air followed. Chill bumps rose along his arms, igniting each and every hair.

I'm still alive after all.

Booted feet entered. Rubbing plates of armor and weapons jangling followed. It was music to Venir's ears—until someone poked him in the ribs.

He jerked in his shackles and moaned.

Bloody bastards!

"Check the cuffs on those leg irons, and unfetter the stockade," a man said. His voice was familiar.

Venir turned his head. It was the leader of the Brigands. The ones posing as Royal soldiers he'd encountered in the gorge. Venir tried to recall how many men the leader had said they had. Less than a hundred, was it? His blood thickened in his veins.

"Tuuth," the leader said, "keep that spear on his back in case he makes any sudden moves."

The orc snorted. "He's not going to move anywhere. He won't be able to walk. Look."

Venir could feel the light from a lantern on his face. The others came closer.

"Gad! That is disgusting!" the leader said. He covered his mouth. "Give me that torch."

"No," the orc said. "The underlings like this. It's not ours to mess with."

Venir felt a lump form in his throat. What was going on? What was wrong with his legs?

"Give me the torch, Tuuth," the leader said. "The Bone with the underlings. This man's a warrior, and he doesn't deserve to die with his legs eaten off."

"It'll be your legs sticking out of the ground, not mine, Fraggon," the orc said. "You humans are so soft. Like buttered bread."

"And you orcs are rotten like basilisk eggs. Look at this!" Fraggon held the light closer. "So vile."

Venir heard another man squat down beneath him and gag.

"Blecht!" Another one spit a mouthful of bile from his mouth. "All these years, and I still can't stomach it."

Tuuth shoved one man onto his back and hunched his big frame down in the light. "Bone. That is nasty. Heh. Heh."

Venir raised his neck from the stockade and groaned. His head felt like it weighed a ton. He mumbled something incomprehensible.

He was trying to say, "What's wrong with my legs?" He couldn't even feel them.

"Keep him steady while I burn these things," said the leader, Flaggon. "Hold him, men."

Tuuth clamped his arms around Venir's chest. Pinning his arms at his sides.

The others grabbed his legs.

"It's for the better, Stranger. An act of mercy I don't normally give, but you've earned that much respect from me," Tuuth said into the bag over his head.

"Mercy?" one brigand soldier started. "He'll need more than that. These grubs have eaten holes so deep in his flesh I can see the bone." Venir heard the man swallow. "Ah slat, I'm getting sick again."

"He's lucky for the leaches; that much is certain," Fraggon said. "They suck the blood and numb the pain. Gad, you don't usually see both like this." He took a dagger out and sliced one off that was bloated with blood and as big as his hand.

"How this man lives, I'll never know," the other brigand said. He spit more bile from his mouth. "He should be dead."

"Well, the grubs eat the skin, but they cauterized the holes somehow. I've seen men with tunnels of holes all over them that still live. But you're right; he should be dead, and I don't think the underlings want that yet."

Venir felt heat on his legs. His heart pounded inside his chest like a war drum. He'd seen grubs and leeches and what they did to the flesh. It horrified him.

What have they done to me!

Fraggon continued. "You've been blessed and cursed it seems, Stranger. The grubs and leeches are enjoying their meal, and a big beefy man like you can feed them for days. Well, what's left of you, anyway. But I don't think the underlings want you dead just yet; else they wouldn't have sent for you. But, I can't guarantee you'll live through this next step either. I mean, you might live, but I don't see you ever walking again. A shame too. You have him secured, Tuuth? I'd say there be some fight in him."

"Should I take the bag off and let him breathe? Let him bite down on something?"

"Are you volunteering your finger, Tuuth? My, so compassionate you've become for the stranger. No, just leave it on. It'll muffle the screams well enough. Not that the underlings would mind that one bit anyway. Stranger, may Bish be with you."

I don't have the strength to – "YEEEEEEEEAAAAAAAAWWW!"

It felt like the tendons of his muscles were being pulled from his skin. Inch by inch. It was unimaginable. Excruciating. Mind numbing. His body shuddered from toe nail to chin. The top of his skull was on fire.

Flaggon pulled cord after cord from within and seared his skin with the torch.

Venir screamed. Stopped. Screamed some more.

"My, he's a gusty one," Tuuth said.

"That grub's as long my innards!"

"Keep pulling it out!" Flaggon said. "It's almost out! Get the knife ready so we can cut the head off!"

It felt like a cord of thick rope was being pulled through his body. He yelled at the top of his lungs, "GET THAT BLASTED THING OUT OF ME!"

"There's the head! Oh slat! What's in the mouth of that thing! Keep it still!"

"Kill it!"

The sound of steel cut through the air.

Slice!

"You got it! Bish! Barely! It almost got us!" Flaggon said. "How's the man, Tuuth?"

Tuuth shrugged his broad shoulders. Venir wasn't moving. "He's breathing, not that it matters. He's crippled now. A peaceful death being eaten alive would have been better."

What have the underlings done to me!

Thoughts were racing through Venir's mind despite the agony. How much suffering would they put him through?

Someone pulled the bag off his head

When he managed to look up, it was into the big pale face of the orcen man, Tuuth.

"His eyes still have some fight in them, Flaggon. Look at this?"

Flaggon stepped into view, eyed him and said with avid curiosity, "Can you stand, Stranger?"

40

"Can underlings die?" Venir said. He pushed against the stockade. Wobbling on his feet.

Tuuth and Flaggon looked at each other, astonished.

"Can you walk?"

Venir took his first step and collapsed face first to the stone floor.

"Help him up," Flaggon said.

"No!" Venir said.

He was free. Despite all the pain, he was going to enjoy it. Unable to use his hands because of the pain in his wrists, he rolled onto his elbows. He pushed himself over and sat himself up. He felt like he would pass out.

Bone!

He saw his legs. They were raw. Scarred. Pale as the orc. There was a hole in his thigh that led to the bone. That was the first one he saw. To the side, the grub lay dead on the floor, six feet in length. It looked like a hairy earthworm as thick as his thumb. Its head as big as his knuckles and filled with tiny teeth. His stomach churned bile up to his throat, but nothing came out.

"Well, Stranger," Flaggon said "you can't walk, but we'll let you crawl if you like. Else we can carry you."

"No," Venir said.

He was numb. Looking at his arms, the bracers on his aching wrists were loose. The bulges in his arms were gone. What had been done to him? The only thing left whole on him it seemed was his beard.

"Then get moving, Stranger. The underlings are expecting you." The brighter tone that Flaggon carried changed. "And seeing how you survived this much, I can only warn you that the worst is yet to come."

Venir swallowed hard. On elbows and knees, trembling, he crawled forward.

Tuuth rubbed the bracers on his wrists. The haggard form of Venir crawling stirred him. In the little amount of time the man had been imprisoned, he'd become a husk of the man Tuuth had battled earlier. Tuuth would never forget the shock in the man's granite face when he cracked his wrists. It should have broken the man. But it hadn't. The Stranger still had fire in his eyes. An anger. A thirst.

Watching Venir crawl up the steps, he shook his head. Tuuth unslung the man's backpack from his shoulders and pulled out the sack. He'd already been into the woods and back again, searching for the man's armament. Opening the neck of the sack for what might as well have been the hundredth time, he reached inside and found nothing. Stuffing the sack inside the backpack, he hoisted it back over his shoulders. There was something going on. There had to be. Magic had to be the answer; he'd keep the stranger's clothes.

Grabbing the cloth bag that hung on the stockade, he caught up to the stranger and stuffed it over his head.

"What'd you do that for?" Flaggon said. "It's bad enough he crawls on all fours, and now you've blinded the man too. At least let him enjoy the sights before he gets there. Heh-heh."

The torchlight flickered over Venir's haggard form that kept crawling inch by inch up the steps. Tuuth wasn't the only one that grimaced a little as Venir dragged his mangled legs over the steps.

"It'll take him hours to get there at this rate," Tuuth said. He picked Venir up and hoisted him over his shoulder. "Let's get this over with."

"Suit yourself, Tuuth. I've not the interest to carry the big lout," Flaggon said. "Come on, men. Let the friendly orc handle this. Seems he has an interest in big helpless men."

Snickering, they headed up the steps and out of sight.

Several steps up, Tuuth set Venir back down. "Where are your weapons and armor, Stranger?" Tuuth tore off the burlap bag and grabbed him by the head of hair. "Where is it? Is it magic? Can I summon it?"

Venir's eyes fluttered open. He shook his head. "Comes and goes," he said.

Tuuth wrapped his hands around Venir's thigh and squeezed.

Venir groaned and sputtered.

"Do not lie, Stranger. I will have those weapons and armor. Tell me, and maybe I can get you some water."

"Humph," Venir said. He spit out a laugh. "Like the wind, fool orc."

Tuuth squeezed again.

Venir groaned. He stared back in Tuuth's eyes. "Maybe you didn't look hard enough, Orc."

"Perhaps I should break your ankles as well," Tuuth said. He squeezed harder.

"Perhaps," Venir said, "you should take a bath, you filthy or—" Venir's eyes fluttered up into his head, and his body slumped forward.

"Borsch!" Tuuth said. He grabbed Venir by his head of hair and dragged his heavy body up the stairs.

CHAPTER 8

BENEATH THE CLOUDS ABOVE THE City of Bone, the most beautiful woman on Bish stood, watching the unraveling chaos below. Trinos. Her world. Her rules. Life and death meant nothing. Meant everything.

Running her elegant fingers through her thick locks of platinum hair, she sighed.

"What to do? What to do?"

In the past, she'd been detached from the lives and deaths of all the colorful people, but now, watching them suffer and cry out, she felt something.

"I wonder where Scorch is, and what he's doing."

Scorch had meddled with her creation for his own entertainment. She sought him out, to hold him accountable. It was the most alive she'd felt since she was immortal. She was feeling all kinds of things.

She imagined Scorch was feeling the same, or was he? Shortly after their encounter at the Void, the two infinite beings had agreed that rather than suffer the endless expanse surrounding the tiny world, they would share a fate on the world of Bish. Each had buried the majority of their power in the heart of the world's center and set out on their own. They hadn't seen each other since.

Soaring the sky, the high winds billowed the robes along her perfectly figured body. She stopped. Hovered and touched a cloud.

"I imagine he isn't nearly so attached as I feel. I wonder what he will do?"

Below her, The City of Bone was in turmoil. The Royals that ruled it had made conditions unpleasant enough to begin with, but now the citizens were in deeper straights. The underlings came. A black menace of small people designed to bring nothing but restlessness and terror to the world.

"Humans win; underlings lose. Underlings win; humans lose. I've seen it so many times before. But they come up with the most interesting ways to destroy one another."

Bodies fell. Burned. They were dragged over the cobblestones and torn to bits. It was having an effect on her. The longer she stayed on Bish, the more attached she became. The world itself, a living and breathing thing. She felt it. So many people were dying, screaming, wailing, and begging for life to be over. Some fought. Most ran, and the Royals, the so called protectors, ignored their pleas. The people pounded on the walls of the castles. Their cries were not heard.

Trinos's fists clenched at her sides when a woman and her children were shot down as they tried to force their way through a gate to find safety. She wasn't sure which angered her more: the underlings or The Royals.

"The hearts of men are so unpredictable."

With little thought and a few gestures with her fingers, the Royal soldiers were lifted off their feet and dropped into the street. Two seconds later, a score of underlings appeared and tore into them. She smirked.

"Well, that was entertaining. What else can I do? Should I bring the underlings to men or the men to the underlings?" She closed her eyes. Her mind probed the thoughts of the people within the castle. "Ah, there you are, you catty little sorceress. I've got another surprise for you, Manamis."

With a wave of her hands, a score of underlings were lifted from the street and dropped into one of the courtyards of Castle Kling. Several more were vaulted onto the rooftops and others through the windows.

She heard one voice in particular shriek out. She laughed. Trinos had dropped two underlings into the bedroom of Manamis Kling, the haughty old sorceress who had challenged her at the fountain.

"Surprise!" Trinos said. She clapped her hands together and smiled. "I like it!"

Manamis shrieked. She shouted. White light burst through the window. The shingles crackled. A loud explosion followed that tore the walls down, hurling underlings through the air. Dead. Smoking. Trinos laughed again as the leathery old woman stood in the smoking hole where the wall once stood, looking around. Trinos grinned. Manamis screamed out orders and blasted the underlings with balls of blue fire.

"Bitter, but strong that one is. Crafty, too. I better keep an eye on her."

Trinos moved on from one incident to the other, observing, interfering, while trying to sort it all out in her mind. Below, she heard many of the people crying out for her in the 21st District.

She'd known the underlings were coming, but she hadn't warned the people. She wanted to see what happened and was curious how it would affect her. Corrin, Billip, and Nikkel had survived, while most of her people fell. The fountain was bloody and marred with death. The survivors had dragged the bodies of man and underling from the fountain, and the waters had cleared.

Why did I let this happen to them?

The men were valiant in their efforts, but the price was great. The big black man with a wonderful smile and cavernous voice, Mikkel, had fallen. His son was on his knees, sobbing and drenched in tears. Even Corrin's hard eyes were dampened.

Trinos felt something stir inside her. Sympathy. Worry.

Focusing, she located Georgio. She liked the young man that was full of hope. Determined to find a friend he so admired. There was something special about him, good, honest and pure. He and his friends were in a bind. The underlings had chased them down the streets and cornered them in an alley.

Georgio and another strange large man stood their ground, each of them battling with the ferocity of many warriors in one, but it would not last forever. They would all die. Even the shaggy bellied animal called Quickster.

"I can't save them all, but I can at least save the ones I like."

BLINK!

The colorful eyes of the underlings widened in the alley when the men, women and pony disappeared. Below Trinos, alongside her fountain in the 21st District, the small party re-appeared, dismayed.

"Where in all Bish did you come from?" Corrin cried out.

It was music to Trinos's ears.

CHAPTER 9

"MERCY!" JOLINE SHOUTED INTO THE kitchen, "Get out there and take some orders. We're busy, you know."

"I'm coming, Joline, just give me a moment."

The past several days had been the hardest in all Joline's life. Her best friend Kam was gone. The baby girl, Erin whom she adored, was kidnapped, and for all Joline knew they were dead. She'd taken word of the predicament to Kam's family, but they'd made their thoughts perfectly clear. Kam was on her own. Her daughter too. Of course, she hadn't spoken to Kam's mother but some other family member who was supposed to send the word out. *No wonder Kam left.*

Mercy bustled through the door. Her pretty eyes dull. Long hair tied in a knot on her head. She refused to let anyone fix up her appearance with an enhancement spell.

"Look at you, Mercy," Joline said. "You're too pretty to go around looking like that." Joline straightened the young woman's apron and wiped a smudge of batter from her face. "And pull that lip up. The customers want smiles, not pouts. You look like a frog when you make that face—so straighten up."

Mercy's eyes began to water.

"Ah, now don't you start that again, Mercy. Mother of Bish, we can't both be crying, not now. Not right now." Joline stammered. A lump formed in her throat.

There had been a lot of tears since Kam and Erin disappeared, a lifetime's worth if not more.

And everyone else fun was gone, too. Joline had grown fond of Billip in particular. The man was ornery but a protector. And

Mikkel, the Big Charmer, she liked to call him, had the gutsiest laughs she'd ever heard. It seemed like she'd had a new family that she'd grown quite fond of. Tears dripped down her cheeks as she thought more about the halflings, Lefty and his wonderful friend Gillem, who brought the most beautiful flowers. What in all of Bish had happened to them? She couldn't shake the dread that overcame her when she thought of them.

"I miss Georgio," Mercy said. She didn't bother to dry her eyes.

"Are you crying again, Mercy? What are you crying for?" one of the other serving girls said, darting towards the kitchen. "We're busy, you over-grown child! Get out there and help!"

"No need to be nasty," Joline shot back, but the girl was gone.

The Magi Roost was almost at capacity and had been every day since the underlings showed up and attacked. The Royals had taken action, and soldiers had been dispatched. The City of Three was ready, and the citizens liked nothing more than to head into a tavern and talk about that.

Mercy was shuddering. "When's he coming back, Joline?"

"Oh, Girl, you are too young to fall for a man!"

"I am not too young. I'm older than him."

"Well, er..." Joline started, but she didn't know what to say. Mercy had teased the younger man from day one, but Joline had figured she was only being ornery. She remembered those days. But when Mercy found out that Georgio had left without saying goodbye, she'd been heart-broken. "Mercy, all men are the same. You'll meet someone when the time is right. Most of these men are plenty kind to you." Joline rubbed her shoulder. "You know that."

"They aren't like Georgio," Mercy whined. She blew her nose in a rag Joline handed her. "He was sweet and adorable."

True. Joline liked Georgio, and she figured if Billip and Mikkel didn't spoil him, he'd become an excellent young man. Still, she tried to think of something bad to say.

"He ate like a pig."

Mercy's eyes faded to the past. "I loved watching him eat. He really loved it. It was as if every time he ate, it was the first time."

Joline huffed a little. "Well, his hair was always a mess and dirty. And he didn't bathe much either."

"I loved all those curls, and his hair was so soft and thick."

"And his manners were horrible. Just horrible. He couldn't pass from one room to another without farting."

"That always made me giggle."

"You're hopeless," Joline said. She started fixing some drinks at the bar. "Now, wipe those tears away and drink th—"

"What is it?" Mercy said.

"Uh ..." Joline stared at the entrance of the Magi Roost. "Nothin but a-a ..."

Mercy followed her gaze to the figures at the front door. Her tears and sobbing stopped.

"I'll get him a table!"

"No, I'll ..." Joline said, reaching out.

Mercy avoided her grasp and headed over to the two people in the doorway.

One was a man, adorned in a fine looking traveler's tunic. His face was impossibly handsome, every feature perfectly formed from his chin to his teeth to the golden blond hair on his head. When his eyes met hers, he nodded at her, and she was at a loss for breath. The man was striking, mysterious, and incredible all at the same time.

He must be a Royal, maybe a member of Kam's family.

"Shall I find you a table, Sir?" Joline heard Mercy say.

"Something by the bar, little thing," a stocky woman said. She was taller than most women, garbed in outdoor leathers. Had a brassy voice. She was rugged too. A knife strapped to her wide hips and a bow and quiver slung over her shoulder. "And, do you have any pickles? My friend here really likes pickles."

"Uh ... well, yes, we have some pickles. Does is like them raw or fried?" Mercy said. She hadn't taken her eyes off the man.

The man, surveying the room, didn't say a word, but the mention of the word pickles brought the slightest smile to his lips.

The outdoorswoman stuck her hand in Mercy's face and snapped her fingers. "Honey, I didn't ask what kind you had. I just asked if you had them." She looked around at the curious faces. "Now where is our table? We need a seat; my feet are aching."

"Certainly," Mercy said, looking at Joline.

Joline nodded at two stools at the end of the bar where Mikkel and Billip used to sit. Joline usually didn't let people sit there unless it was very crowded.

As the two were about to take a seat, an exhausted group of travelers pushed their way inside.

The stocky woman stormed at them and yelled at the closest one. "March your arses out of here! Wait until we come out."

"But we're hungry, Darlene," one man said. He was old. Eyes pleading. "We have some money."

Darlene grabbed the man by his jerkin and pulled him down face to face with her. "I don't care where you eat, as long as it isn't here. Scorch wants to dine alone, and I've already warned you to keep your distance. And you know what can happen if you don't."

The small group of people shook their heads, averting her gaze.

"Idiots, do I have to remind you?" Darlene held out her fist and flicked open her fingers. "Poof! Just like the underlings."

They started backing through the door, their eyes filled with horror.

"Eat somewhere else, and I'll let you know when he needs you."

Darlene walked towards Joline, spun on her heel and whistled. "Nice place you have here. Mmmm-Hmm. So what do you have that's special to drink? I tell you what, Miss. I'm so thirsty, I think I could drink a goblet of goat pee."

Taken aback, Joline said, "We don't have any of that here, but you and your companion might like this." Without thinking, she reached up and grabbed a half-moon bottle of Muckle Sap from the shelf and poured a sample into a tumbler.

What am I doing?

She glanced at the end of the bar, toward the jaw-droppingly handsome man called Scorch. He seemed to be watching everyone in the room at the same time.

They might not even have any means.

She pushed the tumbler to Darlene. "Try this, a, Darlene, is it?"

"You are pretty quick, uh —"

"Joline."

"Yes, Joline. You know, I had a cousin named Coline, but she stopped talking to me when we were children."

"Oh, why is that?"

"I kicked her in the crotch for being ornery. She said she couldn't pee straight after that, but how can you tell?"

Joline tried to hide her laugh but couldn't. The woman, for all her abrasive manners, was likeable.

Darlene took the entire glass, knocked it back, smacked her lips and smiled. "Mmmmm. That is good. Very good! Scorch, you have to try this ... uh ... what is it?"

"Muckle Sap."

"Muckle Sap, Scorch. It makes Jig taste like goat piss."

Joline briefly looked up, wondering if indeed the woman had ever drank goat piss.

I certainly hope not.

"Would you like the entire bottle, Darlene? That first taste is a courtesy sample, and it is our most expensive."

"Oh, well, I... Scorch, do we have any coins?" She nodded. "He says we can buy all the Muckle Sap we want."

"But he didn't say anything?" She looked over, saw his smiling face and blushed. "Did he?"

Mercy walked past the bar beaming, a large jar of pickles in one hand and a plate of fried pickles in the other. She set them before Scorch.

"Mercy, I didn't hear him ask for that?"

"I didn't either."

Another barmaid crossed Joline's path, a plate of cheese, bread and meats in her hand. She dropped it in front of Scorch, smiled from ear to ear, bowed, and giggled away.

"What in Bish is going on here? The man hasn't said a thing."

Darlene reached over and patted Joline on the shoulder. "Don't you worry about what is going on here, and everything will be fine. You see, my friend Scorch, well, he pretty much does anything he wants. And you don't want to be on the side of what he don't like."

Joline took a long look at Scorch. She couldn't tell if it was a thrill or a chill that went down her spine. But something wasn't right.

"This place is a lot better than Hohm City, isn't it Scorch?" Darlene wiped her sleeve across her mouth and burped. "Did you try this Mu-Mookle Surp? It's something. Like, really good."

It was the best Darlene had felt since she could ever remember, being here, in a wonderful tavern full of all different sorts of people. No doubt the City of Three was the place to be. She was never bothered before by the misty city she called home, but she didn't see herself going back now either. She shook her head, rubbed her red eyes and took another drink. "To the City of Trees!"

At her side, Scorch had been eating one pickle after another, washing them down with Muckle Sap, and he hadn't stopped for hours. His broad smile was all Darlene needed to see to tell that he was having a good time.

"Barmaid, tell me—Joline is it?" Scorch smiled.

Her face lit up as she nodded.

"So, you take the pickles, wrap them in cheese, and dip them in boiling..." he paused.

"Lard," she said, wiping the same spot on the bar she'd been at for over an hour.

"It's one of the most incredible things I've ever experienced in the entire universe!"

"The what?" Joline said, cocking her head.

"Universe!" Darlene blurted out, slapping the bar with her hand. "He talks about it, but I don't get it. I think it's in the Underpants—*Hic*—I mean the Underlands."

"And this Muckle Sap isn't half bad either," Scorch said. "I bet Morley would enjoy this." Scorch looked around as if he was searching for an old friend. "Oh, never mind."

"Who's Morley, Scorch?" Darlene said. "And why are you always talking about him?" Whenever she heard that name, her jealous side came to life. Scorch was her friend and her friend alone.

"Darlene," Scorch said, "I told you not to think like that."

She grabbed his sleeve, started petting it with her dirty hands and said, "I'm sorry, Scorch. *Hic*. Won't happen again. *Hic*."

Hopping off her stool, she'd started teetering away when she heard Joline say, "Is she going to be alright?"

"She'll be alright, Joline," Scorch said. He reached over and patted Joline's hand. "But please, tell me about all your worries."

"I'll be alright!" Darlene said. She knocked a bottle from one table only to excuse herself and knock a bottle from another.

The men laughed behind her back as she sauntered away, ignoring the obvious stares. The place was nice, very nice, but the people she wasn't so sure about. Many of them were impeccable in clothing, even the handful of dwarves that smoked around the tables. But their manners were lacking. *Oh!* The fire was welcoming on her back as she took a seat on the corner of the fireplace hearth.

"Woo!" she said, slapping her knees. "Sure is nice in here." She fanned herself. "Getting really hot, though."

The tavern chatter was about many things, including underlings, but there was something else going on she couldn't put her finger on. A couple of robed men's faces were masks of concentration, staring hard into one another's eyes inside a small group that gathered around and added more coins to the piles on the table.

"Ten seconds," one said, rubbing his chin.

"Twenty."

Sweat beaded on both of the robed men's foreheads.

"Thirty seconds," the man said.

The bigger of the two men locked in a stare jumped from the table, banging his knee and holding his head.

"Fodor wins!"

Darlene applauded along with the rest of the men, even though she didn't have any idea what was happening. "Say, what kind of game is this, anyway? A staring contest?"

A couple of the scholarly robed men chuckled while another man sneered and walked away. The smaller man in a bright green tunic seated at the table smiled and waved her over.

"Please, come over here and have a seat. I'd be happy to explain," he said, smiling.

"Really?" Darlene said, "My, you men sure have a different way about you. And your clothes." She grabbed the sleeves of one man's robes and rubbed them. "They look more like something a woman would wear. By Hohm, that sure is soft. What kind of fabric is this?"

The man named Fodor cleared his throat. "Ahem, Miss, what was your name?"

"Oh, Darlene. I'm from Hohm City. Home of the Mists, and that over there," she pointed, "is Scorch. My friend. He kills underlings."

Fodor made a polite nod. "I see. Well, Darlene, let me tell you about this game we play..."

"Excuse me, but are you Royals?" She grabbed another man's sleeve. "Where can I get a shirt like this? It's so pretty."

He leered at her and pushed her hand away. "This clothing is made for Wizards, not for a grubby sheep herder."

A couple men chuckled. Others gathered around.

Darlene looked them over. "I'm a hunter and a trapper, and a fine shot with a bow. I bet I could out shoot any of you. And you better watch your manners." She slipped a knife underneath the man's privates. "Or for certain you'll be wearing that fancy shirt as a woman."

The man gawped, eyes wide.

"Certainly, Darlene," Fodor said. He lay his hand on her shoulder. "Please, put the knife away. My companions don't have the best manners when it comes to travelers."

Darlene slid her knife back into the sheath and burped.

"You can say that again. So," she drummed her fingers on the table, "tell me about this game again, Fodor. Is it something I can play?"

"Certainly," he said, clasping his hands on the table. "And it's really quite simple. Even for you."

She swayed forward.

"Well, what do you mean by that?"

"I say that because it's your first time, is all. No insult about your intellect intended."

She nodded. "That's what I thought you meant."

Fodder smiled and continued.

"So, it's called a Mind Grumble. It's a game for everyone, but a mage or wizard must link it. What happens is our minds are linked together and we engage in a mental arm wrestling contest. A test of wills. Do you understand, Darlene?"

"I think I've heard of this before. I had an uncle that was a wizard, or at least my mother said he was, well said he was my uncle, but I'm not so sure why she'd be sleeping around with my uncle." She shrugged. "Maybe it was on account that my father, my uncle's brother, was no longer around. But he said he did something like this and gave a man a bloody nose for it."

Fodor shook his head. "Who said he gave a bloody nose for it?"

"My uncle."

Fodor looked at her for a long moment as if waiting for her to speak.

"Huh ... I see, Darlene. Are you finished?"

She rubbed her nose. "Will this give me a bloody nose?"

"It's unlikely, but it has been known to happen before. See the floor?" He pointed with his eyes and chin.

There was a dark stain on the floor near their table.

"Is that from blood?"

"Aye, for the bloodiest nose I ever saw. Fogle Boon, one of our kind, arrogant and mysterious, locked minds with a stranger, somewhat like yourself. A rugged wilderness warrior whose name I can't recall."

"What happened?"

"To our shock and amazement, the big fellow won and Fogle Boon's nose was broken."

Darlene gulped, covering her nose.

"Darlene, that won't happen to you, I promise. That night, if anything, was an unfortunate accident. Rather unexplainable, it was. But, in the spirit of things," Fodor snapped his fingers, and a pretty waitress in a short white tunic dress strolled over, smiling, "I treat you to a bottle of wine. Are you ready?"

She eyed the men that surrounded her and the table. They had a shifty look about them, but she felt all right. "You promise it won't turn my mind to mush or anything?"

"It's already mush if you ask me," one wizard said. He had a crook in his jaw and a partially bald head. "Shouldn't hurt a thing."

Darlene's hand dropped to her knife.

"I don't like you."

He stepped away.

Fodor continued.

"Don't mind him, Darlene. He never wins. And if you find yourself feeling uncomfortable, you just need to close your eyes, or look away. It's quite simple. And for all I know, you might give more than I can handle." He smiled and chuckled. "Such things have been known to happen before."

She rapped her fist on the table. "I'll try anything once! Let's do this!" She learned forward on her elbows and stared into Fodor's eyes. "You have nice eyes." She licked her lips. "Now what?"

Fodor loosened the top button on his tunic, nodded to one of the other wizards, and then turned his focus on her. The petite man's eyes were like ice blue water, hypnotizing like a snake.

The men around the table quietly talked among themselves in a strange gibberish and gently laid coins on the table.

"Are they betting for me or against me?" she said.

The mage with the crook in his jaw muttered quickly, twirled his fingers, and then touched her forehead with one finger and Fodor's with another. "What's he doooooo ..."

Darlene didn't feel anything, but the man across from her's face turned snake-like, red tongue licking out of its mouth and striking. It was her, watching herself standing in the dark woods facing off a great snake. She didn't scream, just whipped out a knife and cut off its head.

"Is that it? Is it over? Did I win?" Her voice echoed. But the scene changed. A white mist surrounded her, and the sound of rain filled her ears. "Say, where's the rain?"

In the distance, a man stood waving.

The mist turned from clouds to an Outland desert, and she was hot and thirsty. She watched the man drop a canteen. She was trotting towards it when an orc came from out of nowhere. She shot it with her bow. A gnoll popped up behind her, swinging a bastard sword. She ducked and stabbed in in the thigh. It disappeared. The suns beat down on her as she crawled hands and knees towards the canteen. She grabbed it, tipped it up to her mouth—and drank a mouthful of sand.

"Ugh! No!" she sputtered.

Nearby, Fodor stood, hands on hips, laughing.

"Have you had enough, Darlene?" he said. There was something mocking about him.

She threw the canteen at him. "No!"

He picked it up and poured water down his throat and all over himself. "Ah!"

"This game is stupid, Fodor," she said. She tried to yell, spitting sand from her mouth. "I quit." She closed her eyes and opened them. Nothing happened.

"Why am I still here?" she said, looking around.

"You half-wit!" he said. He stormed across the sand, sneering. "This game isn't over until I say it is over! And you, such audacity to speak with me and sit at my table. Oh, you shall pay for it. After this, you'll tell no more of your stupid stories to anyone again."

"What are you doing!" Darlene cried out.

"Teaching you a lesson you'll never forget, inbreed!"

Darlene grabbed her head. Her nose was bleeding! The sound of laughing voices was all around her now, jeering and making fun. Her fears overcame her, and darkness closed in.

NO! STOP THIS!

"Ha! Ha! Ha! Look, she peed herself," someone from somewhere said.

Angry and embarrassed, Darlene tried to fight back. Lashing out, her figure struck at Fodor with a knife. He rose above it, laughed, clapped his hands, and the knife was gone.

"Foolish woman, you are not clever enough to beat me!"

An invisible force squeezed her mind, suffocating her.

What is going on?

She felt a sudden loneliness that she'd never felt before. Deep down, painful despair. No one liked her. No one needed her. No one cared for her. Not even her father or mother. Her brothers and sisters even abandoned her. She had no one. She was no one.

"That's right, Darlene, no one cares about you at all. Your life doesn't even matter," Fodor laughed.

Tears were streaming down her cheeks, dripping onto the table.

I'm not so bad. I'm not so terrible.

A giant snake coiled around her and spoke through its fanged mouth.

"But you are!"

It took the breath right from her.

She deserved to die. She had no friends at all she could count on. Or did she?

SCORCH!

Joline had just spent the last several minutes pouring her heart out to the man named Scorch. He was a wonderful listener and something to look at, too. She'd just finished telling him about what happed to Kam and the baby Erin when he turned his attention away.

"Pardon me," he said. He was looking for his friend, Darlene.

"Oh my, how did she wind up with them?" Joline said. "I'm sorry, I wasn't paying any attention."

Darlene sat in her chair, catatonic, while the men laughed because she'd peed herself.

"I'll take care of this," Joline said. She rushed from behind the bar straight for Darlene's table.

"You men cut that out! She's my guest—"

Plerf!

The first man that looked up's head exploded.

"Mother of Bish—"

Plerf!

The man next to the man whose head exploded's head exploded as well.

An arc of red sprayed across the room like a rainbow.

Plerf!

Plerf!

Plerf!

One right after the other, three more men's heads exploded. Five bodies fell. Blood was everywhere. Silence fell.

Joline was shaking. Blood was sprinkled all over her hands and apron. At the table, Darlene wiped the blood from her face, gaping at her.

"Did I do that?" Darlene said.

Joline's tongue clove to the roof of her mouth.

Darlene turned and looked at Fodor. He sat wide-eyed, blood-coated and trembling in his chair.

"Did you do that?" Darlene asked him.

He shook his head.

Plerf!

His head exploded.

"Guess not," Darlene said. She grabbed the bottle of wine, pulled the cork out of the bottle with her teeth and started drinking.

Scorch was laughing. Everyone else screamed.

CHAPTER 10

T HE NEST WAS IN CHAOS.
   Find Diller! Save Erin!

Lefty picked his way through Palos's blood bath and into the streets, where skirmishes among the thieves had broken out everywhere. Screams, shouts and cries of alarm echoed up and down the alleys and across the docks, where members of the thieves' guild sought escape from one another—and from another predator: the wrath of Zorth's blade.

Two thieves tumbled through a storefront. One collapsed in a heap, begging for his life. The other drove a dagger into his chest. Lefty darted away.

I have no idea who is on whose side. I need to find Jubbler!

Wind rushing past his ears, Lefty made his way to the docks that had become the battleground of the bloody revolt. Somewhere in the throng, a deep eerie voice rang out.

"I am Zorth! Vanquisher of all evil!"

The pleas and cries of men came to an abrupt halt.

"Get that halfling!" someone cried. "He's responsible for this!"

Glancing over his shoulder, he saw two men and one dwarf coming his way. Behind them was the orcen Quarter Master.

The big orc cracked his lash over his head. "Bring that little blond head to me!"

Lefty dashed down into the Quarters, wedged himself between the crates, and began pushing himself to the other side. Booted feet rushed over the planks.

One. Two. Three. He counted as they passed by his spot.

That was close!

"That's a dead end, rogues!" The Quarter Master yelled. His broad back blocked the narrow space between the crates. "Wait a minute. I smell something. *Sniff. Sniff.* I smell fear!" The Quarter Master turned and peeked into the space." Ah, there he is!" He reached inside the space, fingers clutching, catching hold of Lefty's shirt. "I have you now!"

No!

He pulled away, but the grip of the orc was strong.

Come on, Lefty!

He dug his little fingers into the next crate and held on for dear life.

"Hah! Hah! Hah! You aren't going anywhere, little halfling, except into the murk when I'm through torturing you!"

The orc's pimply and pitted face was pale, merciless. Lefty never imagined facing death would be so horrible. Desperate, he bit down on the orc's finger with all his might.

The orc roared, but held tight, yanking him out from between the crates with one powerful tug, skinning his face. The Quarter Master held him up by the scruff of his collar and stuck the long yellow nail of his finger in his face. He bared the canines of his teeth.

"You bit me like a yellow-headed rodent; now I'm going to bite you!"

The three other thieves gathered round.

"Take a hunk off his leg!"

"No, bite his ear off!"

The dwarf pulled out a long knife and said, "Let me cut off his toes."

Lefty kicked and flailed.

The orc laughed.

"What's the matter, rodent? Are you offended that I won't cook you first?"

"No! I'm offended by the smell of sewage in your mouth."

"Hah! Ha—*urk*!"

Lefty drove his foot into the orc's throat.

The orc hoisted him over his head and slammed him into the ground.

He saw bright spots and felt his shoulder pop out of place. His eyes watered.

The orc stood over him, rubbing his greasy neck.

"Ooo, that little fit cost you, didn't it, Halfling? Hah! The little bird cannot fly away with a busted wing. Tie him up. Once this fight is over, we'll put him on a spit!"

"Heeeee!"

"Hooooooo!"

"Huuuuuuuuuuuh!"

Three burly figures leapt from the crates over them, each landing on a different thief.

One was Jubbler. The crusty dwarf drove a short sword into the neck of the dwarf. The other men's bellies were run through with spears.

Huffing, three dwarves stood there, squaring off on the Quarter Master. The orc ripped his swords from his scabbards.

"Come on then," the orc said.

Lefty scooted back behind Jubbler. The dwarf with pig tails in his beard stepped between him and Jubbler.

"The revolt is over, Quarter Master. Palos's reign is done. Drop those blades of yours, if you want mercy! Huh!"

"Huh!" the orc said. "Fool babbler! Think you I'll surrender! Think I want mercy?" He beat his chest. "The only thing I'm going to do is skin the hide from your thick dwarven necks, you loon, Jubbler!"

The Quarter Master sunk his blade in the nearest dwarf's chest.

"Hah! I'm a warrior, not a thief!"

The other dwarf jabbed his spear at the orc's knees. The Quarter Master spun away, knocked the shaft aside, and stuck his other blade into the dwarf's skull. The orc flashed them a nasty grin. "I'm gonna carve you both into troll food. Tiny little bits that are easy to swallow."

Lefty felt like he was going to vomit. Jubbler was dragging him back, but the dock was running out of room.

"I've a confession to make. Huh. Lefty. Huh. I can't swim," Jubbler said. The dwarf eyed the lake and the orc.

"Everybody knows dwarves can't swim. Don't feel bad. I don't think I can now either," he said. He was wincing and holding his shoulder. He could maybe run if he had to. Dash right past the

Quarter Master. He couldn't leave Jubbler though. But he needed to find Erin.

What to do!

The orc wrenched his dripping blade from the fallen dwarf's skull.

"I'm going to enjoy this!"

Can life get any worse in this world? I've failed at everything!

"Tis a shame, Lefty. Huh. We have this thing won! Huh. Huh. Palos's rule is over!" Jubbler said. He shuffled back another step. Only a few feet of planks left between them and the water. "Tell you what. Huh. I'll fight. Huh. You run. Huh. Tell them I need help. Huh. They'll run this pile of pig slat through. Huh."

"Bravery, the blood-letter of fools," the orc said. The Quarter Master was within striking distance.

Jubbler stopped, stood up and wrapped both hands around his sword.

"Nice knowing you, Lefty. Huh. And remember. Huh. Master Gillem would be proud. Just make sure you master those absidium chains." He raised his sword. "My hide and skull much thicker than my brother's, Orc!"

The Quarter Master banged his steel together. "We'll see about that!"

Lefty's heart sank. He didn't have many friends left. The last one he'd lost, Gillem, he wasn't close to getting over yet. Something swelled inside his chest. With his magic feet, he might be able to run right past the orc and find safety. After all, he had to find Erin. But the thought of another friend dying tore at him.

NO!

The orc swung.

Jubbler parried.

Slice.

Chop!

Bang!

Clatter!

Jubbler's sword skidded over the deck and plopped into the waters.

"Run, Lefty!" the dwarf said.

Fight or die!

On magic feet he charged. "NOOOOOOOOO!" He slammed into the Quarter Master's chest, barreling him over.

"What!" the orc cried out.

Lefty kicked. It was all he could do. His shoulder was useless. Jubbler did the same.

Whop!

A steel pommel hit Lefty in the head. Blood oozed over his eyes.

Crack!

Jubbler fell face first onto the deck.

The Quarter Master gathered his feet under him and stood over them.

"Nice try, little people." He snorted and licked his lips. "But now it's time to die. Mmmm. I'm going to be eating good tonight." He raised his swords over his head.

Exhausted, Lefty couldn't move an inch. Beside him, Jubbler lay face first on the deck. Out cold. Lefty spit blood. He'd fought with all he had in him.

It was the right thing to do. Save a friend a little longer. It had to be. Fight or Die.

He closed his eyes.

I'm sorry, Kam and Erin.

"I am Zorth!"

Lefty's weary eyes snapped open.

Thorn's face and haggard figure quickly approached, wielding a gleaming sword as long as a man in his hands.

"Vanquisher of Giants! Dragons and Evil Doers!"

"What! Thorn!"

The Quarter Master roared and charged.

"You'll not be robbing me of my —"

SLICE!

Thorn swung through the big orc, shattering his blades with one stroke. Blood spilled from the slit in his waist. The orc gawped. The great sword sung again, ripping the head from his shoulders. It bounced off the deck and splashed into the waters.

"I am Zorth! The end of all evil is at hand!"

Lefty leered up at the tall and rangy man. His face was charred and pink. His eyes black. The man he'd known as Thorn was gone and wouldn't be missed. But now, whoever had him possessed was a far superior threat. Lefty lost his breath when Zorth looked down on him with burning black eyes. Blood was dripping from the blade.

"I am Zorth! No evil shall remain!"

Am I evil?

Lefty watched the blade go up like it was a mile high in the air.

Or is he insane?

Blue eyes wide as saucers, he watched the blade descend.

Clatch-Zip! Clatch-Zip! Clatch-Zip! Clatch-Zip! Clatch-Zip!

Crossbow bolts ripped into the big man's body.

Thorn turned and faced his agitators. Filled with bolts in his chest, legs and neck, he stormed up the deck.

"I am Zorth! Avenger of Good. Vanquisher of Evil!"

A dozen thieves greeted him. Crossbows rocking.

Clatch-Zip! Clatch-Zip! Clatch-Zip! Clatch-Zip! Clatch-Zip! Clatch-Zip! Clatch-Zip! Clatch-Zip! Clatch-Zip! Clatch-Zip! ...

Zorth crashed into the ones at the top of the bank. A dozen bolts in his chest. The Sword of Zorth rose and fell. Bones were splintered. Cries went out. Many rogues twitched on the bloody deck. Others searched for their limbs.

"I am Zorth! Destroy —

Clatch-Zip!

A bolt went inside his one temple and stuck out the other.

The great sword clattered to the deck. The remaining rogues chopped Thorn into ribbons.

Lefty wiped the blood from his eyes.

Thank Bish!

A strong hand squeezed his bad shoulder. He flinched.

It was Jubbler. "You alright, Huh!"

"Aye!" Lefty said, swallowing.

Erin!

"Jubbler! Do you know where Erin is?"

CHAPTER
11

T HE WORLD OF PALOS WAS dark, sadistic, perverted and dreary. Kam was choking in the man's darkness with only his laughter echoing inside her ears.

"Kam," he taunted. "I told you that you'd be my whore forever. Now I have you."

Light of a candle flared, illuminating a small wood paneled room with no doors. Tears swelled up in her eyes as she sat on her knees, now a little girl with all the insecurities in the world. Bugs the size of her fist scurried over the room. Each with a different facade of Palos for a face. One crawled up her bound arms and spoke with antennas twitching.

"Are you afraid, little girl? Do you fear the night?" He shape-shifted into a rat. "The rodents. The creatures that slither across the floor!" He turned into a burning green snake and coiled his tail around her neck. "Shall I burn your mind the same as you did my belly?" He hissed. "Hmmm... you lactating witch!"

She couldn't tear her gaze away. She was hypnotized with his power.

"What am I doing here?" she cried out. "Where am I! Where am I!"

The candle went out. Everything was gone. Only the sound of her sobs remained.

What am I doing inside the mind of Palos?

She had to find him. Find something. Find a way out of his maze.

"You never should have come here, Kam!" His voice screamed. "I'll never let you out!"

The sound of a heavy metal door banging closed. She found

herself inside a room, her full adult body bound up in chains. It was freezing. She shivered without control. Her chin quivered. Her teeth clacked.

Palos appeared before her, dressed in warm white clothes, handsome and captivating. He lifted her trembling chin into his soft hands and looked her straight in the eye.

"Kam, swear yourself to me. Be my slave, and I'll end this misery," he said.

She tried to look away, but his words, his warmth, were so inviting.

But I hate you.

A tear dropped down her cheek and froze on her chin.

He kissed her forehead.

"You don't hate me, Kam. You desire me. You want me. Give in to me, and all will be well again," he said.

Why am I here?

She shook her head and looked down at the frosty chains that covered her naked frame. Her breath was frosty.

"So cold ... I can't think," she said.

She was disoriented, lost and frozen. All of her memories, her passions, feeling and anger were gone. If she had an issue with Palos, she couldn't remember it. Why would she be angry with Palos? He was such a charming man.

Isn't he my friend?

"Of course I'm your friend," he said. He stroked her hair with the back of his soft hand. "I'm your only friend now. I can save you. Just swear yourself to me. I'll protect you and your daughter."

"What ..." she said, fighting against her dream-like state, "daughter?"

The one you are looking for ... A dark, powerful voice spoke.

"Who?" she said. She looked around.

"Who are you?" Palos demanded, jumping back from her. "Who is this, Kam? Who are you?"

There was fear in the voice of the Prince of Thieves now. It was an alarming sound. An awakening. The cold chains that bound her faded away into her green mage's gown. She shook her head.

The dark voice spoke again, more demanding this time. *Where is her daughter, Palos?*

"Erin!" Kam screamed.

A dark figure of shadows emerged between Kam and Palos. Its eyes were two burning rubies, and it had a hooked nose. Its gaze sent a chill straight through her.

Palos's face filled with horror. "Get away from me!" He drifted back into the metal door, panic in his eyes. He turned and pulled at the handle. It would not open.

"Where's my daughter, Palos!" Kam shouted. Her strength was returning.

"I'll never tell! I'll never — AYEEEEEEEE!"

The black figure's fingers stretched out like tendrils, filling Palos's nostrils and mouth, burrowing into his ears.

Where is the girl, deceitful one?

Palos shook his head. He ground his teeth.

"No!"

Then I shall dig it out myself!

The black figure reached deeper into Palos's mind.

The Prince of Thieves screamed.

The black figure ripped out his mind.

Kam's eyes popped open. She was gasping. Lying in a pool of her own sweat by the fireplace on Palos's apartment floor. Rubbing her head, she looked up and found the Prince of Thieves still bound to his chair. His eyes were rolled up inside his head. He babbled. Drool spilled from his mouth onto his chest.

"What happened?" Struggling to her feet, she scanned the room, worried. "Where are you? Where is Erin?" She looked down at her hand. It was glowing like fire. The red gems she no longer held. They were now embedded inside her hand.

"No! What madness is this?" She tried to rake them out on the chair. On the table. She screamed. "You said you'd help me find my daughter. Tell me what you found out from Palos!"

His mind did not escape the inquiry. Time to serve, Kam!

Exhausted, Kam fell to her knees, gaping at her hand. What had she done? She'd wanted to live so desperately that she would have done anything to see her daughter again. Now she was bound with a force she couldn't have dreamed of. Only moments ago, she was going to be the slave of Palos, and now she was the slave to something else. And she still didn't have Erin.

Wiping her sweaty locks from her face, she said, "What would you have me do?"

I must return to my home.

She glanced at Palos. He was drooling like an imbecile.

Serves him right.

"And where is that?" she said. "What!" Her body was propelled to the table.

I'll tell you when we get there, but for now, I need to see through your eyes and ears. Ah ... it's good to smell again, even though it's not like my home.

She grabbed a carafe of Palos's wine to her lips and drank.

The voice inside her head, eerie and dark.

This is good, a fine, exquisite taste, but I have no need for more.

Kam forced the carafe away from her lips and set it down. "Can I—or we—at least try to find my daughter on your way home? Please!"

Not likely. I've waited long enough already.

"But—"Kam said. The front door burst open. "Lefty!"

The halfling boy limped inside, holding his shoulder, face bleeding.

"We've got Diller, Kam," he said. He eyed her then looked at the ground. "But no word on Erin ... I-I'm afraid to say."

A dwarf with a strange beard entered along with four other rogues who dragged a chained Diller in and slung him on the floor. Palos's reliable lieutenant Diller's eyes widened when he saw his boss.

"What happened to him?" he said.

"He didn't tell me what I wanted to hear!" Kam said. She stepped forward and stretched out her glowing hand. "And if you think you will get off any easier than him, Diller, you better think again."

Lefty, Jubbler and the rest of the men moved backward. Diller struggled in the absidium chains.

"You might break me, Princess, but you'll always be Palos's whore!"

With a wave of her hand, Kam slammed Diller into the ceiling and back down into the floor face first.

"LAST WARNING, FOOL!" she yelled. The entire room shook.

Lefty trembled.

"Huh-Huh-Huh. Mercy, never seen the likes of that—Huh—before," Jubbler whispered. The other men ducked out of the room without a glance. "You sure she's a friend of yours? Huh."

Kam whirled on the old dwarf, green eyes like blazing emeralds.

"*I tire of you tiny people,*" she said. Her voice was not hers. "*Away with you!*"

Jubbler was lifted from his feet and went sailing out of the room. The door slammed shut behind him. "*Don't move, Halfling!*"

Lefty tried not to shake but couldn't help it.

"Where is my child, Diller?" Kam's words lifted him in the air, slowly spinning him around, upside down.

Nose dripping on the floor, he rolled a bloody toothpick from one side of his mouth to the other and stared at Palos's vacant, babbling face. "Promise you'll not do that to me. Your word. I was going to protect you from that monster, Kam. I swear I was."

There was some truth to his words. Kam could feel it, but he was a liar. They all were.

"That's the risk you'll have to take, Diller, but the longer you delay, the more dire your future will become." She slapped him so hard he spun in a complete circle. Two gemstone scorch marks were on his cheek. She was losing control.

I'm losing my patience, Kam.

"TELL ME NOW, DILLER!"

"She's here!" He stammered.

"Where!"

"Below. In the tunnels. I'll show you! Oh Kam, I don't want to die. I'll take you right there. I swear it! My word!" He eyeballed Palos, who was vomiting on himself. "Anything at all!"

Diller's body fell hard on the floor. Groaning, he rose to his feet.

"Do you know about these tunnels, Lefty?"

He started to move his neck.

"SPEAK!"

"No Ma'am!" he said. "Never been or heard of there."

She released her spell. Diller fell to the floor and slowly got up to his feet. He rubbed his head.

"Lead, Diller, and if you do anything stupid, you'll be eating your drool with a spoon."

"Certainly. Certainly, Kam!" he said. He headed out the door and shuffled down the steps.

"Come," she said to Lefty. "Shoulder hurt?"

"Yes."

"Good."

The once lively tavern was occupied only by Jubbler, a few other rogues, and the dead. All the living eyes were wary as Kam passed. She could feel their fear. Clutching her hand open and closed, she felt great power—and liked it.

Diller made his way into the kitchen, put his shoulder into a cupboard, and shoved it across the floor, revealing a set of stairs.

"It's Diller," he yelled. "And I'm coming down, with company." He turned towards Kam with a worried look in his eyes. "She's not alone down there, but I can't speak to her condition. Not seen her in a while."

"Go!" she said.

A torch was lit at the bottom of a tunnel that burrowed straight through the ground. Wooden rafters held it up like a mine tunnel. A series of chambers and tunnels greeted them at the bottom.

"This is where Palos keeps his hoard," Diller said. "Josh! Are you back there?"

A man in chainmail lumbered forward from the gloom with a longsword ready. He had a hard face, but was stout with a neck full of muscles.

"Where is Palos? And who are these two?"

Time to serve, Kam. I grow impatient!

"Not without my child," she said.

"Who is she talking to?" Josh said. The guard eyed her. "Is this the mother of the baby? The baby is not well."

"Shut up, you fool!" Diller said.

A charge of fire shot from Kam's hand. Josh was incinerated.

"Erin! Erin!"

Somewhere, a baby cried out.

"Erin!

She ran through the ashes and into the darkness.

"Kam, wait!" Diller shouted. "There's more men in there. This is Palos's—"

A grown man screamed. Another followed, echoing in the chambers. It was a horrifying sound. Lefty pulled out his dagger. Even though Diller's arms were chained behind his back, he was still dangerous, and it had only been minutes since they tried to kill one another. But the man didn't move. He didn't move a muscle.

Lefty looked at his sweaty feet. They'd been like that ever since he entered Kam's room. The beautiful woman he so admired was no longer herself. She was something else. Something dark and powerful had overtaken her. He thought of those gems. He'd given them to her, so her possession was his fault as well.

Can I do nothing right?

"Do you think she's going to kill me?" Diller said. His eyes were fixed on the dark tunnel.

"I think she's going to kill both of us if her Erin isn't alright."

Diller shook his head. "If I live through this, I swear to Bish I'll never do bad things anymore. That Palos, I was scared of him, but nothing like this angry mother."

Diller was spooked. Lefty was astounded. The man had been nothing but cold and cruel since the moment they met, but now there was something different about him. If Diller could change, perhaps he could change too.

Kam's eyes were glowing as she stormed up the tunnel, a baby swaddled in her arms. The baby cried and coughed, a wrenching sound. It was Erin; Lefty could feel it inside his bones. She was alive, but not well.

"Kam, anything to help, I will," Diller said. His eyes were pleading. His arms open. "I'm so sorry for all of this."

She clenched her fist and twisted.

Crack!

Diller's neck snapped. He fell to the ground.

Lefty gulped.

She's going to kill me.

She glared at him, shook her fist, and stomped up the stairs. "Don't ever lose my baby again, Lefty! Now find my father's sword! Whatever might bring Erin comfort, and meet me at those docks."

Tears dropped from Lefty's eyes. His tongue clove to the roof of his mouth. He wanted to say thank you out loud but could not.

Oh mercy! Thank you!

"And quit crying! You've shed enough tears already!"

Time to serve, Kam!

She didn't care who she served now that she had her baby. Erin nuzzled her chest as Lefty shoved the gondola off and waved good bye to Jubbler and his ilk.

"We better not wind up here again, rogues, else I'll kill you all!" Kam shouted.

"Huh! No worries, Crazy Lady. Huh! None at all!" Jubbler waved.

Irritated, Kam summoned a flaming snake onto their deck, bringing fire to everything in their paths. "Piss on them and you." She eyed Lefty. "Row, blast it!"

"My shoulder. I-I can't."

"Is it broken?"

"N-No. Just dislocated."

She held out her hand and spread her fingers.

Lefty's eyes widened like saucers. His head beaded with sweat.

"That hurt?" she said.

He shook his head.

Pop!

"Better now?"

He nodded and rubbed his shoulder.

"Don't thank me," she said. "Just be quiet. Be still."

Time to serve, Kam! I'm losing patience.

"We are leaving, fiend!"

She snapped her fingers.

The oars came to life, whisking them over the dead waters and away.

Time to serve! Time to serve! Time to serve!

CHAPTER 12

C ASS HELD ON TO CHONGO for dear life. She was exhausted. The big dog was fast, but not tireless. She could feel him laboring for breath. For over an hour they'd run, chased down by underlings that rode on the backs of spiders as big as horses. It sent a chill through her.

"Run, Chongo! Run!"

Thirty minutes into the chase, she was certain she'd lost them, but that's when more spider riders appeared. Not just a couple either. An entire patrol. Their riders had weapons raised. The spiders' fangs were bared. They scurried right after them.

Sheesh! Those are sick looking things!

Animals were one thing with Cass, but bugs were another. Many druids like the bugs, but they weren't part of her nature. It was fine when the blue bees made honey, but spider webs and slimy toads grossed her out. As a girl, she was fed crunchy bugs once, and she'd never gotten over it.

Chongo dashed into a large grove, paws ripping into the ground beneath him, stirring up dust. Cass hunched down. The branches whipped over her face and legs, stinging her and drawing thin lines of blood on her pale skin.

What have I done?

Digging her nails into the thick mane on Chongo's neck, her free thoughts turned to regrets. She'd left Fogle Boon to blindly chase a two headed dog she now shared a bond with, much further than she ever imagined. Chongo, tongues hanging from his mouth, was going after his master. He'd made it clear he wouldn't stop for anything until he got there. Now she was lost.

"I hope you know where you're going!"

All she could see were glimpses of the sky as they ran under the trees. They needed to hide, outdistance themselves or do something. Behind her, she could hear the spiders crashing through the trees, getting closer.

Don't look back!

She did.

A spider and rider were so close she could see the red in all their eyes.

I've got to do something!

She couldn't think of anything.

Something!

Wind whipping through her hair, Cass struggled to hang on. Chongo raced full speed through the grove and into a ravine. His feet were trampling through a wide creek, bend after bend, when he came to an abrupt stop at the edge of a drop off. It was unlike anything Cass had ever seen before. The creek dropped over one hundred feet, waters crashing into a pool below. She gasped. The underlings and the spiders had caught up with them.

Chongo turned, lowered his heads, and growled.

There were five spiders in all, hairy legs creeping over the creek waters while the underlings chittered and hooted. Cass summoned every ounce of magic she had left.

Bish, give me strength!

Chongo's barks echoed up the ravine. The hairy black spiders hitched up on their hind legs and spewed webs, covering the ground and sticking to Chongo's legs. He let out a howl, trying to tear free.

"No, Chongo! You'll make it worse."

Cords of webbing caught her by the waist. They tugged at her.

"Never Insects!" Magic swelled inside her chest. Fire burst from her hands. She stroked the big dog and moaned. In an instant, both she and Chongo were consumed by flame. The webbing burned away. Chongo charged the nearest spider, jaws tearing off its legs and chomping the underling rider. Everything Chongo touched caught fire. The brush, the spiders, the underling soldiers. The beast tore into them with ferocious fury.

Hold on!

Her strength was already waning.

Two spiders and riders twitched and burned in the creek.

Chongo pounced on the third, slinging Cass to the ground. She hit her head on a stone.

"Ugh!"

The flames left Chongo, surrounding her and her alone. She regained her feet.

Focus Cass! Focus!

Thickt!

Thickt!

Thickt!

Cords of web shot all over the big dog, sticking him to the ground. Chongo's jaws remained locked on an underling. The two heads tore the screaming underling in two parts.

Two underlings on spiders closed in on the beast. They launched black lances into his side.

"NOOOO!" Cass yelled. She dove onto one spider's legs, spreading her fire all over it.

It pitched upward, bucking its rider and sending the underling to the ground. She dove on top of it, wrapped her hands around its throat, and watched its flesh burn to the bone.

Too-wah! Too-wah! Too-wah!

Arching her back, hands out, she felt sharp things lodge deep inside her back and shoulders. Her flames went out. She couldn't move.

What's happened?

A forceful hand grabbed her by the hair and pulled her around. A pale blue-eyed underling in dark mail armor, holding a blow gun, stood over her, flashing a row of sharp teeth. He laughed and stepped away, clearing a view of Chongo.

Chongo was coated in webs so thick she could barely see him.

What have I done?

And the ravine, where they'd fled, was filled with the speckled eyes of underlings as far as she could see.

This can't be happening!

There was nothing she could do. The underling reached down, fondled her hair, and wrapped a rope around her neck. Chittering an order, another hulking albino underling, the likes of which she never imagined, grabbed the rope, jerked her stiff body to the ground and dragged her up the ravine through the creek.

She could feel everything.

CHAPTER 13

"JUST TELL ME," BOON SAID.

They were doubled up on the horse's saddle, and Fogle had gotten tired of telling Boon no. It did feel good however to have his grandfather by the short hairs of his beard for a change. Still, he wasn't going to tell his secret about how to find the underlings.

"No!"

It felt good saying it.

Ahead, Barton led the way with great strides, swinging his heavy arms that almost dragged on the landscape. Fogle still had a difficult time wrapping his head around people being so big. It didn't seem natural or possible, yet in the City of Three, there were three giant statues in the park he remembered seeing as a boy. The stone-faced figures seemed so real at the time, but as he got older he gave them little thought.

And all this time they said the city was named after the great waterfalls. How many other lies have I been led to believe were true?

Boon hopped off the saddle, scowling. "I'm tired of riding."

"Good," Fogle said.

It was dark, overcast above, the clouds giving off a dull light from the moons.

"Tis a good way to travel, with the clouds out. The moons cast too many shadows, making it easier for things to hide," Boon remarked.

"Well, what are you up to now?"

Boon was floating along his side, arms crossed over his chest, smiling.

"Are you using magic? I thought you told me to save my power for battles. In the book it says, and you wrote it yourself, 'Not for frivolous use'." Fogle's brows were knitted.

"I didn't write that for myself, but for you. Besides, I have a great deal more power than you."

"What?" Fogle began to object.

But Boon floated high in the air, stretching his arms out exclaiming, 'Weeeeeeeeeeeeee'."

Fogle huffed.

Madman!

As he watched his grandfather swoop up and down in the sky, he couldn't help but be a little jealous. He wished he could be carefree and dangerous at the same time. He wished he had Boon's fearless edge.

How did he get like that?

Barton stopped, eyeballing the floating wizard. He pointed his log of a finger at the man, looked back at Fogle, and giggled. "Barton wants to float like birdie too, Wizard. Can you send me up there? Hee hee!"

I'd love to send you both sailing away. Nothing would delight me more.

Fogle rode his horse alongside the giant, stared into Barton's good eye, and smiled. "No."

"Aw." Barton kicked up a chunk of dirt. "I've never flown before. If I could fly, I could beat that dragon!" He punched his fist into his hand. "Hate that dragon!"

Dragon?

"Barton?"

The giant was staring into the sky, looking for Boon, who'd disappeared.

"Barton!"

"Hmmm?" Barton still eyed the sky.

"What dragon are you talking about?"

"Blackie." His fingers clutched in and out.

Whatever Blackie is, Barton really doesn't like it.

"Eh ... can you tell me more about Blackie?"

Barton yawned and started walking away, watching the sky and craning his neck as he did so. "I can tell you about Blackie. Barton hate Blackie. Barton hides and Blackie always finds him. Picks him up and flies him home."

"Picks you up? All of you?"

"Blackie's big. Strong wings. Picks Barton up like a hawk and rodent. Hate Blackie. Hate him."

Oh great. Giants, underlings, and dragons are after us. And all I have is this horse to ride on. Bish! I wish Mood were here! What else is there in this world?

"Barton, tell me more about where you come from. Are there many giants and dragons?"

"Oh yes. Many of both, but more giants." He scratched his head. "I think so. Barton likes to hide in the Mist. Many things do."

"Is this dragon, Blackie, coming after you now, you think?"

"Hmmmm ... well, little man with axe said he chopped Blackie's wings. Maybe, maybe not, but you'll know. 'Whump. Whump. Whump.' You'll know. Hate that sound. 'Whump. Whump. Whump.'"

All of his life, Fogle had seen many things named after dragons. Taverns. Streets. And so on. But he never knew anyone that admitted to seeing one until now.

I wonder if Mood has seen one? I wonder if it's true.

Fogle dug his heels into his horse. It lurched forward and caught back up with Barton.

"What else can you tell me about where you're from? Is it just like this, but bigger?"

"I guess so. But, I've only seen little of this place. More water though. Much more water. Splash. Splash. I like the water. I like to drown Blackie in water. Yes! Yes! Drown Blackie!"

He's demented.

"Are there people my size?"

"Yes. Many."

"Are there underlings?"

"Those little black peoples that try to kill Barton?"

"Yes."

"No."

Feeling a little foolish, Fogle realized that if he ever got the time, perhaps it would do him some good to ask his grandfather more about where he'd been and what he'd seen. And to remember that Venir had been there too.

Barton stopped.

Fogle pulled on his reins. An eerie feeling fell over him as he watched the backs of Barton's ears bend up and down with a life of their own. Thoughts of a giant black dragon dropping through the clouds raced through his mind.

"Woof. Woof."

"Blackie?" Fogle said. He crouched down, eyeing the sky.

"No. Woof. Woof. Like dog. Big one."

"Like Chongo?" Fogle said, sitting up, excited.

Barton nodded and pointed.

"That way! Uh oh." His ears wiggled.

"What!"

Barton looked back at him, scratching his shoulder, sniffing the air. "I hear many of those little black things too."

"How far?"

"Pretty far for you, not so far for me," Barton said. He turned and jogged off.

Fogle snapped the reins. Inky, his ebony hawk, swooped down from the clouds and soared above him. Focusing, his eyes and Inky's became one.

Scout ahead.

Inky darted through the air, a black streak in the night, soaring by Barton's head and out of sight.

Cass! Is she close?

"Slow down!" Boon said. He dropped from the sky. "I can only float so fast!"

Fogle wasn't listening. He was galloping.

Come on! Come on! Cass, where are you?

Inky's vision was different than a man's. Where a man saw shadows and the dark shapes in the night, Inky saw pale illuminating lines that separated one object from another. Ahead, rocks and brush, typical of what they saw, but they weren't heading south anymore. They were heading west, or so Fogle thought.

"Barton! Slow down!"

The giant kept going. One mile became two, then three.

How far can he hear, anyway?

Inky, flying ahead, didn't pick up anything extraordinary, but a series of jagged cliffs was ahead. Fogle whipped the reins. He was right on Barton's heels.

The giant labored for breath, clutched his side, and slowed. He waded into a pool of water. He pointed towards the top of some cliffs, where a small stream of water gushed like a waterfall.

Fogle's horse clomped into the water, bent its neck and began to drink.

"Hold on, Barton," he said. He closed his eyes.

Inky soared along the edge of the cliff, and Fogle could see everything.

Trees. Trees. Bushes. Creek. Is that a giant spider? "Mother of Bish—Underlings!"

Speckled eyes were like bright dots in the forest as Inky sailed by. A series of crossbow bolts assailed the bird.

Fogle lurched in his saddle and toppled into the water.

"What happened? Barton said. He helped him up.

"Slat happened! That's what! They're up there, Barton." Fogle pointed. "I can feel it."

Barton dug his hands into the ravine rock and began climbing up. "I know."

Fogle sent Inky into the fray above.

"I'll be ready this time," he said, wringing the water out of his robes.

Inky sailed above the top of the grove, dove down and landed high in the branches. He could see the pale figures of the underlings heading back up the creek, dozens of them. And clumps of black hairy flesh on the ground were burning.

What is that?

Bringing up the rear, they were dragging something, something shaped like a—

Woman! Cass!

Grabbing the vines at the base of the cliff, he climbed. Ten feet up he went. Ten feet down he came.

Splash!

Wiping the water from his face, he yelled, "Come back and get me, Barton!"

But the giant was already halfway up a hundred foot scale.

"Save Cass!" he said. "Bone! I have to get up there qui—*ulp!*"

Two strong arms hoisted him for the pool and took him upward.

"You need a lift, I see," Boon said. "Prepare a chain of energy, Fogle."

"No! That will kill Cass! This is a rescue, not a battle!"

"How many, Fogle?"

"Dozens at least." They floated alongside Barton. "And giant spiders too."

Barton laughed. "Many fun. Wizards make many fun."

"Hurry up, Boon," Fogle said.

The thought of Cass being dead rattled him. He could still see her limp form being dragged away.

"We need a plan," Boon said. "Barton, when you crest that edge, get after them. Fogle, you and I will grab the woman, but you need to focus. They'll have darts, poison, paralyzation at their disposal. We'll need thicker skin to drag her out of there. Much thicker."

Fogle knew immediately what Boon was talking about and summoned his power. He'd readied the spell in his mind earlier. His skin toughened like hide leather. Boon dipped under his added weight.

"Well done. Now, when you get her, grab her and get out of there. I'll handle the rest," Boon said. He stopped just below the crest. Barton hung on the rock at their side. "Can you make that jump if you have to, Barton?"

His big face leered down. He said, "Barton will make big splash!"

"And don't forget about the dog," Boon said. "Now listen to me, Fogle, don't come back for me. Get to safety. I'll catch up if I have to. Ah, and one more thing."

Boon led them over the edge and set Fogle down. Barton cleared the lip and rolled to his feet. Fogle could see the underlings and spiders heading back up the path less than thirty yards away.

Boon held out his hands.

"Barton, give me your finger."

Barton extended his hand.

"You going to make me fly?"

Boon wrapped his hands around the giant's finger and smiled. "No. I'm going to make you fast. Very fast! But it won't last long, so make the most of it."

Barton's face brightened like the suns.

"Go! Go! GOOOOOO!" Barton said. He smashed his fist in his palm. "This is gonna be fun!"

Fogle could see every underling stop and turn. Like black coyotes, they dashed down the ravine. Angry. Chittering. Two spiders the size of horses scurried over the waters at full charge.

Barton met them all head on. His fists drummed like giant flails. "Barton hate bugs!"

The first spider and rider were turned into piles of goo. More underlings and spiders piled on the giant. Barton was a hurricane of flesh in their midst. Snatching, stomping, tearing and rending them like bugs.

"I see the dog." Boon pointed. "Move now, Fogle. I'll try to cover you."

Without thinking, Fogle ran up the wall of the ravine. Through the ebony hawk's eyes, he could see Cass's form still being dragged along. He pushed his way through the branches and caught one in the face. *Blasted trees!* His chest was heaving when he emerged in the clearing. He cut into the underling's path.

The underling stopped. Pale blue eyes leering at him. It pulled a short jagged sword from its belt and charged.

Fogle summoned a word of power, shattering its blade.

The underling kept coming. Slammed into him full force, driving him into the ground. In an instant it wrapped its claws around Fogle's throat.

He couldn't breathe. It was strong as a man, but Fogle was stronger. The iron skin he'd summoned saw to that. He grabbed the underling by the wrists and started pulling them away.

"Must! Save! Cass!" he said. He gave it a heave, tearing its arms away.

It hissed, sinking its teeth into his shoulder.

Fogle didn't feel a thing.

It bit again. Its claws ripped at his robes.

"These are my only robes, you fiend! The Bish with you!"

Grabbing a round rock from the stream bed, he clocked it in the head.

The underling held on, determined, like a hungry badger.

Fogle muttered a word of power, ignited his rock-filled hand, and smote the underling again in the skull.

Crack!

Its head busted open like an egg. Its jaw slackened.

Fogle shoved its dead body off him, gasping for breath.

"Cass!"

Pitching the rock, Fogle scurried alongside her. Removing the rope from around her neck, he lifted her limp form up in his arms and backtracked.

Ahead, the battle raged on. Barton's bellows echoed up the ravine like thunder, and bright bursts of energy sizzled and crackled into the underlings from all directions. Even the barks of two angry hound heads could be heard. But the woman in his arms was not moving.

"Hang on, Cass." He was shoving his way through the thicket. Inky, in the branches above, shrieked. Fogle stopped. Something else was moving their way, and moving fast. He surged through the forest.

"Boon! Boon!" he said. Finally, He emerged where he'd started.

Barton and Chongo were finishing off the underlings. Boon's hands were smoking.

"I see you got her!"

"Boon, you know that spell for the portal?"

"Yes, why?"

"We could use it now." Fogle tried to contain his panic. "Underlings are coming. I can see them. Hundreds are close and beyond them, thousands!"

"Go then! Continue your quest, Grandson! I'll slow them down. Use the spellbook!" He looked over the falls. "Make it count!"

Fogle could see Barton and Chongo's work was finished. Both were bleeding, but the underlings and spiders were pulverized.

"We'll all flee together, Boon! You gave your word."

"To save the girl and the dog, not the man!"

"But, he has all the power, you said." Still holding Cass's limp body, Fogle muttered, summoning a cushion of air along the falls. "Barton, Chongo, come!"

Obeying, they came, stepping off the drop into mid-air where they slowly lowered.

"Come on, Boon! They're close! You can't take them all!"

Boon stared back at him with a grim smile on his face. "They're so much more fun to kill in bunches!"

Drifting down past the lip, he lost sight of Boon. He shook his head until they landed at the pool in the bottom.

Barton rinsed the blood from his hands. "That was fun. We do that again soon, right Wizard?"

Fogle draped Cass over the saddle and swung himself up onto the horse.

"Sure, Barton." He dug his heels into his horse.

Barton and Chongo followed.

Inky soared above the grove, showing Fogle swarm after swarm of underlings piling inside. They coated the landscape like black moss.

One moment, the grove was calm and quiet. In the next was a series of explosions and bright colorful spots.

"Enjoy, Grandfather." Fogle didn't look back. He couldn't fight the feeling he'd never see his grandfather again. *No one could survive that. Not even The Darkslayer. Come, Inky.*

CHAPTER 14

T *OOWHIP.*

    Toowhip.

Toowhip.

Venir opened the heavy lids of his eyes, squinting in the brightness. It was daytime. It was pain time. Everything from head to toe throbbed.

Toowhip.

Toowhip.

Toowhip.

Something struck his face again and again, like tiny stinging insects. His arms rattled, and his wrists ached. From the corner of his eye, he saw a long metal needle jutting from his face.

What?

There were needles in his arms, dozens of them, each leaving a red swelling mark. His head felt like it weighed a ton. He lifted his chin and locked eyes with a ruby eyed underling. One of many. His arm trembled in his bonds. *This can't be!*

It was Outpost Thirty One, but filled with a different ilk, underlings. Hundreds of them were at work within the walls of the huge fort, pushing carts over the courtyard, hammering steel by forges, and ordering motley assortments of men, orcs and kobolds about. Remnants of the Brigand Queen's army. It was a vision of Venir's world turned inside out. A nightmare.

Toowhip.

Toowhip.

Three underling soldiers, little more than five feet tall, adorned in black leather armor, had Venir surrounded. Each reloaded a small blowgun and spat a needle at him. One chittered, pointed at his face with the long nail of his finger, and spat.

Toowhip.

Struck him on the tip of his nose.

"Come closer, Underling, and I'll shove that up your arse," he said. But it was unintelligible. His tongue was thick as wool.

Ignoring the throbbing, Venir scanned his conditions. He was on a set of scaffolding two stories tall and shackled to the wooden blood-stained deck. On the corner of the deck, a bucket sat, with moisture on its lip. He thirsted. Below him, underlings were at work, some staring up with gemstone eyes to catch a look at him. They chittered and gestured. Some laughed before looking away. He'd never heard an underling laugh before. It was a disturbing sound. Shrill and creepy.

One of the underling guards made his way down a ladder, hopped to the ground, and disappeared into one of the buildings below the massive catwalks. It seemed Venir's awakening required the attention of somebody.

Dying of thirst, Venir eyed the other two underlings. He fought the urge to ask them for water. He'd never ask an underling for anything. He'd die first. Despite the ache and stiffness in his wrists, he plucked out a dart and flicked it away.

Toowhip.

Toowhip.

For every dart he picked, a half dozen more replaced it. His arms, legs and torso were covered with a hundred little stings. He kept plucking. Watching. Fighting the pain and ignoring the mocking chitters of the underlings.

Two underlings were whipping an orcen man in the stockades. Other humans pulled carts with weapons and armor, while underlings clad in black armor trained. The underlings moved about the confines of the fort like parts in a well-oiled machine, running drill after drill. Their sharp blades moved fast, glinting in the light of the two suns.

Venir's thoughts drifted to Slim and Commander Jans. Did the underlings know they were near? "Ugh!"

A dart caught him in the lid of his eye.

He reached to pluck it away.

The underling grabbed his wrist.

"Get your claws off me, Fiend." Venir said.

One underling clocked him in the head with a long stick while the other kicked him in the thigh.

Venir yelped. "Bone!" He reversed his grip, snatched the underling's wrist, and jerked it to the ground. Wrapping the underling's neck in the nook of his arm, he squeezed, ignoring all the needles being driven farther into his arm.

The other underling guard beat on his head with fury.

Whack! Whack! Whack!

Venir held on. He'd kill one more underling before the day was done. He heaved. The underling's tongue writhed out of its mouth. Claws stretched out for its last grasp of life. It shuddered and convulsed. Venir crushed its throat. The sound of steel being ripped from a sheath caught his ears. He whipped around. The underling guard's arm coiled back to strike his throat.

A commanding voice shouted out in underling.

The underling sentry stayed his hand, chest heaving. Nostrils flaring.

The platform groaned as a figure made its way up the ladder.

A burly underling warrior, the size of two in one, appeared.

Venir had never seen such an underling before. Dark plate covered its chest, and its arms and chest were as thick as an ape's. Dark ruby eyes glowered at him as it walked over and struck him in the face with its mailed gauntlet.

Venir saw spots. Tuuth's big pale frame appeared behind the underling commander, holding the canister he had carried to signal for the Royal Riders.

A moment of awful clarity. Venir realized his plan was not such a good plan after all. He'd never considered the consequences of the canister falling into underling hands.

Bish, I'm a fool!

All he could do was hope the underlings wouldn't figure out what it was there for.

The burly underling commander grabbed Venir by the hair and pounded the tiny needles deeper into his chest, one blow after the other.

The excruciating pain was blinding. He cried out.

Tuuth was wincing.

"Big human. You should have known better than to kill underlings. Now tell us, why are you here?"

Clutching his chest, he replied, "Hunting red-eyed arseholes."

The underling commander looked up at Tuuth and asked, "What is *arsehole*?"

Grimacing, Tuuth pointed at his butt.

Chittering with anger, the underling grabbed Venir's hair by both hands, dragged him over the planks and slung him off the platform.

He landed flat on his back. "Ooooph!" All the fight he'd had left in him was gone.

Above, the underlings and Tuuth peered down at him.

The underling commander snatched the canister from Tuuth and waved it in the air. "I know about your Royal army. I know what this is. We are ready. Very ready to slaughter them all." The underling ripped the top off the canister, pointed it skyward and whacked it on the bottom.

A ball of energy shot high in the air, darting over the giant logs of the fort and out of sight.

The sound of the Southern gate being opened caught his ears. The underling tossed down the canister, and it clocked him in the head.

"Get a rope, Orc!" He pointed down at Venir. "And drag this *arsehole* back up here by the neck. I want him to see the devastation we shall inflict on his people."

CHAPTER 15

I T WAS HOT AND HUMID. Just another day on Bish. The Royal Riders had just about finished breaking down their camp when a myriad of bright spots sparkled and sizzled above them. Every Royal Rider in the area stopped and stared.

Slim was among them.

Commander Jans held his hand over his visor and exclaimed. "Ready your horses, men!"

New energy spread over the spirits of the hard-driven men.

"Seems your friend hasn't perished after all, Healer. Look!"

"I'll be. He did it," Slim said. A surge of energy coursed through him. "Jans! What do you say now?"

All eyes in the camp were on the commander as he pulled himself up into the saddle. The Royal Rider stroked his long mustache, watching above as the twinkling lights from the signal fizzled out. When he raised his sword above his head, the rustling armor of all the hardened men fell silent as Jans opened his mouth to speak. Jan's voice was like a canyon filled with thunder when he spoke.

"Today, men … We ride!"

A chorus of cheers rang out, steel gleaming in the air.

"Ride! Ride! Ride! …"

Jans's war horse reared up on its hind legs as he cried out.

"RELEASE THE HOOVES OF CHAOS!"

It was a moment. One of those moments when the will of men convinced them they could do anything.

Slim, still weary from the sand spiders that almost took his life, teetered over to Jans.

"Shields ready! Spears! Leave the lances on the bottom!" Jans ordered the nearby Lieutenant. "I want two columns going up, a tight formation. I want them ready."

The man saluted. "Yes, Commander!"

"What is it, Healer?" Jan's said. There was nothing but fire in the exhausted commander's eyes. He and his troops were as weary as men could be, but the thought of battle gave them new energy. "Are you riding? If you are, you'll need heavier armor." He smiled. "Can you poke a spear or swing steel?"

"Neither, Commander, but I've been known to play the lute on occasion. Do you think that might help?"

"Not without a lute it won't, and I don't see one." He looked around. "So what worries you, Healer?"

Slim's long frame standing was almost eye to eye with Jans on horseback. "Trap, Jans."

"Aye, Healer." Jans shoved his sword back into his sheath. "We've been trapped for days, if not weeks."

"No—and call me Slim at least once before you die."

"Certainly, Slim, but elaborate your meaning."

"Maybe it wasn't Venir who released the signal. Maybe he's fallen. Maybe the underlings fired it off."

"So?" Jans stroked his mustache, eyeing the hill.

Slim felt silly. Clearly, Commander Jans had considered everything.

"Healer... er... Slim, keep these worries between us. I don't need my men's heads filled with doubt." He spat out some brown juice and wiped his jaw. "We've got the black fiends all around us now. Our best chance of survival is within the walls of that fort. So we are going to ride up that hill and trample every fiend we can find into a spot of greasy slat." He spit again. "And I wouldn't worry yourself about healing my men. You need to be worried about killing underlings, if you can." He reached over and put his hand on Slim's shoulder. "See you at the top of the hill, Slim. And if that gate's closed, we'll try to ride through it. Hope you make it."

They're crazy!

Slim had to admit: the sense of foreboding that had overcome him was alleviated by the energy of the men. The Royal Riders had survived this long, and any fear they had before going into battle had now fled. Still, how was Venir going to open the gate without the underlings finding out? It was a bad plan, a silly plan to begin with. But, anything was possible on Bish.

If I only had more strength.

Slim wanted to shape shift, fly into the sky and scout from above, but he didn't have the strength. He'd patched up several men and sealed some bleeding wounds. He was spent.

Over the next several minutes, all the men in camp got on horseback, their energy flowing and nervousness settling in their eyes as they headed up the dark hill of the forest.

Slim felt useless as he stood in his sandals and watched them trot by.

"You, Healer!" A soldier in a full suit of chainmail was riding his way. "Get on."

Slim extended his arm, and the stout soldier pulled him up into the saddle.

"Commander Jans charged your protection with me. My, I don't see how I can protect a man so tall, but I'll do what I can."

"I'll be careful of the low branches," Slim said. He reached down and grabbed the shield on the saddle hitch. "And, can I use this?"

"It should cover your neck, but I don't know about the rest of you."

Slim chuckled. *Might be the last laugh I ever have.*

Column by column, up the hill they went, leaving nothing but thunder and hoof prints.

CHAPTER 16

"Easy, Corrin," a stout dark-headed man said, "it's Georgio." The man, shifty and lean, whirled his blades back into his belt. "I can see that, Billip, but I've no idea about the rest of them. Where did they all come from?" He peered into the sky. "Out of nowhere. Meaning," he rubbed his chin, "maybe Trinos is afoot."

Brak didn't know any of these people, aside from the skinny man named Melegal, slumped over the saddle.

Beside him, Jubilee hugged his leg, blinking, whispering. "How did we get here, Brak?"

He shook his head and slung the dark blood from his cudgel. They'd been running through the streets, dashing from corner to corner, avoiding the underlings, when fortune ran out and they were cornered. He and Georgio had fought like wolves, stomping and hacking at every moving underling in sight, but it wasn't going to be enough. They'd been a moment from being hacked up and forgotten. His stomach groaned.

"Who are you?" the one called Billip asked. "And where do you come from?"

As Brak opened his mouth to speak, Melegal slid from the saddle and collapsed into the street.

"Slat, Georgio!" Billip grabbed Melegal and dragged him over to the fountain. "What happened to him?"

"I don't know. He was like this when I found him at the stables. He had been fighting an imp or something."

"Nikkel," Billip ordered, "Fetch that pail and fill it with water."

The young black man frowned, slumping his shoulders as he did so.

Brak heard Billip speak to Georgio under his breath. "Mikkel has fallen, Georgio. Tread Nikkel with caution."

Georgio fell onto his haunches, holding his head. Brak could see sadness in the young man.

Eyeing the streets, Brak lumbered over to the fountain and took a long drink. It was cool and refreshing.

"You're not a horse," the one name Corrin said, "get a pitcher or use your hands."

Brak kept drinking. He also soaked his blood-stained fingers in the water, only to see the blood quickly wash away.

"Did you see that, Brak?" Jubilee said. "I've never seen water do that." Pale eyed and haired like her grandfather, Jubilee scooped her hand in and drank. "This must be water from the Everwell, but they remain below. How did it get here? How did we get here? Ew!"

For the first time, Brak noticed the scores of dead bodies scattered everywhere. Men, women, children and underlings were dead. Many mutilated. But the most disturbing figure was the black hairy bulk of a long legged monster that lay in the street, some of its barbed tendrils still twitching.

"What is that thing?" Jubilee pinched her nose. "Is that what stinks?"

A sad looking young black man with pale blue eyes walked over with a pitcher of water and handed it to Jubilee. "That's the thing that killed my father." He nodded over to the corpse of a large black man laid out on the cobblestone road. "Who killed that beast to save me. Trying to save us all."

"Doesn't look like there's many of you left," Jubilee said.

Brak nudged her in the back.

"What? We're all going to go sooner than later if we don't get out of Bone. Besides, it's not like you didn't just about die less than second ago, Brak." She took a drink from the pitcher and offered Nikkel her hand.

Nikkel pulled her up.

"I'm Jubilee, and I'm sorry about your father. It seems families don't last very long around here. My grandfather..."

Brak didn't pay her any more attention. Instead, he made his way over to the woman named Haze, who lay alone on the blood-smeared cobblestone road. She was light as a pile of rags when he lifted her up in his arms and poured a swallow of water from the pitcher down her throat.

She sputtered and flailed, eyes blinking.

"Get that thing off me!"

He held her tight.

"It's gone," he said.

Her scrawny neck whipped around, left, right, high and low.

"Where in Bone are we?"

Brak shrugged. By the looks of things, they were still in the city, but where exactly, he had no idea. He was lost again. And it bothered him. All he wanted to do was find his father. The Bone with the rest of these people.

"Can I have some more of that water, uh... what's your name again?"

He set her down. "Brak. And sure."

She took another drink.

A commotion started by the fountain.

"Where's my hat, Georgio? And where's Quickster?"

"He's right over there, Me." Georgio was pointing, and he looked angry.

Quickster lay on his back, facing the suns, legs up, knees bent downward.

"I'll kick your fat arse if he's dead, Georgio."

"I just saved your arse, Me. And you better watch what you say to me."

"Get my hat!"

"Son of a..." Georgio stormed away. "Jubilee! Get over here and bring me that hat."

"Ah, the skinny man lives," Jubilee said. "Drat! I like this hat. Makes me feel smarter." She tossed it to Georgio. "But if he dies, I've got dibs on it, got it?"

"Gladly!" Georgio threw it at Melegal.

The Rat of Bone snatched his hat from the air and scowled as he placed it on his head.

"Where's that case of mine?"

"It's on Quickster's saddle. Now will you —"

"Be quiet," said a voice as smooth as polished silver and as strong as hammered iron.

Brak felt his limbs go numb.

A magnificent woman with platinum hair had taken a seat by the fountain. The edgy man named Corrin stepped to her side, eyeing them, guarding her. No one else moved or said a word.

Trinos found the group before her both interesting and colorful, bonded together for one reason or another. Like the rest of the men and women on Bish, they were survivors, but with something in common. All had been in contact in one way or another with the equalizer, a powerful force Trinos had put in place to keep the scales of good and evil in balance. Something that she had almost forgotten about. Something that whispered in the burst of hot air called The Darkslayer.

Gracefully, she walked over to Georgio and tussled the curly hair on his head.

"You seem disappointed, young man. Don't you realize I just saved your life and the lives of your friends?" She gestured towards the rest of them. "I saved you from certain peril." She folded her hands over her chest, waiting. "Well?"

No one moved.

The skinny man who'd complained about his hat was eyeing her with suspicion.

Billip wiped drool from his mouth.

Corrin's fingers twitched over the pommels of the daggers on his belt.

Even the girl with a penchant for talking was mute.

"Oh... I see." Trinos dipped her chin and waved her hand past her face.

Corrin sighed. "I hate it when she does that."

Blinking their eyes and shaking their heads, the rest of the people took a closer study of her rich brown hair, sun browned skin, common though somewhat exquisite garb, and softer Bish-born features.

The question now was, would they still listen to her.

"As you can see, Bone, your home and my home, has been

invaded by the underlings. There are now hundreds of them taking over the streets, and thousands more below and all around us..."

Melegal raised his nose at her. "And who might you be, a Royal? A do-gooder mage from the castles coming here to what, help us?"

"Shut your vile tongue!" Corrin edged between Melegal and Trinos.

"Or what, you saggy jawed bastard?"

"I'll poke a dozen holes in you!"

Billip stepped between them. "Corrin, stay yourself. Melegal's not known for his manners." He dipped his head at Trinos. "Please forgive him and continue, Trinos."

"Forgive? Forgive what, you sawed off slackard!" Melegal said.

Billip grabbed Melegal's sleeve. "That's it, Melegal. Everything was fine until you showed up. Show some respect for our friend over there, will you? She saved your life, you know."

Melegal pulled his sleeve loose. "Oh, pardon me, pretty lady with impossibly perfect teeth. Thank you for saving my life." He bowed slightly. "Without my permission, I might add."

"Fool!" A blade appeared in Corrin's hands.

Haze gathered herself alongside Melegal, a long knife in her hand.

Words and expressions the likes of which Trinos never experienced before came forth.

"Slat sucker!"

"Orcen whore!"

"Sweat from an ogre crotch!"

"Your father bites the heads off chickens!"

"Vomitus Pisswiller!"

Trinos didn't know whether to be amused or offended. "Enough!" she said.

They kept arguing. As if she wasn't even there.

She put a little more power behind it. "SILENCE!"

Everyone stopped and turned to face her.

"First, I am not a Royal. Second, I do command magic, much of it. Third, you don't owe me any 'Thank you' that you don't want to give. But, as surely as my suns rise and fall, you," she pointed at Melegal, "would have perished without me."

Nikkel stepped forward. "Couldn't you have saved us from that monster? Saved my father?" The young man's eyes watered. "Where were you then, Trinos? One moment you were here, and then you left—and the underlings came!"

"Mind your tongue, Boy." Corrin said, "She doesn't owe anyone here anything."

But Nikkel was right. She could have stopped it if she wanted. She couldn't be there for everyone all the time, but in this case, she'd offered these people protection and then abandoned them, all just to see if she could let it happen. People were dying on Bish all the time. Some in the most horrible and violent of ways. Was that indeed how she wanted it? It was, wasn't it? *How cruel. I wonder how Scorch is doing.*

Melegal looked up into the bright lights of the sky.

'My suns'? What a loon! Very pretty. Even smells nice despite the decay, but I've got things to do.

As Trinos continued to enamor the crowd by the fountain, Melegal made his way into the shade behind the walls.

What in Bish is going on?

The last thing he remembered was fighting the imp. Ordering it to stop killing Haze, who now sat slack-jawed by the fountain, hanging on Trinos's every word.

She's a scrappy one. I'll give her that.

Alone with his thoughts, he slid his back down along the wall and checked his pockets.

One. Two. Three. Four. Five. Six. Seven. Excellent.

The imp wanted the Keys for the underlings. The vile little monster was by far the most terrifying thing he'd ever faced. He wiggled his fingers and toes.

All there.

He took the hat off and rubbed his head. It still ached, but wasn't anything so sore as before he blacked out. And he'd been blinded too.

Slat. I've used it too much. Can I use it again?

He placed it on his head.

We'll see.

So much had happened over the past few days, he didn't know where to start. Rayal, what happened to her? She wanted him to find Tonio. Lorda wanted him to find Tonio. Lord Almen, he didn't know if that man was still alive or dead. But what had Rayal said on the matter?

Nothing. I can only assume Lord Almen is alive.

The image of the half-naked cleric emerged inside his mind.

Kill Sefron!

He'd almost pulled it off once already in Castle Almen's arena, but the cleric still lived. He rubbed his dart launchers on his wrists.

Perhaps it's time I used poison.

Closing off the sights and sounds of the other people, Melegal closed his eyes and mediated.

Put it all together, Melegal. What to do next?

The City of Bone was his home. He had no intentions of leaving it again, underlings or not. He had no desire to fight those nasty little creatures or that imp, but they were coming for him.

Perhaps it's time I slid out of here. I'm sure the City of Three would be nice.

Rayal wanted him to find Tonio.

Slat on that.

But she might be his only protection if Castle Almen came after him.

All Royals are the same.

He fingered the Key that had taken him from the chamber below Almen's study to the place he and Haze called home.

Now that's power.

And where would all the other Keys lead? What could they do?

I must know.

He looked around the wall, watching the group still gathered around Trinos. Brak stood tallest of them all, thick arms folded over his chest. Melegal shook his head, ducking back behind the wall.

Things were so much simpler with the big lout around. All I had to do was bail him out. Of course, he's probably the reason I'm in this mess to begin with. But with all the underlings, you'd think he'd be here in the thick of it.

Melegal contemplated many things: Haze. Brak. Trinos. The

Almens. Rayal. Mikkel. Quickster. Georgio. The imp and the underlings. Hours later, he concluded his thoughts. Out of all those people, only one promise came to mind.

Get on with it, Melegal. Kill Sefron. The Bone with everything else!

The detail was horrifying. Trinos, despite her elegance, didn't sugar coat what was going on in the world of Bish. Instead, she made it perfectly clear that everyone's nightmare was coming to life. The underlings were taking over.

It was the least of his worries, however. All Georgio wanted to do was find Venir.

"Georgio, where are you going?" Billip took him by the nook of the elbow.

Georgio jerked his arm away. "I'm going out. After my family. After Venir."

"Me too." Brak stood behind Georgio.

Over the past hour, everyone had come clean, thanks to Jubilee who'd blabbed to everybody about everything.

"This is Melegal's sister, Haze, *wink, wink,* and droopy face over here is Venir's son."

Georgio, startled as he was by the statement, felt a connection. Brak had disclosed how he'd come to the city to begin with and lost his mother, Vorla, in the process. The big man who turned out to be no older than him had asked Georgio questions about his father, which Georgio had been more than happy to answer.

Billip put his hands on his hips. "And where exactly do you two fools plan on going?"

"South," Brak said.

Georgio nodded.

"Did you not hear Trinos?" Billip motioned at the woman, who was busy assisting the wounded with Haze and Jubilee. "The south is covered with underlings. The west is too. You wouldn't make it from here to the Red Clay Forest. If you're smart, you'll go north to The City of Three, Georgio. At least up there, Kam will look after you."

Georgio scowled. "I don't need looking after, Billip."

"Ah, you're still mad at Lefty, aren't you? Why else would you not go there?"

"Lefty who?"

"Hah! 'Lefty who' my eyeballs. Sheesh, you haven't been the same without him." Billip thumbed through the feathered shafts in his quiver. "As for you, eh, Brak is it? Let me tell you something about your father. Venir, that is. He can take care of himself. And it might do you some good to go north and meet with your sister, or half-sister. Erin, that is. I'm sure Kam wouldn't mind the help."

"What?" Brak scrunched up his face.

Georgio hit Brak in the arm. "That's right, you've got a little sister. Congratulations. Bone, Billip. How many urchins —"

Brak walloped in in the shoulder.

Georgio's jaw dropped wide.

"Ooooooooow! I felt that!"

Brak glared at Georgio. His father's fire was in his eyes.

"I'm not an urchin."

"Er ... Sorry, Brak. But how many Venirs are scattered across Bish, do you think?" Georgio rubbed his arm and looked at Billip. "Are you a father too, Billip?"

"I don't think that's something we need to concern ourselves with now, seeing how the entire city is coming down around us." Billip rolled his shoulder. "Feels great. Strong. That woman Trinos did something to me. I feel ten years younger." He grinned. "So, what will it be, boys? And make it quick, before the City Watch comes back with the Royals to recruit you."

The City Watch, henchmen of the Royals, had made their demands known. Any able bodied man was to be drafted into the ranks to battle the underlings. They'd be given weapons, possibly armor, and the great honor of defending their city.

Billip and Corrin laughed out loud.

"We'll send the Royal soldiers back to get you," one of the two Watchmen had warned. "And see to it you make it to the front of the ranks."

It wasn't a laughing matter. No one, formidable as they might be, could overcome the Royals when they came for you. 'Either fight the underlings, or fight the underlings and the Royals.' Both Corrin and Billip had seemed torn, but after many minutes of heated deliberation, they had agreed that the Royals were still the lesser evil of the two. They had even spit on it.

"North or South, Nikkel?" Georgio asked. "Or are you staying?"

He shrugged and looked over at Billip.

"He's sticking with me, I guess."

"What do you think, Brak?"

Jubilee jumped in. "He wants to go north, to the City of Three! Right, Brak?"

Slowly, he nodded his head.

"Aw, is everyone going?" Georgio whined.

Billip slung his bow over his shoulder. "Before long, no one will be going anywhere, by what Trinos says. There's enough underlings out there to surround this entire city. Georgio, get out now, while you can, else you might not ever be leaving."

Georgio rubbed his rumbling stomach. "Well, a bowl of Joline's stew sounds awful good."

Brak's stomach growled so loud that Jubilee jumped.

"Whoa, and I thought my stomach was loud." Georgio eyed Brak. "I bet you can't out eat me."

A grim smile formed on the corner of Brak's thin lips. "We'll see."

"And what about you?" Georgio asked Billip.

Tugging at his goatee, he smiled as Trinos approached, followed by Corrin.

"I'll be fighting alongside her."

"That's sweet, Billip," Trinos said, brushing her arm along his. "But I cannot guarantee your safety. The underlings are many, and they could overtake these walls any day now."

"They say no force can take this city. We have the walls. We have the Everwells. We just need to vanquish the scourge that is among us."

"Every city falls eventually, Brave Billip."

"Yes, Trinos," Corrin agreed, "but no other place in Bish is as comforting to a wretch like me. I live here; I'll die here." His blades blinked in and out of his scabbards. "Just give me all the help you can give."

As Trinos, Billip, Nikkel and Corrin stood before him, an itch to fight overcame Georgio.

"I'm staying as well."

Someone laughed.

"Who's laughing?" Georgio said.

It was Melegal, leading Quickster his way and handing him the reins.

"Get your fat arse out of here, Georgio," the thief said, sliding a slender box from the saddle.

KAAA-VOOOOSH!

A burning building collapsed in the nearest district, sending up a tower of flames and grey smoke.

"Go, find Venir," Melegal continued, "and tell him when you see him, he's doing a lousy arse job killing underlings."

As Georgio, Brak and Jubilee headed south towards the stables, Melegal felt some wetness in his eyes. *I'll probably never see Quickster again. Fat Arse better feed him.*

Haze wrapped her slender arm around his bony shoulders. "How are you?"

"I'd be better if you went with them, Haze. You too, Billip. You need to take your knuckle cracking self with them as well. That boy can't handle the Outlands on his own. You know that."

"I'm staying here, you thin-necked copper snatcher!"

"Alright fine, Billip. I'll let you win, just this once."

Go with Georgio.

"You say you want to go with Georgio, fine. But he'd be much better off with me, and you know it."

Go with Georgio.

"And don't you forget it!" Billip blinked and stared at Melegal.

Go ... with ... Georgio.

Billip grabbed his gear and trotted after Georgio.

Melegal pinched the bridge of his nose.

Bone, that hurts!

"What just happened?" Haze said.

A confused looking Nikkel was chasing after Billip, strapping on his pack.

"Interesting." Trinos touched Melegal's cheek.

A tingling revitalization raced through his body. It felt wonderful. His headache was gone.

"Are you shaking?" Haze scowled at Trinos. "What did you do to him?"

Trinos grabbed Haze's hand. The woman's lithe frame gently collapsed to the ground.

"Take her away, Corrin, and see to it she's well cared for."

Melegal stretched his limbs. He felt better than he ever remembered feeling before.

"How did you..."

Trinos put her fingers to his lips. "What is it you want, Melegal?"

He cocked an eyebrow at her.

"Besides that."

"Can you get me inside Castle Almen? I have unfinished business."

His vest clanked when she patted it.

"You already have a way in. Just find a door and go."

You smell so incredible.

"I know." She grabbed hold of his hand. "Be careful. The Keys go many places. Many people seek them. Seek you."

"Sounds dangerous. Perhaps I should destroy them."

"Perhaps."

KAAA-VOOOOSH!

Another building crumbled and fell.

A squadron of soldiers on horses could be heard galloping their way. Like a deer, Melegal took off running in long bouncing strides.

Kill Sefron!

The Royal soldiers on horseback thundered past Trinos, Corrin, and all of the other 21st District survivors, but none of them saw a living thing.

"Did you do that?" Corrin said.

"Certainly."

"So, what are we to do now, wage war on the underlings? If so, we could use more people."

Trinos took her seat on the bench by the fountain.

"No. We'll do what we have to when we have to, but I think I've done enough for now." She stretched her arms out and dipped her toes in the water. An image of the lives on Bish formed.

Corrin's narrow eyes widened. "Is this what I think it is?"

"I would not deceive you. Besides, sometimes all you can do is sit back, watch, and hope for the best. You never know what is going to happen on a world like this."

CHAPTER 17

BATTLE CRIES AND HOWLS OF pain filled the air. Steel punched through bone and metal. Standing on the balcony of Castle Almen's keep, Lorda Almen's eyes were transfixed downward, in awe.

"Kill them, you worthless curs! Kill them all!"

The underlings had laid siege on Castle Almen, and Sefron, standing off to her side, could barely contain his glee.

Oh, you'll be mine soon, Lorda Almen.

He licked his lips, gazing over her hips and legs.

All mine and mine alone.

Her sharp words interrupted his thoughts.

"How many of those fiends are there, Sefron? It looks like hundreds at the wall!" She pointed. "What in Bish are those things?"

"Spiders, and those pale little things, I've no idea."

"Insects!" She recoiled back into his arms.

Oh my, so vibrant, alive … Delicious!

His hands drifted down on her hips.

Smack!

"I should remove your hands, Sefron! You pervert!" She clasped the plunging neckline of her elaborate dress. "Throw him over!"

"Apologies, Lorda, I only meant to comf—*urk*!"

One Shadow Sentry seized him by the arms, the other by the legs, lifting him over the edge of the balcony.

She means it!

"Lorda, your husband, Lord Almen, needs me!"

"Hold," she said. "Hmmm … hang him over by the legs."

Sefron clung to the Shadow Sentry's arm with desperation.

The sentry whipped out a knife and jammed it in his hand.

"Ow!" Sefron let go of the sentry's arm and dangled over the edge, held by his feet. "Lorda, please, have mercy! You need me. Lord Almen needs me."

He tried to pull himself up, but he barely managed to lift his head.

Lorda Almen wasn't even looking at him. Instead, her cat-eyes were focused on the raging battle below.

Every soldier of Castle Almen was fighting along the wall, ramming their blades into the faces of every underling that tried to climb over the parapets. Spiders climbed over the walls and into the gardens, carrying small albino underlings with thick shoulders. The heavy crossbows from the towers rocked out, filling the spider and underling creatures with giant splinters.

Sefron flinched.

A dying creature's maw opened and closed stories beneath him.

The men shouted orders and screamed for help. It didn't seem possible that the underlings could take over, not with one thousand, not with ten thousand, for Castle Almen was well defended. Between the towers, turrets and massive keep, the outer wall of the Castle could be defended from every angle. Archers and bowmen manned the towers and turrets, raining down death with deadly accuracy.

Half a dozen underlings cleared the wall, only to be feathered with many shafts.

"Lorda, let me up please. I'm sorry!"

Outside the Castle walls, underlings came from all directions, filling the streets as far as the eye could see.

Surely someone is doing something, Sefron thought.

The blood rushing to his head had turned it purple. Gazing around, he noticed the bordering Castles firing into the hordes of underlings as well, but they weren't falling, not as fast as they should be.

Slat, this Castle will never fall if I don't help the underlings.

The arms of the sentry started to tremble.

"Lorda, he's going to drop me! Please," he whined. "You need all the help you can get. At least let me check Lord Almen once again!"

"Pull him up," she said, not looking. "And punish him."

Sefron felt his body lifted through the air like a baby and slammed into the ground like a stone.

"Oof," he said.

He felt a punch in the gut. In the face. Then nothing but pain. He heard his blood dripping from his nose.

"One more transgression," Lorda said, "and it's over the parapet for you. My word on that, you grotesque fiend."

Through his one good eye, he watched the sway of her hips as she departed.

Mine, all mine.

Pushing himself up, he swallowed the taste of blood in his mouth.

We'll see who begs for mercy next time.

Rubbing her neck, Lorda moved across the stone floor and took a seat by her husband's cot. The strong visage of the man she knew was gone, replaced by a paler, weaker shadow of himself. Pulling the cloth from his head, she dipped it in a bowl of water and replaced it.

"Lorda," Sefron wheezed, limping over, "I should handle those dressings. It is my honor. Please, rest yourself."

"Get this toad out of my sight," she said.

The sentries grabbed him under his arms, lifting him up, toes dangling from the floor.

It was hard to look at the flabby man, with his bulbous belly and spindly legs. But she needed him, for now.

"Sent him to the bottom of the keep. If he causes a stir, send him out."

Sefron gulped.

"And keep him away from my servants. Send a couple up."

"As you wish, Lorda," a sentry said.

The cleric wheezed and grumbled, but Lorda found relief when the door closed, leaving her alone with the sentries. She was safe. She knew it, but her thoughts were troubled.

What do these underlings want with us?

Underlings had invaded her castle before, and now they were

back again, forcing their way from outside and from within. And the other Castles along the great wall, they weren't drawing near the amount of attention that Castle Almen was.

"What have you done?" she whispered to Lord Almen.

He had many secrets. He always had, and she was more privy to them than she let on. But, the biggest mystery was what had happened to Tonio. He was still out there, somewhere, deranged and mad. And Detective Melegal, he knew more as well, but she liked him for some reason. Maybe it was because Sefron clearly hated him. And because Lord Almen shared information with Melegal that he did not share with her.

"Hmmmmm," she smiled. She liked men with secrets. She liked to find out what was inside them.

She was stroking her husband's cheek when two servant girls entered the room, fell to their knees, and bowed. Their pretty faces were worried, their hair and clothing unkempt.

She sat up. "What happened to the two of you? You look like urchins."

"Apologies, Lorda. We're cut off from our means."

The younger of the two clutched at her growling stomach.

"Humph, well you better keep your little tummy quiet while you rub my feet, else I'll feed you both to the under—Aaaaaaa!"

A pair of dog sized spiders climbed over the parapet and onto the balcony.

Thwipp! Thwipp!

Spider silk shot out from beneath them and snatched the girls. They kicked and screamed.

The Shadow Sentries burst into action. One caught his blade on the web. The other charged onto the balcony. Another spider scurried through the window and scrambled toward Lorda, its mouth full of dripping fangs.

"Eeeeyaaaah!"

CHAPTER 18

DISTRICT THREE IN THE CITY of Bone was overrun. Underlings by the hundreds filled the streets, alleys, and storefronts—slaughtering everything in sight. One building burned, another one fell, all to the bewilderment of the Royals on the other side of Castle Almen's walls. Not a single man or woman remained alive. The humans who weren't killed instantly were burned alive. Smoldering corpses lined the streets, and their heads were tossed over the walls. It should have demoralized the Royals, but it did not.

Verbard hovered alongside his brother, silver eyes glinting in frustration.

"Jottenhiem, why haven't we penetrated the wall yet!"

Jottenhiem wiped the blood from his shaven head. "It will take hours if not days at this rate. We need siege weapons. The walls are ten feet thick. And they hold superior position from the turret and towers. These castles are made to hold through all-out war."

Catten chuckled, rubbing his chin over his lip.

Verbard sneered at him.

Chuckling now are we, you stiff?

He recalled the days he might have laughed the slightest in situations like this, to Catten's irritation. Carefree he was then, unlike his brother, who'd been all too serious about all things. But now, things were different. They had changed. He eyed the nearest turret.

"If it was aid you needed, Jottenhiem, all you had to do was ask."

Taking a deep breath, he summoned energy. Tendrils of lightning lit up his robes, coiled around his arms. His hands then struck out.

A bolt of energy streaked over the wall, slamming into the turret, scattering chunks of rock and flesh through the air.

The underling army howled with glee.

"Excellent, Brother! I like how you are thinking now!" Catten said. He summoned his own blast of light.

Ka-Chow!

Another Turret filled with archers was gone, leaving a smoking hole in the castle wall.

This is more like it!

Verbard's black blood was like rushing waters. He let another scintillating bolt fly, striking one of the taller towers. Bodies of screaming men plummeted toward the ground, disappearing behind the castle's wall.

"What is that, Brother?" Catten said.

Several robed men appeared at the top of the keep, shouting and pointing their fingers. Purple and green lights glowed from the towers and turrets, covering them like a mushroom with a shimmering cloud of energy.

"NO!" Verbard said. He fired another bolt at the tower.

Ka-Fizzzzz ...

"And there be wizards," Catten said. "I suspected as much." He turned to Verbard. "Seems they've drawn us out, Brother. I say we take it to them. Just us. They can't be nearly as powerful as we."

Verbard looked hard into his brother's eyes.

Are you mad?

"Our shields won't hold forever, and we have plenty of magi that can take them. For now, let's try something else."

He's been put into the body of a fool! I liked you better when you were dead.

Catten flashed his teeth. "Well said, Brother. I couldn't agree more."

Catten's smile didn't seem natural. His resurrected brother had smiled more today than in the past three centuries. It unnerved him.

Who is this underling?

Verbard sent a mental signal to the underling magi.

Hold your energy! Send more spiders over the walls! Onto those towers now!

One by one, the robed underling magi's arms went up, lifting dozens of spiders with their albino urchling riders over the wall, sending them off quickly towards the towers.

Let's see if these shields can stop livin —

Verbard jerked his arm up, shielding his eyes from a brilliant light that burst forth from the top of the keep.

BAA-ROOOOM!

The force of the blast sent him drifting back, slamming him hard into a wall.

At his side, Catten was dusting the debris from his robes and Jottenhiem was knocked from his feet. A smoldering hole replaced the spot on the street where over a dozen underling soldiers stood with one mage. The burnt scent of underling flesh was overwhelming.

Verbard grabbed his brother by the collar of his robes. "Did you know they had such power, Catten!"

"Of course I did!" Catten said, trying to push him away, but Verbard held him tight. "Only a fool wouldn't suspect it, Brother! This is war, you know! And their magic, like their rations, won't last forever."

Verbard clenched his fist and socked his brother in the gut. "You are a fool!"

Catten fell to the ground, grimacing, breathless, trying to speak.

"This is only one castle of many!" Verbard said. "And they have power! They have people! If this city organizes, then they'll gallop right through us! Go! Find Kierway, and see to it he penetrates from below. If he does not, we are doomed!"

Catten floated up from his feet, eyes like golden lava. "As you wish, Brother. As you wish!"

With a clap of his hands, a black door appeared. Catten stepped through and vanished along with the door, leaving Verbard floating there, uncomfortable.

Jottenhiem stood, staring at him with an odd look in his ruby eyes.

Verbard rubbed his fist. "I've always wanted to do that."

"Me too," Jottenhiem said. He formed the closest thing he had to a smile.

"Check in with your scouts, Commander, and report back to me quickly. We can't have the Royal forces rallying the city. Keep pressing the wall. We've got to find a way to bring those towers down."

"Yes," Jottenhiem saluted, "Lord Verbard."

Eyeing the top of the keep, Verbard's stomach started to churn. *This is a suicide mission. I know it!*

CHAPTER
19

"**N**OT YET!" KAM SAID.

Lefty tied the gondola off on the dock. He'd seen Kam broken and busted up but not beaten. However, now she was something else. Her red hair frizzed all over her head. Her robes were disheveled over her body. Heading towards the stairs that led up to the city, her sultry movements were gone, replaced by the gait of a man.

"Wait up, Kam. You'll need a lantern to navigate those steps." Lefty snatched a lantern from the post and blew on the wick inside. An eerie green illumination came forth.

Kam turned, her face contorted, her features almost unrecognizable.

"Quiet, Little Halfling," she said. The voice was not hers. "Put that light out. I don't need it."

Lefty gasped, shuffling backward.

What is going on with her!

Earlier, he'd seen her kill Diller, snapping his neck with the flick of her wrist. She'd left Palos in a pile of his own drool. And as they rowed across the dark lake beneath the City of Three, he'd found no relief in his liberation, only fear at Kam's muttering and arguments with herself.

He stayed back. She strolled up the stairs, the twinkling of the red gems embedded in her hand giving off the faintest of light. He didn't know what to make of it.

Is she possessed? By what?

The step groaned. She stopped and looked back at him, her eyes glowing with green fire.

"Did you say something, Halfling?" she said.

He shook his head. "No. No, Kam, nothing at all."

Turning, she growled in her throat and headed back up the steps, clutching Baby Erin in her arm like a loaf of bread.

Lefty followed, feet splashing over the dock and up the steps. They were soaked in his sweat all the way up to the ankles.

What is going on? I should be celebrating my freedom right now. How did it get even worse for me?

He wanted to flee as soon as he got topside, but what about Erin? She had to be in danger. But in the hands of her mother?

This is madness!

Staying back a flight of steps, Lefty fell in step behind her. At the top, Kam pushed the door open. The dim light of the alley gave Lefty new life. He had doubted he'd ever see the world above again, and now he was only steps away. Kam stepped over the threshold, through the doorway.

Don't lose her, Lefty. Don't lose Erin.

Reaching the top step, the door slammed shut in his face.

"What?"

Jiggling the handle, nothing gave. It was locked.

Nooooooooooooooo!

"Kam!" he pounded his tiny hands on the door. "Kam!"

Suddenly, the door shoved inward, the edge cracking on his head, knocking him down to the landing. He rolled up to his feet.

The silhouette of Kam stood atop the doorway. "Get the sword, Little Fool!"

The door slammed shut again.

Downcast, down the steps he went, rubbing the knot on his head.

HURRY! A voice yelled down inside his head, watering his eyes.

Lefty's heart was pounding like a tap hammer when he reached the bottom.

The great sword lay in the gondola, completely wrapped in burlap. He reached in, wrapped his hands where the hilt should have been, put his back into it, and heaved.

How can anyone wield such a long and heavy thing?

He towed the Great Sword of Zorth behind him up the stair. The door swung open at the top. Chest heaving, he stepped out into the alley that guarded the secret entrance to the Nest.

Somebody should be out here.

The alley always had eyes and ears open.

A signal would get an unrecognized thief through. Palos kept strict control on things, and someone should be there to ask questions. It was odd that there was nothing. A stiff breeze whipped down the alley, bringing the foul odors of rotting food and excrement to full splendor. There was something else as well.

Squinting, he saw three forms slumped against the wall, the faint steam from the warmth of their bodies turning thin. At the end of the alley, Kam stood, back to him, chin up, observing passersby. Swallowing, Lefty dragged the sword past the three dead thieves. Their tongues hung from their mouths, and their throats were crushed in. He quickened his pace.

Oh my! Oh my! Oh my! Kam shouldn't be killing people. What is wrong with her? I wish Billip and Mikkel were still here. And Georgio! I've been a fool.

Kam strode down the street, startling the passing folks who came too close. They murmured and whispered while they scurried away.

Behind her, Lefty struggled to keep up, lugging the sword behind him. He wanted to scream at her, "Where are you going?" but the thought of doing so only tightened his neck. So he followed her, past the storefronts, past the high towers, to the edge of the city, where she came to a stop.

"No!" she muttered angrily to herself. The red gems in her hand flared with new life.

Baby Erin began to cry.

"I'll not do this with my baby!" Her body shuddered and convulsed. "Get out of me!" Her knees wobbled beneath her.

Lefty let loose the sword and rushed to her side just in time.

Kam's eyes rolled up inside her head.

Lefty got Erin just as Kam fell. The baby girl was wailing.

Kam lay sprawled out on the ground, bleeding from the nose, her once vibrant form harrowed.

"Easy, Erin," he patted her and bounced her in his arms. "I'll get your mother help. I promise."

There were faces. Some she recognized, others she did not.

"Kam, are you in there?" one voice said. It was Lefty; she was sure of it, but he sounded like he was miles away.

You will do as you promised. You will serve!

The voice inside her was angry, hateful, controlling. But there was something else. Desperation. It needed her; she didn't need it. That much she'd figured out. So she fought. She fought for herself, for Erin, to regain her life again on this world.

"I'll not serve. I'll not fulfill your evil will." Her mind thrashed against the unseen force.

You will!

Something grabbed the inside of her chest and squeezed it.

"Kam!" Lefty wailed.

"Mother of Bish! What has happened to this woman? She is sick!"

A crowd had gathered.

"Possessed!"

"Bewitched!"

"I'm not anything of the sort!"

But none heard a thing she said. Unknown to her, they whisked her frame through the streets of the dark and dropped her on the porch of the Magi Roost.

"You're on your own, Halfling," one said.

"Don't give up, Kam. We're home!"

You will serve me! You will obey!

Kam had agreed to serve in order to save Erin. Palos had almost killed her before she rescued Erin, but she had made a deal with the force inside the gems. It had assured her the safety of her baby. And now, men were dying. She'd even almost killed Lefty, and more death was coming.

"No!"

She would not bring more death into the world. She was not a killer! Was she?

"I'll die first!"

Yes, yes you will!

Her heart pumped slower and slower and slower. A dark force squeezed it. Burned it. Suffocated her with power.

Kam stretched her arms out.

"Erin, where are you? Erin? I will hold you. See you one last time!"

You'll see nothing ever again!

"Lefty!" an excited voice cried out. "Where have you... KAM!"

"Jo – line?" she said.

The pressure on her chest eased.

What is this?

The force inside her retreated.

She lurched up, gasping for breath, clutching baby Erin in her arms.

"Get some water, Lefty!" Joline ordered. "Mercy! Prepare some clothing. Kam! Lords! My dear, where have you been?"

As the darkness that clouded her eyes lifted, Joline's sweet face took shape. The woman was as distressed as she had ever seen her before. She smelled nice, like flowers. Tears formed in Kam's eyes. She hadn't hoped to ever smell flowers again before.

"You don't want to know," she said, coughing.

"You can tell me later," Joline said. Her friend helped her to her feet and led her to a comfortable chair by the fire.

"No," Kam said, eyeing the flames. "I'd rather sit somewhere... *else*?"

Her word froze on her tongue. The Magi Roost was not what it once was. Flies buzzed in the air, and the scent of blood was strong. Four men lay on or near a table with their heads blown off. She puked.

"Oh dear! Get a bucket too, Lefty!" Joline kept her strong arm around Kam's back and led her to the bar. "You look like you could use some Muckle Sap."

A bottle slid across the bar and refilled a goblet on its own.

"Who..." Kam's voice drifted off. An incredibly handsome man, blond headed and blue-eyed, smiled from the other end of the bar. Beside him stood a rough cut woman that looked like she made a living splitting logs.

"Joline?" the man said. His voice was purposed and poetic. "Can I be of further assistance?"

Lefty returned with a pitcher of water and a bucket.

The bucket clonked off the floor, and he began to shiver.

Kam followed his stare to the headless men at the table. She'd never seen so much blood before. Not even when Fogle mind-grumbled Venir. She retched again.

"Look at that! Just look at that, Scorch!" the rough cut woman said. "I've never seen such an adorable halfling before. Can I keep him?" She waved her arm. "Get over here, Little Fella!"

"That's Darlene, and the man's name is Scorch," Joline said. "And you better drink this and drink it fast. The pair of them have almost finished off the entire stash."

Lefty crept behind the bar and disappeared.

Kam sat up, clasped the neck of her robe, pulled her shoulders back, and shot down her Muckle Sap. There was nothing normal about these people. And where were all her patrons?

"My name is Kam. And this is my tavern. And I'd like to know what in Bish you strangers have done to it!"

"Easy, Kam." Joline patted her arm. "They did that."

"Is that your baby?" The rough cut woman, Darlene, reached out towards Erin. "Can I hold her? We've heard so much about her!"

The woman reminded Kam of a feisty raccoon.

"No. But what you can do," Kam said, "is stop answering my question with a question and give me the answers I seek." She tried to summon her powers, but nothing came forth. She was empty, the force inside her silent, hiding and waiting.

"Easy now, Kam." The handsome man, Scorch, formed the words on his lips in an engrossing manner. "We had an incident. The men over there sought to make sport of my friend, so I taught them a lesson."

"I just love the way his mouth moves when he speaks," Joline said. "Isn't it fascinating?"

It was, but not enough to overcome Kam's anger. All she'd been through. She was home now! She wanted answers.

"So you blew their heads off!" She chucked the bottle at his face.

It stopped an inch from his nose and settled quietly on the bar.

Darlene hopped on the bar and ripped out her knife.

Scorch snatched her by the ankle and dragged her down.

She landed hard, her cheek bouncing off the bar.

"Settle yourself, Darlene. This is her establishment, not ours." Scorch twirled his finger. Darlene rolled over the bar onto the hardwood floor.

"Oooch!" Darlene bounced up, rubbing her cheek and hindquarters. "I'm sorry, Kam. I'm not known for my manners." She took another seat at the nearest table, groaning as she sat down. "It won't happen again."

"Here," Joline said, "let me take baby Erin, Kam. You need to rest yourself."

"No!" Kam said. She held Erin tight to her chest. "She won't be leaving my sight for quite some time, not after all I've been through." She eyed Darlene. The woman didn't come across as dangerous. If anything, she seemed bright and friendly, but there was something that just didn't sit right. "Especially a stranger. But, her bassinet will do. Fetch it, will you?"

"Certainly, Kam, certainly," Joline said.

Darlene started whistling and clapping her hands like she was calling a puppy.

"Here, little halfling fella! Come to Darlene!"

Lefty didn't appear. He could have been anywhere.

Returning her attention to the man, Scorch, Kam caught a glimpse of herself in the mirror behind the bar. The locks of her auburn hair were matted and frayed. Her eyes were sunken, and her cheek was swollen. She rubbed her lip that was split in two places. To top it all off, her robe barely covered her cleavage—or the rest of her.

"I wish I had a figure like yours," Darlene said. "My mother always said I had part dwarf in me on account of these stocky parts. But I didn't think dwarves could breed — *hic* — with other peoples." She closed one eye looking at Kam, shaking her head. "Ain't no dwarf in you, though."

Scorch chuckled. "Forgive Darlene. It seems she's over indulged in your Muckle Sap, which I must admit, is quite delightful."

"So, was it *you* who killed all those men?"

"With a single thought," he said. His teeth were white. Perfect. "And I'm sorry for the mess. I just don't understand why Trinos picked such leaky people. But I have to admit, it does offer a more profound effect."

"You should have seen all those people — *hic* — running out of here like their arses were on fire," Darlene said. "I don't know what was funnier. That or all those heads exploding. It was like blowing up pumpkins with whicker wonkers when I was a girl, 'cept there weren't any seeds in their heads."

That's when Kam got a closer look at all the dark stains on Darlene's clothes. She was covered in them from the waist up. She turned away as Darlene started swatting at flies again and calling for Lefty. "Here little ..."

"When did this happen? Haven't the City Watch come to ask questions? There will be a trial for this! And who is Trinos?"

"The City Watch?" Scorch posed in thought. "Oh, I see. The men in the black billed hats that came to conduct an investigation. Simply put, they showed up and didn't see a thing." He waved his hand over at the men at the table. "See?"

Glancing over her shoulder, the main floor of the Magi Roost was in perfect order. The tables were cleaned, the fire crackled, and there was no proof of another living thing other than themselves. A chill went through her.

Bish, he's powerful!

"And I told a convincing tale about how the cause of the rumors and speculation most likely was those dreaded little underlings people have been talking about. I even procured several wild goose chases to keep the Watch of this fine city busy. It'll be days if not weeks before they figure it out."

"Goodness," Joline said. She was coming back down the steps with Erin's bassinet in her arms. "Where did all of those horrid bodies..."

Scorch's illusion dissipated. The bodies, flies and blood returned.

"... Oh." She shook her head and set the bassinet down on the bar.

Kam held onto Erin, keeping an eye on Scorch, fear creeping over her. The man wrapped a slice of cheese around a pickle and stuffed it in his mouth. It only made her situation all the more disconcerting.

Time to serve. Leave now.

"Can I at least change my clothes?" Kam said.

"Of course you can," Joline said. "Mercy, poor thing, as terrified as she is, laid some out on your bed. And is fixing you a bath. All the others left."

Scorch had finished his pickle. His eyes narrowed. "Who are you talking to, Kam?"

Leave now!

Slowly, Kam placed Erin in the bassinet and took a step towards the door. She fought it. Sweat burst on her brow. Her knees trembled.

Scorch rose from his seat, stepping into her path.

"Who said that?" he said, looking around. "I can feel it, hear it, smell it."

"Maybe that little halfling is playing—*hic*—tricks. What's its—*Buuurrp*—name, anyway?" Darlene clapped her hands and cooed again.

Kam was exhausted, and as much as she wanted to fight, she could not hold the force back any longer. It had dug in deep. It was taking over.

"You should move, Scorch," she said. She looked back at Erin. Joline was rocking and singing gently to her. She headed for the door.

"Eh," Joline said, "Where do you think you're going, Kam? You get back here. You get back here right now!"

Tears streamed down Kam's cheek. "I can't. I must go. I must pay my debt."

Leave now!

Compelled, she stepped left.

Scorch was there.

She stepped to the right.

He was there.

"Who are you speaking with, Kam? Show me."

"Lords, help me." She tried to lift her hand, but it would not move. Her lips sealed. Her body lifted up off the floor.

Whatever was inside her had complete control over her now. Its magic melded with her mind, summoning magic and sending her over.

"What is that light from?" Darlene turned around. "Uh! Look! Her hand! It's as red as the suns!"

Kam rose higher in the air, her toes floating above Scorch's chin, her head almost touching the rafters.

He snatched her feet, pulled her back to the floor, and shoved her in a chair.

Get away from him! Get away from him now!

The jewels in her hand flared with life. Her elbow cocked back.

Whack!

Power coursed through her arm. She punched Scorch in the face with all her might. His head rocked back. His nose broke. She waited for him to fall. It should have killed him. At least knocked him out. It didn't. His nose didn't even bleed.

"Darlene!" Scorch said.

He snatched Kam's arm and pinned her glowing hand to the table.

The wilderness woman yanked her shortsword from her sheath.

Shing!

"NO! What are you doing! STOP!" Kam said in a voice that was not hers.

CHOP!

Her jewel-embedded hand was severed from her slender wrist.

Joline screamed.

Lefty screamed.

"Is all that blood…

" Kam's eyes rolled up in her head.

Mine?

CHAPTER 20

OUTPOST 31 WAS A HIVE of activity. Underlings, more than Venir had ever seen before, scurried over the complex, preparing for a full scale assault. Some were decked head to toe in armor; others' chests were bare. They all checked weapons and buckles and stuffed small knives into their boots. All he could do was watch. Above, they readied the ballistas on the towers and pulled large vats filled with burning pitch onto the massive catwalks. The smell of battle tickled his nose, raising the hairs on his neck.

"Hurk!"

The underling commander jerked the rope around his neck.

"Arsehole," it said. "Soon your people shall die. Soon you will follow."

Face beet red, Venir's fingers fumbled at the coarse cord of rope around his neck that burned like fire.

The underling jerked it.

Venir fell to his knees. He groaned.

"Is it too tight, man with holes in his leg? Arsehole."

If he got the chance to kill one more underling, it would be him. He hated that one. He'd never heard one talk so much before. He was going to rip its beady ruby eyes from its skull. "I'm going to kill you, Bastard," he said, wiping the spit and blood from his mouth.

The underling commander jerked the rope again. "Orc, what did this man say?"

Tuuth shrugged his big shoulders. "Something about killing bastards, I think." Tuuth glanced at Venir and turned away.

"Bastard? What is a bastard? Hmmm… arsehole." The underling paced around him. "A mighty tongue this one has." It chittered, glared at Venir, shook its gauntlet in his face. It pointed to one of its bulging biceps, then the other. "Power, Arsehole. Which one has more power?"

Crack!

The underling struck him across the jaw.

"No more words from you, Arsehole." It drew back the other arm.

Crack!

Venir's nose caved in. Blood spurted down his chin and over his chest.

"So which one is it, Arsehole Bastard? The one on the left?" It flexed. "Or the one on the right? I'll point, you nod."

Venir balled up his better hand. Punched at the underling's crotch.

It knocked the sluggish blow away with ease with its boot and chittered. A form of cruel laughter. The underling gave Tuuth another order.

"Put him in the stockade. We'll whip what's left of him when it's over." It eyed Venir, a smile forming on its jagged teeth. "Arsehole Bastard. Almost funny if it wasn't coming from you." It jerked the rope hard once more, lifting Venir from his knees and sprawling him onto the deck.

He'd jammed his aching wrists again, and he was choking.

Bone!

His face felt purple. A pair of rugged hands loosened the rope on his neck, slightly, and pulled him up by the hair.

Venir moaned.

"You should be dead, Stranger. I've never seen a man survive so many wounds." Tuuth eased him into the stockade. "What is your name? It should at least be remembered if I ever make it out of this fort. Heh, never seen a man call an underling an arsehole or bastard and live to tell about it."

Venir couldn't speak. He was beaten from head to toe. The stockade Tuuth shackled him to only added to the agony. Within moments, his back stiffened and burned. The rest of his body shuddered.

How in Bish did I get into this?

Nose dripping blood, he watched through swollen eyes

everything and anything going on. Bish's ultimate survivor had to find a way out of this jam, but in his bones he knew his chances were grim.

Tuuth took his spot against the rail, leaning against it, facing him, grinning.

Turning his head from Tuuth, Venir tried to find anything helpful. A familiar face. An unguarded exit. He could barely think. Everything hurt too much. His head ached, and his eyes were swollen. His hands were almost useless.

I could still strangle an underling if I got the chance.

The platform was over two stories tall. His view was as good as from anywhere but the towers, and there were dozens of those. The ballista alone would be more than enough to skewer a man to his horse.

Coughing, he noticed the South Gate beginning to rise. It was a massive mouth of wood and steel, almost three stories tall and half as wide. It almost rivaled the main gate of the City of Bone. One by one, well organized underling soldiers spilled outside, armed with spears and small crossbows, disappearing into the green foliage of the woods.

"Won't be long, Stranger. Won't be long at all. It should be a good fight for the Royal Riders, but it'll be their last one. And it won't last long after that." Tuuth pointed at the catwalks. "Once they charge in here, they're through."

Hundreds of underlings manned the catwalks, peering down, waiting. No force would be able to penetrate their superior position. But the underlings had, five years ago. Deceived by their own, the Royals had opened the gates, and the overwhelming numbers of the underlings, combined with the Brigand Army, had overtaken the fort. The battle had lasted longer than it should have, thanks to Venir, Billip and Mikkel's arrival, but in the end, it hadn't been enough. The powerful dark magic of the underlings had confused the well-trained soldiers, and they'd fallen.

Over five hundred men fell that day inside the fort, their bones ground into dust. Now, such men, a small force, only a few hundred at best, were being baited into a return. And it was his idea, not that the Royal Riders had much of a choice. They'd survived in the

Outland as long as they could. It was time for one last ride into glory.

Venir shuddered a sigh. He wished he could join them, but all he could do was watch. So long as he didn't pass out.

The minutes passed like hours while the entire fort fell gradually silent.

Venir lifted his head.

Hooves. In the distance, like a machine, they pounded the ground.

The underling soldiers stirred. Every weapon was in place. Every sharp object gleamed.

"They come." Tuuth gripped his weapon, an orcen Fang. "Stranger, let your last day be a long day. At least you'll see more underlings trampled this day. But what they do to the men that survive?" He shook his head. "You won't be ready for that. But if you want mercy, ask for mercy." He held his blade's tip under Venir's chin. "Perhaps I'll cut your head off before the underlings peel your living skin from you."

Venir didn't hear a thing. Just the thunder of hooves coming his way. His heavy head wanted to sag. His fingers stretched and crackled. His heart pumped a little more blood. But his eyelids were heavy.

Stay awake, blast it! Stay awake!

CHAPTER 21

CHITTERS AND SHORT SIGNALS ECHOED through the spreading fog that was as thick as Boon's beard. He didn't need to see the underlings to kill them, but they needed to see him. He squatted in the crooked arm of a moss-covered tree. Waiting. Biding his time to strike.

Come on, black rodents. Your date with death is at hand.

An entire battalion scoured the grove now. Fogle Boon and company had departed while Boon held the underlings off at the edge of the cliff. Clapping his hands together and screaming up a mighty force, he'd sent a shockwave through the creatures, blasting them into the foliage. Now he waited for them to come looking for him.

Below him, a giant spider crawled, unhindered by the fog. Boon could almost make out the riders on its back. They still sensed he was near. He formed an O with is bearded lips and cast forth a soft popping sound. Somewhere, far away, a commotion stirred, sending the underlings away from his direction.

That should keep them busy.

He should have gone, left, fled while he had the chance, but he wouldn't. He wanted to kill them. Kill as many as he could. Trick them. Trap them. Slaughter them. They were many, but he was one.

Blast, I wish that staff still had its extra oomph. Just get on with it, Boon!

He muttered a spell.

On cat's feet, he drifted through the woodland. Up the creek away from the wary eyes of the underlings. His robes blended in perfectly with the fog as he did so. He stopped, heart pounding in his chest, as three underling soldiers chittered past him. With further caution, up and away he went.

This should do.

He pressed his palm into a tree, scorching the bark. One by one, he did the same to many trees in a row, staying parallel to the search line of underlings, all the while maintaining the sound commotion illusion to keep them away. It was tedious work, but the results would be divine. Over a hundred trees later, he sat down, rested his back against the tree, and closed his eyes. He could hear the chitters of the underlings. The sounds repulsed him.

Ah, what is this?

A breeze started to dissipate and lift the fog. Above, a pair of robed underling magi hung in the air nearby.

As I suspected. Perfect timing.

The wind pushed the fog down through the grove, down the ravine towards the falls.

Boon summoned a word of power.

The last tree he touched burst into flame, igniting the next one, and so on. The chain reaction was quick and devastating. The underling magi's spell to rid the ravine of the fog only hastened the affect. The wind sent the flames jumping from tree to tree. In moments, the grove was a crackling bonfire of smoke, sealing off escape for the battalion of underlings.

Laughing under his breath, Boon crept out of the grove. He could picture the underlings now, burning by fire or leaping from the ledge and plunging to their deaths.

It's a good start.

Zzrcak! Zzrack!

Two red balls of energy struck him in the chest, knocking him down. He rolled to his feet. Spit dirt from his mouth. The two underling magi stood before him. Yellow gem eyes boring into him.

He grimaced, rubbed his chest, and coughed. "Is that all you have for me?"

They flung their arms forward. Balls of bright energy shot out towards him.

Boon caught one ball in one hand, one in the other, and shoved them together. "Amateurs!" He hurled the orb of energy into the nearest underling, catching it full in the chest.

Boom!

Flesh and robes scattered.

"Perfect!" Boon said.

Vines burst from the ground, entwining his legs, pulling him down.

"Don't you have anything new to offer?"

The remaining underling let out a shrill whistle.

"Calling for help won't save you from me!"

Boon shot a green dart of energy from the tip of his finger.

Zing!

It punched through its throat. The underling clutched at its neck and collapsed.

"Blasted vines!" He reached down and ripped them away. "You'd think they'd have gotten more creative by now."

The grove was an inferno. Its smoke a black tower. There was no need for the one remaining underling mage to send a signal; the blaze would attract every underling for miles.

What to do?

Ahead, the barren landscape of the Outlands awaited. If he was smart, he'd try to catch up with Fogle and his friends, but something told him he needed to stick around. See what was going on. He had plenty of spells and energy left.

One more strike, Boon. If you can take one battalion, you can take two, maybe three.

It was his way. Trap and ambush. Trick and destroy. He'd drowned underlings in riverbeds. He'd suffocated them in their sleep. He'd burned them alive in fires. With magic, illusions and a crafty mind, he baited them. Fishing for underlings he enjoyed; killing them he relished.

Boon narrowed his eyes, scanning the horizon. He had no place to hide. He was exposed, but over a mile in the distance, another large grove of trees waited. Could he get there before the underlings saw him? And how much longer could he last on his own?

"I swore if I ever got out of the Under-Bish, I'd take the fight back to the underlings again. Let's go, old man, while your bones and muscles still bend."

Running, he headed straight for the grove, sandaled feet digging into the ground. Ahead, the trees weren't tall, but they'd offer sanctuary, a place to burrow in and hide maybe. Rest. Recharge. Renew the fight on the morrow. He didn't want to use all his spells either. He didn't have the spellbook to renew them. The ones he'd memorized for a lifetime were few.

A blur of black sped his way. Faster than the fleetest deer, it stopped twenty feet away. An underling hunter, armed in leathers, clawed fingers wrapped around the jagged blades of a dagger, barred his path.

Boon sent a green missile its way. A foot from its face, it ricocheted away when two more underling magi appeared in the sky. Another underling sped into his path, followed by another, and another. The shock troops had arrived.

Face grim, jaw set, Boon ground his feet into the dirt.

"So be it then!" Boon muttered a spell.

Arcs of light shot his way. The underling hunters closed in.

Rocks exploded beneath his feet. He dove away and rolled up on one knee.

"This is more like it!"

His beard bristled in and out of a see-through suit of mystic armor, which shimmered bluely around him. A shield wavered in one hand, a black sword of energy in the other.

They came at him. Fury and murder in their eyes. Armed and armored, they were the superior force. Experienced fighters. Killers one and all.

Boon's scintillating blade sheared through one's leg at the knee, dropping it. He gutted the belly of another.

Another stabbed its dagger at his chest, skipping off his chest plate.

Boon caught it in the jaw with a back swing. He was a trained soldier, had been part of the old programs in the City of Bone, before he took to wizardry. He liked fighting, but it couldn't destroy things as fast as he could with wizardry.

Zzrcak! Zzrack! Zzrcak! Zzrack!

Bursts of energy careened off his shield, his chest, his mystic helmet, chipping fragments of energy from it all.

The underlings' weapons gouged and cut. They were useless against his magic. Angry, they slung their weapons to the ground and jumped on top of him.

Boon staggered back under the weight and crashed to the ground. His black sword was too long to stab. *I'll try this!* Concentrating, he shrunk it into the size of a dagger and jammed it into an underling's skull.

An underling jumped on his arm, pinning it to the ground, while the other wrapped its arms around his legs.

Zzrcak! Zzrack! Zzrcak! Zzrack!

He jerked his shield up. Energy exploded out of it, cracking it apart. He kicked and flailed at his underling grapplers.

"I'll try this then, roaches!"

His shield transformed into a dagger, his dagger a shield.

He sunk the mystic blade into the underling's skull and ripped it out.

"No more chittering for you!"

Reversing his grip, he slid it between the other underling's ribs, drawing forth a howl. He extended the blade, shooting out the other side of the underling, cutting its breath short, jaws locking in the air.

Vines exploded from the ground, entwining his legs.

"Not again!" He cut them away. Huffing for breath, he rose back to his feet, ready. "Who's ... eh ... next?"

Gem speckled eyes, on the ground and off, had him surrounded. Rows and rows of them.

He banged his mystic sword into his shield.

"So be it then!"

Bolts of lightning struck from all over, shattering his armor, pounding him into the ground. Everything tasted like metal, and his beard was smoking. Flat on his back, his eyes fluttered open just in time to see an iron net drop from the sky.

CHAPTER
22

MILES AWAY, FOGLE BOON COULD no longer see the smoke in the distance. All signs of his grandfather were faded and gone. In front of him, Cass's limp figure was slumped against him in the saddle. His arm held her tight around the waist.

"Cass," he whispered in her ear, "can you hear me?"

She hadn't moved, but she breathed. Fogle felt a great deal of anger when he got a closer look at her face. It was scraped up, bruised and swollen. She looked awful. *They'll pay for this.*

"Where did Puppy go?" Barton said. Scratching his head, his arms were like tree trunks as he ambled forward. "I like the puppy. He has two heads. Hee. Hee."

It was a good question, but the answer was obvious.

"He's going after Venir," Fogle said. He shifted in his saddle. His back was in knots already.

Barton smashed his fist in his hand

"The man with Barton's toys! Get him, Puppy. Get him!" Barton stopped and leered back with his one good eye. "Wizard, how are we going to find the doggy again?"

Fogle pointed upward. Inky, his ebony hawk was circling in the sky.

"Oh ... that's right. Good thinking."

It was good thinking, especially this time around. Taking no chances, Fogle had cut off a lock of Chongo's mane while the beast was licking Cass, then fed it to the bird. The familiar should have no problem tracking Chongo, but he wasn't so sure that the sliver of horn from Venir's long hunting knife would allow Inky to find the man.

We'll just have to wait and see what happens.

Cass pressed her back into his chest. He could hear her smacking her lips. Reaching around, he put a canteen to her mouth and felt her delicate hands wrap around his wrists. A fire went through him as she sighed, drank, gulped and sighed.

"Is that you, Fogle?" She reached back, nails gently scratching the stiff hairs on his cheek. "Did you save me?"

Despite the weariness, he felt his chest swell.

"You could say that," he said in her ear, "but I wasn't without any help."

Without looking back, she gulped down more water from the canteen.

"How did you find me?"

"Barton heard Chongo barking, I believe."

Cass straightened her shoulder and leaned forward.

"He's gone, isn't he?"

"Yes, but I'm tracking him, see?" He pointed into the sky. "We're going right after him."

"Hmmm... I'm impressed, Fogle Vir —, oh, sorry, Fogle Hero. Seems you're getting a knack for this adventuring after all..." Her voice trailed off.

"What? What is it, Cass?"

"Where's Boon?"

Good question. Dead most likely.

"He held the underlings off while we escaped."

"And you left him?" she said.

"No, he could have come, Cass. But he didn't want to, and I couldn't make him, not with a hundred men."

It was the truth. The pair of them had prepared more than enough spells to bail them out in a pinch if need be, but Boon had made it clear. He'd rather save his energy to kill underlings.

Cass turned her hips in the saddle and draped her sensuous legs over his. Her long-lashed pink eyes bore into his. "He's a crazy old man, isn't he?" She brought a smile to her battered lips.

She understands. Thank goodness for that.

He couldn't help but smile back. Despite the bumps and bruises, she was still the most beautiful thing he ever saw. A sparkle was in her eye.

"That might be a mild way of putting it." He cleared his throat. "Cass, I'm glad you're — *mmrph!*"

Cass grabbed him by his thick locks of hair and kissed him. The long, hot wet kiss was beyond words.

She gasped and sunk into his chest. "I'm glad you're well too."

Fogle wanted to jump off the horse and have her right then and there. He pulled her in for another kiss.

She pushed his chest back.

"Control yourself," she said, "We won't have time for that until the danger is over. And that won't be any time soon. So, do you have any idea where we are? I lost track leagues ago."

There had been a time when Fogle took a great deal of pride in knowing everything. He knew all about the City of Three and its histories, its people, its place, the names of all the Royals and the wizards in the towers ... But now, stranded in the Outland, he realized that he knew next to nothing. Torn, he didn't know whether to be ashamed or fulfilled. It was as if he'd been reborn over the past several weeks, and he was uncertain whether he liked it or not. But, judging by the legs that hugged his hips, he was getting used to it.

She still smells amazing.

"Fogle," she said, shaking his chin. "I asked you a question. Are you fantasizing about me?"

"No," he said, matter-of-factly.

She folded her arms under her splendid breasts, pushing them up a little.

"Oh really, so you are fantasizing about someone else?"

"Uh ... no, never!"

Cass wrapped her arms around his neck, giggled and kissed him on the cheek.

"You're always so serious, Fogle, aren't you?"

One second Cass was expressing her concerns about the danger, in the next she was teasing him. He didn't know what to think.

She might be crazy.

He squeezed her thigh.

She squeaked.

But I can get used to that.

"I'm serious about you," he said.

She ran her finger under his chin.

"Oh, I like that, Fogle. I like that a lot." She turned in the saddle. "But, I am concerned where we are headed. Do you have any idea?"

I'm not a Blood Ranger, you know.

He wanted to say it, but held back. He was in charge now, and at worst, he needed to act like he knew something.

"My familiar is in the air, and whatever it can see, I can. If there's any danger, I'll know, but at the moment, things are clear."

Clear as mud.

The terrain was virtually all the same, miles in every direction. Rocky. Sandy. Sparsely vegetated. He didn't let Inky scout too far ahead, for fear he'd lose him. Instead, he focused on the more immediate threats, particularly the underlings. In the back of his mind, something Barton had said worried him. What about the giants and the dragon?

"What can you see now, Fogle? Are there any forests or streams near? I need to rest somewhere that thrives with life." She shielded her face from the suns. "This is not good on my body. I need water. Natural water." She slumped back into him. "I tire again."

The suns above seemed to be beating down on him all of a sudden, sucking his life through his tattered robes. Above, Inky was soaring west at a gentle southern angle. Soaring above the land, he saw only bone trees and cacti scattered about, with little hope for water or natural vegetation in sight. For all Fogle knew, it might take over a week to traverse the Outlands to get where they were going. His stomach growled, and he thirsted.

She's right. I need to find better shelter. We'll never survive out here if it's too long.

"Follow the birdie," Barton began to sing, eyeing the sky. "Go where the birdie goes and find the puppy. A two headed puppy. And find the man that stole Barton's toys. And smash him."

Cass's head flopped over. Exhausted, she slept.

It worried Fogle. What would happen if he didn't find water or shelter? What would happen if the underlings caught up with them? He sent Inky back for a look.

Barton stopped and turned. "Say, where is the birdie going?"

"He's just making sure no one is following us."

Barton sat his big body on the ground and began rubbing his feet. "Tired of walking, Wizard. Barton wants to fly now."

Inky was almost a mile away when he noticed something. The landscape hadn't changed any, and none of their known pursuers were in sight, but something was coming, something dreadful. It was a swarm of some sort. Inky flew right into it. Whatever they were, they buzzed. Had tails, stingers and teeth.

Fogle turned his horse around.

"Get on your feet, Barton—it's time to run!"

"Why?" he groaned.

Fogle was already galloping away.

"Run, blast you! Run!"

A wall of insect creatures was coming after them like a heavy rain.

CHAPTER 23

THE SPIRE. IT HAD AS good a bird's eye view of the City of Bone as one could get, at least within the district Melegal frequented. He climbed the worn stone steps to the top, scattering the pigeons as he did so. Brushing the cobwebs away, Melegal stepped inside the room and made his way to the opening, where the remnants of a window were still intact.

It seemed like a lifetime had passed since the last time he stood here, a place he came to often, for seclusion and fantasy. He envisioned a magnificent castle and family, relatives of his long past, towering over the streets. When he was young, he'd convinced himself he was a Royal and played his own version of Royal games here. He'd commanded the street urchins from this roost for a while, but as time passed he'd grown out of it.

The wind bristled his clothes. He crawled through the frame and gripped the lip of the tower top above him. Whatever that woman, Trinos, had done, he'd never felt better in years. Fingernails digging into the terracotta tiles, he inched his way another twenty feet upward.

Bish, I haven't considered this since I was an urchin.

Tiles slipped under his boots.

Slat!

His fingers gripped the edges of the tile, holding on for dear life. Three tiles skittered off the roof and shattered on the decayed stone walls below.

There are far worse ways to go, I suppose.

The high winds tearing at his clothes, he continued his ascent at an agonizing pace. Near the top, he stretched out his skinny fingers.

A long metal pole, once a place for a castle banner, jutted from the highest point of the tower.

Stretch, you skinny bastard, stretch!

His fingers licked at the metal. His boots scraped, sending more tiles careening off the tower and crashing on the ground.

Almost there, Rat. He stretched. *Almost.* His fingers slid around the pole. *Got it!*

He pulled himself up and coiled himself around the pole. The first time he'd done that, long ago, he'd told himself he could do anything at all. But all he'd learned from it was that he could make an awfully hard climb to an awfully old pole. Still, he kissed it.

I'd like to see anyone else do this.

The viewpoint was unlike any other in the City of Bone. He could see the tops of the buildings and all the way from one massive City wall to the other. None of the intact Royal Castles lined up against the Wall of Bone had as high a spire. How this one stood here so long as it had, while the old castle and everything else around it fell, he'd never know. His keen eyes scanned the chaos.

Smoke from the burning buildings rolled past and beneath him. The massive gates in the four walls of the city were crowded with throngs of thousands of people. Soldiers patrolled the streets on foot and horseback, while squads of underlings darted in and out of the alleys and attacked. The entire city groaned in horror, despair and disbelief.

This place is going to the slatter.

He turned his keen eyes to Castle Almen. His jaw dropped open. Underlings, hundreds of them, surged the main wall. Every tower was lit with mystic illumination, and spiders the size of dogs and ponies scurried over the parapets, up the walls and towers. A chill raced down Melegal's spine. How long could the Royals hold out? And why were the underlings attacking there? His hand drifted to the Keys.

Sefron wanted them. The underlings wanted them. A picture of the imp invaded his mind. *What if that thing shows up here?*

Something was not right.

Think, Melegal. Think!

He squatted down, flattened himself on his belly, and crept back down the steep tower, thinking all the way.

Sefron works for the underlings. Underlings want inside the castle. Sefron is in the castle. Kill Sefron. Stop the underlings. Ridiculous.

As much as Melegal despised the Royals and all their cruel and twisted games, he knew the underlings were a far greater threat. Venir had shown him at least that much. Catching the lip of the tower's edge like a spider, Melegal crawled headfirst back inside.

Whew!

Alone in the tower, his thoughts went to his friends. He hadn't seen Venir since that last time he was here, and despite his anger towards the man, he'd like to be with him now. If anyone knew how to deal with underlings, it was Venir.

I wonder how Lefty's doing as well.

So far as he was concerned, ever since they all left, his life had been far from normal. If anything, it had gotten worse. He smoothed his cap over his head.

"Well, I suppose if no one else is going to defend my home, I'll just have to do it my—"

A small black blur jumped through the outside window over the top of him. Melegal ducked and rolled, the sisters out and ready. A pair of pearl white eyes greeted him.

"Octopus!"

The big cat circled his ankles, lay down and rumbled. Melegal couldn't have been gladder to see his most reliable friend. He reached over and stroked the cat's back.

"And to think, I actually worried you might be underling food."

Octopus stretched out his eight claws that twinkled in the night.

"I should have known better," Melegal said, rubbing behind his ears, "because you have plenty of lives, don't you?"

After the short reunion, thoughts heavy on his task ahead, Melegal made his way down the deteriorating steps. Octopus darted away when he reached the bottom.

Must be a big juicy rat somewhere. Besides me.

Aside from all the distant shouts of alarm and screams, the streets in this quadrant were barren for the most part. Even the urchins and thugs that frequented the remains of the abandoned castle had become ghosts.

Maybe the underlings aren't so bad after all. They're keeping the stink out.

Down the street he went, tugging and knocking on doors as he did so. Reaching inside his vest, he produced a Key. It was the same one he'd used before.

Hmmm. What did the woman at the fountain say? Just find a door and go?

From building to building he went, searching for a key hole, but none were found.

Drat it.

With all the pickpockets, urchins and thieves about in Bone, using keys to secure common doors and entrances wasn't always the securest way to go. Many shop keepers barred their doors from the inside because they lived there. Melegal imagined most were holed up inside right now. Of course, whenever a door was barred from the inside, it only meant someone must be home. Most citizens of Bone never, ever left their home or store empty.

Never cared to rob the places filled with the living.

He made his way farther up the street.

There must be a keyhole somewhere.

He stopped at the next block and stood in front of an entrance to a corner store, where a big black keyhole forged with brass greeted him. Melegal bounced the ancient Key on his chin.

It's not going to fit in there, is it?

Lowering the Key towards the hole, he froze. His neck hair rose. He sniffed.

Smells like a wet dog.

Wapush!

A tail of black leather encircled his wrist and jerked the Key out of his hand.

Melegal twisted his wrist free. *Who in Bone?*

Wapush!

The tail of the whip caught him by the leg and pulled him down.

Bark! Bark! Bark!

An oversized Rottweiler was snapping at his neck.

"Bloody Watchmen!" Melegal cried out. "Back off! I'm a Royal—"

Wapush!

Another whip wrapped around his throat.

"Watchmen! Ha! Hear that, men? This one thinks we're part of the local brute squad." A tall, limber man stepped into view. He was no Watchman. He was savvy. Buckled. Clean. A different breed.

The other two were stout. Menacing. "Ha! Watchmen, and you were about to say you were a Royal! Eh, Melegal?"

He couldn't answer. The whip choked his neck.

Bark! Bark! Bark!

"Heel!"

The dog quieted, but still loomed over him, growling.

That's when Melegal saw it. The insignia on the man's hand. His blood ran cold.

Bone! The Royal Bloodhounds are after me too!

Melegal had heard plenty of stories of the most vicious bounty hunters of all.

The speaking man squatted down beside him, long fingers stroking the finely groomed auburn hair on his chin. His eyes steely flecks of brown and green. Hair brownish red. Intelligent. Cocky. A good manner about him.

"So, a Royal Detective, as I understand. Pretty crafty I'd say, to be serving Lord Almen." He pulled a long dagger from his sheath. "Roll him over, men. Unfortunately, I need to cut those thews behind his skinny knees. Can't have you running off now, can we?"

Melegal started to speak.

Whop!

The Bloodhound leader slugged him in the face.

"No talking," the man said. Almost polite. "Now get him rolled over."

CHAPTER 24

L ORDA ALMEN COWERED BEHIND A chair, trembling.
"All clear!"

It was a man's voice. Strong. Labored. She peeked.

A few feet away, a dog-sized spider twitched, webbing spewed from its mouth and stuck to the floor.

Glitch!

The shadow sentry rammed his sword through its brain, bringing its convulsions to a stop. The sentry wore a helmet of black mesh armor that covered his face. The rest of him was splattered in spider gore. He extended his hand.

"Are you alright, Lorda?"

She shook her head, trying to stand, too weak to speak. Sprawled out on the floor, her servant girls were dead. A Shadow Sentry sat in the corner, coated in webbing, a nasty wound on his face. It appeared the acid from the spider's fangs had burnt straight through his mesh helmet.

You are in command, Lorda. Act like it!

Reaching out, the sentry caught her under the elbow and lifted her forward. He was strong. His girth reminded her of her former high guard, Gordin. She missed him. Her son Tonio had killed him, and Melegal had saved her, so she was convinced. She shook her head.

"Remember these words, Sentry: from this day forward, Spiders are banned from the Castle." She tossed her hair over her shoulder, pulled her shoulders back, and straightened her bodice. Outside, the battle was raging. Explosions, screams and the disturbing chitters of the underlings could be heard from all around.

"Secure the openings, men. See to it nothing again ever enters this room!"

A half dozen soldiers made their way into the room, followed by two more Shadow Sentries.

Making her way to her husband, Lorda lost her shoe. It stuck to the floor. She clenched her fists by her side.

"BONE!"

One of the soldiers grabbed a torch from the wall and burned the webbing. Lorda covered her nose.

Must all evil things stink?

She picked up a small bottle of perfume that lay near a table that had been knocked over, dabbed it on, and stepped in something that splashed.

"What?"

At her feet, water from Lord Almen's bowl had spilled, and the wash cloth from his head now lay on the ground with spider guts on it. Reaching over to grab it, she withdrew her hand.

"Disgusting."

"I'll take care of that, Lorda," the Shadow Sentry said. "Shall I send for the cleric?"

She glanced at Lord Almen.

"Eeeeeek!"

His bloodshot eyes were wide open.

CHAPTER
25

"NEVER SEND AN IMP TO do an underling's job," Master Kierway said, flatly.

It was dark, aside from the glow of the small underling lanterns that cast shadows through the caves.

"What is that, Kierway?" Catten rubbed his gut. His thoughts were still heavy from his brother, Verbard, punching him there. Verbard had changed, changed much. He couldn't decide whether he should admire or hate him.

I'll get him back when the time comes.

"The Keys," Kierway said. "If we had the Keys, we'd have overrun this Castle already. They can get into anything, anything at all, even that door."

Catten remained silent. Master Kierway had a small army at his disposal, filling the caves alongside the Current beneath Castle Almen as far as he could see. All he had to do was get them in there. Time was running out.

Kierway chopped the top off a stalagmite. "Well, Mage? Did you come here to help overtake this castle or to conspire against your brother?" Kierway chopped another top off. "Or both?"

Catten lifted his chin.

"What are you talking about?"

Kierway flashed the sharp grey teeth in his mouth.

"Oh come now. Do you really think I believe you're on your brother's side? You? Then you wouldn't be the Catten I know. And besides, I already know my father can't stand him. Why else would he bring you back to life?" Showing off with his sword, he split a drop of water falling from above. "To see Verbard dead, of course."

"I'm sure there is nothing you'd rather believe, now that my brother has taken over your charge. The one you've spent years on and failed. The Keys. You dare mention them? You should have secured them, but you failed. And my brother, he's not a disappointment to your father, quite the contrary. But you are." Catten's gold eyes locked on Kierway's copper. "Sinway put you at my brother's will and pleasure, and I am here on his behalf. Now, tell me, why isn't this door open?"

Kierway's eyes narrowed. He slid his swords into their sheaths on his back. The master underling had a way of squeezing out of things, but at the moment, both Verbard and Catten had the upper hand on him. It only figured that Kierway would seek an alliance so he could get out from underneath the will and pleasure of Verbard. Kierway made his way to the door. Two robed underling magi were on their knees chittering an incantation, while another made arcane markings along the door's edges.

"It was only wood before when we destroyed it," Kierway said, "but it's been replaced with iron and stone, sealed by magic. There isn't even any key hole."

"So, how would those precious Keys have worked then?"

Kierway shrugged.

"Nothing to say, eh, Kierway?" Catten floated closer to the door. Over eight feet in height, it was more of a slab than a door. "Have you even tried to crack it?"

Kierway motioned to the battering ram propped up by the stalagmites. It was a six foot metal tube with handles

"I was confident the magi could get us in, like the last time," Kierway said. He picked up the small battering ram with a groan and tossed it at Catten's feet. "Perhaps you should give it a try?"

"Perhaps I should... Fool."

With a flick of his wrist, the battering ram lifted from the ground.

"Magi, finish your spell. Kierway, ready your warriors."

"They're ready." He folded his arms over the bandoliers on his chest. "For what, I can't imagine."

Focusing, Catten grabbed the handles on the ram and filled it with energy. It glowed red and hummed with new life, hovering over the cave floor. The symbols drawn on the door flared with life. The underling magi floated backward. The slab door groaned. The light of the battering ram became brighter and brighter as Catten filled it with more power.

No mortal man is more powerful than I!

The giant missile shot forward, striking the door with mind-jarring force.

KA-CHOW!

Stone cracked. Metal groaned. Parts of the door exploded.

A human cry of alarm went up from the other side.

Catten was about to say, "Get in there, Kierway," but the man and his soldiers were already on their way. Juegen in plate mail, Badoon warriors of all sorts, and albino urchlings stormed through the black hole, led by the Son of Sinway.

"Go!" Catten ordered two magi through the opening.

Yes! He clutched his fist.

The underling force jammed at the entrance.

He blew at the wispy fibers of energy that lingered on his fingers. He never would have imagined it possible, but in moments, he was going to be taking up residence inside the walls of the City of Bone.

Perhaps Sinway isn't losing it after all.

An army of underlings with access to the Current could hold that castle forever. It was brilliant.

We'll take them one castle at a time.

Finally, he would have one victory where his brother had failed. He'd penetrated the castle, and in minutes, it would be his.

Elation had filled him, but the underlings up front cried out in disappointment.

"Impossible!" he cried out.

The door he just destroyed had returned. He and the majority of his underling army were trapped outside. Kierway and his men were trapped within.

CHAPTER 26

ALLIES AND ENEMIES. JARLA THE former Brigand Queen had been on both sides of the war against the underlings. Unlike the Royals who had betrayed her, defiled her, humiliated her and destroyed her trust in all men, good and bad, she wasn't heartbroken to see the City of Bone under siege. Instead, she was thirsty.

Dragging her shoulder along an alley wall, carrying an empty bottle in her hand, she was making her way back to the stables. She just needed to find Nightmare and ride out of here. But there was a problem. She was lost.

"Bastards," she moaned. She stepped over one bloodied corpse after another. "Probably had it com-*hic*-coming."

Dried out and tired, she was rubbing her short locks of braided black hair when she found herself staring at a large road known as the Royal Roadway. A team of soldiers trotted down the street, away from her. She tried to get her bearings.

I know where this is. Hic.

Sauntering along the store fronts where the Royals used to shop, her mind wandered back to her life long ago. Her mother, a seamstress, had been the mistress of a Royal. As a little girl, Jarla watched the proud women come and go, but never desired to be one. She was cut from a different cloth, always fancying the work down in the smithy shops. Down there, as she grew older, she helped in a forge, along with her father who was also a soldier.

She recalled the last day she saw him. Taller than her, eyes blue, black hair long, he'd said, "Jarla, if I don't return, be sure to help your mother." He rode off on a horse and was gone. No word ever came of what happened to him, and her unfaithful mother moved within the walls of the castles. She had never spoken to her mother since. Instead, she enlisted. She had the right through her father, and she passed. Her steel was quick, her determination unrivaled, and after years of training and field experience, she carved her way up the ranks. Then, they betrayed her. She'd been the Brigand Queen ever since.

All the doors she passed by were boarded up or locked, and few of the stores had windows. That would be too dangerous. A pair of long-faced urchins shuffled by.

"Can you help us?" one said. He was pitiful, dirty, scraped up and trembling. "Our parents are dead."

She laughed, handed the boy her bottle, patted him on the head and walked away. "And soon you will be too," she said. She crossed the nearest alley, booted feet clopping over the storefront porch, and stopped. Something rustled inside the store. She pressed her ear to the door. A pair of bottles clinked and rolled. She jerked her head back. Someone inside busted a bottle on the door. Looking up at the sign that hung above her, she licked her lips. It read: Wine Blossoms.

"Where there's glass, there's wine."

Stepping back, she noticed the windows were boarded up and the door had no handle. She cast a glance over her shoulder, noting the streets were empty but distant sounds of battle and destruction could be heard. If anything, there should be widespread looting, but it seemed the underlings had spooked even the looters. The entire city was not itself.

Why not? Someone is in there.

She knocked on the door.

The rustling stopped.

She tried to decide if it would be best to be a member of the City Watch or a person in need. *Besides, I don't think underlings would knock.* She tried again, harder this time.

Knock! Knock! Knock!

She considered speaking. Saying hello. Sounding polite and customary, but such manners weren't in her anymore. Over the years, she'd grown accustomed to taking what she wanted.

"Blasted cowards," she murmured. She pressed her ear to the door again, closed her eyes and listened. Nothing. She was thinking maybe there was another way in when she heard more chittering. Closer this time. Coming her way. Her hand fell to her blade.

Now the little fiends show up.

Jarla didn't fear the underlings as most people did. She didn't fear anything. Besides, she'd seen them bleed the same as anything else. She'd battled them by the dozens when she was a Royal Soldier and found out that their skulls split just as easily as men's. She pressed her back against the doorway. The underlings, so far as she could hear, would be upon her any moment. And by the sounds of things, there were many of them, at least a dozen. If she only had her axes and the armament, she could have handled them.

Slat! I hate running!

Thump.

She heard a heavy footstep on the other side of the door, followed by the sound of a bolt scraping over metal.

She turned just as the door swung open. She took a sharp breath.

"Welcome," a man said. "Won't you come in?"

The man that filled the doorway spoke like his throat was full of broken glass. He looked and sounded like nothing she ever noted before. A hole dotted the center of his forehead. It was unnatural. She blinked and took a step back, hand still on her sword.

Neck cracking, the man bent his ear. "Seems company is coming, huh, Little Lady."

Her eyes drifted to the jug of wine in his grip, then back to his face. His eyes were dark, almost black, and a thick scar parted the brown hair on his head and went down past his neck, stopping at the armor that covered his broad shoulders. Jarla felt something in her bones that she hadn't felt in years. Fear.

"Shall you stay or shall you go?"

She fanned her hand in front of her face. His breath was foul and unimaginable. Everything about him defied reason. Her keen eyes noted the fresh blood stains all over his armor. Swords and long knives hung from his belt and behind his shoulders. His rotting smile turned her blood cold.

He shook his jug of wine. "It's been a long time since I drank with such a lovely lady."

She pulled back her shoulders. "And it's been a long time since

I drank with such a fine man." She snatched the jug from his hand and stepped inside.

He closed the door behind her and slid the bolt back in place.

Taking a seat at the bar, the first thing she noticed was what was left of the dead people on the floor. "I'm Jarla." She tipped the bottle her lips.

The man bowed. "And I'm Tonio."

She almost spit all over herself. Something about the half-dead man's name was awfully familiar.

"Bad wine?" He smirked.

Her eyes flittered towards the door. Tonio stepped in the way, a haunting glimmer in his eye.

Slat! I should have snatched the jug and ran.

Staring at the woman, Tonio felt a degree of fascination. Her scarred face gave him comfort and solace. She wasn't like the rest of the people in this world. He grabbed the jug of wine she'd snatched and drank from it.

"Jarla," he said. It had a ring to it. There was something in a portion of his mind that clicked. "Jarla."

Her eyes narrowed, and her sword inched out of its sheath.

He chuckled. Even though his thinking had begun to clear, his memories were still scattered. "You can leave that where it is, Jarla. I have no reason to harm you."

Scowling, she looked over at the people on the floor. "Is that what you told them?"

"Heh, heh, heh... no, they would have died anyway. They were weak, but you," he eyed her athletic frame up and down. It stirred something in him, "are strong."

"You have better judgment than most men I know," she said. She pulled out a dagger and stuck it in the bar. "Just don't get too close."

Tonio grabbed another bottle and poured it down his throat. It warmed his bones, made him feel alive. But in the back of his mind, the nagging continued.

Kill the Vee-Man.

The image of Venir was still as clear as a bell in his mind. The man had mocked him in the jail cell, in front of his comrades. He could still see the man splitting him in half with that axe. The whistle of the blade woke him up whenever he drifted off. Only vengeance would give him rest.

"Kill the Vee-Man," he growled.

Jarla looked at him and said, "What?"

He slammed his fist into the bar. "Kill Vee-Man!"

Jarla jumped back, ripping her sword from her sheath. "Keep silent, you three-eyed fool! There are underlings out there!"

Underlings, they meant nothing to Tonio. Or did they? A memory came forth, the memory of the underling named Oran. Violet eyed. That underling had saved him after the giant dog's chewing almost killed him. That underling had found the Vee-Man before. Maybe underling help was what he needed after all.

He headed toward the door.

"What are you doing?" Jarla jumped into his path and stuck her sword at his belly.

"The underlings will help me find the Vee-Man," he said, coldly.

"Oh no they won't!" She shoved her sword through his belly.

Tonio didn't feel a thing. He shook his finger at the wide-eyed woman. "You shouldn't have done that, Jarla."

Smack!

He back-handed her across the face, sending her sprawling to the floor. He pulled the sword from his belly and tossed it clattering by his side. Outside, he could hear the chittering of underlings gathering at the door.

Jarla dove after her sword. A second later she was ready. "I can't let you do that, you split-faced bastard!"

"I must find the Vee-Man, and you can't stop me." He pulled a blade from the sheath.

Clang!

Metal crashed into metal. He knocked her swings away, parrying one after the other. With his other hand, he reached the bolt and started to pull it free.

"No!" Jarla said. She poked at his eyes.

Tonio flinched.

"Almost got me, Beautiful."

Jarla gasped and turned away.

Angry churts erupted. Bright underling eyes, teeth bared, poured into the room, surrounding them.

"Didn't you secure the door in the back? You idiot!"

Tonio shrugged at her and turned to the underlings. "Take me to the Vee-Man."

One underling chittered a series of orders; the rest bared their teeth, raised their weapons and charged.

CHAPTER 27

O UTPOST THIRTY ONE WAS UNDER attack. Rider after rider stormed through the gate: three horses wide, twenty horses deep. Their banners streamed in the air, bright and colorful, a symbol of hope among the despair.

His fires stoked inside. Venir fought against the stockade.

The big orc said, "Say anything, and I'll cut your tongue out," then turned his eyes on the burgeoning battle below.

At the front of the riders, Venir could see Commander Jans. His long auburn mustache whipped in the wind as he thundered in.

"Let the Havoc begin!" Jans cried.

Perched on the catwalks and in the towers, the underlings fired. Crossbow bolts, spears, lances and ballista bolts ripped into the men. Hot pitch poured down on them.

Venir wanted to scream, "Turn back!" but he didn't have the throat or the breath for it.

The Riders kept charging, thundering through the giant courtyard, looking for an enemy to strike. One barrage after the next punched into the flesh of men, while other bolts were deflected by their heavy armor.

Venir grimaced. Many men caught ballista bolts in the face. Tuuth pointed and laughed.

Ride out, Jans! Ride out!

Venir's mind was racing. More Royal Riders stormed through the gate and inside. It was just what the underlings wanted. The riders thundered straight into the next assault. Crossbow bolts, heavy and small, ripped into them, separating horse and rider. One rider caught a bolt in the neck. Another was pinned to his horse.

Pitch burned horses and riders alike. A dozen horses went down in an instant, and still the riders kept pouring in.

The well-organized ranks of the riders turned to chaos. The underlings splintered the groups, sending them in all directions. Over a hundred warriors rode purposefully around the fort, looking for something to strike. Something to trample. Something to kill. Another volley cut them down.

Blast their black hides!

Venir's fists clenched beneath his broken wrists. He'd cut off his arm to get down to them. They needed help. They needed to get on those catwalks.

Men yelled. Cried out. Horses whined and buckled. The Royal Riders' organized ranks had become chaos. Some circled the courtyard, while others tried to hide. But there was nowhere to go. The underlings fired from every angle, every corner. Venir felt helpless. Miserable. Standing there watching good men get slaughtered.

Run, blast you, Run!

A dark cloud rolled overhead, blotting out the sun as the southern gate was lowered and sealed shut. The Royal Riders were trapped.

"Won't be long now, Stranger. And once they're all dead, it won't be long for you either."

Venir would have stabbed him in in the throat if he could have. But he couldn't do anything right now. He couldn't even hold a weapon. He could barely walk or keep his eyes open. Through his hazy eyes, he caught something. Massive stone towers jutted up from every corner. Smaller towers lined the inner wall every thirty yards, linking catwalk to catwalk. At the bottom of each corner tower was a huge wooden door. The underlings cried out as one of these doors exploded.

A tall lanky man appeared, waving the riders inside.

Slim!

Commander Jans and his steed disappeared inside, appearing moments later on the catwalk.

"What's this?" Tuuth's jaw dropped in astonishment.

Spears lowered, the Royal Riders galloped into the sea of

underlings on the catwalk. Jans caught two on one spear with his first pass.

Venir wanted to jump for joy. *Yes, by Bish!*

Underlings were trampled and gored. Men were pulled from their saddles. Underlings were hurled off the catwalks.

Boom!

Somewhere, another door exploded. Men surged into the tower and up onto the western catwalks.

The underlings were caught off guard. Flatfooted, they scrambled for weapons, only to have their brains dashed into the wood. The Royal Riders cheered and charged, tearing into the underlings with everything they had. Somewhere someone shouted, "Take the towers!"

One by one, the underlings on the catwalks fell under the heavy steel of the Royal Riders. The underling rout was over, but the battle had only just begun. The underlings were many. The Riders were already reduced to half the force they rode in with. The underlings, despite their losses, were somehow still at full strength.

Commander Jans was at the other end of the Catwalk, beside the South Gate entrance, throwing an underling over the railing. He was shouting, but Venir couldn't make out what he said. Were there still more Riders to come? Had Royal reinforcements finally arrived?

KA-CHOW!

An arc of energy struck Jans full in the chest, blasting him into the main wall. Above, a host of underling magi had appeared. Arms spread wide, fingertips aglow, they let the Royal Riders have it.

KA-CHOW!

KA-CHOW!

KA-CHOW!

"Nooooo!" Venir's hoarse voice cried out.

Tuuth back-handed him in the face. "Quiet, Fool!"

Men were knocked from their horses. Bodies of animal and man exploded. The triumph of the Riders took a sharp turn into a dark tunnel. Venir turned just in time to catch Commander Jans rising back his feet. Blood coated his mustache. He kept shouting. Pointing at the towers.

Two ballistas swung in his direction. An underling mage hung in the sky, guiding them. Venir's heart sank. The underling pointed at Jans. The big warrior saw them and beat his chest, yelling.

Clatch-zip! Clatch-zip!

Two long bolts ripped through the sky, striking Jans square in the chest. He was pinned to the wood. He shouted once more, hand rising in the air, pointing towards Venir and died.

"Ew… that must have hurt," Tuuth said. "But there are far worse ways to go. You'll find out soon, I bet."

The Royal Riders fought long and hard, but they were no match for the underling numbers and mystic forces. A wall of fire encircled dozens of horsemen on the ground. The horses bucked and whined. Riders were tossed from their saddles into the fires. More missiles from the crossbows and ballistas came, skewering the men and scattering others. Minute after agonizing minute, Venir watched the brave men get picked off. The underling magi cleared the catwalks, and the dead underlings and men were piled up in heaps of torn flesh and metal. The hot fort air wreaked of death.

Slim!

Venir didn't see any sign of him.

An hour later, the men of the Royal Riders could swing no more. The last twelve of them surrendered.

"Not bad, Stranger. Not bad at all, for Royal soldiers. But I think a host of orcs would have fared much better." He slapped Venir on his back. "At least you'll have some company. And who knows, they might have you peel the skin from them before they peel the skin from you." He snorted a laugh. "Now wouldn't that be something?"

For the first time in his life, Venir had nothing to say.

CHAPTER 28

LEFTY DASHED FROM BEHIND THE bar, shaking his head, tears streaming from his eyes. Everything happened so fast. *What do I do?*

Everyone was screaming at Scorch, but he paid them little mind. Instead, he pushed his broken nose back into place.

"What have you done!" Joline screamed.

Kam's jaw dropped just before her eyes rolled up inside her head.

Joline caught her on the way down.

But Scorch wasn't paying attention to that. It was the hand that held his eyes. It twitched on the table. "Fascinating." Picking it up, he resumed his seat at the bar. "I've never experienced a talking hand before."

"Lefty! Lefty!" Joline cried.

Lefty stood there next to Joline, but still was unsure what to do. There was blood everywhere.

"Scorch!" Joline shouted. "Why, Scorch? Why!" Joline's tone was delirious.

Lefty trembled.

"Oh, put a sock in it, or whatever you people say." Scorch shook his head. "I'll never understand why Trinos picked such leaky beings." He wiped Kam's blood splatter from his forehead. "I can only presume it gives the dramatic more flare."

"Is there anything I can do?" Darlene said. "I can make a fine tourniquet."

"You could've not cut her hand off, you imbecile woman!" Joline said. Tears streamed from her face as she held Kam in her arms. "What possessed you to do such a thing?"

"He told me to. I do what he tells me," Darlene said. The husky woman handed Joline a rag.

"Would you cut your own hand off if he told you?"

"Probably."

The woman defied reason. Scorch defied reason. Everything Lefty had been through seemed to defy reason. But right now, Kam's bleeding had to stop. And Joline needed to stop screaming.

Lefty leapt onto the bar and kicked Scorch in the jaw. "Fix this, you—"

Blink!

Darleen stood by the table, dumbfounded.

Kam, Joline, the Halfling, and the baby were all gone. She wiped the sweat from her brow and swallowed. "What happened to them?" she said. She started looking under the tables.

"Could you bring me your knife?" Scorch said.

Darlene wiped the blood off her trousers and asked, "Sure, what for?"

Without looking at her, he snapped his fingers, popping her ears.

She hurried over, ears ringing, and handed the blade to him, handle first.

He showed her the hand, the gems embedded in it. "Is it customary to wear gems in this manner, Darlene?"

"No." She took a closer look. "I have to say, I've never seen anything like that before." She grimaced. "Looks painful, but you know, there are bugs that'll crawl right inside you and lay eggs. It's the vilest thing. One time this fella was drinking some jig back in Hohm when these eensy weensy bugs came crawling out if his nose and earholes. Huh! He screamed, I screamed, we all screamed for lice cream!" She popped her lips. "I got my chubby arse out of there after that."

Scorch, so far as she could tell, was ignoring her. He always did, but whenever she thought he wasn't paying attention, he'd say something to her. She'd been trying to figure it out, but she'd come to the conclusion that she just wasn't smart enough. Two minds were better than one anyway, she figured.

Scorch dug the knife under the gem inside Kam's palm.

"It seems my little red friends are determined to stay put, Darlene. Any suggestions?"

She propped her elbow on the bar and chin on her fist. "Maybe we should burn it. I can stoke the fireplace up over there, but let me warn you: it'll smell something awful."

The hand twisted away from Scorch's grip. Like a spider, it scrambled away.

Darlene jumped out of her stool. "Great Guzan!" Look at that thing go!" Heart thumping, she chased after it. She knocked over tables and chairs, diving on top of it as it reached the exit door. She held it up with both hands. "I got it, Scorch! I got it!" It felt like a dry wiggling fish in her hands. "Should I throw it in the fire?"

"Hmmm..." Scorch took a bite out of a pickle. "I have a feeling it doesn't want that. Bring it back over here."

"Certainly." Her arms wiggled. The hand was strong. Unnatural to hold. "Maybe you should cut the fingers off. I've got another knife, you know." *Thunk.* She pinned the knife to the table and handed him the hand. "This is the strangest thing I ever saw, Scorch. What are you going to do with it?"

His eyes lit up like infernos. He looked straight at the gems and said, "Time is short." His other hand became a brilliant blue fire. "What will it be?"

The hand clutched and writhed.

"I grow impatient," Scorch said.

The red gemstones popped out of Kam's hand and clattered on the floor.

"Whoa!" Darlene leaned in closer. "You know what, Scorch? Those things kinda look like eyeballs."

Dangling Kam's hand by one finger, he said, "A shame to see such a functional appendage go to waste." *Plop.* He dropped it in the pickle jar.

Darlene let out a snort, watching it float down, but a sinking feeling fell upon her.

Where did those people go?

"Don't worry about that, Darlene," Scorch said. The gems floated up to his fingers.

And that's when things became odd.

Scorch talked to himself, ate pickles and cheese, and sipped Muckle Sap for the next hour. He laughed. Scoffed. Mocked. His handsome features changed from one expression to another. Grim. Scary. Bold. Enlightened. But for the most part, he giggled and used the word 'fascinating.'

Bored, she began to clean up, whistling a lullaby as she picked up the chairs and tables she'd knocked over. She stopped at the dead bodies and smashed a few flies between her hands.

"How am I going to dispose of these guys?"

She had an idea.

"Uh, Scorch?"

He sat there, eyes transfixed on the red stones he'd set back on the bar.

"Scorch, could you?"

Slowly, he turned, a dark look in his eye.

Walking over to him, she tossed a rag over the gemstones.

He blinked at her, eyes regaining their luster. "What is it?"

She jutted her thumb at the headless bodies.

"Oh," he sighed. "Just find some sand and sprinkle it on them."

"Sand?"

"Never mind," he said. He snatched the rag off the gemstones.

Puff! Puff! Puff! Puff! Puff!

"Whoa!" she said.

The dead men had turned to statues of sand. Walking over, she poked the nearest one and watched it implode over the planks on the floor.

"Whoa. Thanks, Scorch."

But he wasn't paying her any mind. Instead, he rolled the gemstones in between his fingers. "I've got to see this." He said more, but that was all she understood.

She tried to ignore the butterflies in her stomach. She'd never had those before, but Scorch had never acted this way before either.

The door to the entry way cracked open, and one of their followers peeped his gray-haired head through.

"Darlene, er … well, any needs?"

She placed her hands on her hips. "Drag in two more of you, and find me a mop and broom."

Glancing over at Scorch, she almost peed herself. Only the hand and the pickle jar remained. Scorch was gone with the red gems.

"I got a bad feeling about this."

CHAPTER
29

"WHAT IN BISH ARE THOSE things?" Fogle yelled. But Cass wasn't listening. She wasn't even moving. "Cass!" Nothing.

Ahead, Barton's giant feet shook the ground. Running full stride, his arms swung like giant hammers at his sides.

Fogle whipped the reins on his horse. "Eeyah!"

Behind him, the angry buzz of the insects got louder, like a hunger. Fogle had heard about swarms before. He recalled the stories of insects that picked the flesh clean from the bone. Inky's vision of the insects, each as long as Fogle's finger, was a chilling site. Sharp rows of snapping teeth, black bug eyes, wings and a stinger like a scorpion for a tail. He glanced over his shoulder.

"They're getting closer! Eeyah!"

They'd made it over a mile when his horse began to labor for breath. Ahead, Barton began to clutch at his side. *No! Think of something, Fogle!*

No spells came to mind that could put a stop to thousands of insects, and anything from the spellbook would take too much time.

Looking over his shoulder, he screamed again. "Cass!" The insects were getting closer. His horse was slowing, and ahead, Barton's feet stumbled. "Come on, Druid! I need you! You're the one that's supposed be able to talk to things in this world."

The buzzing became louder, not so much a buzz, but more like the sound of thousands of tiny metal scissors opening and closing. Fogle fought the image of his flesh being ripped from his skin one tiny chunk at a time, a thousand times over.

Do something, Wizard! What had Mood said? *You can die doing something or nothing. It's your life. Make it count.*

Fogle flung his arm back, flinging tendrils of energy from his fingertips. The energy punched into the grey swarm, creating a hole. An eruption of tiny explosions in the sky followed. A second later, the hole closed. Fogle shook his head. He was angry. Every time he overcame one obstacle, he found himself faced with another that he was even less prepared for.

You can't be ready for everything. Boon had said. *Just be ready to act.*

"I'll be ready to act, all right. Act dead!" He whipped the reins. "Barton! Think of something. We're about to have company!"

He couldn't tell if Barton could hear him on not, but the giant slowed and turned.

"Keep moving, Giant!"

Barton just leered at him, clutching at his sides, huffing for breath.

"What are you doing?" Fogle said, riding up to him, stopping.

"No more running, Wizard. No more. Wooooo. Barton tired." His hands fell to his knees.

Fogle tried to summon his energy but couldn't think of anything to cast. It was too late. The swarm was only seconds away. He pulled Cass tight and looked up at Barton.

"I guess this is good-bye, Barton."

Barton scooped out two massive handfuls of dirt from the ground and reached for him.

"What are you doi—ingggg!"

Barton picked them both up off the horse, set them in a large divot in the ground, and huddled over them.

Fogle tried to squirm away, but an infant could have done better. "Get off—mrph!"

Everything went black. Fogle and Cass were trapped beneath the hot sweaty mass of Barton's belly flesh.

I'm going to suffocate in sweaty lard!

Barton's body groaned and twitched over top of him and Cass. He could hear the muffled cries of the deformed giant's moans of pain. All he could imagine was the insects eating Barton alive. How long would Barton hold them off until they got to him? Would he suffocate first?

"Cass." He caught a drop of Barton's sweat in his mouth. "Yecht!"

He tried to think of something. Anything that might help. He needed air. Barton needed help. He grabbed Cass's face and stroked it tenderly. He held her tight. Above him, Barton's big body shuddered. He didn't know who to feel worse for, the giant or himself. Inside him, he wanted to fight, but there was nothing he could do.

This is pathetic.

A minute passed, then two. Barton's moans and cries subsided slowly.

He's dying! The bugs will be through any moment.

Barton's body stopped shuddering. The only thing Fogle could feel or hear was his own heartbeat. He pushed up on Barton. "Let us out!" He drove his knee into his belly. What if Barton died and they were trapped? "No! Blast it, Barton, get up!"

He summoned his energy. His fist lit up and he drove it into Barton's belly.

Ssssrack!

Barton's body lurched upward and rolled over. Fogle gasped, basking in the white daylight that greeted him. He could breathe again! One last breath of sweet air before the bugs got him. He crawled out of the hole that Barton had dug and scanned the sky. It was empty aside from a few clouds. The humming of bugs was gone.

"Where did they go?" he said, spinning around.

Barton groaned. The big giant lay flat on his back with hundreds, if not thousands, of red welts all over his body. "Oooooh," he moaned. "My belly hurts."

Fogle stood over his side and patted his belly. "Uh... looks like you've had too much bug poison. I'm sure it will go away."

Barton rolled his big neck his way, staring at him with his one good eye. "You alright, Wizard? Barton helped you, right?"

"Indeed, Barton. I'd be dead without you."

"Pretty lady alright too?"

"She just needs something better to drink than your sweat, but she should be fine. Can you get up?"

Slowly, Barton rose to a sitting position.

"Belly hurts," he said, rubbing it. "Like I got whopped by a giant. Did you do that?"

Fogle turned away. "Have you seen the horse?"

Barton pointed east.

"Ah," Fogle said. Making his way over to the mount that stood basking in the haze of the hot day. "Oh." When he got close, a chill ran through him. The horse still stood with the saddle and his bags intact, but every ounce of flesh and skin had been picked clean. Only the bones remained. He glanced back at the giant. Barton's thick skin had saved them all. All but the horse, anyway. He grabbed what gear he needed, headed back, and tried to make Cass as comfortable as he could.

"How are you feeling, Barton?"

"Dizzy. Little bugs stung me and bit me, but Barton too tough. Too strong. Belly still hurts though. They didn't bite my belly. I don't understand why it hurts." Barton scratched his head. "Was something else underneath me with you? Huh, Wizard?"

Feeling guilty, Fogle was ready to confess.

"Barton, I—"

The giant's eye closed, and he fell backward.

Thoom!

"Great! Just great!" Fogle put his hand on Barton's chest. It still rose and fell. "I guess he's alive." He kicked the dirt.

Now what, Wizard? Now what?

Cass had curled up like a baby, and Barton began to snore, leaving him as alone as he ever felt before. He found a place beside Cass in Barton's ditch and took a seat. *Inky!*

Closing his eyes, he tried to summon the familiar. The last thing he remembered was the bird flying into the swarm, and he'd completely forgotten about the bird after that. He gave it a minute or two and gave up. He pulled at the locks of his hair with both hands.

What have I done? What have I done? What have I done?

Little more than an hour ago, he had things under complete control. Cass was fine, Barton cheerful and his horse reliable transportation under his legs. They were going after Venir, the Darkslayer. Following the dog Chongo. His ebony hawk would lead straight to them.

Now, all of his plans were crushed. Inky was gone. Barton and Cass were almost comatose, and his horse was dead. He could only think of one thing. Well, two things.

Go east. Or sleep—and wake up dead.

Going east should have been simple, but it wasn't. The suns and moons didn't always rise in the same places, not than anyone ever thought about using them as a compass. Mood had always complained that getting around Bish would be easier if the suns and moons rose in the same places. Instead, you had to know the terrain.

Look for the signs.

A keen eye could see for miles in any direction, and the layout of Bish was simple. All you had to know was where places were and how to get there. Just don't be too forgetful. To make matters worse, some days, especially in the Outlands, were longer than others.

Probably have our bones picked clean out here.

He noted a bird of some sort circling above.

Great. Probably man-eating condors. Let's hope I can handle them.

Fogle pulled his spellbook from his pack. It fit on his hand at first, then, opening and closing, it got bigger and bigger, until he had to set it on his lap. He thumbed through the pages.

There ought to be something in here.

Meanwhile, Barton's snoring made the ground rumble.

Page by page, Fogle scanned his book, finding nothing immediately useful. He'd need more time and rest to learn anything new, and he had other spells in mind he had to keep until he used them. He nudged Cass. Her pale pink lips were cracked and dried. He poured a little water from his canteen on her lips, bringing forth a sigh. *Poor thing.* The feisty woman seemed so vulnerable right now, leaving him uncomfortable.

He stuck his nose back inside his book and read through more of Boon's spells. A bad feeling crawled through him. Was Boon still alive or not? The old man was crazy enough to fight an entire army of underlings and willing to die for it.

Bish, don't' let me get that crazy.

Spell after spell he read, not recalling hardly any of them. He felt ashamed now at his reluctance. Boon's written pages were a treasure that never should have been ignored. He giggled at one of them. *Breast replenishment*. With a special note. *For aging wife*. Fogle shook his head. Much of the magic in the City of Three was used to upkeep images, a practice which Fogle, unlike most, found detestable. He wondered if Boon was one of those who created such a spell to begin with. Page after page he went. Transfigurations. Polymorph. Elementals. Enchantments. Transmutations. Conjurations. A dozen forms of evocations and illusions, and so on. The ones that were most effective on underlings were highlighted. But there wasn't anything he could find that would give him directions. Fogle marked a few pages and closed the book.

"Now what, Cass? Now what?"

She didn't stir.

If only Mood or Eethum were here.

He sat for a while, before he got back up. Nightfall would be coming soon.

"Don't worry, I'll take the first watch." He stretched out his arms and yawned. "No, no, you two go ahead and rest. I'll take the second one too." Instinctively, he started to gather sticks and pile them up together. "What am I doing? I can't build a fire now, can I?" He shook his head. "Am I talking out loud to myself? Am I?"

I can't be. I can't be. I can't be.

He poked one of the nasty red stings on Barton's arm with a stick. Nothing. Barton kept snoring. "Well, I won't fall asleep with you around, that's for sure. And we can't have you drawing any underlings, giants, nasty bugs or dragons straight to us either." With both hands, he tried to pinch Barton's nose shut.

Barton snorted and started to roll over.

"Not on top of me!" he said, jumping to the side.

Barton lay on his stomach now, no longer snoring.

"Sheesh!" Fogle got up and dusted his tattered robes off. "Aw, what's the point?" He snatched up the spellbook. "I need something else to keep watch in case I fall asleep," he said, yawning.

Every scrape, bump, and bruise began to settle in on him, and he wondered if the Outland was making him tougher or deteriorating him faster.

I'm no dwarf. That's for sure.

Instead, he was a man. A lost man. A lamb in the Outland waiting to be devoured by Bish.

"There's always tomorrow if we live that long," he said to Cass. Something strange howled in the wind. He eyed the sky. "I really hope you wake back up by then, because, even though you're small, I can't carry you too far."

Barton stirred and farted.

"Ah!" Fogle held his nose. "Hmmm... I think I have an idea. Did a fart inspire that?"

Stop talking to yourself!

Over the next hour, he dove into the spellbook, eyes pouring over and committing to memory what he could. He muttered a cantrip after his final yawn. A Wizard's Alarm should wake him if anything got too close. He needed rest. He had to risk it. Besides, he couldn't wake them up anyway. "Forgive me, Cass." After kissing her forehead, he closed his eyes and drifted off to sleep, oblivious to a unique sound in the distance.

Whump. Whump. Whump...

CHAPTER 30

MELEGAL SQUIRMED. HE WAS ONLY a few seconds from being a cripple if he didn't twist away.

"My, you're a shifty one. I'll give you that," the leader said. "Like a big fish in man's clothing."

Think of something, Thief!

Melegal had been captured before, sometimes willing, sometimes not. But when being pinned down by a superior force there were a couple of ways you could play it. Fight with everything you had, or panic.

"Help!" he screamed.

Or at least act like you were panicking.

One of the Blood Hounds slugged him in the gut.

"Ooof!" Melegal groaned.

The one that hit him said, "His stomach's harder than old leather, Creed."

"Is that so?" Creed drew back and also socked him in the gut. "That ought to soften it some. Sorry, nothing personal. Just business, squirmy one." He pinched Melegal's face in his hand, grabbed his hat, and stuffed it in his mouth. "Any more of that, and your gonads will be dog food. Understand, Detective?"

Melegal blinked twice.

"Good. Now, be peaceful about this, or we'll be forced to kill you."

Melegal's eyes widened.

"That's right, but you're wanted alive rather than dead. Good thing for you."

One of the dogs snapped in his face. He resisted less and began to turn over. He forced a hardy cough, spit out his hat, and screamed.

"Blast it! Just knock the man out," Creed said. His voice was refined. Confident. Patient. "Hand me your black jack. We've enough fooling with this. Underlings might be crawling all over us if we're not more careful."

Melegal coughed again, dodging.

He felt Creed's hand rise up with the black jack.

Now or die!

Slick as a snake, Melegal twisted free of all of them and took aim.

Zing! Zing! Zing!

"Aarggh!"

The dart launchers caught one man holding him in the face and Creed in the chin.

He rolled beneath another man's fist.

Zing! Zing! Zing!

The man wailed out, clutching at his eyes.

Zing!

One dog yelped.

Zing!

Another dog fled, dart protruding from its neck.

"Yer gonna pay for that," one said, ripping a heavy sword from his scabbard.

Melegal slid out his swords, the Sisters, and faced off the goon.

"Nice trick, Detective," Creed said, plucking the dart from his beard, watching. "But hardly effective."

Melegal shrugged. "What the dart won't do, the poison will?"

Creed drew his longsword and smiled.

"Then you'll be going down with us."

Run!

It was the preferred resolution for his survival, but there was a problem. His hat and case were on the ground, and he wasn't willing to part with them yet.

'Greedy gets you killed,' they say.

Melegal shifted his footing, gently bending his knees.

Creed nodded to his man. "Let's see what the Detective is made of. Take him!"

170

The man took three quick steps and lunged.

Melegal sidestepped and stabbed.

Glitch!

The man's sword clattered to the ground, and he clutched at his chest. Melegal ripped his sword from the man's heart. His own heart was pounding.

I did it!

He shifted his focus to Creed. The tall man gawped while Melegal slung the blood off his sword.

"Impressive, Detective, I must admit. I didn't think you had that kind of fight in you. But I don't think you'll have the same fortune with me." Creed smiled. It wasn't an evil smile. Just a confident one. A dangerous one. A 'cat about to eat the rat' kind of one. He drew forth another blade that shone brighter than the other.

Oh slat!

Melegal could tell by Creed's stance, his posture, he was ...

"I'm a swordsman. My comrade, not so much. Besides, I didn't like him anyway. Slow and stupid, but a good grappler." He sliced his blade through the air and twirled it with his wrist. "Hmmm... I'm feeling spry this day, and well, I don't think that dart was poisoned after all." He lifted his brow and smiled. "And, I think I can disarm you in six seconds. I can maim you in ten. But, it's nothing personal. Just business."

Melegal stood his ground.

Still time to run if you don't think of something.

He renewed his stance: blades up, elbows down.

"Tell you what, Detective: come along quietly, and I won't turn you into my dog's dinner. Not all of you, anyway."

Swish!

The sword flashed like a stroke of lightening.

Slat, he's good. Melegal narrowed his eyes.

He immediately recalled his battle with Teku in the alley months ago. It had taken everything he had not to die then, and Teku had been just an assassin, not a master swordsman.

"So, you're taking me to the Almens, eh..."

"Creed, Royal Bloodhound Knight."

"Oh please, you're no Royal or Knight, but a scavenger."

"Like you," he smiled.

Melegal shrugged.

"Like me, indeed then."

Creed scoffed. "I hardly think so. Sefron's message was abundantly clear. You are little more than an overachieving urchin. I, however, am of Royal blood."

Creed could pass for a Royal, in some circles, but Melegal knew better. The Bloodhounds claimed to be a Royal house, but instead they were little more than a house of mercenaries and bounty hunters of the true Royal houses. But, because of their unique position and the secrets they kept, the Royals ignored their overstated positions.

It was Melegal's turn to laugh.

"Sefron? You took a charge from Sefron? Ha! You might as well be taking charges from the urchins that scrub pots in the kitchen and clean the slat from the bird cages. Hah! Are you even sure I'm the one he really wants?"

Creed's eyes shifted, sword tips dipping a hair.

Melegal kept pressing.

"Creed, you are a fool. Have you not noticed that the underlings are storming Castle Almen? How do you suppose to get me in there? Collect your reward? It wouldn't surprise me if Sefron was dead right now. Can you imagine him fighting an underling? Have you ever fought an underling? This City's doomed, Creed. A smart man would save himself. Not carry out the charge of a fool when total destruction is about."

Creed was thinking. Melegal could see it, the hardness in his eyes weakening.

"What are you thinking, Creed?"

"I'm thinking that a Bloodhound never gives up on a charge until he gets his man."

"Is that so, then?"

Creed raised his blades, flashing a thin row of white teeth.

"So it is, and taking into account all you've said and done so far, I think it's best for me if I take you in dead."

Melegal raised his blades.

I'm dead if I don't run. Think, Melegal. What did McKnight say long ago? 'The mind is faster than the sword.' He glanced at his hat on the ground. *If I can just squirm my way to it.*

172

"Creed" The man Melegal had shot in the eyes stumbled along the storefronts. "I can't see, Creed, what do I do?"

"Silence, Dolt! I'll tend to you in a moment."

Melegal started left and Creed started right, both men circling.

Good.

Creed stopped, lunged and chopped.

Clang!

The sound of clashing steel echoed through the alley and down the street. Melegal held back his grimace. Creed struck again. *Clang!* Again. *Clang!* Again. *Clang! Clang! Clang!*

Creed pressed, Melegal parried. The man was a true swordsman. His moves perfect. His swing quick and powerful. Melegal's hands were numb seconds into it.

"Not much of an offense, I see," Creed said, backing away, cutting his swords through air. "But, you've an excellent defense; I'll give you that, Detective. I underestimated you. Problem is, how long can those bony arms of yours hold out?"

Not long!

"Long enough to wear you down," Melegal said.

Creed darted in, blades stabbing like striking snakes. "I don't think so."

Melegal battled one blade away, only to shift and catch another. Creed kept stabbing at his legs, a hungry grin behind his lips.

Slice!

Creed caught Melegal in the inner thigh. He felt every bit of it.

"Hah!" Creed said, jumping away. "First blood to me. Oh, that's already staining your clothes."

Run, Melegal! It's not worth it!

Behind him, the hat and slender case lay unmolested on the ground, but he had no chance of getting them. Creed would pin him to the ground if he tried.

"My, your shoulders are already dipping," Creed said, cutting his longsword over the ground. "More of a fencer than a soldier, clearly. But, I think I've summed you up enough." Creed sheathed one sword, left the other one that gleamed like the sun out, and shrugged. "I feel the need to challenge myself." He motioned Melegal closer with his hand. "Come on, Detective. Attack."

Melegal remained wary. Creed might be cocky, but he wasn't a fool either. Even though the odds had shifted more in his favor, he knew better. Creed had something up his sleeve.

"I'll fight my way; you fight yours. Come on then, Hound. I'm curious to see what you can do with a single sword to my two."

Creed leapt and swung.

Melegal parried and struck.

Pour it on, Rat!

Clang! Clang! Clang! Clang!

Creed parried, dodged and ducked.

Clang! Clang! Clang! Clang!

Melegal stabbed, chopped and cut, but Creed anticipated everything he did. Focused. Determined. Waiting for a weakness.

Move, Melegal!

Out of nowhere, Creed's blade licked out like a rod of lightning. Melegal squatted down. Creed kicked him in the face.

Bang!

Melegal felt his sword ripped from his hand.

Bang!

The other skipped over the cobblestones. The next thing he felt was the tip of a sword under his chin.

SLAT!

"Heh, heh, heh—woot!" Creed wiped the sweat from his brow. "I can't believe you still have your head, Detective. Ah! I missed it! You are fast. I'll give you that."

Melegal started to raise his arms up.

"Ah, ah, ah, keep those wrists down. I can't have you shooting anymore holes in me. I must admit: I'm surprised you didn't try something earlier. But, eh, I figured you were out."

Melegal could feel the sword cut his neck as he swallowed.

I should have run! Idiot!

"EEEYAH!"

A block down the street, someone screamed.

"Eh?" Creed grabbed Melegal by his head of hair and pulled him up from the ground, stepping behind him and keeping the sword at his throat.

That's when Melegal saw them. *Underlings!*

"What in Bish is that thing crawling on the ground?" Creed said, unable to hide his alarm.

Both ends of the road were blocked off. Speckled eyes and spider legs were coming.

"I can get us out of here, Creed. But your word you won't kill me."

"I know better than that."

"There's no time, Creed. You can kill me and die. Or you can trust me and live. And I don't want to die. I've no issues with you."

The chitters became louder, the small bodies closer.

"Cut my throat then, Creed! I'd rather die at your hands than the underlings'!"

Creed's rapid breath was in his ear.

"My word I won't kill you. Your word you won't kill or betray me."

"My word," Melegal said.

Hurry up, Imbecile.

"Done!"

Melegal was a blur of motion, swooping over to snatch his cap and case and darting for the door he'd tried to get in earlier. "Come on, Creed!"

The underlings let out evil howls and charged.

Melegal pulled out a Key.

"What in Bone?" Creed said, looking at the lock. "That won't fit!"

Melegal jammed it inside the lock and turned.

"Sweet Mother of Bish! It wo—*urked*!"

Clatch-zip! Clatch-zip! Clatch-zip!

Creed's face contorted as he stumbled forward. The sound of the underlings was overwhelming.

Melegal shoved his shoulder into the door and pulled the man behind him through.

Bolts zipped past his head. He fought to pull the door closed.

Something slipped in past his legs.

What was that! Hmm — I'll have to live with it.

He kept pulling on the door, catching a pair of hands in the process.

The underlings were pulling it back open.

Melegal grabbed the handle and pulled on the door with all his might.

"No!"

He was sliding forward.

A flash of light ripped through the air.

Slice!

Underlings howled and hissed in fury. The tips of their fingers disappeared, shooting black-red blood everywhere.

Melegal flew backward and felt the door close with a bang.

Creed was huffing at his side, wiping black blood off his blade.

"That was close," Melegal said. "And you better hang onto your stomach."

"Why-yeeeeeeeeeee..."

Melegal remembered hearing that and something else that growled as his body and mind were turned inside out.

CHAPTER 31

"Ashur!" Lorda Almen said. "You have awakened!"

The face was hazy, but the voice familiar as Lord Almen tried to rise.

"Ugh!" he said, clutching at his side. The area was tender, painful.

"Easy, Darling," Lorda said, gently pushing him back down. "You don't need to tear the wound." She sobbed. "Ashur, I'm so happy to see you."

She nuzzled him. Gently. Wet tears dripping on his cheeks.

"My darling," he said, "I'm quite alright."

Still, she held on, trembling.

It was a good feeling, the scent of his wife and the curves of her body against his, but despite his awakening, something was wrong. He sniffed.

"What is that smell?" Blinking, the haze from his eyes began to clear. Two Shadow Sentries stood at his bedside with gore of some sort on their armor. "And what is that sound?"

Somewhere, a battle raged. His heart ignited.

"Help me up, Sentry," he said, pushing Lorda aside.

Sitting up, his head began to spin. He collected his thoughts. The last thing he remembered was being inside the arena. The haggard face of Leezir the Slerg was there, and a big man. A very big man that went berserk, chopping up people like wood.

"Dearest, lie down, please," Lorda said.

He slid onto the floor and with assistance from the sentry stumbled towards the balcony.

"Why are there underlings at my walls?"

It was insanity. Castle Almen was under a full-scale attack. Black armored underlings and oversized spiders filled the streets and alleys.

"How long, Lorda? How long have I been down?"

"Many days, Lord Almen. Sefron saved you. It was the underlings that infiltrated and stabbed you. I thought you were to perish."

A flood of memories washed over him. Everything that happened in the arena became crystal clear up to the point where he could feel the dagger sliding between his ribs.

The scowl on his vulture-like visage returned.

"Melegal."

"Pardon, my Lord? I ordered Sefron to send the Bloodhounds for him —"

He cracked her across the face, dropping her to her knees.

"You hired those Gormandizing Bastards? And Melegal! He's not here? He lives?"

Lorda's eyes were narrow, dangerous.

She started to rise.

"What is the meaning of this that you would dare strike me, Ashur? I'm guilty of no wrong —"

He drew back again, causing her to flinch.

"It was Melegal that slid the dagger in my ribs. Not the underlings. Not any other!"

Lorda shook her head.

"No, Sefron said it was the underlings."

"Pah! Sefron! Where is he, anyway?" He grabbed a Shadow Sentry by the collar of his armor. "You, go and fetch him yourself, and do not fail me. And see to it word spreads that Lord Almen lives!"

Melegal. The man had gotten him, and he had to admit it was impressive of the man. He would have admired it if he'd not been the victim... But now his entire castle was under siege! And he knew why. The chamber room. The underlings wanted it.

"How long has this siege been going on?" he demanded.

"Several hours, Lord Almen," a sentry replied.

"And the Keep is secure?"

"Yes, Lord Almen."

"And the castle?"

"Casualties along the wall, Lord Almen. Nothing else to report."

Lord Almen folded his arms behind his back, stepped past Lorda, and began to pace. He wondered if his neighbors would come to his aid. Or would they see him perish first? After all, that's what he would do.

"Hmmm."

He reached down and lifted Lorda up. She slapped him in the face.

"I'm —"

She slapped him again.

"I'm —"

She swung, but he caught her by the wrist. "I'm going to throw you off the balcony if you do that again."

"You wouldn't dare!" She was almost smiling.

He did smile. "Oh, of course not." He lifted her chin and kissed her cheek. "I'm sorry, my dearest."

"I'm glad you're back, Ashur." She hugged him. Then she looked him in the eye. "I'm sorry. I never would have suspected Melegal. But we'll find him, and when we do, we'll throw him off this balcony together. "

"Oh, we'll do much worse than that."

Lorda took the next few minutes explaining to Lord Almen everything that had been going on, but he was confident the Castle would hold for days. At some point, the other Royals would have to arrive.

Minutes later, the sentry that left to find Sefron returned.

"Where is Sefron?" Lord Almen demanded.

The sentry bowed. "Lord Almen, I have grave news. The underlings have penetrated the bottoms of the Castle."

"What!" He wanted to strangle the man. Ignoring the pain in his side, he dashed out of the room. He had to get to his study, secure the chamber and the Keys before it was too late.

CHAPTER 32

IN ONE OF THE BOTTOM quarters of the Keep, Sefron stared in a mirror, dressing his wounds.

"She'll be mine," he said, stitching the side of a nasty cut on his cheek, "all mine."

"What's that, Cleric?" It was one of the sentries posted outside his door.

Fool! "Eh … nothing, just trying a cheerful tune. Oh, how it soothes the wounds." Sefron crept over towards the man, letting the needle and thread hang from his face. "My, you are a fine specimen of a soldier. I bet you have a steady hand." With a shaky hand, he reached towards the man, who jerked away. "I need some assistance with this."

Another sentry appeared and shoved Sefron back.

"Keep your hands to yourself, Toad, or I'll slit your throat. We know plenty about what you do around here." His hand fell to his dagger. "And it'd be my pleasure to cut your throat."

Sefron fell back, hands up. "Easy now. You don't want rumors leading you to something foolish, do you? After all, I am Lord Almen's trusted servant."

"As trustworthy as a slimy weasel in a hen house. Now leave my men alone!" He shut Sefron inside the room.

Sefron resumed his position in front of the mirror.

"My, I'll never understand why people aren't more taken by my charm." He smiled in the mirror, noticing how his eyes bulged outside his dark sockets and folds of flabby skin dangled under his chin. He was a sickly shade of pale, and his belly jiggled over his scrawny legs.

"Never a finer specimen of a man on Bish," he said, wheezing. He licked the blood from his purple lips. Then started sewing the gash in his face again. "That should do it." He took a seat in a nearby chair, crossed his dirty feet and lounged. "Hmmmm..."

He rubbed the eye that Kierway had stuck with a dart. The underlings waged war from the outside. Perhaps they'd found Melegal. Perhaps they just needed a little help to penetrate the wall of the Castle. He could sense the power beginning to shift. He was an agent for the underlings, and now was his time to move.

And then I'll have Lorda Almen and her servants all to myself!

He sat up.

"Time to get out of this Keep."

Reaching inside a pouch that hung from a string belt, he withdrew grains of an unusual sort. Rubbing one between his fingers, he murmured to himself. Seconds later, the mystic energies he tapped from Bish filled him, rejuvenated him. *Yes!* So long it had been since he last harnessed his energies, waiting, plotting, and scheming for the right time to recall them. He had hidden them long, oh so long. His skin tightened. His muscles flexed and stretched. His haggard body replenished, his crooked spine crackled as he rose to his feet. Smoke streamed from his mouth and nostrils, slowly filling the room.

"What's that smell?" A sentry threw open the door.

Sefron blew the grains of dust into the air.

The smoke in the room poured out into the next. The sound of men choking and gagging was music to his ears.

"Not so talkative now, are we?" He crossed the threshold, upright on a solid six-foot frame. He pulled the dagger from the gagging sentry's sheath and stabbed him in the spine. "I've been meaning to do that for quite some time."

Two more sentries remained, hacking and spitting, blinded to his presence.

Sefron stabbed one in the neck and left the dagger in the other's heart. He cracked his knuckles, went back into his room, and took another look at himself.

His countenance wasn't handsome, but strong and dark, his skin no longer pale nor sagging. His stomach was tight and his legs firm. His damaged eye was still gone, but better. He felt good. He'd been saving up decades for this, and now his time had come. "Let the powers of Bish last as long as they can last."

He focused on his personal quarters in the castle, closed his eyes, and drew in more power. A portal appeared. He stepped through it, back into his room.

"Ah yes."

It felt good, being back inside his place. Very good. Incredibly good. He grabbed his robes from the wall and tied another belt with pouch around his waist. From the corner of the small disheveled room—littered with vials, jugs and old bits of food—he grabbed a crooked staff.

"It's been a long time," he said, kissing it before exiting his door.

Despite the battle raging outside, the massive hallways were quiet. Everyone in the Castle was either fighting somewhere or dead. No longer shuffling, Sefron strolled, whistling rather than wheezing, on the legs of a twenty-year-old man. Making his way through one of the living rooms, he pressed a panel on one of the decorative shelves. A hidden door popped open behind it, and inside he went.

The spaces between the walls of the rooms were a set of catacombs that Sefron had discovered years ago. Even most of the Almens had no knowledge of them. They'd been used by servants at one time, short cuts through the castle, but Sefron had seen to it over time that no servant recollected them. They were where he did his spying, and they traversed through most of the castle's main rooms, except for the keep.

He hopped his way down a narrow set of steps, a smile on his face. It had been a long time since he moved so gracefully.

If I see Melegal, I'll kill him first.

Stopping, he pushed aside a peephole door and looked through. A dining room greeted him, undisturbed, still shiny in silver and crystal. No longer would he have to watch behind the walls after this. No longer would he be a servant to Lord Almen. No, he would be the Lord of this Castle. He pictured himself and Lorda sitting side by side. "Yes, she'll be—eh?"

Somewhere not too far distant, steel banged against steel. He trotted through the narrow passageway two dozen yards, the sounds becoming more distinct and profound. He lifted another peephole door open and got an eyeful.

Underlings were in mortal combat with sentries and Royal magi. Two Royal soldiers in plate mail armor swung their broad swords into a mass of well-armed underlings. Barrages of green and red missiles of light were shooting back and forth. Men were howling; underlings were screeching.

Sefron made his way down another short level of steps to a dead end. Opening a peephole on the final battle, he saw a group of underlings being forced down the steps that led down to the Current. *Yes!* It was everything he hoped for. The underlings had invaded from below as well as above, but there seemed to be a problem. The underlings were trapped. They were losing.

CHAPTER 33

Triumph! Master Kierway felt nothing but triumph when the door shattered and he and his brethren blasted through. Leading the way, he bounded up the stairs and greeted a pair of Royal soldiers with his whirling blades.

He drove his steel through the plate covering one man's heart and cut the mailed neck of the other out. Blood, the only shade of red that he liked, dripped from his blades.

"Inward! Inward!" he ordered his underlings. "Nothing human lives! Everything human dies!"

Juegen soldiers, coated from head to toe in black metal armor, surged past, followed by Badoon warriors with crude knives and hatchets, albino urchlings with claws that could rip metal, and underling magi whose fingertips crackled with energy. Their faces told it all. Hungry. Fearsome. Vengeful. Hate filled. One by one they went. Bright colored eyes narrowed. Soldiers of war that meant business. And Kierway had hundreds of them at his disposal.

"Yes, brethren! Go! Slaughter!"

Everything was working. Within hours, Castle Almen would be theirs.

Up the stairs the underlings went. The last one, bringing up the rear, was an albino urchling, all four nostrils flaring.

"What is this?" Kierway said to himself, bounding down the steps. He hissed. The doorway was sealed. "No!" He looked for a handle, a bar, a lock, but there was nothing. "NO! CATTEN!"

Was this a ruse? Had Catten betrayed him and all his underlings? He didn't have time to worry about that now. Trapped or not, he could still pull this off. He had enough underlings, so he thought.

Dashing up the stairs, he was halfway to the top when the wind and the screeches came. Mystic power flowed everywhere. At the top, underlings were knocked head over heels by an unseen force. Fire licked over them. Burning them.

"No! This cannot be!"

A blast of hot air came. One, two, three underlings tumbled backward over the stairs, landing at his feet. At the top, an underling's head was taken from its shoulders, green eyes bouncing off the steps all the way to the bottom. Kierway hesitated. How many Royals were at the top? But there was nowhere else to go. Taking six steps at a time, he charged, confronting a big warrior. A heavy blade came down at his head. Kierway sidestepped and cut the man's wrist from his arm. The man howled long enough to catch a blast of underling energy inside his mouth.

Kierway ducked under a blast of lightning that struck an underling mage full force. He rolled alongside a wall and got a better look at things. All of his brethren underlings that made it up the steps were gone.

Where did they go?

On the far side of the dining room, two robed humans were guarded by three soldiers, and the air shimmered before them.

Hmmmm.

Several feet away, an underling Badoon and one albino urchling were in mortal combat with the Royal Soldiers. Kierway chittered at an urchling that had sunk its teeth into the neck of a dead soldier and pointed at the magi at the other end of the room. Blood dripping from its fangs, it tore itself away and charged across the room. *Blink!* The urchling was gone.

Furious, Kierway sprang into action, assisting his brethren, hewing into one Royal soldier after the other. The battle raged for another minute and then the last Royal soldier fell, leaving himself, one Juegen, one Badoon and one mage left standing. He shook the blood from his blades and faced the Royals on the other side of the room. The faces of the men showed no concern, but rather, supreme confidence.

Kierway banged his blades together, calling a Royal soldier out. None of them moved, except the magi behind them. One gyrated his hands while the other one spoke in tones. Kierway slung two knives.

Sssz!

Sssz!

They disappeared midflight

The underling mage hurled a ball of fire, lighting up the room, shaking the chandeliers. It stopped, hovered in the air, and returned. He jumped out of the way just before it exploded. Tiny fires licked over his clothing while the underling mage burst into flame, screaming.

Whatever barrier the humans had put up, he knew they could not pass. It was a mystic dimension spell of sorts, and for all he knew the underlings that passed through were on the outside of Bone. Possibly imprisoned in a wall somewhere. But the spell wouldn't last forever. It couldn't. He banged his swords together.

The Royal Magi acted. A missile of mystic energy burst from the hands of one, then another, careening towards him.

He flicked his blades up. The missile smacked into them with a shower of sparks, knocking him from his feet. One by one, he and his men backed towards the stairwell. One bright missile soared after the other. Behind the human magi, another man appeared, dark and mysterious. Reaching out, the strange man grabbed the two magi by the shoulders. They choked, mouths popping open. Their skin tightened and shriveled. Their faces sunk in and dried. The space between them buckled, images contorting before returning to normal.

The dimension spell was gone. Kierway could feel it.

"Kill them!" Kierway said.

The two remaining soldiers readied themselves.

The urchling, Badoon warrior, and Juegen sped across the room. Kierway followed close behind.

The Royal soldiers braced themselves, chins down, swords up.

The heavy sword of one Royal chopped downward, burying itself in the Badoon's shoulder, drawing a howl. The Juegen and Badoon pounced on the man, knocking him off balance and to the floor. Focusing on the other soldier, Kierway sidestepped one swing, followed by the other, staying wary of the man who had assisted him moments earlier. The man, holding a crooked staff, was laughing.

Clang!

Kierway batted away the soldier's heavy swings, one after the other, hissing and taunting. The eyes behind the soldier's metal helmet were determined but became weary. Each swing came more sluggish than the last.

Rip!

Kierway struck the man's knee, sending flesh, blood and steel across the room. The man stumbled forward.

"Urk!"

Kierway drove his sword through the man's heart. Yanking his blade out, he turned on the man who laughed. He and the remaining underlings surrounded him.

The man kneeled and said, "Master Kierway, it is I, your servant, Sefron."

Kierway could see it now. The man's good eye bulged a little in his socket, and his disturbing expression, though more vital, remained unchanged.

"Do you have the Keys?"

"No," Sefron said, flatly.

Kierway nodded to his men.

"Kill him."

Sefron's arm shot out.

"Wait! Master Kierway, I may not have the Keys you seek, but I can open the door at the bottom of the stairwell." Sefron's eye glanced over the dripping blades of Kierway's two men. "I am your humble servant, Master Kierway, now and forever."

Kierway held out his arm. The underling drew back.

"Do it then," he said, sheathing his blades behind his back. "But make it quick if you don't want underling steel fileting your back."

Sefron rose, led them across the room and down the stairwell, and stopped at the oversized door.

"Hurry!" Kierway said.

Sefron leaned his staff against the wall, pressed his hands on the door and chanted. One syllable after the other, faster, slower, lower, higher. Sweat dripped from his bald head, and his knees buckled a little. Panting, he turned.

"It's over," he said, stepping aside. "Shall I open it?"

"Of course, you fool!"

Sefron pushed it open.

A sea of underlings greeted him.

Sefron stood aside. Several feet away, floating across the great Dining Hall, Kierway was in a heated conversation with an underling whose likes he'd never seen before. His golden eyes radiated with power, and a mere glance in his direction ran his blood cold. Even Lord Almen didn't command such authority. Still, Sefron managed to pull back his shoulders and keep his chin up.

Show no fear. No fear at all.

His knuckles were white on his staff as a squad of underling fighters dashed by. They spread like a swarm of bees through the castle and into the main courtyard. Their numbers were overwhelming. Sefron knew that within hours, minutes possibly, the Castle would be taken over. He began to have doubts as to whether this was a good alliance or not.

It was inevitable. The Lorda and this castle or another shall be mine.

Keeping his head down, Sefron kneeled. Kierway and Catten approached.

"How many are in the keep?"

"A few dozen, if that." Sefron said. He kept his head down, eyes up a little. He could feel heat from Lord Catten's eyes boring into him.

"Master Kierway," Catten said, "do we have further need of this man?"

Sefron's eyes shot over to Kierway, heart pounding in his chest. Kierway rubbed his chin.

"Masters!" Sefron fell on his face. "I've betrayed my castle for your glory! I know many of its secrets I can share. And I am still assisting with the one that has the Keys. Spare me!" He looked at Kierway. "You promised me, Master Kierway!" His voice echoed in the large chamber.

"I made promises for the Keys, which you did not deliver."

Kierway said. "And we have an imp that can find the man you speak of, and the Keys, whenever we want."

"But, certainly, you won't kill all of us? Underlings and men have held many alliances before. Outpost Thirty-One and Castle Almen were united on that endeavor." He wiped the sweat from his brow with his robes. "Certainly we can be united on this endeavor as well. I killed off two Royal magi who held a pivotal location." He crawled towards the two husks on the floor and lifted one up. "I am not loyal?"

Catten snapped his fingers. The entire room shook, knocking Sefron over and turning what remained of the corpses into dust.

"Kierway," Catten said, "You say this one is a life drainer?"

"It seems he has that craft," Kierway said, checking the bandolier of knives on his chest. "What of it?"

"Give him your hand," Catten ordered.

"Give him your own hand!" Kierway fired back.

"You'll do as I say, Kierway!" Catten's voice shook the chandeliers.

Sefron came forward, his limbs stiffening. The power he got from draining people didn't last forever, but the magi he'd drained would hold him for hours. He extended his hand.

Kierway sneered at Lord Catten, who sneered back.

"You're such a fool, Kierway. Stupid and cowardly." Catten snatched Sefron's wrist with a grip of iron and said, "Drain me, Human!"

Fearful, Sefron hesitated.

"Do it, else I'll have Kierway skewer and skin you like a rodent."

Sefron summoned his power. The dust stirred on the floor, mystic powers flowing through him, giving him more enriching vitality.

"You like that, do you Human?" Catten ran his tongue along his teeth. "A taste of centuries of tempered energy, something your kind cannot comprehend." He pulled Sefron in face to face. "Well, I'll share a secret with you. I'm feeding you my power, Weakling. You are not taking it."

Catten closed his eyes, holding Sefron fast.

An urge to pull away overcame Sefron.

But Catten held him in a supernatural grip.

Something was wrong. He wasn't draining the underling. Instead, the underling was feeding him dark, exhilarating energy.

"Human," Catten said, "certainly you knew that you are only capable of draining your own kind. I, however, can do both, and what I give, I can take away."

Sefron choked. His breath was gone. All of his vibrancy was being sucked dry. He shrunk. He shriveled. He wheezed, fought to stand, and teetered to the floor. He pleaded with his eyes. Catten released him. He fell down and clutched his chest.

"You really should consort with a better class of human, Kierway. But I should expect so much."

Sefron looked down at his flabby belly, and the skin jiggled under his chin. Wheezing, he pushed himself up on his staff.

Just need another fresh body and I'll be fine, thank you.

"Now, Kierway, take your flabby ally away. Take some of your men and secure the Chamber of Keys. Certainly, someone will show up eventually. As for me, I'll see to it the demise of the Castle is completed."

Sefron's shaky legs struggled to move. He was in worse condition than before. His good eye caught Lord Catten's hard stare once more. He turned away. It wasn't likely Lord Catten would keep him around if he didn't think of something.

Kierway shoved him forward, "Lead the way, you saggy piece of meat."

CHAPTER 34

"DIE, FIENDS! DIE!"

Jarla's inner fires ignited with every stroke. Underlings, one after the other, fell under the precise patterns of her blade.

Chop!

Glitch!

Zurk!

She rammed a dagger into the last one's throat. Beside her, Tonio hewed the underlings down with powerful blows. A tireless machine among the chaos. The underlings, as well prepared as they might be, couldn't have been prepared for this; two skilled fighters with an unrivaled passion for killing.

Body splattered with red-black blood and gore, Jarla churned out one death after the other.

Toowah!

Toowah!

Toowah!

The darts struck her arms and legs.

"Cowards!" she said.

Whack!

She split one amber-eyed underling's skull.

Toowah!

Toowah!

Toowah!

Tonio laughed, half a dozen darts in his face, and yelled in his garbled voice, "There is no escape from me, underlings!"

They chopped at the man, jumped on top of him, tried to drag him down, but Tonio shook them off like a dog sheds water.

Jarla stayed close. Her lungs were burning behind her heaving chest. Her sword became heavy, sluggish. Still, she hacked. She chopped. Cognizant of the pounding on the door behind her. The underlings would chop through that door at any moment.

"We're going to have company!" she rasped. "I hope you can hold them all, because I can't."

"Let them come!" Tonio said, ramming his sword through one's skull.

Claws and fangs bared, an underling charged, leaping towards her from the bar. Engaged with another one of the underlings, she caught it in the corner of her eye, but couldn't turn in time.

Slice!

Tonio cleaved through it in mid-air, sending a shower of dark blood everywhere.

Over a dozen underling bodies were piled up, some twitching on the floor, behind them another dozen or so, when they backed off.

Jarla wiped the blood from her eyes, trying to catch her breath. They needed an escape route, but the only way was to carve through them.

"Think you can cut a path to the back through them?" she asked Tonio.

"Certainly, but I haven't the same need as you. I can fight them all day and all night if I have to," he said. "But you won't last that long, will you, Woman?"

Chop! Chop! Chop!

The underlings were still hewing at the door behind them, jostling Jarla's indomitable shroud. She'd never quit a fight before, but at the moment, there wasn't much fight left in her. She was exhausted, out of shape, and disappointed.

How did I let myself get like this? Lazy over-drinking bitch!

A twinkle caught her eye. She wiped the blood from the ring on her finger. It glowed a bright green color.

"What is that?" Tonio said.

Fool! How could I have forgotten!

"A way out of here, maybe." She darted for the front door, sliding over the blood-slicked floor. "Hold them off!"

Tonio's big frame stepped between her and the underlings,

beckoning the underlings forward. "Come on, rodents. My blade thirsts for your blood!"

Where's the Key! Where's the Key!

Chop!

The blade of an axe emerged through the door. A sparkling eye peeked inside.

Glitch!

She jammed a dagger in its eye, let go and grabbed the Key. She jammed it inside the lock.

Chop!

The Key popped out and fell to the ground. She fumbled for it, grabbing it in her sticky hands.

Chop!

The underlings on the other side kept hacking at the lock. Chunks of wood fell.

Clatch-zip!

Clatch-zip!

Clatch-zip!

Small bolts ripped across the room, burying themselves in the door.

Tonio groaned. "Whatever you're doing, Witch, you better hurry. Looks like the rodents are just getting started."

Thunk!

A javelin juttered in the door frame.

Jarla tried to force the Key into the deteriorating lock. It wouldn't go.

"Blast my eyes! Get! In! There!"

The Key transformed, its head matching the lock. She shoved it in and turned.

Clatch-zip!

Clatch-zip!

Clatch-zip!

Bolts and spears filled the doorway. Over her shoulder, she could see Tonio was filled with them, still standing, snarling and chopping. She shoved the door forward and found herself in a black room. She stepped inside, huffing, then pushed the door shut.

Almost.

Fingers emerged on the door's edge, pulling it open. Tonio's blood-splattered face leered at her.

"Not leaving the party without me, are you?"

"Just get your dead arse in here and shut the blasted door!"

"My pleasure." He closed it on the small fingers of the underlings, crushing them in the frame.

Jarla heard their angry screeches and howls cut short. Everything spun. She wanted to vomit. Her world twisted bloody and black.

I hate this part.

CHAPTER 35

EVERYTHING IN HER LIFE HAD been turned upside down. And now, she was home, back inside her own room, and once more a prisoner. Kam lowered her shoulder and pounded at the door.

Wham!

"Will you stop doing that, Kam?" Joline said. She was rocking baby Erin in her arms. "Can't you just be thankful you are home, safe for the moment?"

"That troll cut my hand off, Joline!"

Wham!

"And when I get a hold of her, I'm gonna shove my foot up her—"

"KAM! Enough!" Joline said, setting Erin in her bassinette.

The bassinette started to rock itself, and soothing music came forth, keeping Erin in a peaceful slumber.

Kam rubbed her shoulder with her lone hand and fought the tears coming to her eyes. What in Bish was going on? She'd just escaped the unbearable, only to find herself at home, confronted with the inconceivable. She looked at her stump, stupefied. Less than an hour ago, she'd awoken in her bed, the wound dressed and cleaned. Joline had done that for her, saying the bleeding had stopped on its own and the flesh had mended itself.

Who in Bish is Scorch?

She gritted her teeth.

Wham!

Joline grabbed her by the arm, dragged her over to the sofa, and pulled her down. Softly, the woman said, "Dear, I don't know what you've been through, and I can't explain what we are going through now, but you are home." Joline looked around and shrugged. "And safe as far as I know. You, me and Erin." She patted her knee. "A family."

Her tears flowed like raindrops. Her body shuddered with every breath. Kam's voice was a high pitched squeak. "I don't know what's happening to me. I don't understand. I just don't understand. I was so happy to be home, and n-n-now I'm a handless prisoner. Where's my hand, Joline? Why'd that woman do that?"

Joline handed her a handkerchief and rubbed her back.

She blew her nose and wiped her tears away.

"The truth is, Kam, you look better now than when you first walked in here. You looked possessed. You weren't yourself."

Serve and live.

That voice. It would haunt her forever. It had possessed her, controlled her. Empowered her. What was it? Who was it?

Kam had made a deal.

It had saved her. The power in the stones. A being was in the stones, like one was in the sword, the great sword of Zorth, the Everblade. It was her father's sword, and she was going to return it. Her father would have to answer to her about his dealings with Palos. She shivered. The thought of that man having his way with her. Pawing at her. Humiliating her. Almost killing her. What had happened to him? She'd left him mumbling in his own drool.

I should have killed him!

Joline squeezed her hand. "What is it, Kam? What are you thinking? There's murder in those eyes! You didn't kill anyone, did you?"

The question was like a slap in the face. Diller. Indeed, she had killed a man. Snapped his neck like a twig. And there had been others. In the alley. Broken. Lifeless. Had she killed them too? She looked at the hand that was no longer there. She swore she could still see it, feel it. And the dark energy from it still lingered within her.

She shook her head, sucked in her breath, looked Joline in the eye, and said, "I did what I had to do to save Erin, Joline." She blew her nose again. "And let me tell you, those bastards down below will think a hundred times before they ever come up here again."

Joline's eyes widened.

Kam got up, scooped her baby out of her bassinette with her one good arm and held her tight. "Nobody messes with me or my baby."

"Uh," Joline stammered, "how about some hot tea?"

"Got any Muckle Sap?"

"No." Joline pulled her shoulders back. "And I wouldn't give you any if we did. You need to settle yourself, Woman. I don't know what all you've been through, and you can tell me when you like, but now's no time for drinking. Just rock your baby."

Kam strolled over to the window. The glass was clear, but she couldn't see out. A busted three legged stool lay on the ground beside it. That window, whatever it was, was hard as stone. Kam couldn't help but wonder if it was all an illusion. Was she really here or not? Joline and Erin were real. Of that much, she was certain, but of the rest she wasn't so sure.

Erin yawned and stretched, letting out a little squeak. For the first time in as long as she remembered, Kam felt herself smile on the inside and out. She had the most important thing in the world, Erin. She kissed her forehead and took a seat in a rocking chair nearby.

"That's better." Joline worked the kettle on the stove. "You've got your whole world now, Kam. Erin's all that matters."

Tight as a drum, Kam yawned. Reflecting on everything she'd been through, she realized life would never be the same. Tortured and manipulated, she'd somehow survived. She was sore. Her face was swollen, and her gut hurt from where she'd been stabbed, but she lived. Erin lived. And even though they were prisoners, at least they were together. She rocked and rocked and rocked.

Joline walked over, eyes tired, and handed her a mug of steaming coffee.

"There you go. I put some Allybass in it. It always helps me relax. Are you hungry, Kam?"

Kam nodded.

"I'll fix you something to eat, and how about I run you a tub?"

"No tubs!"

Joline jumped.

"Sorry, just, I'll wash myself off later." Kam shuddered a sigh. "Hopefully, I can still cast a cantrip for it."

"Whatever you say, Kam." Joline fixed herself a cup of coffee and took a seat on the couch, playing with her greying locks of hair. "I might need you to use a cantrip on me, too. I feel like I've been rolled in sow waller."

Kam let out a short giggle.

It was followed by a long silence.

Kam felt safe in her heart. Restless, but safe. And the loss of her hand had been a small price to pay for Erin's life and her freedom. Perhaps Scorch, at least it would seem, had done her a favor. Shown her compassion, though a bit harsh, and merciless. Still, the image of that rough-cut woman chopping off her hand disturbed her. *She's a maniac.*

"Kam, I'm sorry to ask, but was Master Gillem a part of all this?"

Kam closed her eyes. So much had happened that she hadn't had time to take in. She blew a lock of hair from her face.

"You could say that," she said. "He poisoned the well. He seduced Lefty. But, I don't think he had a choice. At least, it was either that or death."

"Oh." Joline sat back. "I, I just really liked his company and the flowers he'd bring. He said the nicest things and told the most amazing stories. One time he told me..."

Kam let her talk, but she wasn't listening. There wasn't any sense in spoiling Joline's memories. 'There's good in everyone,' her mother always said, 'but it's often harder to find in some than others.' Of course, Kam used to believe that, but not anymore. There was no good in Palos. He was rotten to the core.

"Joline?"

"... and those fragrances he made. So... oh, sorry. Did you say something?"

"What happened to Lefty?"

"Well..." Joline looked around. "I, I don't know. I just assumed he was... oh my."

"Oh my?" Kam leaned forward. "What do you mean, oh my?"

"The last I saw him, he was kicking Scorch in the nose." Joline clutched her chest. "You don't think they cut his hand off too, do you?"

"Why'd he kick him in the nose?"

"He was mad. He was telling Scorch to fix your hand I think, then poof," Joline fanned her fingers out, "here we were!"

Kam's chest tightened. What in Bish had happened to Lefty? An image of him stuffed in a pickle jar popped in her mind.

Knock. Knock. Knock.

Kam and Joline lurched up, looking at each other.

Knock. Knock. Knock.

"Uh... er... Do you want me to get that?"

Kam handed her Erin. "No, I better do that." She walked over to the door, grabbed the handle and looked back at Joline.

The older woman mouthed the words, "Answer it."

Slowly, to her surprise, it pulled open. A familiar figure stood in the doorway.

"You!"

It was Darlene.

"Look, Lady." Darlene looked down into Kam's eyes. "I'm sure you're still upset about your hand and all, but I didn't have a choice in the matter."

"Huh!" Kam was baffled.

"But what Scorch says, I does."

"You are a Maniac!"

"A what?" Darlene rubbed her sweaty neck.

"Maniac! A crazy person! Out of your mind! Do you understand that, you featherless turkey!"

Darlene put her hands up. "Easy now, Lady. I'm not a Mannyack or a Turkey. *Hic.* 'Scuse me. Must be that last bottle of Muckle Sap. Anyhow, I'm a hunter, trapper, and a proud underling slayer. And, I'll warn you once: don't cross Scorch again. He did you a favor, and you know it."

Speechless, Kam tried to measure the woman's words. Darlene still seemed amiable, though taller and formidable.

"So," Kam said, "what is it you want?"

"First, sorry about your hand," Darlene said. "I guess you'll just have to learn to wipe with the other." She winked, pushing her way inside. "Say, this is nice. Better than I imagined it."

"What do you want?"

"Well." Darlene grabbed Kam's cup of coffee from the table and took a sip. "Mmmm... that's fine coffee. Did you make that, uh..."

"Joline," Kam said.

The rocker groaned when Darleen sat down.

"Joline. Like Darlene. I like it." She slurped another mouthful. "Mmmm, that's good. Not like that Muckle Sap, but still plenty good." She kicked her legs on the table.

"What do you want, Darlene?"

She scratched her brown hair, stirring the little flakes that fell out. "Things are getting busy downstairs. I need some help."

"Help with what?"

"Serving the people."

"Customers?" Kam said.

"Yes. You see, I don't have much experience running a tavern. I've always wanted to, but I never had the money. But thanks to Scorch, I now own this one."

"This is my tavern!"

Darlene got up and looked down at Kam. "Nope. It's my tavern now. And you're going to help me ruin it ... *hic.* I mean, run it."

CHAPTER 36

B*LINK!*

"Say!" A dwarf, black-haired and mangy, couldn't hide his surprise. "Where'd ye come from?"

Lefty tumbled onto his butt, shaking his head. "I-I don't know."

The dwarf slammed his fist on the table.

Lefty jumped.

The surrounding men and dwarves erupted in laughter.

Lefty shook his head.

What has happened? Where am I?

He was in a tavern. That much was clear by the layout, the drinking and eating that surrounded him. A fireplace sat cold at his back, and suspicious eyes drifted over him and onto the next patron. There was something else, something weird about where he was. It was misty.

Gathering his thoughts, he looked to the dwarf, who now had his nose buried in a tankard of ale. "I'm from the City of Three, I think."

The dwarf eyed him from behind his tankard, gulping it down.

Clonk!

"Bring another and one more for my out-of-the-city friend here. Say!" The dwarf rubbed his beard. "You're pretty small, even for a halfling. Humph. The City of Three, ye say. Well, that might explain your appearance. Are you one of those magi or wizards I hear about there? I didn't think halflings could take to magic with such fashion."

Lefty crawled up on the chair and sat down. He wasn't certain what to say or think at the moment. The last hours of his life had been incomprehensible enough.

"Dwarf, uh, my name is Lefty Lightfoot, and I really have no idea where I am. Can you tell me?"

The dwarf guffawed as the barmaid, heavyset but not uncomely, set down their tankards, laughing as well.

"Can't ye tell?"

Lefty scanned the room. It wasn't the City of Bone; there were no dwarves there. And it couldn't be the City of Three; the distant roar of the falls didn't catch his ears. And other than the few other places he'd been in his life, he didn't really have any idea at all. It wasn't a village or a logged outpost. He shook his head.

"Have a drink, Halfling," the dwarf said, reaching over and squeezing his shoulder. "Hmm. Hmm. Hmm."

Being polite, Lefty took a sip, glancing around as he did so.

There were women, some dressed in thick but scant clothing, and the men were of a dour but rugged sort. A pair of full orcs sat in the corner, quiet and unusual. At the next table over was a man that might have been half-gnoll with a heavy sword on his belt. Somewhere he couldn't see, someone played a flute, another strings. A sad tune, a slow tune that settled over the room.

"Are you going to make me guess … Apologies, but may I have your name?"

"No, you might just ferget it. Dwarf will do, and no, I'm not telling you where you are."

"I could ask someone else, I suppose."

The dwarf's bushy brown brows buckled, and his calloused hand reached under the table. Lefty heard a dagger or knife slip from his belt. The dwarf leaned inward.

"Ye could, but I'd consider that rude. And I don't like rude people. You aren't rude, are you?"

I might as well be. After all, I'm a thief, a liar, a disappointment, a failure, a lousy friend, and a wretched urchin. Why not be rude too?

The dwarf, who appeared as rugged as they come, reminded him a little of Jubbler, just thicker. Besides, it didn't look like Lefty had any friends in the world anymore. Maybe it was time he made a new one.

"I'm sorry, Dwarf. The truth is, I'm not rude, just really confused.

I don't know how I got here. I don't know where I am. I-I—Sheesh, I guess it's for the better!"

"Ho-ho!" the Dwarf said, "Little one, yer frustration will do ye little good. Take a breath, a drink, and tell me a little about yerself, and if I'm satisfied with your tale, I'll tell ye where ye is." The dwarf winked.

Over the planks of the room, Lefty noticed a creeping fog that swirled as the men and women passed through it.

That's odd.

"Where should I start?" Lefty's feet were sweating.

"Wherever ye want, Lefty. Wherever ye want. I've got all the time in the world." The dwarf lit up a cigar, leaned back, and kicked his heels up. "And just so you know, yer a long, long way from whence you come."

A few more solemn faces joined them at the table, each one less friendly than the next. Lefty's feet were as damp as they'd ever been before.

Drip. Drip. Drip.

CHAPTER 37

" CAN YOU HOLD A SHOVEL?"

Venir hesitated, thinking of his aching wrists, then nodded. He was disgraced. Humiliated. Defeated. He reached out with his busted wrists.

Tuuth shoved it in his chest. "Better off digging than dying, for now anyway, Stranger."

Grimacing, Venir wrapped his hands around it and shuffled away, half dragging his feet. He could barely walk. He was dizzy. Thirsty. Hours ago he'd barley had the strength to watch the masses of the Royal Riders be slaughtered, but he'd held on through the bitter end. Watching the underlings chop brave men into bits and pieces was hard. Watching them burn in a pyre was even worse. The stench of burning flesh stung his eyes. It was suffocating.

"Stranger." Tuuth blocked his way with his big body. "What does that tattoo on your back mean, 'V'?"

Venir said nothing. He wasn't even sure himself, so long it had been since he'd even thought about it. Slowly, he trudged forward, joining the surviving Royal Riders, all twelve of them. All busted and broken in one way or the other.

"Stranger, does it stand for Vanquished?"

He looked up at Tuuth through his swollen eyes and said nothing.

"Villain? Vile? Vulgar? Vain? Victorious? Ha! Ha! Ha!"

It happened long ago. Venir couldn't remember if he was drunk when he'd done it or if someone had done did it to him when he was drunk. Melegal used to say it meant Vociferous and claim that he'd done it, but in truth, even Melegal didn't know when he got it. It was almost as if it just happened.

"Start digging, Stranger."

Wuhpash!

"You three, dig as well."

Venir sank the nose of his shovel into the dirt, thinking of all the bodies that would be stuck in the ground. For all he knew, he'd be buried alive again, and suffocated. His thoughts were interrupted when the underling commander showed up.

"Arsehole Bastard can't dig, you stupid orc!" The commander extended his hand towards Tuuth.

Wuhpash!

The underling cracked Tuuth across the arms, watering the orc's eyes.

"Next time you do something so stupid, you'll be digging a hole for yourself. We don't have any need for you, Orc, or any of those men. I'm tired of looking at humans. I'm tired of you all." He held his nose. "And you stink so bad when you burn!" The underling spat on Venir's chest then slugged him in the gut, dropping him to his knees. "I don't like this one, but I like to see him suffer."

Head downcast, Venir listened to the sound of shovels digging into the ground. He hated that sound. It made him think of the day the underlings overtook his village. Groaning, he rose back to his feet.

"Strong, stupid and stubborn, this man is," the underling commander said. "Like an orc." He hissed and chittered to himself. "Let him watch these men shovel until they die. Let him watch us strip the armor from their dead bodies. Let this stubborn man watch it all while you whip him." The underling reached up, grabbed Venir's chin and looked him in the eye. "And if he passes out, wake him up and whip him some more." The underling shoved the whip in Tuuth's chest. "Maybe he'll die before your arm gets too tired, Orc."

"Yes, Commander," Tuuth said.

Venir locked eyes with Tuuth when the commander walked off.

"Men," Tuuth said to some of the brigand army soldiers, "hitch him to the lashing post." He cracked the whip. "Normally, I'd enjoy this, Stranger. But, in your case, I feel a bit sorry for you and your stupid tattoo."

Wuhpash!

CHAPTER 38

THREEP! THREEP! THREEP! THREEP!

Fogle's eyes snapped open.

Threep! Threep! Threep! Threep!

Sluggish, he rolled onto his knees, yawning.

Threep! Threep! Thr —

With a simple thought, he shut off the Wizard's Alarm he'd set it in his mind. It was an awareness, like a familiar, a piece of him outside himself. *Careful, Fogle.* He scanned the harsh Outland. Anything could be coming, be it flesh-eating bugs, giants or underlings. Squinting his eyes, he didn't see anything, but the sore muscles between his shoulders told him something was wrong. *Never felt that before.*

Dust Devils swirled over the landscape. Nearby, covered in a thin layer of dust, Barton snored, flat on his face.

"Am I the only real adventurer left around here?" Fogle said to himself, brushing off his robes. "Ah! Why do I continue to bother with that?" He took a deep breath, scanning in every direction. "There has to be something; why else would my alarm go off?"

He nudged Cass's curled-up form. She looked innocent, at peace. He pushed her white hair back over her ear and whispered into it.

"Cass."

She stirred.

"Cass?" he said, shaking her some more. He was getting tired of being the only one awake. "Cass!"

Her eyes fluttered open. "What? Who are you yelling at? Not me, are you?"

Elated, he couldn't' help but hug her.

Feebly, she hugged him back. "Fogle, where are we?"

He helped her up to her feet.

"And is Barton dead?"

Disappointed with what he had to share, Fogle caught her up, explaining to her what little had happened since she fell asleep. Well, little aside from the swarm of flesh-eating bugs killing their horse and weakening Barton.

She made a shivering face when she saw the remains of the horse. "So, you protected me, did you?" She smiled a little and grabbed his hand. "My big-headed hero." She kissed him on the cheek. "But, if you had some water, now, that I'd be more than willing to give you a kiss for. Oh, and my lips would be so much moister."

Fogle felt his dry mouth begin to water as she turned away, hips swaying as she walked up to Barton. He could make water if he wanted to, but she'd made it clear before that his kind would not help. "I'm sure there is some nearby, but Cass, I've lost my familiar, and the truth is, I'm not the best at determining the direction in the Outlands. But, we were headed that way, east, I believe."

Cass fingered one of the red welts on Barton. "Stingers and teeth?" She continued her inspection, eyes wide with fascination. "Even I've never seen such a thing. Strange."

"How are you feeling, Cass?" He wasn't certain how long they'd slept, but it must have been a few hours at least. He felt a bit better than before, anyway.

"Mmm... not so bad, just stiff." She rolled her neck. "How are feeling, Fogle the Brave?"

"Never better now that I know you're well." He was unable to contain his grin.

"Oh, is that so?" Cass came closer, her busted lip and bruised face all smiles. "And how well am I, exactly?"

Drat! I had one good remark. I wasn't expecting to need two! "As well as a soldier in a tavern full of whores?"

"What!"

"Er ... Better than a dwarf on stilts?"

She folded her arms over her chest.

"Like a cat in a room full of rats?"

She shook her head. "You need to know when to be silent, Fogle Fool. Now —"

207

Suddenly, Barton jerked up into a sitting position, eye alert, craning his neck.

Fogle could see the muscles tense in the giant's back. Something was amiss.

"What is it?" Cass said.

Barton's hand covered her chest and face.

"Hear that?" Barton said, his voice a low rumble.

"Only the wind in my ears," Fogle said.

Barton's head turned towards the cloudy sky. His jaw jutted out, and he grinded his teeth. "We must go," Barton said. He reached for Cass.

"What are you doing?" she said.

"We must hide," Barton said. "Can you not hear that? Can you not hear that, Wizard?"

Fogle, eyeing the sky, shook his head. "I don't hear anything." Still, he grabbed Cass and held her tight. "Barton, what is it? Giants?"

Barton took a stiff breath through his nose and shook his head. "Not giants. Blackie. Barton hate Blackie."

That's when Fogle heard it. Distant. Foreboding. Massive.

Whump. Whump. Whump.

"A net," Boon grumbled to himself. "Of all things, I fell to a net."

Mile after mile Boon was marched, barefoot on the hot land. His bleeding and blistered feet burned like fire with every step.

Surrounding him, underling soldiers marched at his side, one holding a rope around his neck, jerking it hard from time to time.

Boon glanced over at it. Its red eyes glared back like beacons of death.

"I'll kill you first, you black roach," Boon spat. He looked at another. "Then you." And another. "And you." He was certain they didn't understand a word he said, but he understood them.

They hadn't killed him, but he was fairly certain he wished they had. No, they would torture him. Mutilate him. Cut his tongue off and feed it to him maybe. Of all the races on Bish, it was the underlings that delighted abnormally in peeling the flesh from the bones. The single thought of it disgusted Boon. Everything they did, he despised. He remembered the first time he saw them kill a man, a friend of his. They took pleasure in it. It stirred Boon. It made him sick.

"Ooof!"

Underlings shoved him to the ground, chittering with diabolical laugher.

His body wanted to stay down, but he wouldn't let it. He wouldn't give them the satisfaction. "Kill me now, fiends, before it's too late," he said. Rising, his legs trembled beneath him.

Still, they laughed in their own sick way, his threats as meaningless as the ants that scurried beneath his toes. Chests out, sharp teeth bared, the soldiers marched him over the dusty ground, pushing, pulling and jerking him by the neck mile after mile, one agonizing step after the other. *Walk or die, Old Man. Walk or Die.*

Before Fogle realized what was happening, Barton had snatched him and Cass up and started running.

"We must hide! Barton must hide! I won't let Blackie take me again. I won't!"

Over Barton's shoulder, Cass was screaming in the giant's ear. "Put me down!"

Fogle wanted to scream, but couldn't find the breath. Barton had him pressed over his shoulder too tight. *The dragon might want you,* he thought, *but I don't think he wants us!* Reassuring himself, he patted the spellbook in the pocket of his robe.

Barton's feet sounded like giant mallets pounding over the landscape, clattering Fogle's teeth and jostling his senses.

A dragon.

A black one.

Watching the clouds above, Fogle tried to imagine what to expect. There was a wizard's tower in the City of Three with a great hall filled with the most wondrous and colorful pictures. Battles. Cities. Ancient people of Long Ago. Men and dwarves battled orcs, ogres, gnolls and minotaurs. Wizards fought harpies, chimera, dark sorcerers. So many monsters roamed Bish, yet so few were ever seen, but one picture came to mind. A dragon: beastly, monstrous, little bigger than a horse attacking a host of men. It was a terrifying creature, scales a deep red, but other than that, it looked to only be a big lizard.

"Barton!" he said, "you don't even know where you're going!"

"I don't hear any dragons!" Cass screamed over at him, then looked to the air.

Whump! Whump! Whump!

Their eyes locked on one another's. Cass's widened with uncertainty.

Barton picked up the pace. "NOOOOOO!"

Fogle craned his neck, searching in all directions. Above him, a massive black shadow darted through the clouds.

Whump! Whump! Whump!

A powerful gust of air sent a chill right through him

Barton's running came to a sudden stop.

WHUMP!

Ahead, the sound of something heavy hit the dirt, followed by a roar so long Fogle felt his ears splitting. He stuck his fingers in them. *This is it!* Another roar followed, louder than the last. *I'm going to die.*

Barton lowered both him and Cass to the ground, setting them behind him.

"BARTON HATE YOU, BLACKIE! YOU WON'T TAKE BARTON HOME TODAY!"

There was a loud snort and a blast of furnace-hot air.

Fogle could smell sulfur and brimstone. He opened his eyes and looked. *Oh slat!* His knees warbled. His stomach recoiled. His warm blood went cold.

Blackie wasn't only taller than a horse; he was taller than five horses, maybe ten. His scales were black as coal. Hard as iron. His citrine eyes burned with life. Intelligent. Crafty. Teeth tall as a dwarf and sharper than spears. A great tail swiping back and forth like a preying cat. His giant claws dug into the hardened ground like it was mud.

"RAAAH-OOOOOOOOOOOOOOR!"

The sound was maddening. Without realizing it, Fogle found Cass's arms wrapped around him, eyes shut, trembling.

"Please don't roar again," she said. "Please don't roar again."

Fogle could barely hear her words. Even Barton's bellowing shouts seemed muffled compared to the dragon's terrifying sounds.

"BARTON KILL YOU, BLACKIE! BARTON KILL YOU NOW!"

Fogle was shaking his head. *You aren't going to kill that thing.*

The dragon's wings seemed impossibly long as it spread them and roared once more.

Cass was screaming, tears appearing in the corners of her eyes. They huddled on the ground like two babes in a storm. *This is happening!*

Fogle could feel the hot coals of the dragon's breath getting hotter. Then Barton said the unthinkable.

"BARTON HAVE WIZARD TO HELP HIM NOW. ATTACK HIM, WIZARD!"

The dragon's long neck moved his head from Barton down on the ground facing him.

That thing can understand Barton. Stupid giant! What can I do? Think, Fogle, think!

"HA! HA! HA! BLACKIE GOING TO GET IT NOW!"

The giants were terrifying enough, and he'd had help with them. The dragon was something entirely different. It wasn't shaped like a man. It was shaped like a monster.

The dragon snorted and sniffed. A strange cackling erupted in his long neck.

"WHAT ARE YOU WAITING FOR, WIZARD? KILL BLACKIE!"

"He doesn't want me. He wants you, Barton!" Fogle yelled.

That's when Cass looked up at him with weak eyes and said, "Do whatever you have to, Fogle. I'll fight with you."

From behind Barton's monstrous leg, he touched foreheads with Cass and said, "Fight or Die, my sweet. Fight or die!"

"WHAT?" Barton said, leering down at him with his good eye.

Do something or die, Wizard. A spell came to mind. *Huh! Am I ready this time? For a dragon?* He wrapped his arm around Barton's ankle and yelled upward. "Barton!"

"WHAT?"

"How much to you hate that dragon?"

211

"A LOT!"

"Get ready then! Help's coming!"

Closing his eyes, he summoned his power. Words of magic filled his head. Rolled from his tongue. Churned from his lips like hummingbird wings. Seconds later, he sagged, Cass holding him up.

"HAMMER!" he said.

A glowing hammer, with a head like an anvil, materialized at Barton's feet. It was longer than Fogle was tall, radiating with energy. Barton snatched it up and slung it at Blackie, striking him full in the chest.

KAROOM!

The dragon let out an angry screech, flapping backward and away.

Barton charged over the landscape, snatching the hammer up in his mighty arms, swinging.

WHAM! WHAM! WHAM!

Fogle felt the air shake with every blow. Blackie screeched and clawed, angry, hateful.

"BARTON KILL BLACKIE!"

WHAM!

"FEEL THAT, BLACKIE!"

WHAM!

"BARTON HATE BLACKIE!!"

The two titans fought and clawed over the ground, but Blackie was still bigger, quicker, and deadlier. Barton was a man fighting a giant-sized lizard.

Like a snake, Blackie struck, biting Barton's hammer-swinging arm.

"AARGH!"

The hammer fell from his grasp.

Barton cocked his elbow back and socked Blackie in the eye.

The pair thrashed and rolled through the dirt.

Barton was flailing and screaming.

Blackie clawing and biting.

It was an awful sight. Fogle grabbed Cass, pulling her as far away from the Chaos as he could.

"NOOO!" Barton squeezed.

Blackie pinned Barton under his weight, an adult atop a large child.

The giant's fingers clawed at the dirt, clutching for the hammer.

Blackie swatted the hammer away with his tail and hissed in Barton's face.

Fogle could see the giant's futile squirms under Blackie's power and weight. Barton, a giant, yet still a boy, couldn't overcome his adversary, his oppressor. It was a sad thing when the fire in Barton's eye went out, defeated.

"Help me, Wizard?" Barton said, exhausted, fingers feebly clutching at the dirt.

Fogle did nothing. The dragon didn't want him or Cass. It only wanted Barton. Keeping Cass behind him, he watched Blackie dig his black claws into Barton's shoulders.

"OW!" Barton cried. "Wizard, help!"

Whump! Whump! Whump!

Stirring the air like a small tornado, Blackie was up and off, with Barton in his grasp.

The betrayed look on Barton's face would haunt him forever, but he had to protect Cass.

Behind him, Cass cleared her throat.

"What?" he said, watching Blackie and Barton slowly sail away.

"Do something, Fogle Idiot! Shoot that dragon down!" Cass ordered.

The power of a dragon was one thing. The power of a beautiful angry woman was another. Without thinking, Fogle's body charged with power. Flashes of lightning shot from his fingers across the sky, striking Blackie full force.

Blackie roared, this time with pain, not pleasure.

Barton slipped from the dragon's grasp and plummeted a hundred feet to the ground with a thud.

"That's better," Cass said.

Blackie hung in the sky, hovering, flapping his great wings, struggling to stay afloat.

"Whatever you did, I don't think that dragon liked it. Do it again?"

Fogle shook his head. "I don't have enough power to kill it. I'd better protect us."

The dragon's citrine eyes leered at him like burning suns. He'd hurt it. He'd made it mad. Now it was coming for him.

It flapped over towards them, long great neck swaying back and forth.

Fogle grabbed Cass, pulled her close, and summoned a spell.

Hanging like a black cloud over them, Blackie opened his mouth and breathed.

The blast of a thousand furnaces came out.

Fogle stood tall, a mystic bubble protecting them, scattering the flames around them.

The heat was intense, like standing at the mouth of a blacksmith's forge.

The magic shield kept them away from instant incineration. Sweat poured from Fogle's face. The shield would only hold up as long as he could.

How long can this thing breathe! He felt his air begin to thin, his lungs labor, his concentration waver.

"Hold on, Fogle!" Cass encouraged him, her face as red as a beet, "Hold on!"

He couldn't. He fought with all his will, but his will was out.

"I'm sorry, Cass!" He shook his head. "I can't. Cass ... I—"

The fire stopped.

Blackie reared up, screeching. Barton was on the dragon's back, holding onto its wing with one hand and pounding it in the back of the head with the hammer in the other.

Fogle took Cass by the hand and tried to run away.

SWAT!

Blackie's tail licked out, knocking them from their feet.

Fogle gathered his knees beneath him and summoned more lighting in his grasp.

In front of him, Blackie slung Barton from his back. Wary, Blackie's eyes focused on Fogle's glowing hands.

"You don't like that, do you?" Fogle rose to his feet. "Stings, doesn't it, Lizard?"

A growl rumbled in the dragon's throat. The creature was intelligent, thinking, planning.

"Leave us be, Dragon," Fogle yelled. "Else I'll unleash all of my fury!"

Twenty feet from his nose, the Dragons' red tongue licked out over its fangs. There must have been a thousand of them.

"AAAIIEEEH!" Cass screamed.

The tip of Blackie's tail encircled her waist and dragged her away.

"NO!" Fogle yelled after her.

The dragon tucked her into his chest, playing with her in the palm of his hand like a tiny doll.

Fogle could swear it smiled.

Whump! Whump! Whump!

Up it went, Cass stunned in its grasp, leaving Fogle devastated on the cracked terrain as they disappeared into the clouds.

"CAAAAASSS!!!"

CHAPTER 39

ASTLE ALMEN, A CHARACTER IN its own right, had many secrets. Many lost over the centuries, others found. It was spotless; no cobwebs or dust coated the dark wood and velvety furniture. Every piece of metal was polished. Every crystal gleamed.

Lord Almen closed the drapes to a large bay window and sealed the balcony door shut. This was once the bedroom of his father. He and his best Shadow Sentry, a long limbed man, fled the Keep and traversed the castle utilizing the secret corridors, avoiding the commotion caused by the underlings.

Still weak, Lord Almen rummaged through the drawers of a black walnut desk until he placed his hand around a dagger and stuffed it into his belt. Quickly, he made his way over to the fire place and stood on the hearth.

"Come, stand with me," he ordered.

The sentry obliged, stepping onto the mosaic hearth, fingering the pommels of his swords.

"Tell no one of this," Lord Almen warned, shoving back a marble block on the fire place mantle. The colorful tiles shifted beneath their feet, then disappeared, leaving a black hole. The lanky warrior in the black ghost armor cocked his head. Rapidly, they were sinking.

"You may want to close your eyes, Virgil."

A quick rush of air followed, the feeling of one flying, the weightlessness of a feather, and an abrupt halt that bobbled his stomach. Opening his eyes, the first thing Lord Almen saw was his office beneath the kitchen, and the front door was still closed.

Beside him, Virgil's knees wobbled, his long arms stretching out for support. Lord Almen didn't bother. Instead, he searched his office. No one would have suspected a single thing was out of place, but he knew. It angered him. Whoever had been here had some idea what to look for and what they were taking. Tonio's sword was gone. The shelf that concealed the small secret door was out of place, and the door was open. A variety of footprints had disturbed the dust. *Melegal* was the first thought that came to mind. *Sefron* was the second. But, more than that, something lingered in the air. The scent of underlings.

"Virgil, see to it that door is secure," he said, opening a small case full of vials. "You be keeping post and sending warning if anything comes through there."

"I hope it's underlings," Virgil said. He cracked his neck side to side and eased his sword from the scabbard. "Or any arsehole, for that matter."

Lord Almen couldn't see the man's face behind his cloth mask, but Virgil was one of his best soldiers. A survivor of the Warfield. A friend of danger. Lord Almen favored men like that. Cold blooded killers.

Lord Almen drank down one of the vials, followed by the other. He tossed one filled with a pale red liquid to Virgil.

"Take that," Lord Almen said. He rolled his shoulders. He was feeling better and stronger already. "It will give you stamina. Improve your focus."

Virgil pulled up his mask—exposing his rugged chin, split lip and rotting teeth—before he swallowed it down.

Lord Almen took a deep breath through his nose, filling his lungs to capacity and slowly releasing.

Virgil thumbed his blade. "This sword is the finest blade I've ever owned, Lord Almen, and I'll put it to good use in your defense." He pulled his mask back down. "I feel like killing."

"So do I."

Disappointed that Tonio's sword was gone, Lord Almen grabbed another blade, a poniard with an ivory hilt, and set it on his desk table. Opening a wardrobe, he grabbed his own suit of ghost armor and slipped it on. It fit like a glove, coating him like a thick flexible skin. A smile came to the corner of his lips. *It's been too long.*

"Sir, you look dangerous, but I plan on killing them all before they make it to you."

Almen put his hand on Virgil's shoulder. "You do that, and I'll give you your own room in this castle and a personal servant girl, too."

Black masked, Virgil saluted with his sword. "My life for my Lord. Their life with my sword."

With that, Lord Almen stepped through the small door's opening and headed down the stairs on cat's feet. Stopping, he closed his eyes and slowed his breath. He heard nothing. Not a shuffle, nor a scuffle, nor a scratch. Breathing through his nose, nothing caught his potion-heightened senses. As they passed the bottom of the stairwell, the torches came to life. The large chamber cast his shadow. All six doors were closed.

Where is she?

Making his way back to the alcove where all the Keys usually hung, he noticed the empty pegs on the wall. How in all of Bish had they escaped his grasp? *Melegal.* It had to be. Or had they been taken by the underlings?

He chuckled, remembering the first time he and his father found the chamber. There'd been more doors. More pegs. More Keys. And rings. Many came, many went. He tried his best to understand it. It seemed the chamber had a will of its own. It would serve him, so he thought, so long as he fed it. A mystery. An advantage he didn't hesitate to press. No wonder the underlings wanted it. But how did they know about it? Who made it? *Seven Keys last I counted. Eight with the one I gave to Jarla. I hope she still has it.* He looked at the floor. The slightest sucking licked at his boots.

Lord Almen paced around the circle of the great chamber. His castle was under siege. The underlings had penetrated for the second time in days. He could have held out in the keep, but the Keys were what he was certain they wanted. He had no plans to part with them. They gave him power. Control. To go whenever and however he wanted to go. And until several days ago, only few knew about his secret. Now that secret had been compromised.

Standing in the center of the room facing the alcove and the ancient doors, Lord Almen stood, watching and listening. *Where is that Brigand Queen?* He twisted the finger ring that he used to summon her. She never appeared at the same duration, but always she came. Minutes, an hour maybe, but never a day. He frowned.

Perhaps she's dead.

She had a Key and a ring. Her Key would open the doors and give him access and freedom if the underlings took over. And if the underlings had the other seven Keys, the Keys that they knew about, what would they do? They could strike day or night all over Bish if they wanted to. Just like he had. He couldn't fight the smile on his lips.

The minutes passed, leaving Lord Almen alone in his thoughts, his memories.

For years Lord Almen had used the Keys, slipping into rival bedrooms and parlors, strangling or cutting their throats while they slept. Already a Master Assassin, the Keys had made his job all too easy. Castle Almen had moved up the ranks quickly on account of it. The ancient chamber was a recent discovery, come upon by accident by his father. Slowly over the years, they had abused the power of the ancient chamber, never truly understanding it. But he knew, he'd always known, someone would come after the power one day or another. And now it seemed that day had come.

He froze. Up the stairwell echoed the sound of wood exploding into splinters. He shifted his stance. Readied his sword. Chitters and the clash of steel followed. A human cry of alarm went out. Silence fell. The room went cold.

Something clopped down the stairs, rolling to a stop at the bottom. It was Virgil's head. A clean cut through the neck. Blood spilled into the mosaic. A sucking sound followed. Lord Almen sheathed his sword.

The first past the torches was an underling, copper eyed with a bandolier of knives around his chest. He was tall, over six feet, the tallest underling Lord Almen had ever seen. Blood dripped from the tip of his sword, and a fierce grin parted his lips. Behind him, others came: two, then four, then six. Some were in black plate armor that didn't clank or rattle; the others wore little more than leather or a cloak. Blades of many kinds hung loose in their grips, and their eyes were bright with color.

Lord Almen rubbed the sweat from his hands. So many adversaries were to be expected, but everyone else in the castle flooded his thoughts. It was entirely possible that his family were being wiped out one by one. *I hope they made the Keep at least.*

Still, he stood tall, a statue by comparison. "I am Royal Lord Almen, Liege of this castle, and I request a parlay."

Coming closer, the copper eyes of the first underling narrowed to slits, a sinister chuckle erupting in his throat. "Parlay," he said, slipping his sword in the sheath in a wink of an eye. "I don't see any need for a parlay, Human Lord. After all, we've seized your castle, within your city. I think there is little you can do to help us."

About then, a wheezing sound caught his ear. Sefron the Cleric was huffing down the stairs, oversized robes hanging from his body, his gnarled staff clacking on the steps. Lord Almen's usual frown expanded when they locked eyes. *Traitor!* Lord Almen didn't hide his rage as the underlings formed a tight circle around him.

"Sefron, you sickening slaggard! It was you that gave up the castle! I'll cut open that fat belly of yours!"

Sefron groaned, straightening the bend in his back with a chuckle. He rubbed his saggy chin and blinked his bulging eye. "Master Kierway, may I have this one?"

"Fool," Kierway said, "this man will prove to be a better resource than you, certainly."

Sefron came closer, trying to push past the underlings, his hand reaching out.

Lord Almen recoiled back the ever slightest. He knew Sefron's secret and what the man was capable of. It was why he recruited him in the first place.

"Don't you dare, Servant," Almen said.

"Stay back, Sefron, you disgusting fool." Kierway shook his head. "You bother me, but this man, he doesn't bother me so much, other than being a human." He scratched his cheek with his long black nails. "Tell me about this *parlay*, Lord Almen. I'm curious."

Tearing his eyes away from Sefron, Lord Almen cleared his throat. "I've a history with your kind, Master Kierway. It was I who aligned myself with you at Outpost Thirty-One."

"So you are a traitor?"

"A survivor." Lord Almen nodded. "A master planner. My family and my castle are what mean the most in life to me. I dare not guess what the underlings have in mind with my castle or this city, but I will assist you. I'm a man of many secrets. Tell me what you want, and I assure you that I can help."

Kierway moved with the ease of a cat, sauntering through the chamber, tugging on one door handle after the other. Standing in the alcove near the key posts, he said, "This architecture is strange, but similar to many chambers in the Underland. Hmmm, so, Lord Almen, tell me, where are the Keys?"

Lord Almen kept his relief concealed. He'd lost track of much while he'd been down for several days. He eyed Sefron briefly. He could tell the cleric must have had something to do with that, or had he? The wound between his ribs should have been fatal, and he vaguely remembered Sefron coming to his aid, only to betray him now.

"Stolen," Lord Almen said.

Kierway crossed his arms and leaned his shoulder over one of the doors. "So, you are waiting for the thief to return with them? Certainly that wouldn't happen in the middle of a siege. Not unless the person with the Keys would have a reason to come back, and into that question you might have more insight than I." He raised his eyebrows. "Of course, perhaps you are down here because you are expecting someone else. Seven pegs. Seven Keys. Six doors. Interesting opportunities."

One of the most frustrating things that Lord Almen had encountered about underlings was that they weren't stupid. Every one he'd dealt with had a calculating mind and cunning demeanor. He admired that about them. And something else. Unlike men, they weren't greedy, at least not in terms of material things. Instead, they thirsted for something else without distraction. Power.

"I can't readily say, and I cannot refute the possibility either."

There was a long pause. Surrounding him, standing like statues poised to strike, the breathing of the underlings was barely audible. Lord Almen glanced over at Sefron, who now sat wheezing on the stairs. He should have rid himself of the slaggard long ago, but Sefron was so resourceful when it came to digging information from his enemies. And there was another thing. Perhaps Sefron was still his ally. The man gave no sign of it.

One by one, Kierway slid three throwing knives from his bandolier. He juggled them with one hand. The blades flashing in the air, hand moving in a blur. Kierway's expression was lax and bored. "We wait, if need be, Lord Almen, but it might be a very long time. Of course, through our sources, we know where the Keys are. They are with a man, one of your own. What is his name, Sefron?"

"Melegal."

Feigning surprise, Lord Almen said to Sefron, "And how do you know this?"

Sefron sat with his legs crossed and sighed. "He's the last one we saw with them in here." He pointed at his ruined eye. "Thanks to him I have this."

Kierway snapped his wrist.

Thunk!

A knife jutted in the support beam by Sefron's head, causing him to jump.

"No." Kierway's eyes narrowed at Sefron. "Thanks to me you have that." He turned to Almen. "This man, Melegal, created the ultimate dilemma. Acts like an underling, that one. Cool and cunning." He resumed his juggling.

Inside of himself, Lord Almen was astounded. Melegal had found the Keys! But how? And why? *Hmmm... I see. The underlings recruited Sefron to find the Keys, meaning they must have known they were here. But why now? Why after all these years? It seems they have even darker secrets than I.*

"What's this?" Putting away his knives, Kierway drew a sword.

By the stairs, Sefron rose to his feet.

A faint yellow glow outlined the door where Kierway was leaning. "Chit! Chit!" he said. Underlings moved into the shadows. Some in full armor, some little, others none. "You, stay with Lord Almen!" He pointed to one then to another. "You, stay with the other one."

Lord Almen was pushed back into the alcove, where on tenterhooks, he and two of the underlings waited. *Finally,* he thought. *For what little good it will do.*

The yellow light disappeared, and the ancient door swung open.

CHAPTER

40

"WHAT IS THIS PLACE?" CREED fumbled through the dark. "Silence, Creed." Melegal held his stomach.

You'd think I'd be used to this miserable feeling by now.

Creed moaned. "Slat, I feel like I'm hung over. What just happened?"

"You'll see." Melegal searched the darkness for a handle or a knob. "Listen to me, Creed. When I open this door, we're going to be in a chamber. People might be there, and underlings for all I know, so get your guts in order, and be ready for anything."

Creed scoffed. "I'm always ready for anything; just give me a moment."

Melegal pressed his ear to the door. If anything was moving on the other side, he wouldn't know. The door was as thick and hard as stone—and magical, for all he knew. Still, he worried. He assumed the Key took him back to the chamber beneath Castle Almen, but maybe it didn't. Maybe it took him somewhere else.

"What's that?" Creed huffed. "Did you feel something? Something's in here."

Melegal, still frozen, felt a gentle brush between his legs. Looking down, he saw two pale white eyes. "Octopus," he murmured.

"What's that?"

"Don't worry about it, Creed. Now listen to me. Do you want to go in hard and fast or quick and easy?"

Truth was, Melegal had to wonder what would happen if others were in there. Could he slip back in and seal the door? He hadn't thought long enough about it; he'd had no choice. And what if the underlings were inside? He straightened his cap. *Be ready for a nose bleed.*

"I don't suppose there really is a fast and easy way, is there?"

"I don't think we've much choice. Just be ready to fight..." Melegal found the handle and started to pull.

"...or Die," Creed finished.

Quick. Quick. Quick.

Melegal pressed the latch downward and shoved the door open. He darted straight forward, rolled, and rose to his knees, swords ready.

Creed spun along the wall, blades whirling.

The massive chamber was silent, torches flickering, forcing a wavering light.

Narrowing his eyes, Melegal noted the figures lined against the walls in the shadows. Their eyes were glimmering. *Bish! It's underlings!*

Whamp. The door they came through shut.

Leaning against the wall with two swords crossed over his back was an underling as tall as him. His copper eyes glowered at him.

"Ah... you must be the one called Melegal."

The other underlings emerged from the shadows.

The tall underling continued. "I just missed you the last time, it seems. You are the one Sefron calls The Rat."

Stupid! Stupid! Stupid! I should have taken my chances in the streets! One. Two. Three... Seven underlings. No crossbows. No darts. Two torches. Where to go? Where to go?

That's when he caught the heavy stare of Royal Lord Almen. A sword was pressed into the Vulture-like man's back. Wary, Melegal turned in his spot. Sefron's eyes were on him as well.

The cleric shuffled, wheezed, and squirmed at the side of an underling that held a blade to his belly.

Melegal allowed a grin and returned his focus to the copper-eyed underling.

"I am that rat. And who might you be?"

"Master Kierway." The underling pushed himself off the wall.

"Oh, so you are the one that Sefron wanted me to get the Keys for?"

Lord Almen shot Sefron a look, but the cleric remained silent.

"Indeed, and I assume you have those Keys?"

Slowly, Melegal nodded his head. There was no reason to lie now. All they would do was kill him and take them. He searched Lord Almen's face and saw nothing of help. It seemed the Castle was at a loss. But even if the underlings didn't kill him, he was certain Lord Almen would. After all, he'd tried to kill Lord Almen and failed.

How will you squeeze out of this one, Rat?

He glanced at Creed. The man stood tall, eyes darting from one underling to another, ready to fight anything and everything.

"I do have the Keys." Melegal sheathed his swords. "And they are yours to have."

Lord Almen's face turned pale.

Melegal reached inside his pockets.

Creed harrumphed. "Let them take those Keys from your dead body. Don't make a deal with the underlings, Detective. There are only a few of them."

"Mind your tongue, Bloodhound," Lord Almen said. "It's not your back that's dancing with a sword."

"Huh," Creed said. "At least I'll die with one in my hand, not in my back."

"As much as I'd rather not admit it," Kierway said, "I agree with this man over here. I'd rather die than make deals with the enemy. That's the kind of fighter I am. But at the moment, that's not my mission. The Keys are. Let me see them!"

"Certainly." Melegal fumbled through his clothes. *No rush. Not too fast. Not too slow.* Producing the 1st Key, Amethyst, he placed it on the floor.

Every eye in the chamber widened.

"And, Master Kierway," Melegal said, "considering my inevitable death, I would like you to consider another request." He set the 2nd Key, a diamond set in a brass setting, down on the floor. Out of the corner of his eye, he saw Lord Almen fidget the slightest.

Sefron's wheezing picked up.

"Say whatever you like, Human," Kierway said, "as you are intelligent to realize that your death is inevitable."

Melegal stood up and pointed.

"Let me sink my blades into that bug-eyed bastard, Sefron. He's the reason I came back. To cut his throat. I can't imagine you have any practical use for him. He failed to get the Keys. I didn't. And now I lay them at your feet with that one tiny request."

Sefron managed a fearsome snarl.

Melegal jumped. Still, he set the 3rd Key down.

"Let's just fight them, Man!" Creed urged. "I've killed underlings before." He eyed Kierway. "Dozens."

"Perhaps you'll get your chance, Human," Kierway said, still focusing on Melegal. "But first, let me see another Key. And maybe, assuming you do have all seven, I'll grant your request."

It made sense, what Creed was suggesting. If they fought and made it to the doors, they could escape. And so far as he understood it, he could go wherever he wanted, if he used the same door. *Two-Ten City might be nice right now.* As for the other doors, where did they go and which Key fit which door?

Of all the things to forget, he hadn't noted which Key was on which peg next to which door. It had been dark when he took them. *Clumsy fool!* For now, all he could do was buy a little more time and see what happened.

He set the 4th Key down. Its gem burned like orange fire.

As for overpowering the underlings in the room, it didn't seem likely. The ones in plate armor were of the likes he'd never seen before. He ventured any of them would be a match for Creed, who was certainly a superior fighter to himself. And Master Kierway wasn't at all worried. The underling and his brood made the men look wholly inadequate. *He didn't even ask us to disarm ourselves.*

"You'd made a fine Bloodhound," Creed said, "on account of you wanting to kill that Cleric and all."

Melegal ignored him, his shoulders and back tightening as he laid the 5th Key down. So much had happened since Lord Almen had acquired his service and made him a detective. He remembered those days in the man's office, the pressure, the fear the man put into him. He could feel Lord Almen's eyes heavy upon him, but he no longer felt that fear. *I wonder what he has in mind. He must have some plan.* Reaching inside his vest, he felt the long case he had tucked away. *Might not ever get a chance to use this. A shame.*

"Here is the 6th Key, Master Kierway." He knelt and rubbed his hands on his pants. "Can I cut that cur's throat now? Before I hand over the 7th? Just let me take his life, and I'll freely give you mine."

Kierway came closer. "You've made it interesting; I'll grant you that. Perhaps, I'll make you prisoners and lock you in a cage together instead. I think we underlings would find that entertaining."

"Would you want to be put in a cage with him?" Melegal said, unable to help himself.

"Well spoken!" Creed said, shifting on his heels.

Kierway showed him his sharp teeth. "Sorry, Human Called Melegal, but I see no reason to make such a deal." He paused and gestured. "I wouldn't be what I am, giving such consideration to a human. Now," he held out his clawed hand, "the 7th Key, please."

Shing!

In a blink, Kierway had pulled out his blade and put it at Melegal's throat.

For the first time in recent memory, Melegal felt beads of sweat on his forehead.

"You worry me, Human Called Melegal."

Melegal swallowed. "And why is that?"

"It seems foolish that you keep all the Keys on you, understanding their value. If it were me, I'd keep them hidden in many places. A bargaining chip if my life depended on it. A smart man would have hidden them all, would he not?"

I can't be that stupid. Of course I should have hidden them. Am I really going to die a fool?

Melegal's memories flashed to his friends: Venir, Georgio, Lefty, Billip and Mikkel.

I can't be as stupid as them.

But he had thought briefly about hiding the Keys and concluded that so long as they thought he had even one Key, they'd hunt him— the Royals and the underlings—forever and ever. *A clean slate or a clean death is what I'm going for. Let the rest of Bish plot and scheme all they want.*

"I did think of that, Master Kierway, but why risk the torture? They say, 'A quick beheading has no sting.'" Clasping his hands around the final Key, he summoned power from the hat that rested on his head. His mind cleared. Blood and mystic energy mixed in his veins. *Faster. Quicker. One step ahead.*

Everything around him slowed: Sefron's breath. Creed's blinking. The flickering of the torches. The clutching of Kierway's fingers.

Ahead of Melegal, behind Lord Almen, the outline of the ancient door glowed with new life and started to open.

Kierway's sword arm flicked backward.

Move or die! Melegal. Move!

Kierway's arm came forward.

CHAPTER 41

ATCHING HER BREATH, JARLA FUMBLED for the latch on the door. In the darkness, she was alone with Tonio's ragged breathing.

"Don't do anything foolish," she said, brushing against him and pulling away.

"Where are we?" he said, heavy feet shuffling around.

At the moment, Jarla wasn't so sure whether or not it would be a good idea to tell him. It didn't really matter either way. Lord Almen would be waiting, and what other surprises he had in store she couldn't imagine, but he must have needed her.

"Just be ready, you bloodless goon, because you're going first."

She pushed the door open.

Over Tonio's shoulder, the torches were bright beacons. It took a couple of seconds for Jarla's eyes to adjust to the figures in the room. Lord Almen, a few other men, surrounded by underlings.

"Father?" Tonio's body tensed in front of her.

Lord Almen had a look on his face she'd never seen there before. Surprise.

Behind him, an underling had a blade pointed at Lord Almen's back.

It stirred Jarla, her energy renewing, her senses firing a warning.

"Father!" Tonio's garbled voice echoed in the chamber.

Jarla stepped forward.

Another underling stepped between them and Lord Almen. Two long knives were gripped in his hands, ruby eyes glinting, bare muscular chest stuck out.

Across the chamber, two more underling soldiers armed with barbed spears filed inside as well.

Other than that, no one moved.

"The odds aren't going to get any better than this!" an unfamiliar voice shouted.

Clang!

Bang!

Lord Almen moved. Fast as a cat, he spun behind his underling oppressor and drove a dagger in its throat.

The bare-chested underling closed in, cutting out a portion of Tonio's chest armor.

The big man rammed his sword through its belly, lifted it from its feet, and slung it into another wall.

"Jarla!" Lord Almen screamed.

When she turned to his voice, an underling in black plate armor stepped in her path, swords moving like striking snakes.

Clang! Clang! Clang!

Parrying with two hands, she found her back against the wall.

Fast and fluid it came. Jarla parried and countered, stabbing its chest, her sword glancing off the armor.

"What in Bish are you?" the underling yelled at Tonio.

Krang!

Tonio hit it so hard he knocked it from its feet.

A split second later, Lord Almen kneeled down and jammed his dagger under its chin, piercing its skull.

Huffing, Jarla found Lord Almen's eyes.

"Get the Keys!" He ordered.

"What Keys?" she said.

"On the floor! Don't let the underlings have them." Ducking under an underling's arm, Lord Almen ripped out a long poniard and started swinging.

"Keys!" Tonio was pounding his way through his underling assailants. "Get for Father!"

Another underling adorned in black leathers surged at her, two short swords in its hands, sharp teeth bared.

Slice!

It howled and jumped back, clutching its split and bleeding chin.

"Don't you chitter at me, you little fiend."

When Tonio emerged through the door, Melegal swore he heard his heart stop. The Yellow-Haired Butcher had arrived. Behind him, the insufferable woman, Jarla. He was uncertain whether to be glad to see either one of them. They both deserved horrifying deaths so far as he was concerned. *Perhaps they'll get them.*

Tonio's face showed an ounce of humanity as he called for his father.

Jarla's scowling face, riddled with scars, showed creases of concern.

Behind Melegal, Sefron wheezed.

Kill Sefron.

The footfalls of more underlings came down the stairs.

Creed took in a deep breath. "The odds aren't going to get any better than this!"

Kierway hissed through his teeth, glowered at Melegal, and cut at his neck.

Everything in the room moved slowly except the underling's blade.

Melegal jerked his head down and jumped away.

Swish!

He touched the thin red line dripping on his neck.

Slat, that was fast!

With a brush of his foot, Melegal scattered 6 of the Keys in all directions.

Clang!

Whew! Keep him busy, Creed. Keep him busy.

Kierway caught Creed's swords in a crossed sword parry.

"Sefron," Kierway ordered, "get those Keys while I cut this man to ribbons! Brethren, help him!"

Man and underling squared off, lightning fast strokes ringing off each other like bells.

But Melegal had his own problems to worry about. He tucked the 7th Key back inside his clothes. *Slat on the Keys! Kill Sefron! Save yourself!*

The battle was furious.

Underlings swarmed, jumping out from all directions at the human attackers.

Tonio stood in the middle, a one-man army.

Jarla's sword darted at underling throats, her eyes darting after the Keys.

Lord Almen. *Slat! Where is he?*

Melegal let his heightened awareness take over. *Ah, there he is.* The haunting form of a man hung like a shadow near the wall, striking down an unsuspecting underling that crossed his path. *Interesting!*

A dozen yards away, Sefron slowly shuffled over the floor, bending over to grab one of the Keys.

Melegal extended his dart bracers and let Sefron have it.

Clatch-zip! Clatch-zip!

Sefron whined like a dying sheep, falling over, clutching at his legs.

Melegal crossed the room—deftly avoiding the melee—and kept shooting.

Clatch-zip! Click! Click!

Melegal overpowered Sefron and straddled his belly, pressing a knife to his throat.

"Remember my friend, the servant girl? You know, the one you almost whipped to death?"

Sefron's bulging eyes were merciless. "Hard to say. There's been so many." He licked his lips. "And there'll be many more to come, I assure you, long after you're dead."

Melegal felt Sefron's clammy hand wrap around his wrist. It was cold, ice cold.

"No, slug, it's you who'll be dead. And if I had the time, I'd whip you to death myself."

Melegal pushed his dagger into Sefron's throat, but no blood came forth, just Sefron's cackle.

"Fool, do you really think I'm so weak that a rodent such as yourself could take me?"

A wave of nausea overcame Melegal. *What's happening!*

Sefron's grip became as solid as iron, squeezing his wrist to the point of breaking it.

His dagger fell from his numb wrist.

Before his eyes, Sefron changed. His hair thickened. His teeth straighten. His body firmed like a fighter's beneath him.

No! What is this!

Melegal watched his hand curl and shrivel. It horrified him.

"No!" he groaned, trying to pull his rawboned body away.

Sefron cackled and sucked his teeth.

"Ah, such succulent life from such a scrawny man. Surprising."

Creed's father had told him that the first time he picked up a blade and swung, he was three. He'd cut into a leg of mutton and saved the butcher some trouble. He'd been swinging steel ever since.

Bang! Chang! Clang! Swish. Swish. Chang!

His opponent: an underling that weaved steel with skill he'd never seen. He thought he'd seen everything. He'd thought he knew everything.

Creed parried, dodged, ducked, and jumped backward. Forward and followed up with a chop-chop-chop.

Always attacking at the same time, the copper-eyed underling batted every blow away.

Not possible! Creed backed away.

The underling's blades were of the finest craftsmanship, archaic and curved at the very end. They moved like black flashes of lightning. Quick as a blink of an eye.

Creed had trained all his life, defeated every man he faced in fence or battle. The ones that would fight him, that is. Many Royals never gave him the honor. It bothered him. And now, entering his prime, for the first time in his life, he was worried.

"I never believed an underling could be so fast," he stalled. "Quite remarkable."

Kierway showed his sharp teeth. "Remarkable is my lowest level of skill, Human. Whatever it is you've done, I've already done a hundred times a year over a hundred years. You should know: this battle is over."

Creed wiped the sweat from his forehead with the back of his hand.

"Then I suppose this is what I've been training all my life for. Ee-Yah!"

In a flash, his gleaming blade leapt at the underling's throat.

Kierway deftly shifted his body a foot out of the way and swatted into the backs of Creed's legs with the back of his sword.

"Ugh! Blast it!" Creed cried out. He could feel the blood dripping down over his thighs already.

The floor made an eerie sucking sound.

Creed's face showed horror. "What in Bish is going on?"

"Interesting," Kierway replied. "It seems the floor hungers. I think I shall feed it."

Creed banged his blades together. One blade the finest of steel, the other enchanted by a mystic forge master. Until today, he'd always felt himself invincible with them and his skill, but it seemed for the first time in his life he'd met his match. He banged his blades again and muttered angrily to himself. "Come on, Creed! Draw his blood at least!"

Use your reach. You're longer!

Steel scraped against steel. Sweat mixed with blood.

They say, 'When your final battle comes, you'll know.'

His father had told him that, years ago, hours before he died at the Warfield. He'd always wondered who killed his father. A great sword. A great hound. Now he'd never know.

He charged. One sword high, the other low, he swung.

Kierway caught both blades on the outside with a smirk.

Creed's booted toe lashed out into Kierway's chin, clattering his teeth and splitting his lip.

Shocked, the underling hissed.

Creed kept swinging hard and fast.

Bang! Clang! Chang! Chang! Bang!

Back and forth the pair went. One master. One ancient master.

The underling's arms were strong like steel, but tireless and flexible as snakes.

For seconds, Creed pressed the advantage.

Slice.

Kierway ended it with a lightning fast stroke across Creed's thigh.

Slice.

Followed by another one across his belly.

Slice.

A hunk of flesh fell to the floor. It was Creed's.

234

"Hear that, Human? It's the sound of your death getting closer."
Parry, Fool! Parry!

Blue sparks showered the air.

Kierway pounded at his blades. Knocked Creed's steel down, numbing his hands.

That was Creed's plan. To beat his opponent's arms down until they felt like lead. But now his own arms felt like lead. Laboring for breath, he struggled to keep up with the blinding speed of Kierway's blades. Below, something sucked at his feet on the floor.

"You tire, Human." Kierway swatted Creed's blades away like toys. "Drop your blades, and I'll give you a merciful death."

"No. I'm going to cut you just once, Black Fiend. I can't go down like this. I can't."

Bang!

Kierway ripped one of Creed's swords from his hand and paused.

Creed's lone sword arm trembled. He grabbed his wrist with the other to support it.

"You are a fine swordsman, Human. But I've faced many better. All dead now, of course. So take note that you'll die at the hand of the finest swordsman this world has ever known."

Creed labored for breath.

Kierway was barely winded, his eyes darting around, looking for something.

"So be it then, Underling." Head down, Creed took a knee and set down his sword. "Vanquish me."

"With pleasure."

Catching a glimpse of Kierway's nearest knee, Creed lunged forward with everything he had, stabbing with a dagger concealed in his bracer. The blade sank into flesh and hit bone.

Kierway howled.

"I swore I'd cut you!"

Kierway's blade came for his head.

CHAPTER 42

ORRIN RUBBED HIS EYES. FOR hours he'd sat watching the images in the fountain, mesmerized. Trinos had shown him the world outside the City of Bone, the home he'd never left. It was all fascinating and horrifying at the same time.

"What do you think?" Trinos said.

Corrin stretched out his stiff arms and shook his head. "It's a horrible, horrible world out there." He cleared his throat. "And just as bad in here."

Trinos lifted her brows without making a crease in her perfect forehead.

"How so?"

Corrin wasn't sure how to respond at first. After all, he was a murderer and cutthroat, even though he was pretty certain that was all behind him now. Watching all he'd seen—people dying of thirst or getting lost in the Outlands, battling for honor in a place she said was called the Warfield—it seemed as if someone was always fighting something else somewhere in this world. All his years, he'd assumed Bone was the worst the world had to offer, but it clearly wasn't. The entire world was in a struggle, and the driving force behind it all was the underlings. Or was it? He wasn't so sure.

He took an apple from a wicker basket, started peeling it with his knife, and looked into her eyes.

"I always figured there was solitude somewhere in this world. But if there is, I've never seen it. And I've never experienced it. At least not until you came around."

"Well, Corrin, you've only seen what I've shown you. Don't you find it entertaining?"

"I can't tear my eyes away from it, if that's what you mean by entertaining, but I have to ask, is all of this real?" He stuck a piece of apple in his mouth and chewed. "Or is it an illusion? Are these places you've been to?"

Trinos's smile was warm and radiant, creating a soothing vibration in his chest. He almost felt ashamed just for looking at her, and even when he tore his eyes away from her, he glanced at her perfect figure constantly. Trinos was a mystery. Powerful. Unlike anything he could imagine in this world, but real. He didn't know what to make of her, but he'd do anything she said.

"Do you want to keep watching, Corrin?"

He shrugged, staring back into the waters where a new image started to form. This time it was different. His jaw dropped. This time it was people he knew, and they were in danger. He felt his heart speed up inside his chest, eyes transfixed.

"Perhaps you'd rather see something," she stuck out her hand and the waters wavered, "more pleasant?"

"No-No!" he said, shoving his hands over the water. "I want to see how this ends."

The waters steadied, and the image cleared. Trinos leaned towards the fountain and said, "Me too."

CHAPTER 43

MELEGAL FELT HIS STOMACH TIGHTEN into knots.

The cleric's hair grew and thickened. His sagging jawline toughened. Sefron's disturbing features transformed into the countenance of a man full of strength and vitality. It was unlike anything Melegal had ever seen before. In seconds, Sefron went from a hapless weakling to a formidable foe that was about to kill him.

"Oh yes, Rat." Sefron's teeth were straight and strong. "You thought you would take me. Avenge the honor of a worthless little slut, but now, just imagine what I'll have in store for her the next time I see her. She'll think I'm handsome, will she not, you fool? She'll be having me instead of you."

Melegal wanted to scream for help, but his tongue shriveled in his mouth, and his throat was dry. The chaos surrounding him was in full force where men and underlings battled. The Keys skittered over the mosaic floor. In his mind, he could hear them, count them all. *One-Two-Three-Four-Five... Forget the Keys! Save yourself!*

"Oh, this feels so good." Saliva dripped from Sefron's mouth.

In horror, Melegal watched his own age spots and crooked fingers form. It felt like Sefron had the grip of an ogre. *Am I to die like this? A rotting old man?* His doubts overwhelmed him. His anger and surprise turned to shock and confusion. *What do I do?*

"Heh-heh-heh." Sefron gloated, licking his lips. "It's time to die, Melegal."

Die? He let out a feeble cough. The air in his lungs felt thin. For the first time in his life, he wheezed. He was confused.

"Ha! Painful, isn't it?"

Melegal shook his head. *Can't let this happen! What do I do?* His mind was drifting. The pain was growing. His focus deteriorating.

"I think I might have what's left of you for soup. Melegal stew, stirred with your own bones and sautéed with your eyeballs."

Now, Melegal's eyes looked at Sefron like a complete stranger. He tried to withdraw. Fear overwhelmed his feeble mind. *Let go! Let go! Let go!*

The hat on his head ignited.

Sefron's grip popped open, eyes blinking, shaking his head.

"Why — why did I let you go?" Sefron reached over, grabbed his staff and raised it over his head. "No matter, I'll just bash your sock ridden he —"

Glitch!

Melegal stabbed him in the heart, plunging his blade hilt-deep in the chest.

"No!" Sefron coughed up blood, groaned, and gurgled before falling over, dead.

Melegal pulled out his dagger and stabbed him once more.

Sefron's stare was glassy, and the cleric's body reverted back to normal.

Filthy Bastard.

Melegal fell flat on his back, sucking for air. Rolling onto his belly, he groaned. "Slat, I feel like I'm a hundred years old." He crawled over the floor, aching from head to toe.

Nearby, Creed was about to die.

So much for him.

He turned his attention elsewhere. *Get to one of the doors!* He had a Key; he could still feel it, but at the rate he was moving the nearest door might as well have been a mile away. Going up the stairs looked impossible. Everyone was fighting everything everywhere.

Bone, I'm not going anywhere! I might as well die right here.

Clang!

The sound of clashing steel was music to Creed's ears. He rolled away and sprang to his feet, limping. The underling, Kierway, was tangled with a big, ugly menace of a man he would not have known had he not called Lord Almen Father. Tonio had changed.

"I like these odds!"

Rejuvenated, Creed jumped into the fray, stabbing his gleaming sword.

On the other side of Kierway, the big ugly brute hammered away with fast, heavy blows.

Kierway parried, the man on one side, the monster on the other, with speed and expertise Creed never before imagined. Still, Kierway was hobbled, blood dripping from his thigh onto the blood-sucking floor. *Wear him down!*

Bang! Bang! Bang!

Creed pounded at the underling's steel. Now, Kierway's chest began to heave, and sweat dripped from his nose.

Stab!

Kierway poked straight through the monster's belly and ripped it out.

The monster grinned.

"You're no man!" Kierway exclaimed, side stepping a heavy swing and chopping into its leg.

"Nay, underling. I'm a monster the likes you've never seen!"

It chopped high.

Creed sliced low.

Kierway howled, tumbling to the floor.

The Bloodhound swordsman felt his sword hit bone.

Kierway's sword clattered over the stones; with the other one, he still parried. In the next instant, Kierway stuck a small whistle in his mouth and blew.

Creed smacked the whistle from Kierway's lips with his blade.

Two more underlings emerged, but Tonio was already assaulting them.

"Time to finish this!"

"Hah, Human! You think you've defeated me. I still have one sword," Kierway said, rising.

"And a really bad limp." Creed huffed. He didn't have much left in him, if anything at all.

"Tell you what, Human. Let's settle this with a draw." Kierway lifted his eyes and made the motion to sheath his sword.

"You first." Creed panted, wiping the sweat from his brow.

Kierway slid his steel over his back and extended his hands. "Now you?"

Creed did the same, over his hip.

"First one out gets the first swing." A wicked smile formed on Kierway's lips.

Creed swallowed the little spit he had left. He'd never been beaten in a draw, but this underling was quick. At least it was an honorable way to go. At least he'd bought more time to live. *Come on, Creed! Think of all those years of training. All those Royals snubbing you. Fight or die.*

"On my wink, Underling."

"Perfect." Kierway casually dropped his hand over his head.

Creed took a half breath, cleared his mind and focused. *One. Two. Three.* He blinked one eye and drew.

Kierway's blade was already out.

Impossible!

CHAPTER
44

M ELEGAL INCHED HIS WAY OVER the floor towards the nearest
door in sight. *Look away! Look away!* So far, his plan seemed to
be working, either from his hat, or the confusion that was going on
around him. *Not my kind of party. Look Away! Look away!* He had to
go at least two dozen feet more, every movement in his joints stiff
and painful. Still, he was aware of everything.

Jarla cut an underling down with a stroke to its throat.

Lord Almen buried a nasty-looking dagger in the spine of
another.

Tonio and Creed battled the one called Kierway with flashes of
lightning and the resounding sound of steel meeting steel.

No, it wasn't his kind of party at all. *Vee! I need you. Come through
that door any second now.* Grumbling, he slid over the floor: one foot
closer, then two.

Down the stairs the underlings kept coming: one to a man, then
two.

All the while, the floor seemed to wriggle, draining the life of
the fallen, turning their bodies to husks.

They'll never make it out of this.

Everything was happening so fast, but he was moving so slow.
What did that Cleric do to me? He clutched at the Key inside his clothes
and touched something else. *What is that?* Curious, he produced the
black rectangular case he'd take from Lord Almen's study above.
Opening it, he found a wand-shaped rod made of dark wood with
ornate carvings.

Out of nowhere, Lord Almen came and snatched it from his hand.
"You just gave your worthless life a few more precious moments,

Detective. Enjoy them while they last." Lord Almen snapped his wrist. The rod flared with life, a glowing purple tendril of energy extending from it.

Melegal shielded his tired eyes.

WUHPAZZ!

Two underlings whirled on Lord Almen, ruby eyes wide.

"Taste this, underfiends!" Lord Almen stroked the mystic whip of energy.

WUHPAZZ!

It sheered the arm off one, shooting blood over the room.

WUHPAZZ!

It coiled around the other one's neck. Its skin sizzled. Its eyes rolled up under its head.

Lord Almen popped its head from its shoulders with a yank, and then methodically made his way around the chamber.

The underlings, even the armored ones, were cut up with the whip, like butter with a hot knife.

WUHPAZZ! WUHPAZZ! WUHPAZZ!

Melegal, keeping his eye on Almen, continued towards the door. *I'm going to steal that... again.* Less than ten feet away. *I'm going to make it out of this slat hole!* Five feet away.

WUHPAZZ! WUHPAZZ!

Good for you, Lord Arsehole! He reached inside his shirt and wrapped his hand around the Key. He was all alone. Out of the corner of his eye, he caught someone else.

A golden-eyed underling floated in. Surveying the room, it shook its head, sneered, and opened its mouth.

Melegal's hat pulsated on his head. *Move!* Mustering all the strength he had, he lunged for the door.

A single word burst forth from the golden-eyed underling, turning the chamber asunder.

A wave of energy slammed into Melegal, jarring every bone, every fiber. The Key fell from his grasp, but he didn't hear it land. All he wanted to do was cover his head. Instead, he collapsed, unable to move, hands twitching. He'd never felt anything so painful before. *Please don't do that again. Kill me first instead.*

In the center of the room, Lord Almen, Jarla, Creed and all the underlings aside from Kierway were sprawled out over the floor. Alive or dead, he did not know.

Tonio still stood, listlessly dragging a gore-dripping sword around the room.

Melegal's Key twinkled nearby.

He stretched out his fingers. *So close.*

Kierway stepped on his hand and picked up the Key.

Melegal's vision faded. The last thing he saw was Kierway's dripping blade.

Will death be as painful as life on Bish?

CHAPTER 45

"**I**'M HUNGRY." BRAK MOANED.

You aren't as hungry as me," Georgio shot back, pushing back his sweaty brown locks. "Nobody gets as hungry as me!"

"Am too, hungrier!"

"Please stop it! Both of you," Jubilee shouted from Quickster's saddle. "You two idiots ate all our food!"

Billip wanted to kill both the young men. They'd all departed the City of Bone in a rush, but were amply supplied, a couple of weeks' worth anyway. But three days into it, the food was almost gone, with maybe a day left, maybe two, and it was still at least another week to make the City of Three.

"I didn't eat it all; he did," Georgio said.

Brak, whose big feet shoved the dirt like a plow, chucked a rock at Georgio, smacking him hard in the back. "I'm going to cram the next one in your biscuit hole, so you'll be swallowing your teeth."

Good, Billip thought, stopping to look. *I hope they beat each other to death.*

Georgio picked up a rock as big as his hand and slung it back. "Eat this!"

Brak jerked his forearm up.

The rock skipped off his wrist and clocked him in the head, drawing blood.

Brak's eyes widened then buckled, his big face drawing up. "You're going to die for that!"

Georgio widened his arms and slapped his chest. "I'd like to see you try, you droopy face bastard!"

"You shut up, Georgio!" Jubilee shouted. "Go beat the crap out of him, Brak!"

Closing the distance in two long strides, Brak took the first swing.

Georgio raised his arms up, blocking the blow and laughing. "You're too slow for me, Goon. I'm going to pummel you — *oof!*"

Brak upper-cutted him in the belly, lifting him from his feet.

Billip winced.

Jubilee gasped.

Face reddened, Georgio scrambled to his feet and charged. Slamming into Brak, he lifted the bigger young man from his feet and drove him into the ground. Georgio's fists hammered into Brak, hitting ribs, face and gut. "You're gonna pay for that! I'm gonna beat you to death!"

Brak, the bigger and much older-looking of the two, had his hands full.

Georgio, a big young man himself, was the quicker of the two, sneaking in punches through Brak's blocking forearms.

Billip yawned. He'd seen old three legged dogs fight better.

"Get him, Brak!" Jubilee yelled, shadow boxing in the air. "Bust his jaw so he can't eat any more."

Over the dirt they tussled, kicking up dust, yelling and growling at eat other.

"I'm going to kill you!"

"I hate you!"

"You skinny ogre!"

"Potbellied urchin!"

Billip took a small sip from his canteen, which was getting light. They'd run out of water soon. The past day had worried him. Normally, hunting game of some sort, be it a pheasant or an Outland fox, wasn't much of a problem, but thanks to the mass exodus from the south, game was harder to come by. And Billip had led them on a more difficult path as well, fearing that other weary travelers would be after them or the meat of Quickster.

He shook his head.

Only days ago, he'd been dead set on staying in the City of Bone, helping Trinos to fight and battle the underlings. The next thing he knew, he was leading the young men and Jubilee north towards the City of Three. Did Melegal talk him into it, or was it something Trinos had done? *I'm going to get that thief one of these days.*

Turning his attention away from the mirages that littered the barren landscape in the distance and back to the boys, he shook his head.

Georgio had his meaty fingers around Brak's neck, and Brak had his around Georgio's.

"Stop them, Billip!" Jubilee said.

He waved her off.

Crack!

"Ow!" Brak exclaimed.

Crack!

"Ow!" Georgio moaned.

Nikkel stood over them, his father's club in his hand.

Both young men panted for breath. Brak wiped the dust and blood from his nose, and Georgio popped his dislocated finger back into place, grimacing.

Something tugged at Billip's heart as he saw Nikkel standing there with Mikkel's club in his hand. The strapping young man would be a spitting image of his father in a few more years.

Rubbing his head, Georgio said, "What did you do that for, Nikkel? I was winning."

"Were not," Brak said. "I'm so hungry."

"I'm hungrier," said Georgio.

Nikkel, who'd been glum and quiet ever since they left, showed the slightest smile.

"Well, Nikkel," Billip said, "You found something, didn't you?"

Nikkel shrugged his muscular shoulder. "I think so. Come on."

Following Nikkel and Billip, Georgio glanced over his shoulder from time to time. Jubilee sat on Quickster's back, frowning and holding her stomach. The girl looked like she hadn't eaten in days, and her hazel eyes were sagging. Beside her and Quickster, Brak walked in long slow strides, but he was able to keep up, eyes forward, chin up and casting a scowl at Georgio before looking away.

Georgio clenched his fingers in and out of a fist. Even though he healed quickly, they were still sore. Hitting Brak was like hitting rock. The man, or young man, whatever he was, was tough. Unnaturally so, but so was Georgio.

"What are you looking at?" Jubilee said. "You're fortunate, you know. Brak could have killed you. He was holding back."

Georgio turned and stopped.

"You want to walk or ride?"

"I'm a Royal, you should know," she said, folding her arms across her scrawny chest.

Georgio rolled his eyes. Jubilee had made it a point to mention that at least a dozen times since they left, and he was getting sick of it. And if she was a Royal, how'd she wind up with them? *Venir's right: all Royals are a pain in the arse.*

"Quickster is mine, little girl, and if you don't mind your mouth, I'll have him buck you from the saddle." He glared at her and put his fingers to his mouth, ready to whistle.

Jubilee looked away and mumbled something under her breath.

"What was that?"

She tightened the cloak around her body and said nothing.

He glared at Brak.

The big man stood at Jubilee's side like a watchdog.

"You three quit boogering around, else we'll leave you!" Billip said. "And don't tempt us! We'd all have been much better off if we left you to begin with!"

Georgio didn't even bother to run and catch up. He didn't have the energy, and it didn't seem that Jubilee or Brak did either. Instead, they followed the men up ahead, one ravenous step after the other under the blistering heat.

As for Brak, Georgio still hadn't sorted out all of his thoughts on him. He hadn't even seen the big man smile as of yet, and that disturbed him. Brak's face was familiar. Like Venir's but different. If it weren't for the man's blue eyes, he'd have little resemblance at all. Brak was quiet, whereas Venir was loud. It just didn't sit well. Other than that, when they weren't fighting over food, Brak was alright.

He put his canteen to his lips. Nothing came out. "Ah..."

And of all things, the two of them could only talk about food, and that's what got them in trouble to begin with. Staying on watch one night, while the others slept, they got caught up with themselves, talking about food and eating most of it the same night. When Billip woke them up the next day, he was furious. Not only had they fallen asleep, but almost all the rations were gone. It seemed one had been blaming the other ever since, and they were taking their guilt and hunger out on one another.

Ahead, Billip and Nikkel stood on top of a ridge, talking to each other and pointing downward. Georgio climbed the rocky hill and stood between them.

"What is it?" Georgio said, looking over the ridge.

A field of cacti lay below: some tall, others round, some three times bigger than a man.

Georgio held his rumbling stomach. "So, Nikkel found some cactus. I don't see how that's of much help to us. Maybe the round ones would help, but there's no way to get to them. What are we supposed to do, Nikkel? Feed on Cactus needles?"

Billip shot him a look. "There's game in those needles, Boy. All we have to do is roust it out."

"And how do you suppose we do that?" Jubilee said with a smug look on her face. "And what kind of game are we talking about?"

"Pheasant, antler rabbits, and foxes to start," Nikkel said. "Not to mention the water in the round husks."

"There's no way to get to them!" Georgio said. "It's impossible. Let's just keep moving north. All we've done now is waste time by moving east."

All of them were hungry and weary. Eyes were tired and full of grit. Their clothes and armor coated with Outland dust so thick you couldn't tell what color they were. They'd have been better off staying with the caravan, but Billip had talked them away from that. Now they stood, baking in the sun with nothing to eat or drink but sand and needles.

"Get your bows ready." Brak lowered himself over the ridge like a giant-sized sloth.

Jubilee jumped from her saddle. "Brak! What are you doing? Get back up here, Brak! Get back up here!"

"You fool, get up here!" Billip shouted. "We don't even have a plan yet! There're snakes down there, vipers and such. Step in a nest of those and you're in for! Slat, he's still going in."

Brak ambled down the incline another thirty feet before he stumbled and rolled into a wall of needles at the bottom. Groaning, he got up and started to growl.

"Hungry." He pulled Tonio's sword from its sheath. "Tired of being hungry."

Georgio looked at Jubilee and the others, swallowing. "What's wrong with him?"

There was a wild look to the man. An inferno erupting within. The man Georgio had wrestled with moments ago was gone, replaced by something else, something savage.

"Oooooh," Jubilee said. She took her place beside Billip. "I've seen this before."

In a clap of thunder, Brak turned from man to monster, hacking furiously through the impassable wall of needles.

"He's gone mad," Billip exclaimed, readying his bow.

"No, he's gone berserk!" Nikkel said.

"RAWR!"

Georgio hopped back. The maddened sound of Brak's voice rose the hair on his arms.

Brak hewed through the green cacti and needles like tall grass. A wild man.

"That fool's bound to get snake bit in there!" Billip said, drawing his bow string alongside his cheek. "Look!"

Three antlered rabbits, bigger than cats, darted across the valley of cacti.

Twang!

Clatch-Zip!

One rabbit tumbled into the dust with two holes in it.

"You got him!" Jubilee shouted.

"Nikkel, you shot mine!" Billip said. "You take the rear; I take the front." He nocked another arrow. "That's how Mikkel and I used to go."

Nikkel cranked back the line on his crossbow.

"Got it!"

A silence fell. They all watched the rustling of the towering cacti swaying back and forth, many falling down under the sub-human roars of Brak the Berserker.

"What kind of man fights cactus?" Nikkel exclaimed, eyeing Jubilee.

"A hungry one. A very hungry one."

"Georgio," Billip said, "Get down there and fetch that rabbit before a fox gets it."

"But..." He looked toward the path Brak had created. "What about—"

"Get your hungry arse down there! Run back up here if you're scared!"

A bloom of pheasant burst out of the cacti and into the air.

Clatch-zip!

"Hold your shot, Nikkel!" Billip said, "You have to wait till they clear the grove. Slat. Do I have to do it all myself?"

Twang!

Twang!

Two rock pheasants spiraled out of the sky, falling along the jagged rim.

"Get down there!" Billip ordered, nocking his bow and searching the grove.

"RAWR!"

Georgio's boots slid over the slope, over the loose rocks and dirt, until he hit bottom and fell on his back. "Blast it!" He plucked needles eight inches long from his arms.

A dozen feet away, the rabbit lay just outside the cacti, an arrow and bolt in its belly and thigh.

He glanced down the path that Brak had hewn down. Cacti lay fallen and torn, leaving an ugly path behind, but there was room, just very little. He plucked another needle from his thigh. *I must look like a porcupine by now.* He grimaced.

"Toss up the rabbit," Nikkel yelled, his black face glistening with sweat.

"I will!" Aggravated, Georgio snatched it up off the ground and slung it up the hill. "Happy now?"

Nikkel disappeared, but he could see Jubilee's eyes peeping down at him over the lip of the ridge.

"Go get Brak," she ordered.

Georgio yelled back up, "You go get him!"

"You're already down there, Stupid! Besides, you ate all the food too! So go fetch it!"

"Aw, I'm going!" He stomped off into the cacti.

She was right, but he wasn't very comfortable going after Brak, not after the last look he'd seen in the man's eyes. It wasn't human. It was something else. Something that rent flesh from bones with its teeth or bare hands. *He can't kill me. He can't kill me. Could he eat me?* He shook his head. *He would have to be hungrier than I am, to eat me.*

Tip-toeing his way down the path, he was twenty yards in before he heard Brak's mad snarling and mutterings again. It tickled his spine.

"Brak," he said, barely audible.

White-knuckled hand on hilt, he took a deep breath and forged ahead, painful needles biting into him time and time again. He could hear Billip calling out for him. *If they want me, they can come and find me themselves.*

"Blasted needles!" he cursed, wiping the sweat from his eyes. There was no avoiding them, no matter how much he tried, and they burned too.

Twenty feet deeper, he twisted and turned.

Ahead, a small clearing opened up, with Brak standing in the middle, plucking a yellow fruit from a plant Georgio had never seen before. Two at a time, Brak was stuffing them in his mouth, chomping and squirting the pulp down his chin and jaw. The man had more needles in him than Georgio could ever count. They were in his face, his arms, thighs... Tiny droplets of blood ran over his face and down his clothes. It was painful to look at. How Brak ate only fruit and no needles, he didn't know.

"Alright Brak, you win; you're hungrier than I am." Georgio sheathed his sword. "What kind of fruit is that anyway?" He got closer. "I've never seen it before. It might be poisonous, you know."

Turning, Brak snarled, raising his sword.

Georgio froze.

"Easy now! Go ahead, eat all you want. I can wait." Georgio plucked some small needles from his meaty forearms. "But save some for everyone else."

Brak kept eating, grunting and swinging his sword.

"That used to be my sword, you know. Venir gave it to me."

Brak didn't understand. His face was still sub-human, a wild animal ready to strike at any moment. Georgio didn't care. He was too hungry. Too tired. He sat down.

As ten more fruit disappeared down Brak's throat, the sword in his arm lowered, and the growling stopped. Stuffing another fruit in his mouth, Brak blinked at Georgio and held his hand out. "Hungry?"

Georgio nodded, extending his hand.

"Good," Brak said, tossing it over. A smile riddled in needles crossed his lips.

A long shadow rose up behind Brak. It was a snake. Big, thick and hooded. Eyes like emeralds and a red flicking tongue.

"Brak, look out!"

Brak turned, but too late. The snake sank its fangs into the back of the big man's shoulder.

Georgio jumped to his feet and ripped his sword out.

Two more snakes slithered from beneath the cacti, rearing up and blocking his path.

Georgio struck first, clipping one's pale yellow underbelly.

Something like a hot knife sank deep into his thigh, numbing his leg.

Instantly, the bright light of the suns swirled.

CHAPTER 46

T HE GIANT'S FEET MADE A cloud of dust with every step.
Listless and weary, robes dragging on the ground, Fogle
Boon followed Barton. His sunburnt face peered into the clouds.
Cass was gone again, and the suns of Bish had already set twice
since then. He was miserable. Sick.

"Hold up." He fell to his knees.

Barton stopped and turned, scratching his head. "What are you
stopping for, Wizard? We're almost there."

Fogle scanned the area. There was nothing aside from the bone
trees and tiny lizards that scurried across the ground. Still, he'd been
following Barton, wandering aimlessly, empty, with no idea where
they were going. He hadn't had any luck finding the remnants of
his ebony hawk, Inky. If he ever did, he could summon it again. He
wiped his cracked lips on his dusty sleeve and spat.

"Barton getting thirsty. Make water, Wizard. Make water now."
Opening a mouth that was big enough to swallow Fogle whole, the
giant stuck his enormous tongue out, pointing at it. "Dry. Need
water. Make water, Wizard."

He could make water, but he didn't want to. Instead, he wanted
to suffer. He deserved that much. *I failed, Cass. I deserve to die. Right
here. I'll just wither away into the rock and stone.* He pulled his knees
to his chest and dipped his head between them.

"Just go on without me, Barton."

"What?"

Shaking his head, he said it again, louder. "Just go on without
me!" He could hear Barton scratching his head.

Barton took a seat beside him. "Ah. Wizard still sad that Blackie take his woman?"

He felt a big hand patting his back. It knocked the breath from him. "Will you just go away!"

"Sheesh, Wizard getting grumpy. Make water, Wizard, so we can be happy. Barton is thirsty."

He looked up at Barton. The reddened dot inside the giant's disfigured eye stared back at him, unable to blink. The good eye shifted back and forth.

"Barton, what makes you think I can make water?"

"You're a Wizard. You can do anything, right?"

"No, if I could do anything, we wouldn't be lost out here. I'd have killed that dragon too. And Cass would be with me."

"Hmmm." Barton stretched out his arms. "But you can make water, can't you?"

No sense in him suffering. I guess I can make myself not drink it. And I only hope the spell works.

"Maybe." Fogle dusted off his hands and got back up. "But, I need to know something, Barton."

"What?"

"Do you think Cass is dead or alive?"

Barton shrugged.

Fogle felt his face redden. He'd been asking questions on and off, but the giant was reluctant to help with anything. All Barton wanted to do was find Venir and get his toys. And for some odd reason, the giant seemed to know where he was going, which left Fogle feeling more lost than he already was. *I wish Boon were here. He'd know something about that dragon. Why didn't that old fool come with us? Why!*

"Tell me something, Barton. Give me some hope at least." He kicked Barton in the toe.

"Ow!" Barton grabbed his toe and hopped up and down, big eye blinking. "What did you do that for?"

Fogle limped away, clutching his head. He wanted to pull his hair out. *What am I doing? Can I not outwit a giant now?* He looked up at the clouds. "Pull it together!"

Barton got up, looked up into the sky and said, "Pull what?"

"Tell you what, Barton: I'll make barrels of water, more than we could use in a month, but you have to help me find Cass."

"Blackie took her; she's gone."

"That's not going to get you any water, Barton. You'll have to do better than that."

Barton folded his arms over his chest. "Make the water first, Wizard."

The shadow the giant cast when he looked up at him gave Fogle little comfort. It made him feel insignificant. He had once been the cockiest mage in the City of Three, and now he was a rattled mess. It made him angry. He summoned his energy, filling his lungs with power.

"ANSWER ME, GIANT! OR DRINK YOU WILL NOT!"

Barton took a step back, covering his face. Peeking through his forearms, disfigured face bunched up, he said, "Yes! Yes! I will tell! I will tell!"

That felt good!

Fogle hadn't often used the Wizards Voice before, always feeling it was more show than effect.

I'm going to have to use that more often.

"OUT WITH IT!"

Barton's lips tightened.

"BARTON..."

"Ah, Blackie will take her to the giants' castle." He lowered his voice. "Or to his lair. Many bones there. Many bones of the dead."

The way Barton said it didn't seem genuine.

"ARE YOU LYING, GIANT? I DON'T LIKE LIARS!"

Barton covered his face again. "No bones! No bones! Just the castle. Blackie takes people to the castle, and they never leave there. Impossible."

"You will take me there then." The power in his voice was gone.

"No! Barton will not go back there. You'll go yourself. Now make my water. My throat hurts."

Fogle rubbed his throat. It felt like he'd swallowed a mouthful of dirt now. "Hold out your hands and make a cup," he managed in a dry voice.

Waving his hand over his water skin, he summoned the spell.

"Decanterous! Everless! Fill!" He tipped the water skin over. Clear liquid poured out like a rushing spring.

Barton sucked up a dozen handfuls, and Fogle, head riddled with guilt, thoughts only on Cass, drank until his throat no longer burned. He capped the water skin.

"Feel better now?"

"Much." Barton patted his stomach. It rumbled like a giant bullfrog. "Now make food."

Fogle laughed. "Water will have to do for now. Plenty of that. If you want food, you'll have to hunt it yourself."

"Alright." Barton wandered off.

"Barton!"

The giant didn't slow.

"Barton, where are you going?"

Barton stopped and turned. "To find the doggie and get my toys."

"What about Cass? You need to help me go and find Cass!"

"She isn't going anywhere. Barton not going back there, but you help Barton find the doggy and the toys, I'll take you there." His smile was wide and creepy. "I promise."

They walked, suns down to suns up, resting little in between.

Fogle, even with all the water, was exhausted, his legs shaking with every step. He'd given up on trying to convince Barton to go back. The little giant wouldn't listen. And Fogle didn't believe all of what Barton said about the castle and Cass being there and safe. He remembered those citrine eyes of the dragon. They had a murderous intent. *Is she dead?*

He stumbled and fell to his knees.

"Get up, Wizard."

Fogle didn't move. Instead, he lay staring into the sky, hoping to see a black dragon pass by. *I deserve to die here. Bake my flesh, Bish. I'll make a fine meal for the buzzards of this lousy world.*

Barton kept on walking.

CHAPTER 47

PAIN. IT WAS ALL THAT remained of Venir's life. His burning skin looked like raw meat on his back, and there was little left to be seen of his tattoo. Tuuth had whipped him until the rawhide was soaked with blood. Venir had fought the first few hours, making derogatory comments about the orc and his kind.

"That's a nice lash. Did you borrow it from your mother?"

Wupash!

"What's it like being an orc? Stinking and stupid all the time?"

Wupash!

"Is your arm getting tired yet? My back's just getting warmed up!"

Wupash!

"Bone! That's feels good!

Wupash!

"Say, Tuuth, don't they think you can do anything harder than this?"

Wupash!

"If I survive this, I'm going to skin your hide and make a whip out of you!"

Wupash!

It had gone on like that, back and forth, until Venir couldn't say a word, or remember his name. Unable to wake him after the first day, they had dragged him off to his cell, only to drag him back out again and hitch him to the post. That was three days ago.

Wupash!

He remembered watching the Royal Riders stripped of their armor, mutilated, tortured, buried and burning. He saw how the underlings celebrated their handiwork. They'd strolled inside the fort, arm in arm, mugs raised high and chanting strange sounds that would make hound dogs cry. It all made Venir sick. What he could remember of it.

Still, some men survived. Chained and cuffed from the neck to ankles, they served, performing one menial task after the other. Venir caught glimpses of it here and there, but his memories faded until he worked again to suffer another tortuous day.

Now, lying face down in the slime of his cell, he stirred. It was dark, but a pool of yellow light shone through the door. He tried to sit up. Something was on his back, picking at it.

"Wha—?" he mumbled, forcing himself up.

He heard a buzz.

A sharp stabbing pain shot through his back to his chest.

He slammed his mangled back into the moldy wall.

Something crunched and squished.

A sliver of fear raced through him. His blood coursed behind his ears. Something was feeding on him. Something had chewed up his legs, now it felt like bugs were making a nest in his back.

"Nnn—"

He slammed his back into the wall again. Bright spots of light burst in his eyes, leaving him woozy. He sagged down, slumping to the floor.

"Venir."

His eyes popped open, searching.

"Venir."

Somewhere, a tiny voice was speaking to him.

"Lie still, you idiot, and stop squishing the bugs. They're healing you."

"Slim?"

"Quiet."

He felt tiny insect legs crawling over his shoulder to his ear.

"Yes, it's Slim, and I'm getting you patched up... again."

Something crawled off his shoulder and stood before him. It was an insect, like a mantis, but mostly had Slim's face, except brownish green and bug-eyed.

"Uh..."

"Just be still, you big fool!" Slim put his insect arm to his face.

"This wouldn't be so bad if you weren't so stubborn. As soon as that white orc whips you, pretend to pass out. Stop running your mouth. Bish, you've got a lot of nerve calling him stupid and stubborn. You should be dead already, you fool, but I've been having the bugs patch you up. You heal fast. Very fast."

A bug the size of Venir's finger that looked like part cricket, part spider scurried up to Slim's mantis-like form. Its antenna twitched back and forth in short furious motions, then it scurried away.

"Listen, you big lout: you smash any more of them, they're leaving, so just lie there and be still. I can't keep you alive forever, you know."

"Water."

Motioning to a stone bowl that was tipped over, Slim shook his head. "You already drank it. You don't remember, do you?"

"Just get out of here, Slim. Escape, tell others. There's nothing more you can do here. If I die here, then I die here. Enough have died here already. You don't need to die too."

"That's a great idea, but the safest place right now is here, under the enemy's nose. I've been keeping a look out. More underlings have come since we rode in here, and they talk as if the City of Bone has fallen. They talk as if they've conquered the world, Venir." Slim blinked his glowing bug eyes. "I've seen it pretty bad on Bish before, but this? I've never seen it this bad, but something's got to happen. It just can't keep going like this. It can't."

Venir never figured Slim's age, but for all he knew, he was as old as Mood. As for the underlings, he'd never seen them with such an upper hand before either. Usually, he'd been able to face them with the mystic armament when things got bad, but now it was gone. Perhaps the underlings had it. *If I could wrap my paws around Brool's handle one last time! Bone!*

"Just do what you can and go, Slim. It's like you said, 'Bish Happens.'"

"I did say that, didn't I? Huh, that's a good one." He scurried over Venir's shoulder and spoke in his ear. "Now you just be still while I have the bugs stitch you up. And remember, keep your mouth closed tomorrow. You're better off dying digging holes than being whipped to death, I'd figure. Of course, I'm a lot smarter than you."

"Thanks, Slim—Yeouch!"

It felt like something crawled into his spine.

"Be still, I say! It's going to hurt, you know. Yesterday you slept right through it, leaving me wondering if you were getting better or worse."

"Worse." Venir bit his lip. Helpless, he lay there listening to Slim guiding the creatures all over his back. "Don't you have any of that blue ointment?"

"Heh, the underlings would sniff me out in a second if I used that. I've got it hidden. Besides, I'm saving the good stuff for me."

"Great…" Venir said just before dozing off.

Slim the Healer kept his astonishment to himself. Venir should have been dead. The man's back was a grotesque mat of blood and skin. The first time he saw it, he felt his own skin turn inside out. Yet somehow, Venir had prevailed.

The bugs scurried over Venir's back, attacking the puss that seeped through the pores. *If he gets the fever, he will be dead.* If he did, there was no way of helping the man, no way at all. Still, it was a mystery. What kept Venir together this long? One by one, the bugs pushed the flaps of skin back into place and sealed them up with a thick gummy spit.

"Aside from all the blood, you don't look half bad," he said, dusting his insect hands off. "I can even see the tattoo. 'V'. Hmmm, what did that drunken fool put it on there for? What was her name? Vorla? Ah, time to crawl back into my hole. Sleep well, Venir, and don't run your mouth tomorrow."

Venir snored.

"That might be a good thing."

On his six insect legs, he made his way from Venir's cell and followed the other bugs into a small hole they had bored into the interior of the fort's wall. Squeezing through the dark and narrow path, he popped into a hollowed-out room inside the massive log from the Great Forest of Bish, big enough for several men. Exhausted, he reverted back to his normal form and stretched out in the dim green light provided by the Elga Bugs from the glowing sacks on their bellies.

Resting the best he could, he couldn't help but worry—as he had on all the previous nights—that Venir would not return alive.

"How much will the underlings put up with, and how much more can he take?" Closing his eyes, he whisked his hand, and the Elga bug lights went dim.

If Venir's no longer The Darkslayer, then who is?

CHAPTER 48

CASTLE ALMEN WAS NO LONGER under siege. It was overtaken. Lord Almen sat on the marbled tile floor, arms shackled behind his back, and sighed. A corpse of one of his prized Shadow Sentries lay dead at his side, his mesh mask melted to his face. The rest of the room, his throne room, was in good order. But now, where there had been one high-backed chair of mahogany wood trimmed in the finest metal and jewels sat two. Both were empty at the moment.

His stomach rumbled as he shifted on the floor. He'd been fed, but very little, and he was stripped down to his shirt and trousers. All of his rings and baubles were gone. Closing his eyes and leaning back, the same thought raced through his mind.

How could I let this happen?

He rolled his shoulder and cracked his neck side to side. Something scurried out of the corner of the room. A spider, big as a dog and quick as a cat, on silent legs crawled over towards him. Another nearly his size dropped from the ceiling, jaws opening and closing. They were the underlings' watch dogs. Creepy things. Hairy black creatures with white stripes and venomous teeth that he'd seen suck the marrow from his own nephew's bones two days hence. The revolting sound still rang inside his head. The sucking. The screaming. The anguish. For the most part, Lord Almen delivered quick and silent deaths, but the underlings enjoyed the torment at another level. They delighted in the suffering of others.

He remained still, beads of sweat dripping from his nose onto the floor. A minute passed, then two before the spiders backed away and curled up out of sight.

How did I let this happen?

Until now, there had never been a day when Lord Almen hadn't felt in control, but other things had led to his fall. Melegal had undone him. Sefron had betrayed him. Most men dared not look him in the eye, nor did they have the courage to attack him. But Melegal had. As for Sefron, the man's own lust and fear of the underlings clearly led to his betrayal. However, Lord Almen could not imagine why Melegal had tried to kill him. He raced through that day. What had happened before Melegal stabbed him? Had Melegal done it on his own? Certainly he'd wanted to. Or had Leezir the Slerg pulled off a suggestion? *Hmmm…*

Lord Almen thought through it until his lids became heavy and he drifted into sleep.

Clap!

His head snapped up.

"Almen," a silver-eyed underling named Verbard said, "rise up."

He nodded.

The underling sat on one of the thrones, his golden-eyed brother, Catten, at his side. Between them stood another creature, a hulking black humanoid that reminded him of a panther. The underlings' eyes pierced him as he rose up to stand tall. With a single word, he felt one or the other could destroy him. He'd dealt with underlings before, but not like this. The cleric Oran had been formidable, but the might of these two? Another scale. No, these two had made his finest magi look like carnival enchanters: leaving one in a pile of ashes, the other with a gaping hole in his chest.

"The time has come to negotiate," Verbard said.

"With?" Almen replied.

Catten tapped his fingernails on the arm rest, a callous look on his face.

Verbard took a deep draw through his nose.

"Do you smell that, Almen? The delicious scent, so pungent, so sweet? A dead child? A dead wife, perhaps?" Verbard rubbed the rat-like fur under his chin.

It wasn't what Lord Almen smelled that bothered him so much as what he didn't smell. His castle had always been filled with fresh flowers and the burning of scented candles, oils and such. Now, the beauty of his Castle—that he and Lorda took so much pride in—was gone. The gardens trampled and smeared in blood. Many of his men buried in them. As for Lorda, he had no idea if she lived or was dead, but the Keep had fallen a day later, after the rest of the castle fell. He could only presume she was dead. It was the best way to avoid manipulation.

"I smell death. Decay. What else is there?"

"More, much, much more." Verbard floated off his chair and right past him. "Come. I'll show you."

Lord Almen glanced at Catten and the Vicious. The underling filled his goblet with a bottle of wine, and the Vicious fell a half-step behind him and shoved him forward. He limped but kept up as Verbard made his way through Castle Almen as if it were his. Underlings were posted throughout the castle, their countenances evil and alert.

Grimacing, he followed Verbard into the keep, taking the stairs that led onto the roof. He was panting when he reached the top, rubbing the bandage on his leg where he'd been stabbed at the battle in the chamber.

Verbard floated still higher in the air, robes billowing, turning towards him. *Can you see it? Can you smell it?*

He heard it in his mind.

He did see it and smell it. Black smoke was rolling up over the great wall of the City of Bone, not on the inside but on the outside. Eyes watering, he covered his nose.

Play along, Almen. Play along.

Walking across the top of the keep and stepping into a small tower that led to its highest point, he got his first glimpse over the wall in years.

Underlings. Legions of them.

They were everywhere. It wasn't just underlings either, but giant spiders and strange creatures he'd never seen before, tossing one dead human onto one flaming pyre after the other. His fingertips went numb.

He looked Lord Verbard in the eye. "Would you have me negotiate the terms of surrender for the City of Bone?"

"Serve us well, Lord Almen. You and a select few of your choosing can be our liaisons."

Lord Almen had made deals with the underlings before. He'd

supplied Oran with people for various poisons, potions and such. He'd even conspired with others to see the fall of Outpost Thirty-One. It had led to his rise from the 6th house in the City of Bone to the 3rd. But now, in hindsight, it seemed that move might also have led to this.

"I welcome the opportunity." He bowed. "How may I assist?"

"We just need to know which Castles need to fall first. You see, with the Keys, we can infiltrate any of them and slaughter them all. But 'Which falls first?' is the question."

Lord Almen wanted to laugh. *I can send the underlings to do my bidding for me! But to what end?*

"After that, you can negotiate with the weaker houses and on down. Once we control them, then we control everything."

"I see, Lord Verbard. And once they surrender, what are your plans for them? Slaughter? Slavery? A mass exodus into the Outland?"

"Those are excellent suggestions and most likely a great deal for them all, but you shouldn't worry about that. Not for your own sake."

Verbard pointed at Almen's chest and hissed.

"No, you should just worry about yourself."

CHAPTER 49

THE DUNGEONS BENEATH CASTLE ALMEN hadn't changed any over the past few months, but the guards had. Now, they were underlings. Wiry with gem-speckled eyes that didn't hesitate to punish if you so much as snored.

Melegal sat with his head between his bony knees, contemplating. Contemplating his next move. He'd been doing it for days, but he didn't have a next move.

Keys. Keys. The Keys. Wretched things got me into this mess. The wretched things could get me out.

Two underling guards in dark leather armor dragged a tall man in and shackled him inside an adjacent cell. Stripped down to his trousers, the man's chest was bruised and knotted with painful lumps.

Melegal could feel the man's green eyes on him, but he kept his head down.

The underlings didn't whip the quiet ones, but Creed, he couldn't help himself. You'd think someone of his ilk would know better.

"Ooof!"

An underling kicked Creed in the gut, locked the cell and walked away.

Don't speak. Don't speak. Don't speak.

Nearby were the rest of the survivors.

Jarla lay in her cell, facing the wall in the back. The Brigand Queen hadn't acknowledged any of them since they'd been there. Instead she, despite her condition, maintained her air of superiority somehow. Melegal wouldn't be surprised if she was there as more than a prisoner, but a spy. After all, she had assisted the underlings in getting into Outpost Thirty One.

What are you going to do, Rat? What?

Stripped down to his own trousers, Melegal might as well have been naked. His hat was gone. Worry gnawed at his stomach: that an underling had discovered its powers, powers that he himself had only recently begun to unlock. It had been long ago when he acquired it, and it had become a companion of sorts. He wasn't comfortable without it. Not at all.

Get the hat, get the Keys. Get the Keys, get the hat.

Hiding his yawn, he couldn't stop his stomach from rumbling.

One of the underling guards stepped over and banged on his cage.

He kept his head down, but was unable to contain the next loud sound his stomach made.

The ruby-eyed underling, brandishing a black club, opened the door to his cage, stepped inside, and cracked him in the head, drawing bright spots in his eyes. The underling drew back again.

Slat on this!

In a single motion, Melegal swept its legs out from under it, snatched its keys, scurried out, and slammed the door shut, locking the underling guard in his cell. He tossed the keys to Creed's outstretched arm.

Slice!

The jagged teeth of the other underling's sword ripped over his head.

Melegal leapt over a torment table, snapped up a spear from the wall, and braced himself. The creature, swift as a cat, batted the weapon away and lunged inside. Melegal twisted away, the underling's blade slicing the skin on his back.

What am I doing? What am I doing!

He knew he couldn't overpower the underling. They might be small and lithe, but their bodies were hardened like animals. He'd seen them rip overconfident men to pieces a time or two. The underling came at him, hard and fast. Melegal sidestepped again, pinned its sword arm on the table, and drove a long metal torture needle through its hand.

It screeched, ruby eyes widening, and then back-handed Melegal in the jaw.

His knees swayed.

The underling pounced on him. Its clawed fingers wrapped around his neck and dug into his skin.

Melegal's eyes bulged. *At least I killed Sefron. I'd kill him again if I could.*

Glitch!

The bloody tip of a sword burst through the underling's chest. It fell over dead.

Creed stood tall, eyes cold and dangerous.

"Now this is more like it. Just what I've been saying all along." He grabbed Melegal's arm and pulled him up like a doll. "What's the plan now?"

"Yes, what is the plan, Fool?" Jarla pressed her angry face against the bars. "To get us all killed?"

"'Die doing something, or die doing nothing.' That's how I saw it." Melegal hunched over, catching his breath. "And I don't recall making you part of any plan. Any of you, for that matter."

Creed gave him a look.

"No offense. I needed you to kill that underling, but I didn't figure it'd take you so long to operate a keyhole."

"Why you sneaky little scarecrow," Creed was smiling. "I like it. But, I took a moment to kill that other underling first." He pointed to Melegal's cell.

The other underling lay back against the wall, a large gash in his head.

"At that point, I wasn't certain I needed you either." He winked. "But you won't be going anywhere without me." He wagged the dripping sword in Melegal face. "At least not without my sword sticking through you."

"Hah, hah, hah." Jarla was still sneering. "You don't have any plan. Do you, Fool?"

Actually, I do. Just not a very good one.

Melegal had learned many secrets about Castle Almen in his stay here, many thanks to Sefron. He knew of the secret rooms and corridors, not all, but some. He figured that should be enough to save himself.

"No, no I don't, but right about now, you're in the cage, not me."

Creed grabbed his shoulder and squeezed it. "We'll need all the strong arms we have if we're to carve our way out of here."

"Let out! Let out!"

It was Tonio's voice, crying out from behind a wooden door with a closed-off portal.

Melegal hadn't forgotten about the man, but he wished he had. The deranged man rattled even the underlings, who seemed to avoid him.

"We're going to need that big fellow too, you know." Creed was making his way around the room, gathering up weapons. "I don't know what he is, but he swings a heavy piece of steel like a needle. Let the monster out." Creed gazed at Jarla up and down. "Perhaps this raven-headed princess can control him."

"You dare! You, a misfit from the Royal hounds of the sewers?"

Creed forced a laugh, shoulders dipping.

"You have the cell keys, Creed. Do what you want." Melegal made his way over to the iron door. It didn't appear to be locked. He pressed his ear against it.

"Let out!" *Wham!*

Melegal shook his head. So far as he could tell, the way past the iron door was clear, for now, but they needed to move fast.

Just lead them out, Melegal. Once they start swinging, you'll disappear and be fleeing. Heh. Heh. Crafty as a serpent, I am.

"Let the monster out then," he said, looking at Jarla, "and Tonio too."

I hope she dies first.

Sword ready, Creed unlocked Jarla's cage.

"Idiot." She made her way across the room and sorted through the weapons on the table.

Melegal kept his eyes on her.

Tall, dark and arrogant. A Queen of Brigands indeed. Other than those hips and legs of hers, I'll never understand what Venir saw in the evil hag.

"Your word: you won't be stabbing any of us in the back, Jarla."

Her smile looked as dangerous as a viper. "Unlike you? No, I'll not be giving you my word, you little ghoul of a man. As a matter of fact, I see no reason to follow you." She came closer, sword ready. "For all I know, you'll lead us into a trap."

Creed stepped between them. "The underlings are the enemy now, Jarla. Survive their invasion. We can settle our differences later. Now, I'll give my word. You give yours, Jarla, and Detective, yours as well."

Bang! "Let out! Give Word! Let out!"

"The word of a liar is as useless as the slat of pigs." Jarla stuffed a dagger in the waistband of what was left of her clothes. "All men are liars. All men are filth. But I'll give you both my word—and my word is 'Slat on you both.'"

Melegal huffed a laugh.

That's good enough for me." Creed eyed her up and down again. "And if we do indeed survive this, I'll like to share some drinks."

"Pig!" She slung a pair of shackles at Creed.

He caught them against his chest and winked. "Just lighting a fire in you, Man-hater. Now, let's get on with this." He tossed the cuffs to the ground. "You've got some ornery ideas for such a fine woman."

Jarla's face reddened. "I'll clip your—"

"That's enough!" Melegal stepped around Jarla and strapped on a sword. "Creed, get the door."

Creed unlocked Tonio's door.

The tall half-dead man stepped outside, morbid and scary, rubbing the hole in his head.

Melegal's spine tingled.

Hate that man.

Even Jarla's breath hastened.

Creed's eyes were wary. "Grab some metal, Tonio. Detective, lead the way."

Swinging the dungeon door inward, Melegal felt something crawling in his stomach.

Why haven't they killed us already? What do they need with us, anyway?

He remembered what he'd seen and what he'd been told. The underlings would mutilate some and send them out to spread fear in the world.

Shouldn't we be dead or crippled?

Up the stairs he went, followed by Jarla, Creed and Tonio's heavy steps.

He'll get us all caught.

The dungeons beneath Castle Almen weren't deep, but more or less a sublevel of the basement with a lone entrance at the top. In this case, Melegal knew where he was, but there were places in the Castle he'd never explored. A lone door awaited them at the top. He knew it led into one of the main basement corridors. It was perfect. All they needed to do was overpower any guards, and Melegal knew a few secret corridors with hiding spots down there.

Alright, Rat. They fight. You run.

Running his fingers through his salt and pepper hair, he felt naked without his hat.

Forget it. Just run, Rat. Run!

He mouthed the next words to his followers.

"Ready?"

Creed nodded.

"One."

"Two."

He grabbed the door handle.

"Threeeeeeeeeeee...."

The door transformed into a black mirage and enveloped them.

Suddenly, Melegal was free falling.

Creed was yelling.

Jarla was screaming.

In the next instant, he felt himself land hard on the ground. Spitting the dirt from his mouth, he sat up only to face the heads of many spears lowered in his face.

I know this place. All too well.

They were inside Castle Almen's arena.

"What kind of bloody magic was tha—ulp!"

Creed bit his tongue thanks to the barbed spear at his throat.

"Well, finally, some new opponents come." It was Master Kierway. "And just when I was beginning to wonder whether or not you would show."

Kierway wasn't alone. He was accompanied by several underlings, warriors one and all, being served by men and women, barely clothed, and shackled at the neck. One was kneeling by his side, holding up a plate of fruit. It was Lorda.

"Ah," Kierway rose up, "these will be much better opponents

for my Juegen to spar with. The others," he gestured toward the wall of the arena, "didn't last so long."

At least a dozen human heads on spikes encircled the inner wall.

So this is what they were saving us for. Games. Underling games.

Melegal's head felt heavy, and he couldn't stop his chin from dipping. His stomach rumbled. All he could think about was Brak here in the arena. His wailing. His moaning.

How in Bish did I get here?

It was pretty clear that nothing was going to save him now. Not Brak, not Venir and not himself. All those years he fought to escape the horrors of the Castle, and he still wound up here. He locked his eyes on Lorda. She was still captivating despite the scrapes and bruises on her face, and he'd never seen her voluptuous body in such revealing clothing before.

"Who's that?" Creed whispered in his ear.

An underling jabbed the butt of a spear in the back of the Bloodhound's head.

"I hope they let me fight you first," Creed said, "Black fiend!"

Whack!

Creed hit the ground.

"Secure them all, except the skinny one," Kierway ordered, copper eyes on Melegal. "We'll whittle what little is left of him down first."

Melegal raised his brows and allowed himself a smile.

Lorda showed a grim smile back.

Well, it's over. Nothing like a little flirting before you're dead.

CHAPTER 50

"W**ATCHA LAYIN' THERE FER?**" A gruff voice said. "That ain't what I had in mind when I taught you about adventurin'."

Fogle didn't move. He couldn't. Instead, he lay in the sun, baking like a biscuit in a roasting oven. Still, he forced his eyes open, trying to blink the hallucination away from his mind, his thoughts.

"Go away, Mood. I'm done for," he said with a dry throat.

"What's the matter? Did ye lose your little druid friend? And now yer tender heart is broken, so you quit? This is Bish. You quit, you die. Now get up!"

Fogle didn't. Instead, he closed his eyes, but the scent of Mood's cigar drifted into his nose.

This is one powerful hallucination.

For hours, maybe days, he'd lain there, letting his inner self fight it out. He'd failed. He wanted to go home. Crawl under a rock and bury himself.

He'd been here before. Back when Venir beat him. Busted his mind and his nose. A broken man, he'd left the Magi Roost. It had taken him years to understand his failures. His fears.

Now, those fears returned with a vengeance. The Outlands. The sweltering heat, the chronic battle to survive, and the threat of the unknown had rattled his brilliant mind.

I can't do this anymore. I can't.

"Just leave me alone," he said, rolling over.

"Get up, Wizard!" the gruff voice prodded. "Get up, else I'll kill you myself."

He curled up, covering his face.

"Go ahead," Fogle said. "If my hallucination doesn't kill me, I'm sure something else will. Perhaps a giant will step on me, or some bugs will eat my flesh," he cackled, "or a dragon will roast me like a log." He cackled again. "Or the underlings will cut my throat. So many ways to go. Getting killed by my imagination seems more soothing than the rest. So Mood, my long gone friend, I'm prepared for the worst."

A silence fell. Even the hot winds slowed. The scent of Mood's cigar drifted to his nose again. Fogle sighed. "That's much better." He curled up and pulled his robes tighter. "Sorry, Cass. I failed you."

A minute passed, maybe two.

"GET UP, I TELL YA!"

Fogle's eyes popped open. In the next moment, water was pouring over his head. Down it came, second after second, soaking his hair, his robes.

"GET UP!"

Spluttering a mouthful from his lips, he forced himself to an upright position. Water was still being poured over his head by the figure of a large stout man. When the water finally stopped, he wiped his eyes.

Two emerald eyes under bushy red brows were staring right at him.

"Mood? Are you real?"

"As real as a mole on an ogre's fanny." Mood puffed on a cigar stuck between his two meaty fingers. "Are you finished belly aching now?"

Fogle stretched out his arms and hugged him.

"But how? You were, well, in such bad shape." He patted the rocky muscles in Mood's thick shoulders.

"True, but I was still breathing. And I'm King of the Dwarves. Soon as I fell, the lady dwarves came running. They patched me up leagues away, where Eethum caught up with me."

That's when Fogle noticed Eethum, the big black dwarf, arms crossed over his long blood red beard, standing like a mighty oak. He wasn't alone either. More Black Beards, each just under five feet tall, but stout as keg barrels, sat on the back of dwarven horses.

Fogle couldn't hold his tongue from catching Mood and Eethum up on everything that had gone on.

"A dragon, ye say? Woot! It's been a long time since I've seen one of those," Mood said, taking a knee, wincing.

"Mood, you aren't fully well, are you?"

The ancient dwarf shot him a look. "Ye need to mind what you say, Wizard." He grabbed Fogle by the forearm and squeezed. "I'm well enough to snap you in two."

Biting his lip, Fogle tried to pull away. "No need to be so cranky. I was just concerned."

Mood squeezed harder. "You were what?"

The fingers on his hand went numb. "Nothing! Nothing!"

Mood released him and blew a puff of smoke in his face.

"Mind yer manners." Mood reached into a pouch on his trousers and tossed him something in a cloth.

Fogle unfolded it and found the remnants of Inky.

"Thanks," he said, fanning the smoke. "How'd you find me?"

Mood rolled his thick neck towards Eethum, who said, "We're Blood Rangers. Once we got yer scent, we could track you anywhere, but we did lose you for a bit." He glanced at Mood.

"I hate to admit. You disappeared into thin air."

Fogle knew what he was talking about. It was the spell Boon had cast that got them out of the jam when they fled a wave of underlings.

"Still, why can't you follow Chongo?"

"He doesn't have a scent."

Fogle raised an eyebrow. "I guess not."

Mood handed him his water skin. "Yer gonna need this. We've a ways to go." He grunted as he swung his leg up on his horse. "Get on."

Mood looked like a giant atop his dwarven Clydesdale, large axes strapped across his back.

"Where are we going? What about Cass?"

"We're going after that giant," Mood said, "Find him, most likely we'll find her. Now get on. Time's a wasting, and I suggest you find ye some good spells."

"Why's that?" Fogle said, getting on.

"'Member them giants that socked it to me?"

"Yes," Fogle said, looking over his shoulder as the horse lurched forward.

"Well, they ain't done. YAH!"

As the first dusk settled, Fogle got his first glimpse of green tree tops in the distance, but it brought him little relief. When he wasn't focusing on his spells, he was thinking about Cass and those piercing eyes of the Dragon that Barton called Blackie.

I'll get you back, Cass. I swear it. Even if I have to find a way to the Under-Bish all by myself.

Eethum led the way, followed by the Black Beards, then Mood and himself. The King of the Blood Rangers had little to say, however, unlike before. He seemed grim and angry for some reason. Fogle was about to ask him if something else was wrong when Eethum brought them to a halt less than a mile from the lush branches of the jungle.

Mood rode forward.

"You want two ranks or one?" Eethum asked, bushy red brows raising up and down.

"Two. But no more than thirty yards between us. It's as thick as my beard in there."

"Well, I'm certain the giant left a noticeable trail," Fogle said, dropping from the saddle and stretching his limbs.

Mood huffed.

"Wouldn't he?" Fogle said, gulping down some water, looking around. None of the dwarves had taken a single drink, now that he noticed, and now that he'd gotten used to it, he'd been sipping every hour. He held it out to Eethum. "Drink?"

The dwarf showed his teeth and shook his head.

"Trusting the giants are ye now, Little Wizard?"

"Well, no, just following him. But he's helped me, and I've helped him. I see no harm in it." He plugged his ever-flowing water skin. "Besides, he seems to know where Venir or Chongo is. Where else would he be going?"

Mood and Eethum just looked at him.

Fogle shrugged. "What? I'm not a dwarf, you know."

"A good thing fer us you ain't, Wizard. Now hush your mouth and get back on. We've got a ways to go."

Fogle pulled at his sweat-soaked robes. Hoping for relief in the shade of the jungle, as opposed to the dry Outland heat, he instead found himself overwhelmed by the chronic dampness of the humidity.

"Like walking through water," he muttered.

"Aye," Mood agreed, "but don't worry: you'll never get used to it."

They'd traveled through night, the jungle as black as a cave, before the dawn of a new light. Fogle found little comfort in it, swatting at mosquitos as big as his hand and smashing them on Mood's back.

"Ye want something?"

"Uh…" Fogle wiped his hand on his robes. "No… But, shouldn't we have caught up with Barton by now?"

"Barton? Is that what ye call yer friend?"

"Never mind."

Mood had been plenty clear on his hatred for the giants. He'd even shared a horrible tale of another one called Horace. The insane giant had slaughtered more than a hundred dwarves. Some of Mood's sires. One of his wives. But, how Mood captured the giant, tethered and killed him was another thing. It seemed the giants had a mystic way to come and go as they pleased. Fogle was curious about that.

"Look." Mood pointed his sausage-thick finger toward an opening in the trees.

Squinting, Fogle shook his head. "What?"

"Not thata way." Mood grabbed Fogle's chin and turned his head. "Thata way."

A stark log-made structure like a giant's home sat atop a mountainous hill.

"What is that?"

"Men call it Outpost Thirty-One or somethin'."

"Are you serious?" Fogle knew the history of the fallen outpost that gave the underlings the upper hand in the southern lands. 'Nothing on Bish has been the same since the fall of Outpost Thirty One,' the travelers from the south said.

It was rumored that whoever controlled Outpost Thirty-One controlled the South and would gain a foothold on the North. Now, it sat there alone, abandoned so far as he could tell. The logs that made up its framework were five times as thick as the surrounding forest trees. That was the other odd thing. The fort, a safe-haven for men, had been built by giants, they said. It reminded him of the City of Three, where a few structures still stood that marveled the others in size.

"Mood, you're a giant dwarf. Who built that? The giants?"

"It don't matter who built it. It only matters who's in it."

"Then who's in it?"

Mood shook his bushy bearded head and snorted the air.

"Well, I'll be slat on a stick. I think Venir is in there."

"Alive?"

"Don't know, but there's only one way to find out." Mood dug his boots into his horse and lead the Black Beards towards the mountain.

"I thought the fort was run by an army of underlings."

"So?"

"Well, there's only fifteen of us. Can I assume the King of the Dwarves has a plan?"

"I'll let ye know before we get there. It's still a bit of a ride ahead."

"That's not a plan."

"It's better than whatever you got."

CHAPTER 51

"ORDER UP! ORDER UP! ORDER up!" Darlene clamored. "Move your boots, ladies! There's hungry fellows out there!"

"I heard you, Darlene!" Mercy said, grabbing a tray of food from the kitchen and rushing it over to a loud and eager table.

Kam had been rubbing the black polish on the bar for over an hour, trying to ignore the rough cut woman. Now, her elbow was sore, and her cheeks burned.

I'm going to kill her!

Over the past few days, the Magi Roost had been turned upside down and inside out. No longer the quaint establishment it once was, it was now a seedy den for travelers from all over the land. It hadn't ever been this bad before, not even when Venir was here. Not by a long shot. And all of Kam's patrons, many of whom she adored, were gone, replaced by anything from an orc to a halfling. The City of Three had become a harbor for Southern refugees, and it was a problem.

"I hope you aren't planning on going through with that."

Taking the dust rag off the stump of her hand and slinging it over her back, she turned and faced Scorch. The man's comely looks were startling. He'd been sitting in the same spot at the end of the bar for days. He never left, and she couldn't get used to it. But, she'd gotten used to it enough.

Eyeing her hand in the pickle jar and blowing her red locks from her face, she said, "And if I am? Are you going to cut off my other hand?"

"Certainly not. It was Darlene who did that, not I. But Kam, I must warn you: I'm not comfortable with murderous thoughts."

He refilled his goblet. "I want this to be a happy place. A place of celebration. A place of fun."

She could feel her missing fist clenching. Through gritted teeth, she said, "A place I cannot flee, because you will not permit me to. No, Scorch. If you want this place to celebrate — then leave!"

His blond brows creased a little.

She felt her breath thinning.

"Kam!" Darlene said. "We're shorthanded. Get over to that table of half-orcs. I like those guys. They tell the filthiest jokes. Here," she held a pitcher out, "they need replenished!"

Cheeks flushed, Kam shot her a dangerous look. "You do it!"

Go! Scorch's voice rattled her head.

More on his will than her own, she grabbed the pitcher of ale and started over.

"And show more cleavage," Darlene shouted after her, "they'll pay extra for that. And hide that stump of yours. I don't want the patrons uncomfortable."

CHAPTER 52

"How's he doing?" Billip asked.

Shaking his head, Nikkel wiped the sweat from Brak's head with his sleeve.

"He's still burning up. I could fry an egg on his big head."

Brak lay still, his big swollen face creased in a frown. His back was red and purple where the snake had bitten him, leaving the man bloated.

Georgio groaned on Quickster's saddle. He was swollen a little himself, and his stomach still hurt. He didn't remember anything after the snakes struck. Instead, he'd awoken on a stretcher of sorts, being dragged by Quickster. That was two days ago. All he could figure was his body's special gift for healing itself had saved him. But Brak, he wasn't so sure about.

"He's still chewing," Nikkel said, widening his blue eyes. "I've never seen a man who could eat in his sleep before." He shrugged. "At least he isn't dead. But it doesn't look like he's going to get up for a while."

Brak's body convulsed, and thick saliva dripped out of his mouth.

"Yech," Nikkel said, tossing Jubilee a rag. "You can wipe that up; he's your friend."

Jubilee lifted her chin up and strutted over to Brak. "I'd be happy to."

Georgio felt miserable. Part poison, part other things. Brak hadn't done anything wrong aside from being hungry, and in all truth, it had been Brak's berserker's fit that saved them, all of them. The man-boy had scared up plenty of food, and Brak's clearing in the cactus pit had revealed many round cacti filled with water. He had filled them all up, but Georgio didn't feel like eating any more.

He pulled at the locks of his curly hair. *It's not my fault.*

"This is all your fault, you know," Jubilee said at him. "If you hadn't gotten him all riled up, he wouldn't have gone berserk, Fatboy Idiot!"

"That's enough, Jubilee!" Billip intervened. "It's not anyone's fault. Things like this happen in the Outlands. You *children* just aren't used to it."

"But—"

"But!" Billip turned on Jubilee, nostrils flaring, knuckles cracking, "I'll tell you about *butt*, Little Girl. I'm going to bust yours from two halves to ten if you don't close that big mouth of yours."

She folded her arms across her chest and stuck her tongue out. "No one's ever whipped me, and no one ever will."

"Don't tempt me," Billip said, taking out an arrow and smacking it into his palm.

"You'd enjoy that, wouldn't you, Rogue?"

He smacked it into his hand with a loud whap. "I certainly would."

"Pervert."

Georgio thought Billip's face was going to crack.

But Nikkel, calm as well water, stepped between them. "Let's not kill each other. Because if we do, who'll take care of Brak?" His smile, which hadn't been seen in days, was beginning to show more.

"Quickster, I guess," Georgio said, starting to chuckle.

"Well, I hope Quickster doesn't understand what she's saying," Billip added, "else he'd kick her in the teeth."

The men started laughing.

"I wish I'd thought of that," Nikkel said, smiling. "Let's give her some rawhide to chew on. That might keep her quiet."

"Stop laughing at me!" Jubilee whined.

They ignored her.

"Stop it, I said! Stop it!"

Georgio felt a little better, and it was good to see Nikkel smile again. He looked even more like his father when he did that. He even noticed a little moisture in Billip's eye.

"How much longer, Billip?" Georgio asked. "This is taking twice as long as it did when we came down here. We aren't lost, are we?"

"No. But we've got a ways yet. I'm certain we'll make it, but I don't' know about Brak. I'm afraid if we can't get him some healing soon... Just keep feeding him bits of the green snake meat."

Everyone looked at Brak again. It was a sad sight. Somehow, he'd managed to save them, but they had no way of saving him.

Georgio fought back the tears in his eyes. He missed Venir. He missed Mikkel and even Lefty. He pinched the tear ducts in his eyes.

"You alright?" Nikkel asked, patting his shoulder.

Georgio pushed his hand away. "It's just dust in my eyes."

"Sure, Georgio, sure. I got some of that too."

CHAPTER 53

"KEEP MOVING," TUUTH SAID.
Wupash!

It was early. The suns hadn't crested the fort's high walls yet, but all Venir could think about was the long day ahead. Everything but his fingernails ached. Every step was full of lead, and his back felt like it was on fire all the time. It was misery, but knee deep in an underling slat hole, he kept shoveling muck from one pit to the other.

"Smells good, doesn't it, Stranger?"

Venir kept his head down. His mouth shut. Tuuth had been taunting him day and night, but he wouldn't take the bait. He had to hold out. He dipped his shovel in the muck and slung it over his sagging shoulders.

"You don't look well, but you haven't died." Tuuth spat a snot ball in the muck. "Even the underlings are talking about it. Funny thing, Stranger, the underlings aren't so different than men. Believe it or not, they're betting on you. How much longer you'll live." He spat again. "I'll tell you this much: I lost my wager days ago. So I don't have any motivation to see you live any longer, so die already, will you?"

Tuuth spat again and took a long drink from his flask before he continued.

"One of my comrades, Flaggon, will win if you don't make it through the night. That's a nice bit of script he'd get with the underlings, and he promised the rest of us enough wine to drink all night." He stuffed a large wad of tobacco in his mouth. "So plan on a few whippings and more digging. They won't be stopping at all today unless your heart gives."

It didn't even stir him. He dug. Busted wrists and all. His once taut muscles now sagging on his arms. The thought of men consorting with underlings had infuriated him once, but now it didn't seem to matter. Now, the only thing that mattered was digging from one day to the other.

"Huh," Tuuth said, walking away, "I think I liked you better when you talked more."

Venir kept shoveling, glancing around from time to time.

Watch. Listen. Learn.

The remnants of the Brigand Army and the renegades from other orders were fewer than one hundred, including Flaggon and Tuuth. But the underlings were a different story. Venir had never seen so many different colored eyes before. He hadn't realized there were so many underlings in the world. He'd managed to count over a thousand of them one day, but the next day when he woke there'd been almost two thousand. They weren't all coming in through the gates either. Instead, squads of them came from inside the Outpost walls, out of a building that was once the Royal Headquarters.

And Venir knew there was no way that building could hold them all. Dread filled him.

Have they taken over the entire world?

Digging, he tried to make sense of what was happening, but he could barely think.

Brool.

His war-axe entered his mind. It seemed his days of devastation were over. What a fool he'd been, to remove the armament and leave it behind. And for what? His pride!

Am I a fool?

He couldn't shake the feeling he'd seen Brool and the rest of the armament for the last time. He'd do anything to be reunited with it again.

Curse me for a buffoon.

He slung more muck over his shoulder. One shovelful. Two. Fifty. A hundred. Two hundred.

Steam rose from the muck. The big flies and mosquitos swarmed.

A tall man walked over with a jug of water. It was Flaggon.

"You seem to attract the rottenest things." He fanned the bugs away. "Here, drink."

Venir took a swallow and made an ugly face.

"What did you put in that?" Venir tried to hand it back.

"Keep drinking, Stranger, and make it quick. That's vinegar added to it. You need it."

Venir eyed him.

"I thought you'd win the bet if I died today."

"Ah." Flaggon's brows lifted. "Tuuth told you about that, did he? Well, the truth is, Tuuth doesn't know what's going on. I already have plenty of wine, and there's no such thing as money here. We barter a little with the underlings." He winked. "But Tuuth's not very good at bartering. Besides, now that you've survived this long, I hate to see you die. Ye've defied the odds, ya have." He scratched his head. "And something's to be said for that."

Venir took another drink, finishing it off, and tossed Flaggon the canteen.

"How long do you think they'll keep you around?"

Flaggon shrugged. "I don't have any choice in the matter. No more than you. But I'll tell you this: the underlings are running the show on Bish now. They aren't going to kill everyone, but they will be killing everyone who opposes them. And I figure I'm better off with 'em than against 'em."

Venir scowled. "You make me sick."

"Ha!" Walking away, Flaggon waved at him. "I see they haven't broken your spirit yet, Stranger. See you tomorrow. Dead or alive. I've a bottle of underling port to crack."

Digging and simmering, Venir filled the other hole, crawled over the ridge between the pits, and stepped in it. Rolling his shoulder, he realized no one, not man or underling, even noticed. Instead, they all went about their business. A digging corpse, he was already forgotten.

They were Chittering back and forth with one another, even smiling, some of them.

Could it be true? Had the underlings taken over? He even saw one playing an instrument, similar to a lute. But the thing that disturbed him most was—he was getting used to it. Their smell. Their gray faces and their faint fur-like pelts.

Another hour passed, then two.

"Dig, Arsehole Bastard. Dig!"

It was the underling commander.

Venir ventured a look at him.

His bulging arms were crossed over his barrel chest. A razor-edged sword hung by his side.

"On your knees, Arsehole Bastard," the underling said. "You are now a servant of the underlings."

It felt like all the eyes of the fort were on him. Those of both underling and man. Dying of thirst, tongue swollen, Venir kept shoveling.

"Orc," the commander said, "is this man deaf? I told him to bow, not to shovel. Make him bow, Orc. Make him bow!"

"On your knees, Stranger," Tuuth said.

Venir kept shoveling.

"He looks like he can't hear." The commander slid a sharp dagger from his belt. "So he doesn't need those ears." He extended it towards Tuuth.

Hesitating, Tuuth said, "You want me to cut them off?"

"No, I want you to carve him a new arsehole, Stupid Orc."

Tuuth snatched the blade. "Fine then. Stranger, get out of that puddle."

"No!" The underling pointed. "You get in the puddle, Orc. What's the difference? You always smell like dung."

The surrounding underlings chittered in agreement.

"Last chance to bow down, Stranger," Tuuth warned, an angry look growing in his eyes. "If I step in the mire, I'm going to do more than cut your ears off. I'll cut your tongue out as well."

Venir glared at them. "What are you waiting for?" He slung a shovel full of muck on the both of them.

Ruby eyes flashing, the underling let out a hiss.

Tuuth roared, jumping in, splashing muck all over.

"You couldn't keep your mouth shut, could you?"

Crack!

Venir's head rocked back, falling into the sludge.

The underlings and men let out cheers.

"That'll shut him up, Tuuth!"

"Bust him again, good!"

"Make him eat that slat he's diggin'!"

Even the underlings chittered words of encouragement.

"He'll not talk after that punch!"

His legs felt like anvils, his arms like sandbags, but Venir got up and raised his hands on his busted wrists, squeezing them into fists. Dripping in muck, he eyed Tuuth.

"Fight or die."

Tuuth walloped him in the belly.

He sagged to his knees.

"He's bowing now, ain't he!" a brigand said.

Venir rose again.

"Cut his ears off, Orc!" The underling commander said as two other underlings wiped the muck from his armor. "I want them for a necklace. I might have you add some fingers and toes as well." He spat and wiped his mouth. "I want the tongue too."

Tuuth grabbed Venir by the hair, yanked him up to his feet, and put him in a head lock.

Struggling, Venir's face was beet red, but a ten-year-old boy would have fared better. His strength, what little he had left, was not enough.

Venir grinded his teeth and tried to pulled away.

"You!" Tuuth ordered to one of the brigands. "Get in here and grab his feet."

"Slat on me," the heavyset man said, stepping in and rolling up his sleeves. "Just make it quick, will you? It smells worse than an ogre's outhouse."

"Try not to scream, Stranger," Tuuth growled in his ear.

Slice!

His ear dropped into the muck.

"Did you hear that, Arsehole Bastard?" the underling commander said.

Every eye from the underling camp was watching now. From the towers, the catwalks, sitting on the parapets. If you were within eye shot, you could see.

Fight, blast you! Fight!

Venir's struggles were in vain.

Slice!

His last ear fell in front of his eyes, floating atop the grime.

"Good, Orc, good," the underling rubbed his chin. "And I like your idea. Cut his tongue out as well. No more talk, Human. Instead, you will scream so we can't hear."

"You two, get in here," Tuuth ordered.

One man rolled his eyes; the other one groaned.

"Get in there, idiots," Flaggon said, shoving them forward.

They sloshed through the muck, one holding his nose.

"Get his arms," Tuuth said, and then looked down on Venir. "Any last words, Stranger?"

"You're all orc, Tuuth. And it smelled better before you got here."

Ptui!

A gob of spit hit Tuuth square in the eye.

Tuuth rose his dagger high.

"Just the tongue Orc! Do not kill him!"

THROOM!

Everyone in the fort flinched, eyes searching the southern gate.

THROOM!

All the men murmured.

The underlings chittered, scrambling to their stations.

The wooden portcullis cracked and buckled.

THROOM!

The alarm was sounded, high pitched.

"Move it, men," Flaggon ordered. "Tuuth, leave him. He's not going anywhere."

"Not until I have his tongue first." He rested the knife on Venir's chin. "Hold him."

CHAPTER 54

S HACKLED TO A STAKE WITH mystic purple bands, gagged, arms behind his back, Boon sighed.

The fight is over.

All his life he'd been in control. Dominant. A powerful force. Even when the giants had custody of him, as powerful as they were, he'd had a say in his destiny. But now, his say had run out.

Surrounding him, in an underling camp in the Outland, were more of the fiends than he cared to count. Thousands, and they were still arriving. He'd never seen such a large force. He hadn't even imagined one so large.

Nearby, a brood of underling magi watched over him. Their light blue and green eyes in study.

He wondered why they kept him alive.

"Water," he said, licking his lips.

They said nothing to him, chittering to themselves from time to time and inspecting his robes. The only stitch he had left on him was a pair of cut-off trousers. Even his sandals were gone. The suns gave a nice red layer to his back.

He tried to stand, but his knees wouldn't bend.

He never thought he'd ever ask an underling for anything, but he asked again, "Water."

Nothing. But it would come. It had come yesterday and the day before. A humpback urchling had fed him some food that was horrible but digestible. And so it had been. Day in. Day out. Hour after hour.

"I always imagined I'd die battling you fiends. Never a prisoner.

Now look at me. An underling's beggar." Again he sighed. "I can't even insult you."

After dozing off, for how long he didn't know, he was rustled. Two underling warriors picked him up, leading him on trembling legs through the camp. The black grey smoke burned his eyes. He closed them until they stopped. An underling chittered at him with an angry tone. He knew what it meant.

Open your eyes, Human.

He knew what to expect. He didn't mean to open them, but he did.

They led him to the edge of camp, where a graveyard of the living and the dead waited.

Trains of people—men, women and children—fell under the lash and spade. They screamed, cried and wailed. Mercy was asked, but none was given. They dug graves. And were buried in them by their own.

A tear fell onto Boon's wispy white beard.

One underling pointed. The other one laughed.

It gnawed at his gut.

"To take such pleasure in it is sick."

They led him through the graveyard until his legs failed.

How could this happen? The armament must be gone. Or the underlings must have it.

CHAPTER 55

A S QUICK AS HE MIGHT be, Melegal was no fighter. He was a thief. A cutpurse. Shadow. Survivor. Rat. The swords in his hands were heavier than those he was accustomed to, his blades, the Sisters.

"Just get in a quick jab between the ribs, Detective," Creed said. "You have it in you."

Tonio and Jarla stood nearby, surrounded by underlings with long spears, leaving Melegal in the center of the arena, all alone.

Still, Lorda's long-lashed eyes intent upon him gave him a bit of a charge.

Master Kierway chittered to one of his men.

An underling with dark ruby eyes stepped forward, a razor sharp sword in each hand. The steel flickered around his body in a lightning quick display of skill and speed.

Great.

"That's all show! Go for the ribs," Creed said. "Like you did to my man. That was a good jab." Creed muttered to Jarla something under his breath. "He doesn't have a chance."

Melegal glared back at Creed, who shrugged.

"Let's get this started, shall we?" Kierway said, raising up his hand.

Melegal swallowed hard and squared off with the underling. *If I only had my hat.* But it was gone. Everything was gone. The Keys. The hat. His friends. *Maybe they'll survive this. But at least Sefron is dead. Was vengeance worth it?* He thought about Sefron. The man had been much more than he appeared to be. Was anything in Bish what he thought it was? He'd seen so many things the past several years.

Melegal glanced at Lorda one last time.

She blew him a subtle kiss.

I'll be.

Kierway dropped his hand.

The underling sprang, swords chopping high and low.

Melegal backpedaled and parried the snake quick strokes.

Clang. Clang. Clang. Clang. Bang.

"Keep 'em up, Detective!" Creed said.

Drained and starving, Melegal didn't have the strength to fight. *Fight or die.* It rattled in his head, but he didn't have it. He didn't have anything. *Die.* He broke it off and threw down his swords.

The underling paused and looked over at Master Kierway.

"Don't go out like that. Pick the blade up and finish like a man!" Creed said.

Skinny chest heaving, Melegal clutched at his sides and dropped to his knees.

Creed frowned. "He's got nothing left in him. Coward."

No, Melegal wouldn't die fighting. He sucked up all the air he could and fixed his gaze on Lorda. *If I go out. I'll go out doing what I want to.* He winked at her and mouthed good-bye.

She clutched her painted fingers at him, eyes watering.

"Finish him," Kierway ordered, dropping his thumb. "And get the woman ready next. Sad, but I bet there's more fight in the woman than the man. Pathetic humans, letting their women fight with them and against them. Weak."

The underling warrior raised his blade, sharp teeth showing a savage grin.

Melegal kept his chin up, eyes on Lorda.

"CEASE!"

The entire room shook.

The underling warrior froze.

Lord Verbard, silver eyes sparkling, floated down the stairs with Lord Almen and a hulking Vicious right behind him.

"How dare you?" Kierway said, jumping up from his chair. "This is no concern of yours, Verbard, you insolent underling! My father—"

"Your father agrees! You can ask him yourself," Verbard said.

"He's coming soon, and no doubt he'll want to evaluate your failures."

Kierway's hard jaw slackened. His ascent up the steps stopped.

"Lord Almen, are these the humans you want?" Verbard said, pointing down into the arena at them.

"Just three of them: Lorda, Jarla, Tonio, Come!"

"Tonio!" Lorda shot Almen a look. "Our son?" She looked at her son. Total shock on her face. She didn't know him.

"Aye, now get moving, Dearest Lorda," Almen said. "I'm out of parlays."

"And that woman, the black-haired witch? Are you bringing your mangy whore along?"

"What about me, Lord Almen?" Creed said. "I'm a loyal Hound at your service! You know that."

Lord Almen shook his head. "A hound, yes. No more, no less. I've plenty of curs at my disposal." He grabbed Lorda by the wrist.

Creed scowled at Almen, muttering to himself.

Lorda twisted away and continued her ascent, giving Melegal one final glance. "If you get her, then I want him."

Lord Almen's jaw tightened. "Be grateful you live, Woman. You can stay with me, or you can stay with Master Kierway."

Lorda called him a bastard, called out for Tonio, and moved away.

CRASH!

A boulder as big as a pony burst through the glass dome, crushing two underlings into the arena stairs.

The castle shook. Shouts of alarm when up.

"We're under attack!" Lord Almen said. "It seems my neighbors have awakened." He looked for Verbard, but the underling Lord was already moving.

"Get your men ready, Kierway," Verbard said. "The next battle has begun."

A large white-yellow ball of energy floated through the broken glass and hovered over the arena.

Kierway chittered a command.

Melegal balled up, covering his ears, closing his eyes.

Ka-Chow!

Something fell on top of him. It was the underling he'd been fighting. He shoved it off.

What in Bish!

Its red eyes were blinking and its limbs were loose. Melegal, despite his weakness, could still move. He grabbed a sword and stuck the underling.

Glitch!

Creed was on the move. Snatching up a sword, he tore a stunned underling's head from its shoulders.

Escape, Fool! Run!

Chaos unfolded. The dazed underlings were gathering their wits, heading for the doors. Kierway and Verbard were moving, ordering, unfazed.

The Vicious, a hulking predator, pounced into the arena and darted towards Creed.

Clank!

Melegal and Jarla froze.

A large leather sack had landed along the arena wall in front of Master Kierway's chair.

Slat on me! Venir?

Long legs churning, Jarla dashed over and dove on the sack. With a ravenous look in her eyes, she opened the sack and reached in.

Tonio was confused. His father was there, calling for him. His mother didn't seem to know him, and then she called for him too. And the underlings were in charge. Deep in the recesses of his mind, he knew he should be able to put it all together, but he couldn't. It was frustrating.

"Mother?" he said.

A rock fell from the sky, and a brilliant white flash followed. He grunted. Clutched his head and shook it. "Mother!"

A creature with a cat-like face shoved his mother down. Down the steps it bounded. He didn't know what it was, but he was going to kill it.

"Tonio kill!"

A pair of underling warriors stepped in his path.

"I'm getting used to this underling steel!"

Stab!

Creed yanked the blade from the underling's neck. Black-red blood gurgled from the hole and seeped into the ground.

The underling, though stunned, recovered quickly.

Creed, Master Swordsman from the House of Bloodhounds, pressed his advantage.

Slice!

He disemboweled one.

Chop!

He chopped another's neck open.

"Who do I have to kill to get some food and ale around here?" Creed shook the dripping blood from his blades. "I'm so hungry I could eat one of you fiends! Where's the kitchen?"

He caught a shadow in the corner of his eye and whirled.

"What in Bone are you?" he exclaimed.

The Vicious. Wicked rows of teeth. Claws like razors.

"I see you're missing some fingers," Creed said. "Let's see if I can even you out and remove a few more."

Creed lunged.

The Vicious sprung away and hunched down like an ape.

Creed felt something crawling in his belly. He'd never seen anyone that big move that fast.

"Yer not born of this world, are you? No matter. I'm still going to gut you with my blades." He banged the swords together. "Give it a go again. I'm ready for you."

The Vicious pounced, arms sprawled out, chest bared.

Slice!

He cut it across the belly and rolled out of the way and back to his feet.

"Let's see how you fight with your guts hanging out."

The monster turned, showed its fangs, and smiled. There wasn't a mark on it.

Creed felt his skin turn pale. "I'm in for."

The Vicious lunged.

Creed chopped with all his might. The blade shattered on its forearm.

The Vicious ripped a hunk of meat from Creed's chest.

"Urk!"

The Vicious snapped him up by the neck and squeezed his neck like a fresh fruit.

Eyes bulging from the sockets, Creed flailed and kicked.

At least I took some more of them with me.

"Mine!" Jarla said, licking her lips, eyes wild.

It was her salvation. Her liberation. The sack, after all these years, was back in her grasp, and nothing would ever stop her again, ever. It would fill her. Restore her. Any kind of enemy Jarla faced, even be they Royal or underling, she would prevail.

Reaching inside, her fingertips tingled in anticipation. The shafts of her axes. The power surging through her bracers. The awesome awareness from her helmet. Down to her shoulder she reached, fingers outstretched as far as they could go.

"Where are they?" She reached deeper. "Where are they!"

Her heart emptied. Nothing was there.

"No," she sobbed.

A shadow fell over her. She looked up. It was the rawboned detective. He held a heavy club with both hands. She sneered.

"That's not yours," he said. "It's Venir's."

"What? Are you mad? I'll never let that lou—"

Whack!

Melegal clubbed her across the jaw.

She tried to speak, but no words came. Only pain. Then darkness.

"That felt good," Melegal said, gathering the sack, "and I haven't forgotten that Lorda wants you dead. But I'll let the two of you fight that out."

Explosions were still erupting all over the castle, so the concerns of Lord Almen and the underling leaders were elsewhere right now.

Hidden along the arena wall, no one had sight of him.

The stunned underlings that were coming out of the mystic blast were focused on the fighting in the middle.

Now I just have to hide until I find Venir. I knew that fool must have caused this.

It was simple. All he had to do was find a place between the walls until he figured out where Venir was. Then he could free him and let him deal with this mess. And he just might be able to get his cap and Keys back. *Just the cap. The cap would be good.*

A doorway, up the steps on the other side of the arena, was open with no one to bar his path.

Move or die.

He was darting along the arena wall, concealed for the first twenty steps, when he heard a familiar voice shout out.

"Seize him!"

It was Lord Almen pointing and shouting, his face filled with rage.

Melegal jumped up, grabbed the lip of the wall, and slung himself up.

Two underlings bolted towards the door, cutting off his path, weapons ready.

He was too late.

Bone!

Two more were closing in from behind. All he had was a club and a sack. Expecting Venir to appear any second, he shook his head.

Where is that brute?

Dropping the club, he sat down, laying the sack on his lap.

CHAPTER 56

"M MMPH!"

Tuuth tried to pry his mouth open, but Venir wouldn't give. Teeth clenched, he fought on.

"Hold him still!" Tuuth ordered.

The brigands, stout as they might be, struggled. Each slipping into the mud from his efforts.

"Blast you, Tuuth! You hold him! I'm not swimming in slat on account of this wretch's tongue! He's done for!"

"Aye!" the other agreed, letting go and crawling out of the slime.

"You'll both be in the stockade for a week, maybe longer!"

"Pah!"

Still in a headlock, Venir's nostrils flared.

Tuuth cranked up the pressure.

"This isn't over," Tuuth said, looking around.

All the brigands and underlings had abandoned the pit, shouting orders and gathering gear, leaving the two of them all by themselves.

Tuuth shoved him down in the muck and held him under, waited several seconds, and jerked him back out.

Venir coughed and spat.

"Enough of this," Tuuth said, trolling out of the muck and slinging it from his fingers. "Let the underlings kill you themselves, like everyone else."

The ground shook.

"What?" Tuuth stopped in place, arms out.

Venir felt it too, but it was of little notice. Sitting in the muck, he was in agony. Reaching down, he plucked one of his dirty and bloody ears from the muck, tossed it aside, and grabbed his shovel.

He pushed himself up with it, legs shaking. Wiping the filth from his eyes, he was watching the southern gate, which was rising, when another clamor went up.

"It's a giant!"

Tuuth tucked the underling's dagger into his belt and looked back. "Don't go anywhere!"

He wasn't. He couldn't. Even if he could, where would he go? Though tempted to at least climb up out of the muck, he remained in what little cover the pit provided, keeping his eyes transfixed on the slow rise of the southern gate. Hundreds of underling soldiers, dark armor and helms gleaming in the sun, stood ready.

A moment later, a collective gasp followed.

There he was.

Tethered by thick ropes and chains, towering more than three times the height of the underlings, a giant stood. They pulled, poked and prodded him. He was angry and confused, each footstep shaking the ground. Bolts and javelins jutted from his body like briars.

Venir's eyes widened.

It was Barton.

The young giant growled and yelled. Slung his weight against his captors to no avail. They had him chained by the neck, the arms, and the ankles. Enough chains to forge an armory.

Venir felt pity. Barton's expression was tormented. A confused child. Miserable.

Barton stomped. Rocked and reeled.

"LET BARTON GO! LET BARTON GO!"

But the underlings had him under control. They chittered. They laughed.

Sitting down on the edge of the muck pit, he watched the underlings bind the giant further. Venir recalled his time in the Mist. It had been Barton who freed him. It had been Barton he tricked, and it had been Barton who said he'd come for him—and he had.

Of all people, he remembered me.

Of course, it wasn't Venir he wanted, it was the armament. The toys. Venir wanted them too, but he was certain the armament was gone.

Barton's going to be disappointed, if he lives to find out.

Barton was bound to the exterior wall, a mere ten yards away, but under heavy guard. He yelled and whined, but after several minutes, he fell silent.

Venir resumed his shoveling. *Nothing I can do. Sorry, Barton.* Whatever happened was going to happen, and there was nothing he could do. Two more hours he dug. He was dying of thirst.

"Dwarves!" One of the brigands shouted from the catwalks. "Dwarves!"

Venir lifted his head up. Stout black-bearded men, shackled, were herded inside like cattle. Some limped. All bled. Hard looks on their grim faces.

"Who's in command of this place?" a commanding voice said.

Mood? He cupped his hand behind his missing ear, peering forward.

"Come on, rodents! Bring yer leader out!"

Venir shielded his eyes from the blazing suns with his hand. Mood, bushy and broad, stood over the rest, a green glimmer under his brows.

The underling commander strutted forward, chest out.

"Blood Ranger, you have no business here. Not on my mountain. The penalty is death."

"Ye'll release us all, Underling," Mood said. "We hunt giants, all over Bish, and where they go, we go. Underlings or no. It's our right. You best let us go, or the entire dwarven world will come for you. Not to mention more giants."

An underling cracked a spear over Mood's head.

The Blood Ranger didn't flinch. All he said was, "I'm warning you."

"Say all you want, Blood Ranger. You'll be dead soon, so it doesn't matter. Bish is ruled by the underlings now, so your threats are of no matter." The underling commander started to walk away. "Flay them. Flay them all. But save the giant for last."

"It's easier to flay a stone than a dwarf, you fool!" Mood said. "We'll dull your knives after the first cut."

Venir shook his head and resumed his shoveling.

"Stay here."

Those were the last words Mood had said to Fogle Boon before he'd departed with the Black Beards and headed towards Outpost Thirty One, leaving him alone with Eethum. That had been several hours ago, and at the bottom of the massive hill they waited. He'd been clutching at handfuls of his hair ever since.

"Eethum, what's the plan?"

Solemn as always, the black Blood Ranger replied, "I don't know."

That was the same answer he'd given five times already, and Fogle was tired of it. He had to know, and even though Fogle didn't question dwarven integrity, he had his doubts.

"So, am I to understand that we are to *stay here* forever? And you're comfortable with that?"

Eethum eyed the long branch he'd been whittling for hours.

"He's the King. I do as he says." He stuck his knife in a tree stump and admired his work. "Look at that. Straight as a dwarven bolt." He smiled at Fogle. "I can make a fine spear with it." He tossed it to Fogle. "Or a Wizard's walking stick. Ha! Ha!"

Fogle wanted to crack it over Eethum's head. He slung it to the ground.

"We can't wait here forever, Eethum."

"We won't," Eethum said, grabbing his knife along with another branch and whittling again.

Pacing around him, Fogle said, "I'm not a dwarf. I can't stand here for a hundred years and do nothing, like you."

"I'm not doing nothing; I'm carving wood. Just find yourself something to do. Study your spellbook. Always be ready for something."

It was easier said than done. Fogle didn't know what was going on. So he turned his attention back to Inky. His ebony hawk familiar stretched out its black metallic wings. It was ready.

He glanced over his shoulder at Eethum. The Blood Ranger didn't pay him any attention.

"Alright, I might have to stay here, but that doesn't mean I can't try and figure out what's happening."

Grabbing Inky, he placed Venir's hunting knife in its talons. "Give this to Venir if you see him. It will be some time before I can connect with you again." He tossed the bird in the air. Black wings flapping, it soared into the sky, disappearing into the tree line.

He turned and faced Eethum.

The Blood Ranger's arms were crossed over his chest.

"What?" Fogle shrugged. "I'm staying here."

Eethum shook his head. "There's at least a thousand underlings out there. Your little bird's done for."

"Why do you think that?"

Eethum batted an eye at him. "Wizard, have you seen a single bird since we've been here?"

Fogle tucked his chin into his neck. "No."

"There's a reason for that." Eethum put a finger to his lips, then pointed upward. "Hear that?"

Fogle cupped his ear. Something hummed in the sky. "I can always bring him back to us."

"Don't do that. You'll just lead them right to us."

"Them?"

"Stirges. Flocks of them. They destroy every flying creature in sight."

"But Inky doesn't have any blood."

"Maybe so, but they don't know that."

CHAPTER 57

"**Y**OU SHOULD EAT SOMETHING, CORRIN."

"What?" he said, blinking.

"Eat," Haze said, motioning to her mouth. "I heard your stomach growling from over there. You've been staring in the fountain for hours. Take a drink already. Or a bath even. Just do something other than sit there."

Corrin gaped at the skinny woman. "Don't you see them?"

She leaned over and peered in. "What? Fish? Spooks? I don't see anything except water."

He looked back in the fountain. The living images were gone.

"No!" he said, reaching in the water, shaking his hand. "Where are they?"

"You've lost your wits," she said, walking away, "but I'll still get you something to eat. Get some shade at least. The suns probably cooked your noodles."

"Aw!" he said, smacking the water. "I'm going to miss it. Trinos!" He looked everywhere. She was nowhere to be found. "Hate it when she does that!"

Trinos had told him strange things. She spoke of Bish as if it were her own child and the things that worried him would take care of themselves. There was order among the chaos, she'd said. Sanity with the madness. Good where there was evil.

But, he disagreed. There wasn't any good in the underlings. He was a hired killer. A murderer. But he took no pleasure in it. The underlings did, and he made it clear to her that despite the Royals' lust for power and control, the world would be better off without the underlings.

"No one is ever in control," she had said. "I have planted many seeds to see to that. But nothing will last forever. I tire. When it ends, it ends."

Corrin didn't understand it one bit. All he knew was people were dying and underlings were living. When it came to the battle for Bish, he wanted in. He buckled on his sword.

"First, I'm going to fill my belly with food, and then I'm going to fill gray bellies with steel."

Trinos sighed.

Her world was everything she'd imagined it to be, but worse. It drained her. The people were strong, full of life, bold—but always shadowed in darkness. Peace had come in the past. Only to go and come again.

Scorch had changed that. Now, peace was a lonely cry from the highest mountain top.

She walked, her toes drifting over the sand in the Warfield. Of all the places in Bish, it was the one most at peace right now. Hot and barren, both underlings and men had avoided it among the turmoil that had broken out everywhere else.

Shall I stay? Can I go? Is this what I want?

She knew she couldn't go. Not without Scorch. They had both buried most of their power deep in Bish when they arrived. One could not tap it without the other.

In the meantime, her own power, vast as it might be, had weakened. Bish was feeding on her. Her powers waned. What had been effortless required effort now. She filled her chest with hot air and slowly let it out. Despite the change, she felt as alive as she ever remembered. Emotions, long forgotten, went up and came down.

Does Scorch feel this as well?

Should I track him?

So she walked, toes sinking into the sand, becoming another part of the world she'd created.

Behind her, two disfigured people followed, covered head to toe in Outland robes, swords hanging from their hips, sandaled but no longer insane.

CHAPTER 58

CREED KICKED THE VICIOUS IN the face. It was a last ditch effort.
It head-butted him.

Crack!

He saw bright spots and stars. He was choking. Sharp claws dug into his neck. His own blood trickled down his chest. He always figured he'd die before he was gray. A match of steel against a younger, stronger opponent like himself. Where he held on with skill and cleverness to the end. But this, to fall in the brutal hands of a monster, was unbearable.

If I only had my sword again.

The brute held him by the neck, pushed him up with its long arm like a child, and shook him like a doll.

Purple-faced, he gulped for air.

Such a cowardly way to go!

He kicked at the Vicious again and again, but there was laughter in its evil eyes.

"Blast you, fiend!" Bloody saliva flew from his mouth.

Creed felt his body closing down. The light dimmed. The pain subsided.

This is it, Bish.

The Vicious released him.

Creed fell to the ground, coughing and choking.

Tonio was there. Arms latched around the creature's neck in a headlock of some sort.

Crawling through the dirt, Creed searched for a blade—a knife, anything.

"Perhaps I'll get in one last swing."

"Mother!" Tonio growled. "You hurt my mother!"

Strength versus strength. Power versus power. Two titans thrashed with one another. The Vicious, an underling abomination of magic brought to life in humanoid form. Tonio, a dead man revived, raging within like a forest fire.

He didn't know what he was or how he came to be. He knew he should be dead but he lived, stitched up by the spiderish arachnamen. Magic gave him life, and nothing could give him death. So he fought. His vengeance unfilled against the yellow-haired Vee-Man.

The Vicious twisted out of his choking grip and socked him in the face.

He staggered back.

The creature pounced on him. It punched and clawed at him, one blow as quick as the other.

His skin shredded. His bone exposed. Tonio didn't feel a thing.

The creature let out an angry howl.

Tonio punched his fist inside its mouth.

Its eyes widened. It pushed away.

Tonio shook the spit from his hand and flashed a split-faced grin. "You can't hurt me!" He pounded his chest. "Nothing can!"

The Vicious leapt. Kicked him in the chest. Knocked him to the ground.

Tonio laughed and rose to his feet. The underling was quick. He matched it blow for blow. He slammed it into the wall.

It bit off a part of his leg.

Tonio hoisted it over his head. Slammed it into the ground. Stomped on its chest. It's head.

Back and forth they went. Two monsters. Evil. Tireless. No quarter given. No hatred spared.

Underlings closed in.

Melegal's instincts took over. He reached into the sack, clutching for a weapon. Something. Anything. Bony fingertips stretching. Tingling. He felt something. Cold. Living.

What is that?

Smack!

An underling cracked him over the head with the pommel of its sword, splitting his vision from two to four.

Spine like jelly, he slumped over the benches, the sack slipping from his grasp.

The one underling grabbed him by the leg and dragged him. The other tossed the sack over the rail, into the arena.

Head bouncing off the benches, Melegal stared at the broken glass dome above. The suns gleamed on the broken glass edges.

Venir, you lout, where are you?

Creed crawled. Huffing. Bleeding. Busted inside and out. A rack of weapons awaited him against the way. And that wasn't all.

"I'll be," he said.

His sword lay on the rack. Steel glimmering under the dust. Tonio and the other monster thrashed behind him. *Move, Creed!* He gathered his feet and stumbled over.

"I bet Pearl can poke a hole in that thing."

He stretched out his fingers and grabbed the hilt.

"Bone! Ah!" The sharp stabbing pain of broken ribs bit into him. Something fell over his head, blocking his sight.

What in Bish?

He tore it off his face and beheld a worn, stitched-up sack of leather.

Where did this come from?

His stomach rumbled. He hadn't eaten in days. A savage instinct overcame him.

Maybe there's a loaf or some cheese. I don't fight well when hungry.

Ravenous and wild-eyed, he set down his sword and reached inside.

Lorda Almen squatted along the wall at the top of the arena, hiding in a doorway, trembling. A boulder the size of a sofa had almost smashed her, and a creature as dark as night had shoved her down. Her home, her castle, had become a den of madness, and it had only just begun.

"Lorda, get out of there," Lord Almen cried out, his long arm waving her over.

Underling soldiers were whisking him away, and two more were coming for her. She shook her head.

Down on one side of the arena, her son Tonio smashed two underlings together. He attacked the hulking beast that had shoved her, and he was about to break the neck of another. On the other side, Melegal, a man she'd become fond of for some reason, was pinned in by the underlings, awaiting a certain death.

She tried to catch his eye, but a strong armed underling jerked her off the ground and hissed.

"Come with me, Woman. I can't have my pets running loose, now can I?" It was Kierway. He looked over his shoulder. "I've got more pressing matters than watching humans die."

"Unhand me!" she said.

He backhanded her.

Her legs swayed.

"Speak to me like that, and you'll never speak again."

CHAPTER
59

C OULD HE BE DEAD?

Slim the Healer crawled out of his hiding spot and scurried outside. Being king of the Elga bugs was getting old. He needed to stretch his legs. Not the six he had now, but the two he preferred to walk on as a man.

This is tiresome.

Still, he would do whatever he had to do to keep his friend alive. Something had to happen. Something always did. But this time things didn't seem right. His friend, Venir, was being whittled away, one chunk at a time.

Crawling up one of the Outpost walls, he found a good spot, away from the soldiers.

Oh my!

A man the size of three men was inside the camp, talking like a loud child and fighting against his bonds.

A giant!

A dwarf was whipping his blood red hair in the air, screaming and yelling at an underling like an angry bugbear.

Mood! And Black Beards? Captured? What in Bish is going on?

Bug eyes shifting back and forth, he glossed over a man shoveling in the muck.

Ew! But that's what Brigands should be doing.

Still searching, he couldn't find Venir, so he looked for the orc called Tuuth. The big orc was watching over the dwarves, arms crossed over his chest. Fluttering his wings, Slim found another spot and started searching faces all around.

Venir? Where is that brute?

The man was nowhere to be found. Turning back to the man in the muck pit, he took a closer look. Earlier, he'd been looking for blond hair and muscles. But the markings of a 'V' tattoo still shown through the muck. *Venir!*

A sinking feeling started inside his insect belly. Doubt flooded his mind. Over the centuries, he'd seen many things, but he'd never witnessed such a dire scene before.

The underlings singled out one dwarf and chained him to the wall. Above, in one of the fort's turrets, a pair of underlings grabbed the winch and cranked back the draw string on a ballista. Then loaded a bolt as long as a man. The black beard looked up at the underling, set his chin and raised it high.

Slim closed his eyes.

Ballista bolt sticking out of his chest, the Black Beard let out his final gasp, "For the King!" His head dipped. His helmet fell to the ground.

The underlings let out a loud raucous cheer. Venir had never witnessed underlings celebrating so. They danced and jumped. Loaded another ballista. Replaced the dead dwarf with a live one.

"Yer gonna pay for that!" Mood bellowed, fighting against his bonds.

Venir's heart dipped. Mood's rescue attempt was going to cost the lives of all his men, and then that of Mood, himself. This wasn't how the giant dwarves were supposed to end. They should have known by now that his friendship only brought death.

"King of the Dwarves," the underling commander said, flexing his arms and pumping up his soldiers, "what is it like to see your subjects die? It is customary that we kill the leader first, but I like to watch your eyes. I want to make them water. Making a dwarf cry will be a first." He pointed up at the fort tower and dropped his arm. "Fire!"

THWACK!

Another Black Beard fell. The bolt sticking out of his skull.

"That probably stung," the commander said, "but not for very long."

The crowd chittered, sharp teeth gnashing in agreement.

"Two down, many more to go."

Venir was used to people dying, but not when they weren't in battle. Not without a fight. Watching the dwarves fall ate at him. It wasn't right. It wasn't natural. Hands white-knuckled on the shovel, he thought of Brool. The white hot power surging through his hands. A hollow feeling overcame him. An old friend lost. Lost forever. He had lived this long without it, but could he live anymore? He was broken. What there anything else he could do to help this savage world?

"You?"

Barton's hanging head tilted up and looked right at him. The giant sniffed the air.

"Ah-hah, you are hiding in the stink, Venir?"

Tuuth faced the giant. "What did you say, Giant?" He pointed at Venir. "Are you talking to him? Is he *Venir*?"

"Go away, Orc! I do not like your stink!" Barton's eye rolled back over to Venir. "Give me my toys!"

"Gag that giant!" Tuuth ordered his men.

"What's going on?" the Brigand Flaggon said.

"This man, Commander, has a bounty on his head. A big one. This is Venir the Outlander, the one who destroyed the Brigand Army."

Flaggon rubbed his chin. "I thought there was something familiar about him." He kneeled alongside the pit. "Your bounty is big, and the penalty is death. Get his shovel, men. Tuuth, clean him up a little before you cut off his head. We'll want to bring it as a trophy, if we ever make it back to the Brigand City."

Throughout the fort, everyone's heads snapped up.

The sound of trees snapping like twigs echoed in the distance.

"What now?" Flaggon said.

Tuuth kept his eyes intent on Venir. "Get him out of there."

The ground shook. Not like before, but worse.

Thoom!

It shook again. More trees snapped and cracked. Branches sounded as if they were being crushed into the ground.

Thoom!

Above, Venir glimpsed several robed underlings soaring above the walls, clawed hands filling with color.

Wumpf!

An uprooted tree soared over the wall, smacking into an underling mage and crashing them both into the ground.

"Oh No!" Barton said. "They've come!"

The underling magi fired balls of energy over the wall.

The soldiers in the towers fired their ballistas.

Rocks bigger than men flew over the wall.

Men and underlings scrambled.

A rock smashed into a turret. Underlings fell to their deaths.

"They're after the dwarves!" The underling commander cried out. "Prepare for parlay! We'll hand them over!"

"Hah!" Venir heard Mood say. "If there's anything giants hate more than dwarves, it's the underlings!" Mood snapped his chains and punched the wide-eyed underling commander in the face. "But none hates more than I do, Fiend." Mood let out a gusty word. "*SHARLABOTZ!*"

The leather and metal that bound the Black Beards withered and snapped. The dwarves burst into action. In seconds, they were an armed force. Hacking and slashing into the off-guard underlings.

Venir stirred. A fire ignited within. He raised his shovel and brought it down on the back of Tuuth's head.

Snarling, the orc turned, grabbed Venir by the hair, and slung him to the ground. The orc pinned him down. Wrapped his fingers around his neck and squeezed.

Venir couldn't breathe.

"You're done for now, Venir!" Tuuth pushed him towards the muck pit. "And your grave's even ready. Your bones will be right where they belong, Outland Scum."

CHAPTER 60

T *HUMP.*
  Thump. Thump.

Boon's heart still beat. His nose still breathed. But that was all he could to. Beat and breathe. Barely. *Is this all I have left?* The mystic cuffs tightened with every move. Biting into his wrists and burning at the same time. Inside, his own mystic fires still burned, but he could not summon them. His mouth was bound tight as well. Eyelids heavy, heart skipping and slowing, it was his magic that kept his fiber together. Without it, he would have died long ago.

Oh, to wield the armament one last time! I'd give these fiends a show.

Sagging on the ground, he was oblivious to the commotion that stirred the camp. His mind was somewhere else, fighting to keep his body on this side of the threshold between life and death.

Fire fell from the sky.

"Eh..." He opened his eyes.

Smoke began.

The hairs on his arms and beard curled and singed.

Hot smoky air filled his nose and lungs.

A cry of Chaos went up.

A clamor spread through the underling camp. Underlings barked orders. Flames spread from tent to tent.

Someone grabbed hold of him. Pulled him to his feet. Cut his bonds and yanked the gag from his mouth.

"Eat this!" his rescuer said. A fruit of some sort was stuffed in his mouth.

He sunk his teeth right in. Juice dripped down his beard.

"Come with me!"

He followed, blinking the dark smoke from his eyes. Flames surrounded them. Underlings screamed out. They burned. They burned alive. The sound of underlings suffering was music to his ears.

Is this real? Or am I dead?

"Grab this and get on!" the voice ordered, placing his hands on a rope.

"What?" he started to say, but was cut off.

Something huge lurched beneath him, stirring up a cloud of dust and fire. Off the ground they rose. Boon fought to hold on. He slipped, but a strong arm grabbed him and held him tight.

"Am I on what I think I'm on?"

"Keep silent, and hold tight!"

CHAPTER 61

C REED'S FINGERTIPS TOUCHED LEATHER. HE dumped out the contents of the sack. A sword belt. Different. Two pommels with a dull gray finish were shoved in short scabbards on it. Compelled, he strapped it on. *Two short blades are better than none.*

"Food! There must be something." He reached back inside.

Behind him, Tonio and the Vicious were still having it out, but it didn't matter to him if either one died, so long as it wasn't him. "Just a morsel, eh? Or maybe a skin of wine? Please?"

Instead, the sack served up soft fabric.

"What's this?" Creed held a dark, intricately woven cowl, big enough to cover his head and shoulders.

The cowl throbbed with a life of its own, telling him something.

He traced the tiny swirling rows of stitches with his fingers. "Bish, what kind of garment is this?" Creed's keen eye understood fine craftsmanship. He'd crafted his own blades with intricate designs. But what he now beheld was nothing short of marvelous in his eyes.

"Huh, a bit much for keeping the rain off," he said. He put it on. And forgot his hunger.

The Cowl filled him with great awareness.

He jumped from the ground. "Mother of Bone!"

The Vicious caught Tonio in the nose, rocking the half-dead man, flattening him. It turned on Creed, jaws snapping, claws bared.

Tonio moved, but slowly.

Creed didn't have a stitch of armor on him aside from The Cowl. He wasn't worried. He felt thick. Tough. He sized up the monster.

Its arms were long like an ape's. Its skin tough, like black steel. The claws on its fingers were ten blades to his two.

Creed's hands fell to the steel pommels at his hips. *Maybe they can cut this thing.* He jerked them out. Steel. Dark. Razor sharp.

"Great Bish!"

The blades were long! And heavy, but light in his hands.

The Vicious charged.

Quick as it was, Creed was quicker. Like a cobra he struck.

Slice!

Slice!

One monster hand fell, then the other.

The Vicious howled, fangs dripping with saliva.

Glitch!

The tip of one blade punctured its eye.

Glitch!

The other its throat.

The Vicious sagged to the ground, dead.

Creed looked at his blades. "I'll be." Spun them around. "I could get used to this."

His head throbbed. Underlings were coming. His eyes glimmered. Two underlings surged down the steps and leapt into the arena. Behind them, Detective Melegal's scrawny body was sprawled out on the benches, unmoving.

Creed smiled. He twirled one sword in his hand. Held the other behind his back.

Flanking him, one underling came in low, the other high, curved swords licking out like serpent tongues.

Creed swatted their blades away.

They pressed.

He pressed back, laughing. *If the Royals could see me now! Hah. They'd never face me.*

All his life, he'd been training to fight. We wanted to be respected. Fight the Royals in their arenas. Be their champion. But they wouldn't let him. He wasn't their blood. They claimed he wasn't worthy. Still, he continually perfected his skill and craft. Designing his own steel and other weapons. Now he wielded two as easily as sticks. He felt like he could swing forever.

"Hah!"

His steel flashed.

He clipped through the nose of one.

Zitch!

He tore the lip from the other.

Bleeding, the underling's eyes were focused. Ready.

Creed folded his swords behind his back, stuck his chin out and shook his head.

Chittering, they came at him.

Creed lunged. Stabbed both through the chest.

Their swords fell. Their bodies right after.

"If only my hounds could see this."

He slung underling blood from his swords and scanned the arena. Only one underling was left. Its eyes furrowed beneath its brow.

Creed waved him down.

"Time for a rematch, you copper-eyed roach."

Tonio pushed himself off the ground, shaking his head. The black creature was fast. It confused him. Still, he would make it pay.

Turning to face his predator, he saw something he didn't expect. The Vicious was face first in the dirt, hands missing and dead. He had a sinking feeling when he looked over and saw the next thing.

A faceless man battled the underlings. His swords were fast. Strokes of lightning.

A chill went through Tonio. He looked at the scars on his arms and ran his hand down the split in his face. Something about that man distraught him. He had to get away.

"No," he said, recoiling. The black forest came to mind, the webs. He noticed a gleaming sword near the arena wall and took it. Then, he headed to the nearest door and ripped it open. His mother, Lorda, was screaming after him, but he didn't hear her. He had to hide. He had to plan.

"Detective."

Melegal groaned.

"Detective." It was the soft voice of a woman. Her lips brushed his ear. "We must hurry."

Melegal found himself gazing up into the beautiful eyes of Lorda Almen. His heart thumped in his chest. He reached out and grasped her hand, feeling her breasts brush against his chin as she held him. He savored the moment.

"We must go," she said, lifting his chin to face her.

A moment ago, he'd been ready to let his suffering in Bish end. He'd had enough of facing one bad day followed by another. But for now, he had a new purpose. He fought the pain and discomfort and wrapped his hand around her sensuous waist. *Fight and fondle.* He was going to help the Lorda.

"How many underlings?" he said, coughing a little.

"Hundreds. They come and go. From where, I don't know. It's an army." She pushed her black hair from her eyes. "It's madness, is what it is. We have to get out of here." She pushed him. "Let's go."

Melegal started to go, then froze.

"Venir?"

In the arena, a man in a dark cowl was squared off against the underling, Kierway.

The sight sent chills through Melegal.

The man under the cowl was tall and muscular, but not savage and brawny like Venir. His face was obscured a little. The man moved like a predator, dark blades whirling at the underlings like storms at small boats out at sea.

Melegal then noticed the pants. Well-trimmed auburn hair around the mouth.

Creed?

Sadness fell over him. Despair filled his belly. If his friend was no longer The Darkslayer, then was his friend no more?

"Fool!" Lorda said, pulling him along. "You're supposed to be saving me; I'm not supposed to be saving you."

They made their way to the door Melegal had tried to approach earlier. He passed through it before her.

A corridor led around the arena toward many other exits. There was a clamor everywhere. Chandeliers fell. Vases were busted.

Footsteps scrambled over the marble. Castle Almen was under attack, but the usurped were fighting back.

"C'mon," Melegal said. He took her hand. One corridor was blocked off by rubble. Another was overrun with underlings. "There should be more options in a castle so large." Jogging back down the corridor by the arena, they took another path. Melegal had spent considerable time following Sefron and learning many secrets. Others, he'd discovered on his own. He eyed the framework of the wall. "Aw, where is it?"

"What?" Lorda said.

Chitter. Chitter. Chitter.

Underling soldiers were prowling the halls, coming from both directions.

Dripping with sweat, chest heaving, Lorda's eyes locked with his.

Melegal caught her voluptuous form in his arms and kissed her on the mouth.

She dug her nails into his back. Kissing him back. Her soft lips were hungry. Passionate.

They finished, gasping.

"You know," Lorda said, "death is the penalty for that."

Underlings cut them off at both ends.

"Obviously," Melegal answered, pushing her behind him, "but it was worth it."

CHAPTER 62

T HE CASTLES IN THE CITY of Bone were all lined up against the
great wall: some looking over, some not as tall. On both sides of
Castle Almen, the other two attacked. Small catapults hurled heavy
stones, and piles of logs and ballista bolts crisscrossed.

Standing on top of the keep, Lord Catten laughed.

"It seems the Royals have decided to engage," he said to his
brother, "but it's a bit too late."

Verbard knocked debris from his shoulders. "Or, perhaps it's
their way of taking down an enemy. Putting an end to the Almen
house, which has betrayed so many."

Lord Almen stood tall and stone-faced. Nails digging into his
palms. He would have done the same thing, but seeing it happen
to himself and his people and family was a hard thing. "Spare your
people, Lord Catten and Lord Verbard," Almen said. "This isn't a
full assault, but rather a test of strength."

"And how long will this test go on?" Catten said.

"Several minutes at most," Almen said, giving a quick nod.
"Perhaps after that I can begin a parlay with them. Certainly their
eyes are on me." He gestured at one of the other castle's towers.
"They'll be expecting something."

Floating inches above the roof of the Keep and staying half a
head taller than Almen, the molten eyes of the underlings bore into
him.

"Mind your place, Human," Verbard said. "Your suggestions
are annoying."

"And your Castle is boring," Catten added.

Out of the corner of his eye, Lord Almen glimpsed a missile

coming his way. He ducked. The ballista bolt splintered on an invisible shield of magic.

"Such a fool, Brother," Verbard said. "Did you pick him out?"

"Nay, Brother," Catten said. "I believe it was you who suggested we keep him around, but I see little need for a man who flinches at such a feeble attack."

Lord Almen regained his feet. Eyed the attacking castle turret next door. They were reloading. He caught the glimmer of a spy glass turned on him.

"Interesting, Brother," Verbard said. "I don't even think that attack was meant for us, but rather meant for him."

"I agree, but there is only one way to find out." Catten floated to Almen's left.

Verbard nodded and took a place on his right.

"Stay right where you are, Lord Almen. My brother and I have a wager of sorts."

It was hot. Sweat dripped off Lord Almen's brow and nose. In all truth, the underlings didn't have any need for him. They had his Castle. Key sections of the City.

It would take a unified Royal force to prevail against the underlings. *Not likely.* His only sanctuary was knowledge, but he was certain the underlings would risk losing that. They could just learn it for themselves.

Rocks and pitch-coated burning logs sailed overhead, slamming into the castle. Soldiers in the turret were winding the ballista winch back. The one with the spy glass had pointed right at him; he was certain.

"Any last words, Lord Almen?" Catten asked, arms folded over his chest.

Lord Almen took a silent draw through his nose.

"If I die, kill all those bastards."

"They'll die anyway," Catten said, "but if it makes you feel better, you can believe we did it that way."

Don't blink. Don't flinch. Don't move.

Lord Almen didn't have any idea if they kept their shield up or not, but certainly they'd protect themselves now, wouldn't they?

Twack!

The bolt sailed. Lord Almen's quick mind watched in slow motion. Closer. Closer.

Rip!

It tore straight though his leg. He spun to the ground. Three feet of wood jutted through his thigh.

"Hmmm... Brother," Verbard began, "it seems their aim isn't very good. Not good at all. I can't really say if they were aiming for him or us. It was such a bad shot."

"Agreed, Brother," Catten said, turning away, "but I can't fool around here all day. And I don't think our enemies are interested in this human's parlay. No, let us leave him up here and we'll check back and see if they spared him or not."

"Fair enough. Besides," Verbard said, "I think we need a better eye on our neighbors. I think our imp would be a much better ambassador."

"Agreed."

Lord Almen watched them walk away, a hard grimace on his face. Through the door they went, closing it behind them. Lord Almen and his Royal enemies were all alone.

The spy glass reflected in the suns.

He stood up, bit his lip, and searched for cover. *Get to the ledge.* He hopped as fast as he could. Another bolt ripped through his shoulder.

CHAPTER 63

Tuuth applied pressure to Venir's throat. "I'm going to enjoy this, Outlander." Saliva dripped off the orc's canine teeth. "I want a clean-cut earless trophy."

Venir's kicks glanced off the big orc's sides. He tried to speak. Tuuth squeezed harder.

"No more words from your loud mouth," Tuuth said. "Perhaps it's another challenge you want? Perhaps another insult towards my kind? If I had your ears, I'd stick them in your mouth."

Venir's eyes rolled up in his head. Sound faded.

"NOOO!"

WHAP!

An oversized hand sent Tuuth spinning away. There stood Barton. Fists clenched at his sides. Chest heaving.

"Get my toys first!"

Venir gulped for air. Gasped. "I... I don't have them."

Barton slammed his fists into the ground.

"NO!"

"Giant!" Tuuth beckoned with his finger, one hand still behind his back. "I know the toys you're looking for. Stoop down, and I'll tell you where they are."

Barton grunted, leaned downward, cocking his head.

"Where are they, Orc?"

Tuuth's gauntlets flashed.

WHAM!

He struck Barton in the jaw.

Barton quavered. His eye rolled up into his head. He collapsed.

Tuuth thumped his chest.

"I just broke a giant's jaw." He looked down on Venir. "Imagine what I'll do to you."

The ground shook.

Three giants jumped off the walls, crushing a dozen underlings.

"Can you knock them out too?" Venir said.

"I'm not worried about them." Tuuth swung.

Venir blocked the punch. His bones clattered. He fell in a heap.

"I can't die like this," he said, looking up. "Not to an orc."

Tuuth glowered at him. "You can, and you will." He kicked Venir in the gut.

Everywhere, underlings by the hundreds swarmed the giants. Cutting, Stabbing, and screaming. They crawled over them like angry black ants.

There was another explosion.

The southern gate was shattered. A giant bigger than the other three, with brown hair tied in knots, stormed inside. He swung a hammer as big as an ogre. Dozens of underlings were crushed and swept aside. Their bones powdered on impact.

Tuuth snorted and gawped.

"Where in Bish did they come from?"

Something from the sky fell at Venir's feet. It was a long knife in a scabbard.

"Huh?" Tuuth said.

Venir dove for it.

Tuuth kicked it away.

"Nice try, Venir!"

The orc grabbed him by the hair and pounded his face and chest. Ribs cracked.

Venir lost his breath and collapsed.

Tuuth readied the underling's knife and thumbed its edge.

"This is it for you."

Venir groaned, struggling to rise. He couldn't even open his eyes.

Tuuth pushed him down with his boot.

"No, you won't die on your feet. You'll die in the muck."

Something growled.

Venir's eye popped open.

Tuuth turned.

There stood a giant a two-headed dog. Fangs bared. Hair raised on its necks.

"What the…"

Chongo pounced. Sank one head's teeth into Tuuth's arm.

Tuuth punched the giant dog's other face.

Chongo held on. Growling. Snarling. Shaking his heads.

"Let go of me!" Tuuth screamed, still punching, his gauntlets charged with energy.

Venir crawled over to his knife. A new fire in his belly. He closed his fingers around it.

Chongo's massive jaws crunched the bone in Tuuth's arm.

Still, the orc kept swinging.

Pow!

One head yelped. The other let go. Shaking, Chongo backed away. Sluggish, Growling. Teetering.

Arm limp on one side, Tuuth shook his glowing fist.

"I'm going to kill you, dog."

Venir stepped between them, knife behind his back, swaying.

"You have to kill me first," he said, "and you haven't done that yet, orc."

"I'm going to rip your head from your shoulders, Venir." Tuuth came at him.

Venir braced his feet.

Quick. Quick. Quick.

Tuuth drew back. Gauntlet glowing. Everything was in his swing. The big fist came.

Like a panther, Venir leapt up out of the muck pit and struck. Venir cut through armor. Muscle. Bone.

"Urk!"

The orc's yellow eyes widened. Blood filled his mouth. Tuuth punched.

Venir held on. Driving the knife deeper, he drove Tuuth to the ground. Twisting the blade one last time.

"I hate you, Out—"

Tuuth died.

Shaking, Chongo came by his side and lay down. Both heads licked the muck off of him.

Venir grabbed his mane. "You're too good to me, Boy."

A black bearded dwarf sailed high overhead, slamming into one of the ballista on the towers.

"No time to rest now," Slim said.

"What?"

Slim appeared from behind a wall of cornmeal barrels. "This party just started. They'll need your help. Ew, Chongo! Oh well. Now grab some weapons and gear, Venir. You've got underlings to slay."

"I've got a knife, Slim. I can barely lift it. The armament is gone, Slim. It's gone."

Snap!

With two underlings on his back, Mood continued to pummel the underling commander into submission.

Crack!

"Ye little underlings think yer a match for a Blood Ranger? Their king at that? I'll make a greasy smear of all of you."

Face broken, the underling commander jammed a dagger in Mood's side.

"Ho! Poking me with a tooth pick, now that's just insulting, stabbing me with anything smaller than a sword."

He brought his ham-sized fist down like a mallet into the underling commander's face, knocking it out cold. He tore the other two underlings off his shoulders and threw them to the ground.

Black Beards hacked them down.

Mood yanked the dagger from his shoulder and sunk it in the underling commander's heart.

A Black Beard, grisly from beard to toe, handed him his axes.

"By the bearded goats," he said, assessing the chaos, "we've got work to do!"

Underlings swarmed from all directions, their focus on the giants—the dwarves an afterthought. All the Black Beards huddled in a battle circle, striking with planning and precision, but they weren't here to roust the underlings. They were here to save Venir.

The giants were just a distraction. A good one. But Mood had led them here.

They might be big, but they ain't so smart. They'll be after us soon enough.

One giant, with black hair down to his back, was scooping up underlings and throwing them over the wall. Another, heavyset as an ogre, stuffed the black fiends in his mouth like roaches, crunching bone and metal like canes of sugar.

"Get along the walls! Away from the giants!" Mood commanded. He swung, splitting an underling's face in half.

It was a battle. It was war.

I should've brought more dwarves.

A giant swinging an axe stepped into the fort through the southern gate. He was chopping up the catwalks like kindling when a blast of magic caught him in the face, sending him reeling into a store house. The giant's twin followed, helping his brother up before jumping up and destroying a fort tower with a lethal strike.

Underlings were dying. By dozens now. It was a great thing.

"Black Beards! Find my friend!" Mood said. "We need to get our wrinkled hides out of here!"

Days earlier, Mood and the Black Beards had tracked down a lone giant and killed it. That was what they did. Now, the giants were not only after their kin, Barton, but they had vengeance on their minds as well. Mood would deal with them when he had to. He never imagined Barton would lead them to Outpost Thirty One. They'd let themselves be captured. It couldn't have worked out better. The giants caught right up with them. He couldn't have asked for a bigger distraction.

"Hurry, Dwarves!"

A shadow fell over them. A giant with a gore-splatted club in his hand attacked. The first swing crushed two dwarves.

Fogle sat on the back of Eethum's horse, grinding his teeth.

The jungle erupted. Trees snapped, and footsteps shook the ground.

"Giants?" he asked.

Eethum shook his head yes.

"Aye, let's just hope they're not too late. Come."

"Late?"

"Hold tight, Wizard, and have your craft ready. Ee-Yah!"

Less than a mile away, they galloped up the mountainous slope. Fogle readied a pair of spells on his lips, squeezed his eyes shut, and summoned his powers. He was used to fighting underlings now. For a change, he'd be prepared.

"What are we supposed to do when we get there?" he shouted in Eethum's ear.

The big dwarf was silent, long red beard whipping in the wind.

Bloody dwarves are nothing but secrets.

Something big crashed into the branches above them and fell to the ground. Two underlings lay dead, one with a broken branch stuck in his eye. Fogle smiled.

Good. But what in Bish did that?

The horse burst through the trees and onto the road, hooves thundering over the path.

"Yah!" Eethum whipped the reins. A giant wearing a one horned helmet stepped in their path.

Fogle's neck stretched upward.

The giant was as tall as the oaks. Three underlings floated in the sky, surrounding it, shooting lighting from their hands.

Zzzraam!

Zzzraam!

Zzzraam!

The giant roared, swinging blindly, covering its eyes with its arms.

The underling magi pressed their attack, shooting out the lightning that coiled up and down their arms.

"I'll show them," Fogle said.

He pointed and shot a bright green missile from the tip of his finger.

Zing!

It pierced one underling skull and entered another before blowing out the other side and into the third one's mouth. It gagged, hissed and swallowed a moment before it exploded. All three forms fell from the sky and thudded to the ground. The giant stomped each and every one of them, grinding them into the ground before moving onward.

Eethum stopped the horse, turned and eyed him.

"Don't do that again."

"What, kill underlings?"

"We're not here to kill underlings. We're here to save your friend—and my king, if need be. Protect yourself and your friend. When the time comes, you'll know."

"Killing underlings does protect us," Fogle said. "Killing giants does too, for that matter. And since when do you dwarves decide when killing is and isn't allowed? I say we go in there, kill them all, and sort it out later."

Eethum flashed his teeth and harrumphed.

"Aw, I like the way you think, Wizard Warrior," the Blood Ranger said.

Did I just say what I thought I said? I must be going mad.

Fogle thought of the image of his grandfather's blazing eyes and wispy white beard. The man enjoyed killing underlings more than anything else. *I'm not like that.* He glanced back at the giant footprints of underling goo and laughed. *Well, maybe I am a little.* He jumped off the horse.

"What are you doing?" Eethum growled, grabbing him by the cloak.

Fogle twisted away.

"Why wait to kill the evil bastards later when you can kill them now? I'm going in."

Eethum jumped off his horse and slapped it on the rear. Whipping out his axes, he said, "Mood was right, as always."

"About what?"

"The best wizards are the crazy ones."

CHAPTER 64

Master Kierway entered the arena, head high. The underling's eyes were more curious than they were fearful.

Creed's confidence dipped.

The Cowl on his head urged him forward.

Blood charging through him like a rushing river, Creed faced Kierway for the second time. Chill bumps ran down his arms.

"Fool, no man nor underling can best me, no matter the steel he swings." Kierway eased his swords from the sheaths on his back. "Your death was only delayed by circumstance." He shifted his stance. Circling.

The underling grandmaster of the sword was the fastest he'd ever seen. When they battled in the chamber, it had taken all of Creed's skill just to parry. *I'm faster now. Better now. Aren't I?*

The Cowl assured him he was. The swords in his hands said they were parts of him now. Like a snake's head and tail.

"I beg to differ," Creed said, "It was your death that was delayed."

Creed lunged.

Kierway spun out of reach.

Stabbing a fly would have been just as easy.

"Blast!"

"So, you grumble already, Human. Good."

Eyes flashing, Kierway attacked.

Ching! Ching! Ching!

Creed was on the defensive. Parrying the lightning fast blows. He'd never seen anyone move so fast before. It was astounding.

Rolling his wrists like a human windmill, he batted the attacks away.

The underling's blades were unrelenting.

Rip!

Kierway clipped him under the ribs.

Rip!

Across the thigh.

"Bone! You can't be so fast," Creed said, jumping away.

Kierway twirled his blades and laughed.

"Maybe you should stop talking and start fighting. You've swung once to my twenty," Kierway said. "Still, it's entertaining." He pressed forward.

Creed backed away. It was embarrassing. He'd been taught everything there was to know about the sword. Offense. Defense. Counters and strokes. But in seconds, the underling had negated all of it with superior speed and power.

'Loosen up, Bloodhound,' his mentor once said. 'Being too stiff will kill you. All the skill in the world won't save you when your instincts fail. Trust in them.'

Creed always had good instincts. He could size up an opponent quickly. A dipped shoulder. A slouched posture. Too much weight on one leg. Short arms. Long arms. Everyone had a weakness to exploit. Not this one.

Holding one sword behind his back, Kierway swung.

Clang!

"There. I'm making it easy for you. Swing back."

He wanted to swing.

The Cowl on his head wanted him to swing.

But one mistake would be fatal. He almost died the last time. He didn't want to die today.

Clang! Clang!

Kierway swung.

Creed parried. Backward he went. Stepping around dead bodies.

"Are you going to bleed to death?" Kierway said, eyeing his wounds. "I thought you wanted to fight. Give me a challenge, Human. Give me a fight of some sort before you die like the coward you are."

"Coward?" Creed said, his voice a little less mortal. It made him mad. His mind surged. "You—whose kind strikes at women and children in the darkness—are calling me a coward?"

"Yes, a soft one. A coward and a shoddy swordsman."

Torn between caution and rage, Creed had to choose. *Sometimes you have to trust your instincts and let loose.* He lowered his chin. *Swish. Swish.* "Let's finish this."

He attacked.

The Cowl rejoiced.

But Kierway was already spinning away. He'd seen the move before it happened.

Slice!

Creed clipped Kierway's shoulder. Red-black blood was spilled.

Kierway snarled and cut at his belly.

Creed sprung backward ten feet.

"Did you feel that, Underling?"

Kierway's eyes were molten.

Creed noticed something. An awareness. A second sight. *Go with it, Creed. Go with it!*

Steel crashed against steel like an armory caught in a tornado. Back and forth they went. Blood was let. Sweat dripped. Attack. React. Anticipate.

Creed's mind, body, and blades were one. His skill and instincts melded together. He turned. He changed. From a swordsman into a fearless fighting machine.

Slice!

Kierway ducked and countered.

Chop! Slice!

The underling's blade ripped into Creed's shoulder.

He drove his pommel into the underling's chin.

Kierway stuffed his knee in Creed's gut.

Steel flashed again. A pair of tireless storms trying to wipe out one another.

Duck!

Jump!

Parry!

Strike! Strike! Strike!

Creed didn't know if it was him commanding his body or The Cowl, but he was doing things he'd never done before. The underling's strikes came, precise and fatal, but they missed their mark, time and again. He bled. He fought. He learned.

"Such improvement, Human." Kierway said, "Unexpected. Impressive."

Master Kierway's hardened face lathered. His thin coat of fur showed a sheen.

Creed's own chest was heaving. He'd never fought so long. So hard. Pressed. Possessed. He fought on. *Kill the underling!*

Seconds passed that felt like minutes. Sparks of hot metal flew in the air.

Clip!

He caught Kierway below the knee cap.

Clip!

And under his left sword arm. His blades cut armor like bread.

"What manner of man are you that fights like many?" Kierway said, breaking off his attack, wiping the blood from his lips. The underling lowered his blade and stuck one in the ground. "A parlay, perhaps?"

Creed opened his mouth to speak.

Whish! Whish! Whish!

The underling's knives flicked through the air.

Creed battled one away, then two, catching the third in his chest.

"Now that's just dirty! Who's the coward now, Underling?" Creed plucked it out and slung it back.

Kierway ducked under it and laughed.

"Such words have no meaning to our kind. Your time to die has come, Human."

Chest burning, Creed shrugged is broad shoulders and stood tall in the face of his enemy. He might not have much time left to live, but he still felt like fighting. *Make the most of it!*

Kierway's swords came at his neck and thigh.

But Creed had seen them coming two steps ago. Lunging forward, he punched his right sword through Kierway's side.

Bang!

He head butted Kierway in the face, breaking his nose.

Kierway hissed, tearing himself away and clutching at his bloody side, copper eyes wide as saucers.

"Impossible!" he said, eyeing Creed as if he were someone else.

"Nothing's impossible!"

Creed charged. Inspired. He spun. He swung.

Kierway's swords were ready.

Creed shattered both of the underling's blades with his first blow.

Slice!

Kierway's head popped from his shoulders with the second blow. Blood sprayed. The underling fell.

Creed clutched at his chest and fell to his knees, sucking for breath and spitting blood.

"Now that was some glorious fighting. If I can only live to tell the ladies about it."

CHAPTER 65

IT WAS STRANGE, STANDING ALONGSIDE one of the most powerful women in the City of Bone, having her huddle in his arms.

If we had a soft bed and a secure room, I bet I could teach her a thing or two.

In little more than a stitch of clothing and without even a weapon in hand, Melegal prepared for his last stand.

"They won't kill you, Lorda," he said, pushing her between the wall and his back. "But I don't think they'll spare me."

"True," she said, her nails wrapped around his belly "but I may be able to convince them otherwise."

The idea had promise, but sooner or later, the odds of surviving were bound to catch up with him. *Cats have many lives, but perhaps rats have more.*

"I appreciate that," he said, "but you don't need to risk yourself. No one lives forever. Save yourself."

"How noble, Detective. You have a charming tongue. I wish we had more time."

Melegal's ears perked up, and Lorda Almen gasped.

Two underling soldiers came closer, black hair braided and old gold hoops in one's ears. One scraped his hand-axe along the wall, and the other let out an unfriendly chitter.

Melegal's grip tightened over Lorda's hand as the other pair closed in. Dark faced and armored in leather, there was something evil about them. Something sinister. Melegal never meddled in the affairs of underlings; he let Venir The Darkslayer handle that. The stories he heard and the things he had seen were more than enough to keep him away from the twisted breed.

Lorda pressed her soft lips into his back. "Sorry, Detective." She stepped into the clear.

The underlings stopped.

She pointed at Melegal. "I am the Lorda of this castle, and this man is my servant. No harm should come to me or him, Underlings." She had a convincing way of speaking. "Seize him if you must, but don't you dare lay a hand on me."

The nearest underling, red eyes glimmering, lowered his weapon, walked over and back handed her in the face.

"Silence, Human."

Lorda fell to the ground, gaping, rubbing her reddened cheek.

Another underling lowered a spear at Melegal's belly.

Melegal crept back into the wall, the spear tip nicking his exposed belly.

"This man will die, a painful death," the underling said, "but you, Woman, your death will look like an accident."

"You wouldn't dare," she said, shocked. "My husband is in good standing with your Lords. They'll punish you for this."

"No," the underling said. He pinched her face in his hand. "Human life has no meaning to us. No use to us. They'll be rid of you soon enough."

"You overstep your bounds, Black Swine. You've no order to kill or harm me, just him," her eyes flicked to Melegal, "... maybe?"

The longer they talk, the longer I live. His stomach groaned. A shadow darted between the walls. *What was that?*

"Put a hole in the noisy one's stomach."

Chop!

An underling's skull was split open.

Slice!

The head of another underling leapt from its shoulders, freeing Lorda.

Melegal twisted. The spear tip jabbed at his center.

Slice!

The underling spear-wielder lost both hands from forearm to finger.

Melegal turned.

Taller than him the battle-splattered warrior stood, eyes glowing a pale green through a dark cowl. Melegal blinked, thinking of Venir, but his man was different. Agile and swift. Quick and merciless. The face was obscured somehow. But he was certain it was Creed.

The last underling charged Lorda Almen, cutting at her throat.

Melegal dove for her, but he was too far away.

In one long stride, Creed cut the underling off and ripped his sword across its belly, spilling its bowels.

Creed sheathed his swords and clutched his chest. Reaching down, he lifted Lorda back to her feet.

"Who are you?" she said. Her fingers grazed his broad chest. "You're wounded."

"Aye, but it's already getting better." He bowed a little. "I'm Creed the Bloodhound, Lorda."

"No," Melegal said, getting back up, "that's not what you are, not right now." He craned his neck. "And more soldiers are coming." Melegal grabbed her arm. "Anything left in the arena?"

"Just the dead."

"Good," Melegal said. "That'll be our way to sanctuary then. Come on."

Through the entrance, down the steps and over the wall they'd gone when Melegal's keen eye caught something in the rack of weapons.

"I'll be," he said. He rummaged through the rack, strapping his swords, the Sisters, around his waist and finding something else. "Yes!" He grabbed his dart launchers and snapped them on. "Where is it?"

"Where is what?" Lorda said, trying to help.

"My cap."

"I'll buy you all the caps you want," she said, running her finger over his ear.

"No," he said, looking at her. "Have you seen it? Do you remember—"

"Yes, I remember. Last I saw it, well," she picked at her lip and shrugged. "It was in my husband's throne room, under heavy guard."

That bothered Melegal. Had they discovered the secret of his cap? Why else would they guard it? *Must get it back.*

"And the Keys?" he said.

"Same place."

"How many did you see?"

"Five, I think. But Kierway had one."

Finishing the last buckle on his dart-launchers, he searched the headless body of Kierway. Nothing. "Are you sure he had a Key on him?"

"I'm certain."

His neck snapped to the last spot he'd seen Jarla. She was gone. "Slat! The witch has it!"

"What's so special about those Keys?" Lorda asked, brushing her hair out of her eyes.

The question struck him. There was little reason to believe that Lorda knew anything about the Keys. Lord Almen was a man of many secrets. As for the Keys, the easy way out of this was gone. He had no idea which Key went where, or what they all did. Did they need a door from the chamber or could they be used elsewhere instead?

"Did you notice the gemstone in it?"

Lorda's perfectly plucked eyebrows scrunched down.

"Sapphire, I believe," she said. "I only caught a single glimpse of it."

I didn't matter. It wasn't the one Melegal had used anyway.

Swish. Swish. Swish.

Creed was whirling his blades around his body in a marvelous fashion.

"Astounding," he said, "I cannot tell if it's the blades or me." He extended the keen edges outward, eyeing them. "I don't prefer hand guards." *Swish!* "But these are so flexible."

"And how about that... cowl... on your head?" Melegal started.

Creed slipped his blades into their sheaths. He didn't move. Instead, he stood still, cocking his head back and forth.

"Are you coming?" Melegal said. "Or are you waiting for more underlings to arrive?"

"There are so many," Creed said. "I can feel them running through the halls. Their hearts beat in my ears." He cast a dark foreboding glance at Melegal, and his voice changed a little. "I can kill them." His body tensed. "I can kill them all."

"No," Melegal said, "if you could do that, they'd be dead already."

"What makes you say that?"

"I know. Now..." He tossed Creed the sack. "You'll need that." He jammed two fingers down his throat.

"Ew, Detective, what are you doing?" Lorda asked. "Are you ill?"

Melegal spit a metal gob into his palm and rubbed the spit off. He flashed the light of his coin in their eyes and grinned.

"Follow me."

"You're resourceful, Detective. I'll give you that," Creed said. The man was chewing on jerky and flipping his coin of light. "This is the best jerky I've ever tasted."

"You don't have to call me detective, Creed. Melegal will do." He was sifting through a trunk in what used to be one of Sefron's hidden rooms. "Or not."

If Castle Almen didn't have so many secrets, we'd be dead already.

Of that much, Melegal was certain. And as for Sefron, his pasty nemesis, the cleric had been storing up for something. This room barely held the three of them, but it was filled with provisions, and it was only one room within a sprawling network. *I could spend a year exploring this castle, maybe more. I wonder how many secrets are in this world.* He looked at Creed and crunched into some fruit.

The man had finally pulled his cowl down off his head so it rested on his shoulders, and Melegal could make out his face. *Good.* For the time being, Creed was himself again. An overachieving thug in the ranks of Royals.

At least he doesn't have his loud and smelly dogs with him.

"Melegal," Lorda said, chin down, rubbing her arms. "Do you think all my family are dead?" She sobbed. "I saw them gut my niece and butcher one of my uncles before my eyes. They're monsters, aren't they?"

Just a little more so than your husband.

"There's no time to mourn, Lorda. Just escape."

"But?"

He put one hand on her shoulder, lifted her chin and looked into her eyes. "Be strong."

A tear fell down her cheek. Lorda had family, and they meant something. He was certain they were wiped out. Most all of them anyway. If he understood anything about underlings, he knew they didn't need people for anything, other than amusement. They were like cats that played with mice.

He fondled a small ring he'd found in one of Sefron's chests earlier. It was a flat metal with odd symbols, dust coated, and set with a variety of smooth gemstones. There were other baubles, but he had no pockets to stick them in.

"You're gorgeous," Creed said, staring hard at Lorda.

"What?"

Creed game closer, adjusting the bracers he'd pulled out of the sack and put on his arms earlier.

"You're more gorgeous," he repeated, "than the morning light in the gardens. Captivating."

Lorda pulled tighter around her form a gown Melegal had scrounged up for her.

"Mind yourself, Bloodhound," she warned. "I'm not some tavern trollop who'll swoon at your clever phrase of words. The finest troubadours in the land haven't swayed me, so how could a smelly hound like you?"

"Pardon, Lorda." He bowed with a grin. "It's a sincere compliment. But I'd be lying if I didn't admit that I'd cut my own arm off just for a — "

"Don't you dare, Heathen!"

"Shhhh! The both of you," Melegal said. "There's a hundred underlings out there looking for us."

"A taste of those sweet lips," Creed said, "was all I was going to say. What did you think I was going to say, anyway? I'm a Royal too, you know."

Lorda scooted farther away.

The last thing Melegal needed was a conflict with Creed. The man wasn't a brute, but he was all fighter. They needed him. They might have to carve their way out to escape.

Creed resumed his seat and tore back into his jerky. "What's the plan, Melegal?"

Melegal envisioned the last thing he'd seen from his spire before he came in here. Underlings were everywhere. The only safe way out was the same way he'd come in. With a Key.

Slat! And to think: I had seven of them, along with my freedom, and I came right back into this infernal Castle. What a vengeful fool I am!

"We need a Key, Creed. I think one Key is all it will take to get us free and clear. It's either that, or we're going to have to lay low in here, and it won't be long before the food runs out or they find us."

Eyeing Creed, Lorda said, "I'm ready to get out of here. I don't think this man can be trusted with me in these close quarters."

Creed perched his eyebrows. "My intentions are nothing but honorable. You'll need protection, Lorda. You can't expect me to believe you'd prefer the company of underlings to me?" He shrugged and looked at Melegal. "Then again, maybe you prefer the small gruesome kind. No offense."

"None taken."

Creed slipped The Cowl back over his head. "Let's be about our business." He held a finger up. "Wait, something comes."

Melegal stepped in front of Lorda, pushing her behind him. He hadn't heard a thing when a dark shadow slipped into the room.

Creed drew his sword.

"Wait," Melegal said.

"What is that?" Lorda said.

"It's my cat. Octopus."

Lorda let out a sigh.

Creed flipped him his coin. "That's the ugliest cat I ever saw. And those eyes. What is it, blind as a bat?"

"Blind as a bat and meaner than ten of your dogs."

"Huh."

Octopus rumbled, the hairs raising on his back.

Creed froze. "They're close."

"How close?"

Dust and debris fell from the ceiling above.

Wham!

Something pounded the floor above.

"Is that close enough for you?"

Bone! They're onto us.

CHAPTER 66

SLIM DANGLED THE PINK FLESH of Venir's missing ear in his face. "Hold still. This is going to sting. I can put it back on, but, I'm sorry, I couldn't find the other one."

"That's alright," Venir said. "I never listened much anyway. I don't think putting my ear on is going to do me much good eith—*urk!*"

Grabbing both sides of his head with extra-long fingers, Slim's hands glowed.

"Argh!"

Venir's bones crackled. His skin felt like it was on fire. It wasn't pain, not like all the other torments he'd faced the past few days, but it was uncomfortable. Disturbing. Unnatural.

"Bone! What are you doing, Slim?"

A storm raged between his temples. His bones moved. His skin crawled. His arms and legs thickened.

Slim's long, youthful face changed. His hair thinned. His eyes sunk back in their sockets.

Venir blinked hard.

Slim's red lips turned gray, and the skin on his body became mummified and dry.

"No, Slim! No!"

He tried to push his friend away, but Slim's lanky arms didn't budge.

Finally, Slim let out a ragged sigh, released him, stepped back, and fell to the ground. His long frame little more than a husk of skin and bone.

"Slim! Slim!" Venir said.

The cleric's teeth were cracked when he smiled.

"Don't worry about me, Vee. I'll be fine. Go get you some underlings."

One of Chongo's big heads licked the man.

Then Slim's eyes rolled up in his head.

Venir's head dipped to his chest, and his hand was white-knuckled on his knife. He was whole. So far as he could tell, he was as whole as he'd ever been. He'd been living in such pain.

Grabbing Chongo by the mane on his neck, he swung himself into the saddle. "Let's find me an axe and shatter some bones!"

Chongo surged forward.

Outpost Thirty One was in total disarray. A hundred underlings or more dragged one giant to the ground. A dozen underlings at a time were being stomped, leaving black smears in the dust. A wagon cart was tossed into one of the towers, and a giant bigger than all the rest beat his chest and roared, slamming his weapon across the ground, sweeping underlings away like bugs.

"Now that's an axe!" Venir yelled.

Chongo barreled through the sea of underlings, biting some and trampling others. Venir's eyes locked on the battle axe of a fallen brigand who'd been smashed into a bloody mud hole. Riding by, he snatched it off the ground. A second later, he gored an underling's head.

"It's sharp! It's metal! It ain't Brool. Yah! But it'll do!"

He brought the heavy axe down, busting armor and splitting through a clavicle. He was free. Unfettered by his helm, he had clarity. Sweeping the battle axe from one side to the other. In seconds, gore coated his arms and chest.

The distracted underlings didn't see him and Chongo coming.

Crush!

Crumble!

Chomp!

"Over there, Chongo!"

Venir had spied an ailing Black Beard surrounded by a thicket of underlings. Chongo pounced on them. Venir dove into the ones he missed. Swinging left and right with all his might, opening chests and crushing in skulls. *Who needs the armament!*

Two strokes later, his corded arms turned to lead. His lungs caught fire. Out of the corner of his eye, he saw another pack of underlings closing in on him.

"Seems fear of the giants has rerouted their attack," he said, raising his axe over his head. "Come on, get them!"

Eethum led. Fogle followed. The Blood Ranger's axes sang to the underlings. A tune of death and destruction. Fogle tasted their oily blood in his mouth and spit it out. Above, the towering giants had failed to take over. Scores of underlings kept coming. Overwhelming the giants with sheer numbers. They crawled all over.

Fogle was torn. *Whose side should I be fighting for?* Even if they defeated the underlings, wouldn't the giants turn on him and the dwarves?

Thump!

Thump!

The entire fort shook. One of the giants, eyes close together, was slamming himself into one of the corner towers. Underlings spilled out, screeching on their way to the ground.

"Help the dwarves, Fogle!" Eethum said. "Keep your eyes out for Venir!"

Find Venir! And get out of here!

Wading through underlings and dodging oversized feet and weapons, Eethum led them up the stair onto the catwalks.

"See anything?" Fogle said.

"No!" Eethum said. The Blood Ranger was holding them off.

"There!" Fogle pointed.

Two Black Beards were fighting for their lives in the corner. Fogle unleashed his power. A bolt of lightning leapt from his fingers.

Sssram!

The chain of lightning ripped through one underling, then another. Piles of ash were scattered in the air.

A giant, bald and cock-eyed, leered down at him, raised his axe and swung. Eethum shoved Fogle out of the way. The catwalk shattered. They tumbled hard to the ground.

Breathless, Fogle got back to his feet just as the giant reached down for him.

Wham!

The ugly giant roared.

Somebody swung a club the size of a tree into its knee. It was Barton.

"Leave my Wizard friend alone, Haddad!"

Whack!

Haddad struck Barton across the face, knocking him from his feet, and turned back to Fogle.

"I'LL EAT YOU, WIZARD!" He patted his belly. "YOUR MAGIC MAKE HADDAD STRONG!"

Eethum burst into action, chopping into the bone below the giant's knee.

"ARGH! BLOOD RANGER! YOU SHALL PAY!" The giant was quick. It snatched Eethum off the ground and squeezed him.

Fogle drew his arms back, summoned his words, and started to cast.

Clonk!

A sling stone ricocheted off his head. Blood trickled in his eyes. The next thing he saw was Eethum flying through the air and the giant reaching for him.

I don't want to fly like that.

Fighting to lift his arms to swing, Venir's knees buckled when an underling's shield clipped the back of his chin. Trying to shake it off, he was too late. The underlings piled on top of him, clawing and tearing at his throat.

"Heeyah!" a familiar voice rang out, scattering the underlings like bloody moths.

Mood's arms pumped those axes into one underling after another, rekindling Venir's fire.

Venir caught his breath and burst into motion.

"Ain't so savvy without that helmet on, are ye?"

Venir, arms high, sunk his axe down into an underling's chest, shooting black and red blood up everywhere.

"No!"

Two more black beards joined in, the five of them forming a circle, keeping the underlings at bay.

"Where in Bish are all these roaches pouring out from, anyway!" Mood shouted, deflecting a chop at his neck on the blade of his axe.

"Northside War Room! There must be a tunnel in there!"

Hundreds of underlings lay dead, but where one fell, two more were coming. So far as Venir knew, the underlings never had a tunnel to the Outpost, but they could have dug one over the past few years. Chopping away, he watched another giant fall, leaving only three.

"What was your plan, Mood?"

"Carve a way in and rescue you! Carve a way out to freedom!"

That wasn't going to happen. The underlings covered the gates, and many were watching the giants fall. Ropes, grappling hooks, and magic cords wrapped the giants' legs and pinned their arms. Another giant pitched and stumbled, his head slamming into the wall. He roared while the underlings cut and stabbed at his back.

Thwack!

One of the Black Beards caught another ballista bolt in his back. "Bone!"

"Tis a shame," Mood said, still swinging.

"What!"

"We could have made it, if not for all the extra underlings."

Fogle's plan had unraveled. He'd had on his lips the same spell he'd used to fight Tundoor and his breed. It was lost. Now, mind addled, he tried to recall another spell before he was crushed, then eaten.

One foot from his nose, the giant's fingers stopped. An enormous black shadow fell from the sky, shaking the ground.

WHUMP! WHUMP! SNORT!

Fogle's heart skipped. Two citrine eyes bore into him.

Blackie!

A tide of flames ripped through the underlings.

Ka-Chow!
Ka-Chow!
Ka-Chow!

Bolts of lightning fell from the sky, blasting underlings off the ground. Every portion of the battlefield was either lit up in a spectacular array of fireworks or consumed by flame.

Venir's attackers paused. Their hesitation was fatal.

Chop! Hack!

Two underlings fell.

"Head for the North Gate," Venir said. "The south is on fire!"

In front of them, the giants waded through the flames like they were water, stomping and chopping at every underling in sight. The black bodies were burning and dying by the dozens now, the others trying to flee.

Venir led Mood and the remaining Black Beards north under the catwalks, picking their way through the dead.

"We can take the drainage tunnel, if we can get to it."

"MOOD!"

The loud voice shook his bones. The biggest giant of all, hefting a battle axe over its shoulder, was coming after them.

"I'VE GOT YOU NOW!"

The Black Dragon was the last thing Fogle expected to see, until he saw Cass, sitting on its back.

"Cass!" he yelled, but nothing cut through the chaos.

Inspired, Fogle launched a magic missile into the hesitating giant's eye.

"ARGH!" it roared, stumbling backward.

He sent another one past Cass's face.

She jerked back, pink eyes hot with anger before she caught his gaze.

He waved and ran toward her at full speed.

Blackie whipped his serpentine neck in front of him, opening his mouth that was full of flames.

"No, Blackie!" Cass cried. "He's on my side."

One spell. One spell. One spell.

Boon soared off Blackie's back and floated into the sky.

Above Outpost Thirty One, five underling magi hovered, attacking the giants. He let them have it.

Ka-Chow! Ka-Chow! Ka-Chow! Ka-Chow! Ka-Chow!

Lightening ripped out of the clouds and through their robes, sending them twirling and smoking to the ground. Below him, Blackie, flames shooting from his mouth, landed on the ground.

"Burn them! Burn them all, Blackie!"

The smoke was black and thick, and the smell of burning flesh foul, but Venir and Mood waded through it, trying to avoid the giant.

"I CAN SMELL YOU, MOOD!"

CRASH!

The giant was destroying everything in its path, trying to get at them.

"GIANTS! SECURE... THE... GATES! THE... KING OF THE DWARVES... IS HERE! KILL HIM... AND... HIS KIN!"

Ka-Chow!

The giant's face was lit up by a lightning strike.

Venir stopped and took a look.

"Are ye mad?" Mood said. "Keep moving."

Venir gazed up at the man floating in the air. It was the old wizard, Boon, scraggly hairs whipping in the wind, eyes filled with power.

Where'd he come from?

"PARLEY!" Boon said in a voice that was loud like thunder.

The giant, Haddad, rubbed his temples. "WHAT, WIZARD? HAH, YOU... CANNOT... PARLEY... WITH US. WE... HAVE... YOU. ALL... OF...YOU."

Venir tugged at Mood's shoulder. "Let's move."

Mood rose his hand up. "Nay, let them parley, Venir. It buys us time, if nothing else."

Behind Haddad the giant, another one had Barton slung over his shoulders. The deformed giant was kicking and screaming.

"TOYS! VENIR, GIVE ME MY TOYS! BARTON WON'T GO BACK WITH YOU, HADDAD! BARTON HATES YOU ALL! AND BLACKIE, TOO!"

"THE TOYS ARE GONE, BARTON!" Boon said.

"LYING WIZARD TRICK BARTON JUST LIKE VENIR DID BEFORE! BARTON WILL SMASH VENIR. CRUNCH HIS BONES. HE IS A LIAR!"

Haddad the giant reached back and walloped Barton in the head.

"NO MORE... TROUBLE FROM YOU... TEASER OF DRAGONS!"

Barton's hand went to his eye. He started to cry.

"HE STARTED IT!"

"SIIIIILENCE!" Haddad said, shaking everything on the ground. "WIZARD, I OFFER THIS! I TAKE PRISONER THE BLOOD RANGER KING, MOOD. BLACKIE THE DRAGON AND THE TINY GIANT," He pointed at Barton, "MUST COME HOME." He spat a giant gob onto the ground. "THE REST CAN LEAVE."

Another giant stepped forward, squeezing a black beard between his fingers.

Venir swore the black-faced dwarf was purple.

Giants are liars. But are they good liars?

Remaining still, Fogle's eyes were transfixed on his grandfather, who was negotiating with the giants. Out of nowhere, a pair of warm pale arms wrapped around his waist.

"Miss me?" Cass said. She kissed him on the cheek.

He struggled to choke out the words. "I thought I'd lost you, Cass. I'm so—"

She put her finger to his lips.

"Shush, Fogle, I'm alright." She gave him a reassuring embrace. "And Blackie, believe it or not, has been quite good to me."

He glanced over at the dragon. There was jealousy in those yellow eyes.

"But, how?"

"I'm a druid, remember. I can communicate with all living things. And Blackie and I," she said, nodding at the dragon with great admiration in her pink eyes, "we understand one another."

Fogle chewed on his lip. He'd seen that look in the eyes of women before. Her arms around his waist had already slackened. *No. This can't be happening.* What had Venir told him on the trail before? *'Bish is full of surprises. And women even more. Get used to it.'*

"You're going with the dragon, aren't you? Over me—A man!"

She caressed his face, looked up into his eyes, and said, "Oh Fogle, you knew it could never last, me and you."

It tugged at his chest, but he knew she was right. The two of them couldn't be any more different, but what they had shared had been wonderful. He didn't want to let that go.

"I never really thought about it. I was too worried whether you were alive or dead." He stepped away from her a little. "And now," he glared at Blackie, "you choose a beast over me?"

"Don't be that way, Fogle."

"What way? Sane?"

"No," she said. Her cheeks reddened. "A grown man acting like spoiled child who lost his favorite toy. Shame on you, Fogle. I'm not yours to claim. I never was."

"I risked my life for you! I fought that dragon! And this is the thanks I get? Come on, Cass!"

"Oh Fogle, don't be so dramatic," she said, walking away and onto Blackie's back. "It's not manly. An adventurer should know that." She sighed. "At least you'll know what to do with the next pretty woman you meet."

Fogle turned away.

Of all the ridiculous things.

"Here," Mood said to Venir, handing over his axes.

"For what?" Venir said, feeling a little foolish for some reason.

"Cause you'll be needin' them, I'm certain. I'll not where I'm going."

"You can't be serious, Mood?" Venir said. He looked at the giant that talked with Boon. He couldn't understand it. He turned back to Mood. "You're the King of the Dwarves. You can't leave your people."

"It's better to be a live King than a dead one." He winked. "And don't worry; they can't hold me forever. I'll outlive them first."

Venir took the axes. Mood walked out to the giant. "Alright, Haddad! I'll come with you, but all my dwarves and people stay!"

Chongo stammered his paws on the ground. Black tails flicked back and forth like whips. His big jaws snapped.

Venir got in between both heads and hugged Chongo's necks. The dog would do anything for him. He'd do anything for the dog. But things had changed. He could feel it in his bones. Without the armament, the underlings would catch up with him sooner or later. They would catch Chongo too, if he stayed with Venir.

He couldn't protect his dog. The dog couldn't protect him.

"I've got to let you go, Boy." He rubbed his forehead on Chongo's big chest. "Go with Mood." He pointed at the dwarf.

Mood stood, shoulders stooped, holding his side a little.

"Mood needs you, Boy. He's getting old."

Both of Chongo's heads licked Venir one last time.

Venir rubbed his dog behind all four ears. "Take care of him, Chongo. If anyone can lead the old curmudgeon out of there, you can." He hugged the muscular necks once more.

Chongo, with one head looking backward, walked away. Venir wiped the blood from the corner of his eye.

"Dog come with Barton? Good. Barton like that." Barton sighed in the clutches of two other giants, like the child he was. He struggled in vain. His chin dipped. They were bigger and stronger than him.

The other giant set Eethum down, and one by one the giants faded into mist, along with Chongo, Barton, and Mood, whose thick arms crossed his bearded chest.

Whump! Whump! Whump!

Cass and the dragon lifted off the ground and into the sky. Fogle's head was down, but Boon waved goodbye to Cass, a big smile on his face. Only three men, a handful of dwarves, smoke, fire and carnage remained.

"Now what?" Fogle said. "Is it over?"

353

"Or has it just begun?" Boon cried out, pointing.

The underlings that had fled earlier were coming back now. There were well over a hundred.

Venir readied his axes and dug into the ground.

"So be it, men!" He yelled out at the top of his lungs, "RELEASE THE HOUNDS OF CHAOS AND CRY BISH!"

"Wait, Venir. There has to be another way to get out of here," Fogle suggested.

"To the last, Grandson! The time for a final stand has come!" Boon said, lightning racing up his arms.

Eethum the Blood Ranger shouted over all of them.

"Over there! Look!"

One of the Black Beards was waving them over from the entrance to the War Room.

Venir growled. "That's where the underlings came from earlier."

"Well, they're not coming from there now!" Fogle started running.

"Slat! Let's go then!"

Dashing across the courtyard, the small party barreled through the doors, stepping over dead underlings, ignoring the ones that still burned.

The Black Beard led them through a panel in the wall that Venir had never noticed before and down a wide set of carved out steps. At the bottom, a long corridor ten feet tall and just as wide led to another door, which was open.

"Fool! What does this do, lead to the Underland? I'm not going in." Fogle turned away.

Behind them, the underlings were coming. Chittering and screeching as they entered the War Room.

"We either fight them out here, or in there, but having that big door between us will buy us some time to prepare, at least," Boon said. "I say we go in."

"Well, time's a wasting," Venir said, watching the underlings tear up the corridor. "It's now or never, Wizard."

"Fine!" Fogle said, being the first to enter.

Boon was next, followed by the Black Beards, Eethum and Venir, who pulled on the door handle, trying to close it.

"See any underlings yet?" Venir said between clenched teeth.

No one said anything.

Venir and Eethum kept pulling, but the underlings fought them on the other side.

"Heave!" he yelled.

Eethum grunted.

Venir pulled with all his might, pinching underling fingers around the edges.

"Hurk!"

The door sealed shut. Eethum slammed the bolt in place.

"Whew!"

Suddenly, Venir's instincts caught fire. He knew he'd made a big mistake. In the distance, something evil chittered and twisted.

CHAPTER 67

"DOGS," CREED SAID. "HAS TO BE."

Melegal could hear nails scratching at the ceiling above them.

"It's your cat that led them to us, Melegal," Creed said, "but I can handle them if they catch up. Just lead us."

With Lorda hanging onto his hand, Melegal led the way through the winding secret passage until the clawing above them came to a stop.

"See? They're stuck in one room, and we're beneath another, so it's not my cat." Shining a tiny beam of light forward, he realized Octopus was no longer around. *Good.* He wasn't going to admit it, but Creed was probably right.

"They're still going to catch up with us," Creed said, eyes glowing in the dark through The Cowl.

Melegal shook his head. Something about the man disturbed him. Creed was eerie. Unpredictable. And to make matters worse, he was a Bloodhound. Part of a notorious bunch of chaotic goons. *Keep your back in the front and front in the back.* There was no telling what the man would do, and he had the armament now. Melegal remembered Jarla, who had it before. She was the most evil woman Venir ever knew.

"Just keep your swords ready, Creed. We've still got a shot at getting out of here yet."

"Are we going to the Throne Room?"

"Aye. We're going to steal a Key." *Or as many as I can get my hands on.*

Melegal's eyes glared through a peep hole.

The Throne Room was empty. No guards. No underlings. No Keys. No hat.

Where in Bone could they be?

"What is it, Melegal?" Lorda clung to him. "What do you see?"

"Nothing," he said, "see for yourself. It seems they've moved the bloody things."

"If I were a Key, where would I be?" Creed said, oddly.

On the one hand, Melegal was relieved he didn't have to face the underlings. On the other hand, he'd have to start all over again, with the underlings already looking for them.

"Perhaps I can find out, Melegal," Lorda suggested. "Lords Catten and Verbard are working with my husband. If I can get to them…"

"No! They tried to kill you once already. Besides, I can only assume they are either in the Keep or the Chamber."

"Perhaps the Chamber is where we should go. The Keys will be there at some point, won't they?" she said, pressing up against him. "We could hide and wait them out."

"I've already thought of that," he said, rubbing his aching neck. He brushed up against Lorda who brushed back. *So amazing. Even in perilous times.* "But they probably have more guards there than anywhere."

"Then I'll have to kill them all," Creed said.

The madness never ends.

All Melegal wanted was his hat, at least one of the Keys, and his own castle. He was pretty sure his own castle was the most attainable of the three.

"Move or die, Detective," Creed said. "Move or die."

"I'll be," Lord Verbard said. "He's butchered."

Lord Catten was holding up Master Kierway's head, unable to hide the shock in his golden eyes.

"Do you think Master Sinway will be angered or pleased?" Catten said, handing the head to one of his Juegen.

Verbard gawped at the mutilated Vicious on the ground. "Probably more angered about the Vicious than his son." He shook his head. "What do you make of this, Jottenhiem?"

"A swordsman," the red-eyed commander said. "An outstanding one at that. Master Kierway was one of the finest swordsmen in the Underland, after me and a few others, of course."

"You boast, Commander," Catten said. "Much as I hate to admit it, Kierway's skill was without rival."

Jottenhiem glowered at him. "If you say so, Lord Catten."

"Stay close, Commander," Verbard said. "Whoever did this... well..."

"Might be The Darkslayer, Brother? Is that what you're thinking?"

It was exactly what Verbard was thinking. It worried him. It more than worried him.

"Eep!"

The bat-winged imp buzzed up to him out of nowhere, rubbing its taloned fingers together.

"Yess, Lordsss. Is it time to kill?"

"It's always time to kill," Verbard said, "but the hunt must go on first. Find who did this, imp, and report back to me, immediately."

"As you wish, Lordsss Verbard," Eep hissed and looked at his brother, "and Catten."

Blink.

With Eep gone, Verbard and Jottenhiem were continuing their brief investigation when he discovered something else.

"We've another problem," Verbard said.

"Oh, and what is that?" Catten replied.

"Master Kierway's Key is gone."

"Well, Master Sinway won't be happy about that either, but he said we only needed one Key. We still have seven. Kierway's Key didn't do much of anything."

"It did enough to help anyone escape."

Catten twirled a dark gray cap on his fingertip. "Are you suggesting The Darkslayer fled?"

"We don't know that it was The Darkslayer." Verbard's nails dug into his palms. "And what is that on your finger?"

"A mystical item."

"What does it do?" Verbard's hand slid inside his pocket over his Orb of Imbibing.

"I don't know yet, but I will soon."

"It's ugly."

"It's charming."

"Well, I wouldn't be wearing it when Master Sinway arrives."

Catten slid it into his pocket. "I suppose the time has come to greet him." He pulled a Key from his pocket. "Shall I let him enter, or shall you? I could lead him to your Throne Room, if you like."

"Or I could lead him to yours, Brother. But we'd better be rid of this scourge first."

Verbard tossed Lord Almen's whip to Jottenhiem.

"Soon you might get your chance to prove who is better: Kierway or you, Commander."

CHAPTER 68

Venir felt like one side of his body was going out the other.

"Bish! What is happeningggg?"

He felt the wind whoosh through his hair. A split second later he stopped.

"Fight, Man! Fight!"

It was the old wizard, Boon, yelling. Yellow strands of light licked from his fingertips, striking at the hive of underlings surrounding them.

Choking down the queasiness, Venir lashed out.

Slash!

An underling warrior fell dead with its neck open.

"You fight well, Warrior." Eethum banged one attack away and countered another. "But can you fight long?"

Glitch!

The Blood Ranger gored the underling's chest.

Venir, brow buckled, did what he did best. He swung and swung, giving no thought to where he was or what he did.

"Fight and die!" he cried

Fogle's first question wasn't 'Where am I?' but 'How much longer am I going to live?'

He blasted the first underling he saw in the face, knocking a hole in it and barreling two more over. In the dim light, he caught glimpses of a large chamber that was rows deep in underlings.

I can't be in the Underland! I can't be!

He summoned a mystical shield and glanced over his shoulder. The door they'd come in was sealed.

There must be another away out of here.

Two underlings converged on him, mouths wide, curved swords low. The first struck hard, its edge glancing off his shield, cracking it. The other slammed into him with its full weight, pushing him backward. They kept swinging, chipping away shards of magic one piece at a time. Something ignited in Fogle.

No!

The underlings. They'd caused so much anguish. So much pain. He'd lost Cass because of them!

NO!

He shoved his arms forward. His attackers were flung backward, clearing a hole at the bottom of a wide torch-lit stairwell that was otherwise filled with more underlings coming down.

"Hahahaha," he heard his grandfather laughing, "Brilliant, Fogle! Brilliant!"

Boon flung a ball of smoke up the stairwell. It exploded in a puff of air, leaving behind it a wall of stone. Those underlings were sealed outside the chamber.

"Have at them, warriors!" Boon cried, eyeing the hoard of underlings that still surrounded the party. "Let's route these fiends once and for all! Hahahaha!"

Like two Juggernauts, Venir and Eethum gored every black thing breathing.

"Bish!" Fogle lifted his feet from the suction of the floor. The fallen were being sucked dry. Dry husks in an instant. A nasty chill went through him. "What is this place?"

"Eight!"

Chop!

"Nine!"

Slice!

Arms heavy, chest filled with fire, Venir kept swinging. Mood's well-crafted axes could cut metal, but they weren't as light and balanced as Brool's keen edge that he'd grown so accustomed to over the years.

Gashed from chin to toe, he fought on and on, mindless of anything else. He'd gotten his wish. He'd sent more underlings to the grave. He could die complete. Happy. He buried one axe in the next underling's chest.

Large drops of dark blood showered the odd mosaic floor, which sucked every bit up.

"Venir!"

Eyes blazing, he whirled.

"They're all dead," Boon said. "Look around."

Twenty underlings, maybe thirty, were being sucked dry by the floor, their flesh withering.

"Aw." Eethum knelt down at the armored shell of a Black Beard. The dwarf was one of only three that now remained.

Venir's wounds dripped like sweat, feeding the yearning floor. His skin crawled. "We need out of this cursed place." He walked over and tugged on the handles of many doors. "Hurk! Get over here, Eethum, and help me!"

The dwarves remained kneeled, holding hands, heads bowed over their fallen comrade.

Venir tried the next. Then another after that.

"You need a Key, Venir," Boon said, with Fogle standing by his side, panting.

"I've got my own Key." Venir swung Mood's axe into the wood, juttering his arms. "Son of a Bish! It's harder than stone."

"It's magic," Boon said, taking a stroll around the room. "Hmmm... six doors." He peeked into the alcove, where seven lonely pegs remained. "I'll be. Strange. Tricky."

"What?" Fogle's face was drawn up as he shook underling guts from his robes.

"This room," Boon said, his voice filled with wonder, "I believe is an ancient device I've read about before. It's a Chamber of Transportation. As I understand, it can take you anywhere in the world. Very mysterious magic this is. Ancient. Dark. Dangerous." He ran his hand over one of the doors. "If the underlings have the Keys... my... well, that would explain a lot of things."

"Any idea where we are now?" Fogle asked.

"If you still have a map in that spellbook, we can certainly find out."

"And what of that barrier you created, Boon?" Fogle said. "How long will that hold?"

"Hours, unless they bust through it or have a mage to dispel it, and I don't think they do."

Venir made his way around the room, testing the doors anyway while he gathered his thoughts. Fogle had changed a great deal. The lines on his face were hardened, and his skin was darkened and tough. The wizard even had a ragged beard covering his face, giving him a dwarfish look.

Fogle caught him staring. "I'm glad we found you, Venir. And I'm sorry about your dog—and Mood. I spent a great deal of time with the both of them, looking for you."

Venir nodded and turned away. So much had happened. He didn't know what to think. His friends, the best ones he'd ever known, were all gone on account of him. The armament was gone as well. He felt naked without it. Still he lived. And Slim, what had happened to him? Had that man given Venir his very life?

"Aw, give me that book, Fogle," Boon grumbled, taking it away. "You're got mintuar hooves for fingers. It's a wonder you managed to write down anything."

"At least I don't waste what I've written."

"Pah, here it is," Boon said, fingering the book. "Just give me a few minutes."

Leaning against one of the doors, Venir squatted down, took a deep breath, and closed his eyes. He was tired, and his bones were aching.

Boon and Fogle stretched out a mystic map on the mosaic floor and gawped. Then one said to the other, "We're in Bone!"

"What?"

"Venir," Boon said, waving him over. "Look at this."

Venir raised his big frame off the floor and sauntered over. Boon's aged and crooked finger was pointing down on a map that shrunk and grew with a wave of his hand. Venir could see everything. He pointed at a red dot that was located on a drawing of a castle.

"I can see the entire city," Venir said, wiping his brow with his forearm. "I can even see the alleys. Huh, that's Castle Almen."

"Are you certain?" Boon asked, perching one eyebrow.

Venir glared at him. "I'm certain."

Boon rose to his feet and tugged at his white beard. "Hmmm... They've taken over a Castle. Possibly many of them."

"Or the entire city," Fogle said.

"Then that means they'll be coming right back for us," Boon said, eyeing the stone wall that protected them. "Any minute now. We're at the very heart of the battle now. Hah! We may have just squandered their plans after all. But I sense something. Someone familiar."

"I sense something too, Grandfather," Fogle said. "Are you thinking what I'm thinking?"

Venir didn't know nor care what either one of them was thinking. He just watched. They clasped hands.

But knowing that they were back in Bone? A place he thought he'd never see again? That sent a charge right through him! He was ready now. Ready to tear the wall down and carve a bloody path back to the Drunken Octopus. He warmed his hands on the glow of one of the torches.

Boon and Fogle cried out. The pair, fingers locked, were shaking. Eyes rolled up in their heads.

Venir tried to separate them, but Eethum stayed his hand.

"No," he said in a stern voice, "there's nothing we can do now. They're in a battle they must fight on their own."

Crack.

Boon's wall of stone cracked and began to crumble.

Eethum and the two other dwarves surrounded the interlocked wizards. "We'll protect them as long as we can."

Venir took his place at the bottom of the steps. "I'll kill underlings as long as I can."

CHAPTER 69

"Lead the way, Detective," Creed stepped aside.

Still holding Lorda's hand, he brushed past Creed's chest.

"Beg Pardon," the man said. "But that's worth risking your life for."

"You incorrigible, Piiii—"

Two clawed hands burst through the wall. Lorda was yanked through the wood and plaster, leaving a gaping hole.

"What in Bish was that thing?" Creed said.

Melegal darted through the hole and found himself facing his worst nightmare. It was Eep the imp, hovering in the air, holding Lorda Almen by the neck in his clawed fingers.

"We meetsss again, Skinny One," the imp said. Its long tongue licked up and down Lorda's dangling body, which kicked and flailed.

Melegal only had one dart in his launcher. He took aim.

Better make it count.

"Drop the woman!" Creed said, stepping into the clear, swords ready. "Slat, you're an ugly thing. What in Bish are you?" He looked at Melegal.

"An imp."

Creed shrugged. "Drop her, Imp, or taste my steel."

Eep laughed, rose twenty feet high into the throne room, and dropped her.

I've found them, Mastersss.

Found who? Verbard replied.

The Skinny Man who had the Keys, a woman, and the murdering swordsman you seek.

Where?

In the Throne Room.

"That was fast," Catten said. "Even for an imp."

Suddenly, Verbard's and Catten's eyes locked.

It cannot be, Brother, Verbard thought.

"But it is," Catten hissed through curled lips.

Someone was searching for them. An old enemy. A great foe. An enemy they'd fought decades ago.

"Boon! And his grandson, Fogle!"

"How did they get here? Where did they come from?"

"They must be in the chamber."

Verbard fingered the Keys in his pocket, as did Catten. They were all there except the one Kierway had lost, the one that led to Outpost Thirty-One.

"So they were the source of all the commotion? They're here? How did they make it through an entire army?" Catten was outraged. The surrounding castles were still attacking, and he'd sent all their reserves to Outpost Thirty One for reinforcements. How many giants had arrived down there?

"What do you want to do, Brother?" Verbard said.

Catten slipped the cap on his head. "Boon is not what he was; I can sense it. And his grandson is still green." Catten rubbed at his side where Fogle had zinged him months before. "I think I can hold them."

"Then I'm after that swordsman, whoever he is," Verbard said. "Jottenhiem, come with me and bring every soldier you can spare. We'll wipe this out quickly."

CHAPTER 70

FOGLE'S KNEES KNOCKED. HIS CHIN rattled. His mind rocked and reeled. The image of the golden eyed underling Catten snickered in his head. He and Grandfather were somewhere else. A battlefield in the inner mind, inescapable and chaotic.

"Grandfather! Grandfather!" he sputtered out, fingers knotted around Boon's.

The old man's body withered and sagged to the ground, making a feeble gasping sound.

Fogle remembered the last time he'd locked minds with Catten. It had almost killed him, and now, the underling was prepared. Enlightened. More powerful.

"You will die, Human. You and the old man both."

Biting into his lip, Fogle felt his mind collapsing on itself, turning dark and filling with despair.

Hold on, Fogle. Hold on.

The voice was weak and distant.

The underling was slowly ripping Fogle's mind from his grandfather's. A great gaping maw filled with razor sharp teeth was ready to devour them. Swallow them into an abyss forever. A long yellow knotty tongue lashed out around his grandfather's waist and reeled the old man in. Boon's face was sagging and withered, his grip, once strong as iron, struggled to hang on.

I won't let him go! Fogle's feet anchored themselves to the warbling floor. *I beat you once! I can beat you again!*

Catten chuckled and spiked a shard of power in his head.

"Aargh!"

The pain stabbed between his eyes. Excruciating. His entire body felt like it was melting into a gooey drop, ready to be swallowed whole.

Think, Fogle! Think!

His fingers slipped from his grandfather's.

On the other side of things, Catten was laughing and dusting his long nails on his robes.

"This cap is amazing," he said to himself, making his way out of the arena. He thought of his brother and Master Sinway. "It gives me that edge I've been seeking."

The stone wall crumbled. The first underling rushed through. Its head was splattered all over the walls.

"Ten!" Venir roared.

But the stairwell was three beasts wide, and the ranks of underlings deeper than a well.

Hack! A clawed hand was lost.

"Elven!"

Crunch! A chest caved in.

"Twelve!" Blood spurted from an underling's neck.

Glitch!

Venir took a punch to the shoulder, lost his footing and stumbled backward.

"Blast yer hides!" he screamed, swinging wildly, keeping them at bay.

"Get over there, Black Beards!" Eethum yelled and ran at the same time.

Three dwarves in heavy armor rushed forward, plugging the stairwell. Steel clashed on steel. Axes splintered bone. Long knives sifted through weak points on armor. Slowly, the dwarves, busted and bleeding, were being pushed backward.

Venir took a quick glance over his shoulder. The wizards had collapsed on the floor. Like their bones were missing. They twitched. He growled. The underlings had taken his friends, and now they had taken his city. He was tired of losing. A raging storm ignited inside him.

"Rrrrrah!"

Charging, he leapt over the dwarves into the underlings.

Yes, Fogle. Yes! Boon said to him, his withering voice stronger than before. *Do it! Do it quick!*

Fogle hung on. Struggling for his sanity, bearing every cruel twist and turn, searching for a weakness in the underling's probing mind. He summoned The Darkslayer. The underling laughed. One door slammed closed. *Find another.* Fogle found something. *Yes.* The green amulet that he'd given to Venir to track him. *Yes.* He'd put it in Catten's robes when he exchanged them for his spellbook. It was a little something he'd planned on sharing with Boon when the time was right.

The time is right now! Boon said. The old wizard's eyes were opened wide. He grappled with the tongue that held him. Grabbing the lip of the beast that tried to swallow him, his arm now held a pick-axe, which he sunk into its lip and held on. *I can hold on! Let me go and strike!*

"NO!" Fogle said, "I can't risk it!"

You've no choice now. The iron in Boon's eyes had returned. *Do something. Quick! Before he finds out!*

"I can't get out of here." Fogle said.

Do it!

Boon, geared up in his mystic armor and sword, dove into the belly of the beast and disappeared.

"Noooooooooo!"

CHAPTER 71

Melegal and Creed arrived at the same time, catching Lorda, who'd fainted.

"Nice catch," Creed said, looking upward.

Eep's wings buzzed. He was laughing. *Blink!*

"Watch out!" Melegal said.

Eep popped up behind Creed. *Slash! Slash!* Tore into his back. *Blink!*

"Argh!" Creed said. "Bish!"

Melegal's head swiveled on his shoulders. He'd seen the imp tear men into dog food in seconds. *Run! Get Lorda and get out of here!*

Creed turned his back to him and said, "How bad is it?"

Two bloody gashes formed a nasty X beneath his shoulders.

Eyes intent, Melegal took a quick glance.

"Just a scratch."

He moved away. *Where is that thing?* His eyes drifted towards the only exit. "No," he said, shoulders sagging.

"What?" Creed said, looking around.

Several underlings entered the room.

Eep buzzed alongside a floating underling with bright silver eyes. Accompanying him was a burly underling soldier with a shaven head and dark ruby eyes. Lord Almen's whip glowed in his grip. Four other underlings in dark chain armor escorted them. The floating underling hesitated in midair a moment, pointing at Creed as it spoke.

"Jottenhiem, Eep, kill him. Leave the skinny one to me."

Creed could feel them. Sense them. They were going to kill him.

"Let's give it a go then. Shall we?"

One by one, the four underlings, brandishing a variety of sharp blades, surrounded him. He glanced at Eep, his keen ears keeping track of the buzzing. *Not going to let that happen again.*

The bald underling with the whip chittered out a command. The well-trained team of underlings struck in unison.

Creed was already moving. He stepped into one underling. *Stab!* Piercing its heart in a lightning fast strike. *Swish!* He ducked under the next cutting blade.

Clang! Slit!

He ripped the sword out of one's hand and took its throat.

Gulch!

Gored the face of another.

Slice!

Tore the innards from the third.

Chop! Chop! Chop! Chop!

And butchered the fourth's head like a melon.

He took a bow.

"Next."

The imp and the whip-wielding underling circled him.

Blink!

The imp was gone.

The bald underling uncoiled the mystic whip and grinned.

Wupash!

"Oh, Great."

He backed towards the thrones. He had no sense of where the imp was. He needed a barrier on his backside. *You won't be getting to my back again.*

Blink!

Eep re-appeared right in front of his face and latched onto his chest.

"NOOOO!" Creed yelled. He dropped his swords. Grabbed the imp by the throat. The creature was solid. Muscle. Hard knotty skin and bone. He was no wrestler. "Get off me!"

Eep was merciless. Talons dug deep into his flesh. Its oversized jaws bit hard into his shoulder.

Creed punched the imp. It was like hitting a rock. He'd been in hundreds of fights, but he'd never faced anything supernatural like this. He punched and punched.

Wupash!

Eep blinked away, reappearing alongside Jottenhiem.

Creed sagged to his knees, fingers searching for his swords.

Wupash!

The whip coiled around his neck and jerked him to the ground.

Creed's head was burning hot. He clutched at the air.

Melegal's feet were lifted from the ground. He sailed right into Lord Verbard's powerful grasp. The underling squeezed his neck.

"Interesting for a human, you are. A survivor. I might have a use for you yet."

The words registered, but the meaning was lost. *I'm choking to death.* He twitched and recoiled from the depth of evil in those silver eyes.

A long shiver went through him when Verbard said, "Of course, it all depends on how long your breath can last. Can it last longer than my grip, Little Rat?"

CHAPTER
72

"Eh..." Catten mumbled, his golden eyes flaring.

Boon, a forgotten nemesis, had become a great fish hooked and struggling on his line.

"So be it, Enemy! I'll kill you first and take your grandson next."

He released his grip on Fogle Boon's mind, blasted every stitch of armor from Boon's body with a single thought, and started shoving Boon's broken form into a deep, dark, grave.

Fogle gasped. Breathing again, recollecting his senses, he crawled over to his spellbook and thumbed through the pages. Blinking hard and trying to block out the sounds of battle that echoed in the chamber, he found the page he needed.

He pressed his finger on the first word.

"I never thought I'd do this." He touched his grandfather's unmoving form. Boon was ashen and cold. Knowing it would erase the spell, Fogle read straight from the book.

The first word was soft, like a drink of sweet wine. The next syllable exploded in his mind, taking it yonder and back in a split second. His face lit up. His back straightened when the last syllable fell. "Eethum, get ready!" The page of the spellbook faded into smoke.

The air sizzled, shimmered and crackled.

Underling Lord Catten materialized before them, his wizened face gaping.

"What!" he said, outraged. Bewildered. "You shall pay for—"

Slice!

Eethum's stroke took his head from his shoulders. Its bright golden eyes rolled over the ground.

"I did it," he said, looking at Eethum. "He's dead. He's really de—"

Clang! Bang! Crunch!

Fogle whipped his aching head around. *Venir!* Buried in underlings, the big man was in for.

The underlings. Their hatred was deep. Venir's was deeper.

Chop!

Rage. They ignited it. He hated them. The smell of them. The sight of them. The oily stink of them. And he was going to kill them. Kill them all.

Hack!

He was a hurricane. Dwarven steel gone wild.

He launched a fatal blow into a bright blue-eyed underling's chest.

Sixteen!

Venir was no longer a man, but now a savage animal. Hungry. Starving. Battling for survival. For supremacy!

He brought both axe-blades down hard on a helmeted underling's head, splitting its skull to the teeth. Wrenched his blades free.

Two underlings jumped on top of him, pinning down his arms.

Slice!

A curved blade lashed out across his leg.

Down he went with five underlings on top of him. He fought like a tiger. He fought like a beast. He lost his blades. Something hard, heavy, struck his head. He could not feel. His vision blurred. He swallowed blood. He spit blood. He saw blood.

Small blades rose and fell.

He was going to die. He was certain. He booted one in the nose.

"Remember," he said. "I killed a thousand of you, and you only killed one of me!"

Crack! Stab Slash!

Venir didn't feel a thing. *Fight and die.* Everything faded. Fuzzy. Black.

Chop! Chop! Chop!

What was that?

Something was stuffed in his mouth. He tried to spit it out.

"Chew!" the Blood Ranger ordered. The Black Beards, the two that were left, kneeled along his side, beards dripping wet.

It hurt to swallow, but he did. Then he glanced at his burning belly. It was open, in more places than one.

"Got any Elga bugs?" Venir looked over a Black Beard's shoulder. "Say, what happened to that underling?"

The stone wall was back. A breathing underling was stuck inside it.

Eethum tore a piece of string off his sleeve with his teeth, threaded a fine needle, and started sewing Venir's belly up.

"Hold on," Venir said to Eethum.

Rising to his feet and holding his innards in, Venir limped over, grimacing, and jammed his axe in the trapped underling's head. Sat and lay down again.

"Here," Fogle said, holding a canteen to his lips. "Drink."

Venir pushed it away. "I'm not an infant, and I'll have no part of a bearded nanny."

Boon forced himself up into sitting position and put his throbbing head between his knees.

"Did you get him?" Boon said, holding his stomach.

"One of them," Fogle said, holding Catten's head up by the hair.

Boon blanched.

"You cut his head off! With a sword!"

Fogle smiled. "Eathum did. With an axe as big as my head."

"Well, that's a big axe alright, but," Boon paused, "the other one, Silver Eye?"

"Haven't gotten him yet."

Boon sighed. "How much have you got left?"

"About as much as you, I'd guess."

Boon rubbed his forehead and held his trembling hand out. The fire was back in his eyes. "Give me that spellbook."

CHAPTER 73

J OTTENHIEM YANKED ON THE WHIP, jerking Creed from his feet and slinging him across the room into the hard wall behind a tapestry.

Creed felt every bit of it.

Wupash!

The dark purple light of the mystic whip ripped the skin from his arm.

Wupash!

It coiled around his other arm, burning like fire. Jottenhiem pulled him across the floor.

Creed screamed. The pain was maddening. It shocked every inch of his body.

"Let me eatss him!" The imp said, wringing its taloned hands and gnashing its over-sized jaws. They opened so wide, Creed could see his entire body fitting inside the imp's mouth.

He grabbed at the whip and cried out.

Jottenhiem slung him into another wall.

Wupash!

He cracked the whip into Creed's blood-seared back again and again.

Wupash!

The whip coiled around his neck with only The Cowl protecting him.

"Go ahead, Imp," Jottenhiem said, flashing his sharp teeth, "I'll hold him still. You eat."

Eep smacked his thin lips and slowly buzzed over.

Creed tried to scream, but he couldn't. All he could do was scream in his mind.

NOOOOO!

Rage mixed with helplessness. The urgings from his cowl now shrouded by the pain. Creed outstretched his arms and flexed his fingers.

I'm not going to die like this!

The imp was fifteen feet away. Ten. Five.

No! Not like this! Where are my swords?

Two sharp objects shot across the room into his hands.

My blades!

Eep paused and blinked.

Creed sunk one blade through its eye before the lid could open.

Slice!

He cut the whip away. The imp twitched and howled, sporadically flying all around.

Slice! Slice!

He clipped one buzzing wing, then the other.

Blink! The imp vanished.

Creed took a deep breath. *That was close.* His arms were shredded. He dripped blood. He hobbled when he moved. He wanted to rest. Heal.

The Cowl wouldn't allow it.

Suck it up, Creed.

Jottenhiem tossed the broken whip away and came running with his swords. They collided at the center of the room, sword hilts locked together. Shoving back and forth, Jottenhiem held his ground. The underling, though smaller, was far stronger than he looked.

Jottenhiem cracked Creed in the jaw with his head, bringing painful spots and slicing right at him.

Clang!

He deflected a blow.

Clang!

Then another.

Jottenhiem sneered, reversed his grips, and came after him slicing, stabbing and spinning. The bald underling was almost as fast as Kierway, but a different skill of fighter. Hours ago, Jottenhiem would have been far better, but that was hours ago. Much had changed in the past few hours.

Creed whipped his blades under Jottenhiem's nose in a flurry. "Smell that, Underling?"

Jottenhiem's lips twisted.

"Smells of death, doesn't it?"

The underling tore into him. Blades clashed. Showers of sparks went everywhere. Creed felt his hatred growing. His skill increasing. The battle led out of the Throne Room and into another.

Clip! Slit! Clip!

Jottenhiem bled from three separate wounds.

Slit! Clip! Slit!

One ear dangled, and an X on Jottenhiem's forehead dripped blood into his eyes. He broke off.

"Thinking about running, aren't you, Underling?" Creed shrugged, gasping. "But there's no honor in being a coward, is there? Come on, then." He waved him over. "At least you don't have a whip around your throat."

Something propelled him forward, attacking the underling with unrelenting fury.

Bang! Bang! Bang!

Jottenhiem's corded arms started to give, snapping back up slower and slower. It was fatal.

"Enough of this!"

Creed ripped at Jottenhiem with all his might, tearing one sword from his hand.

Jottenhiem gasped.

Flash!

Creed tore the other one out.

Jottenhiem's ruby red eyes were full of hatred. Anguish.

He shook his head, took a knee and bowed.

Creed's next stroke was lights out.

"No!" Verbard moaned. "No!" His silver eyes darted around. Looking for a ghost.

Clutching Melegal with both hands now, the underling's silver eyes filled with anger and dismay. Whatever happened had been bad for the underling. Whenever bad things happen to underlings, worse things happen to people.

Melegal clutched at the underling's wrists and tried to kick at its guts.

Let go!

The ring from Sefron's chamber glimmered on Melegal's finger, and a charge of energy coursed through him.

Zzzzt!

Verbard's brows lifted. His face contorted. His jaw dropped open. "Argh!" The underling yelled, releasing Melegal and clutching his head.

Coughing, Melegal hit the floor, legs moving towards Lorda. The woman had sat up and was rubbing her head, blinking. "Get up, Lorda. Head for that door!" He glanced back.

Verbard spun in the air, shaking his head, arms coiling with mystic energy.

Here it comes!

Zzzzram!

Tendrils of lightning leapt from Verbard's finger, striking Melegal full in the back.

He skittered across the floor, reeling in pain, mouth tasting like metal and stone. Teeth screaming. He couldn't move, but he twitched, fingers curled, stomach knotting, his nose filling with the stench of his seared skin and hair.

Verbard floated over, gloating, and raised his arms.

This is it, Melegal. He found Lorda's eyes once more and mouthed the words, *So long.*

She reached for him.

Melegal crossed is arms over his face.

Zzzzram!

Boom!

Creed didn't stop with Jottenhiem. He didn't stop with the imp. He kept going. Limping. Hunting. Sliding from one room to another like a shadow, he slaughtered every underling he honed in on.

I know where you are.

Most of them didn't see him coming. For those who did, it was too late. One dead underling became two. Two became four. Four became eight. It was a glorious thing.

Melegal's shaking slender fingers patted over his body. *I'm still intact!* He wasn't alone either.

Two robed men stood in front of him, coated with transparent swords and shields. One's hair was long white and wispy, the other looked like he'd just crawled out of the woods. They were accompanied by a blood-bearded giant dwarf and two smaller black beards.

Melegal didn't stick around to thank them. Instead, he scooped Lorda up and headed for the door.

"Heh..." he breathed, stretching his aching fingers into his clothes and grabbing one of three Keys he'd pilfered from the underling Verbard's robes. He shoved the Key in the nearest door and turned. The door opened. "Let's get out of here. Shall we?" He'd hesitated, starting to turn back, when the room shook in its entirety. Shards of marble careened through the air.

A powerful figure shoved him inside and closed the door behind them. His mind and body started to spin. *Creed!*

CHAPTER 74

"You first," Boon said after opening up a black dimension door.

Fogle gave him a look.

"I cast the spell, and I'm your elder. If it makes you feel any better, take the dwarves with you."

Fogle summoned his power, coating his body in a transparent layer of blue energy and a shield. Armor, mystical or not, wasn't something he was at all accustomed to. As a matter of fact, he'd never worn so much as a bracer before.

"Let's go," he said to Eethum.

Holding his stomach, Venir said, "I'll go too."

"No, we'll need you to pull us out if things go wrong," Boon said, handing him the end of a rope tied to his waist. "If you hear us scream, tug it."

"Let the dwarf tug it," Venir growled. "I'm going in... oof!" Clutching his stomach he took a knee.

"Go, Fogle," Boon said, "I'll be right behind."

Stepping through, they found themselves in the Throne Room facing the back of a robed underling that hovered over a man and woman he did not recognize.

Fogle flicked a green missile into its back. *Zip!*

The underling's arms sprawled out.

Zzzzram!

Boom!

The underling's energy, meant for the man and woman, shot up into the ceiling.

Eethum and the Black Beards charged.

The underling, Verbard, whirled around, silver eyes flashing. With a wave of his hand, he knocked the dwarves around the room, slamming them into the wall.

"Let him have it, Grandson!" Boon yelled, energy erupting from his hands.

A bolt of power slammed into the underling's chest and dissipated. Fogle fired his own charge, which careened towards the underling and disappeared into the underling's robes.

The underling reached into his robes and pulled out a glowing orb of power.

Fogle started to fire again, but Boon stayed his hand.

"This is not good for us."

Verbard laughed.

A burst of energy blinded them.

Fogle heard his grandfather scream.

Facing the black doorway, Venir tugged at the rope. Nothing happened.

"I better get in there," he said, staggering towards the black door.

Srrit!

It disappeared.

"Slat!" He rubbed the back of his head. "Stupid mages! I knew I should have gone with them."

He could see it now, the two of them fighting the underling mage with the silver eyes. He knew it was him. They had said so. Now, he was trapped inside the blood hungry chamber with nowhere to go.

Fogle's wall of stone cracked again.

Venir picked up Mood's axes.

"It's just you and me, underlings."

Creak...

Behind him, one of the six doors opened.

Venir's jaw dropped.

Out came Melegal, whose eyes were as wide as his.

"Vee?"

"Me?"

"I knew you were behind all this!" Melegal said.

"Uh!"

A beautiful black-haired woman was shoved to the floor behind Melegal. The skinny thief jumped away and whirled.

"Creed, what are you doing?" Melegal said, backing away.

A tall rangy form stepped from beyond the threshold. He pointed a gleaming sword at Melegal's scrawny chest with one hand and held a jug of wine with the other.

Venir wiped the sweat and red grime from his eyes with his forearm and locked eyes with the man he'd all but forgotten about months ago.

"Tonio!"

"Vee-Man!"

Nullified.

That's what happened to the plan.

Boon had planned on overwhelming Verbard with his grandson, spell after spell, while the dwarves wove in and out, attacking. It might have worked if it weren't for something Boon hadn't foreseen. The Orb of Imbibing.

"Defend yourself, Fogle!"

Zzzram!

Zzzram!

Verbard launched one blast into them after the other, shattering their mystic armor and skipping them across the floor.

Boon tried to summon the dimension door again, but could not.

Verbard pressed the assault. Not letting him get a word out. The underling hovered over them now, draining their powers.

"Which one of you killed my brother?"

"I did," Boon lied, "and it was quite satisfying. Like a tender piece of veal cooked just right." Boon licked his lips. "The death of underlings is an excellent dessert."

One Black Beard had been crushed inside his armor. The other was out cold. Eethum lay on the floor bound up by yellow magic cords. Fogle's grandfather was a horrible negotiator.

Be silent, Fogle wanted to say, but his tongue was made of wool. Fogle had thought he was ready for anything by now, but he wasn't ready to not be able to use magic.

He gazed at the orb that pulsated in Verbard's hand like a beating heart. *Bish is just one excruciating surprise after another.* He tried to lock minds with Verbard.

"You dare!" the underling Lord hissed, squeezing his telekinetic fingers around his neck. Fogle was choking. Beside him, Boon clutched at the invisible fingers wrapped around his own neck, face turning purple. Verbard was getting stronger as he got weaker. There was nothing, nothing at all he could do. Was there? Searching the deepest recesses of his mind, he had to find the answer. He had to find the key. He heard his neck crack. Or was it Boon's?

"Finally," Tonio said, shattering his wine jug against the wall, "I'll have your head."

Shoulders lowered, axes bared, Venir charged in. "No! I'll have yours!"

Krang!

Tonio's gleaming sword tore Venir's axe from his wrist. The half-dead man was powerful and fast.

Venir ducked under a decapitating cut and tore a gash across Tonio's belly.

Tonio laughed. "You already killed me, Vee-man! You can't kill me again. Sorry yet?"

Whack!

Venir cut across his leg, but Tonio countered, punching Venir's bullish form in the face, cracking his nose open. Spitting blood from his mouth, Venir squared off again, shoulders dipping, belly aching. Whatever Tonio was, it wasn't mortal.

"I've been searching for you a long time, Vee-Man." He ran his fingers down his gash. "I'm going to split you in half as well. Show you how bad it feels. You ruined my life. You ruined everything!"

Venir forced a laugh at him. "Especially your face!"

Tonio grunted and stuck his sword into the stone. "Come on then," he said, walking over, "see what you can do with that little axe of yours."

"I'll be glad to show you, Tonio!"

Slic—

Tonio caught his arms and wrenched the axe free from Venir's hands.

Venir dug in, punching at the monster's ribs with his hardened fists.

Tonio didn't feel a thing.

Whop! Whop!

Venir's head snapped back. His knees buckled.

Melegal had seen Venir brawl with anything from underlings to half-ogres, but he'd never seen him fight something that couldn't be hurt or broken.

Tonio's speed and strength were Venir's match. Toe to toe, blow for blow, they fought and wrestled over the mosaic floor.

Come on, Vee!

Venir hammered away, an angry juggernaut, but his strength was fading.

A lightning fast strike caught Venir in the chin, wobbling him.

"Your head is mine, Vee-Man!"

Tonio wrapped his arms around Venir's head and squeezed. It turned red, then purple, his blazing blue eyes rolling up.

Move, Melegal!

Fogle thought of Cass. Dying, he still found himself angry with her for abandoning him—for a dragon of all things—and now, leagues from his home that smelled of flowers and sweet wine, he was going to die.

Verbard's fading face was gloating from above, sneering at him and his grandfather.

"I'm disappointed. I thought the pair of you would have more power that I could store in my orb. But the power I have should be enough to bring my brother back, once more, if I must."

Glitch!

A dark bloody sword burst into Verbard's chest and disappeared.

Glitch!

Another blade followed. In and out.

"No," Verbard said, incredulous, turning on his captor. "Where did you come from?

The man in the cowl with the glowing eyes stood tall, swords held in his thick wrists.

"Are you The Darkslayer?" Verbard said, splitting up blood and sagging to the floor.

Creed swung both swords at once.

Slice!

Verbard's head slid from his shoulders.

"I guess I am, Underling."

Fogle clutched at his chest, gasping.

Boon was doing the same. The old man, coughing, reached over and grabbed the Orb of Imbibing.

"Grab my hand, Fogle, so I can restore you. Quickly!"

Melegal whipped out the Sisters and struck Tonio in the back of the knee, tearing out tendon and flesh.

"What? You skinny flea!" Tonio teetered, losing his balance.

Venir bull rushed the man onto the floor and started to 'ground and pound' him, one blow after the other.

Tonio swatted the blows off and clutched at Venir's throat.

Stab!

Melegal pinned one of his swords through Tonio's shoulder.

Tonio caught him by the ankle and jerked him down.

Melegal tried to twist away from Tonio's grasp.

Snap.

His ankle cracked.

"You break like a twig!"

Venir was drunk with battle. He punched, kicked and clawed, almost oblivious to his opponent, but the arrogant tone in Tonio's voice kept him going.

"Ahhh!"

Melegal, his best friend and confident, cried out.

Tonio had the man's leg and still hung onto Venir's throat, holding them both in his vise-like grip.

Venir's instincts took over. He fumbled for a weapon. Found his long knife strapped to his leg. With both hands, he raised it over his head and drove it straight into Tonio's heart.

Crunch!

"That won't work, Vee-Man!" Tonio said. His grip was getting stronger. "I have no heart!"

Venir twisted the knife inside Tonio's chest.

Tonio's eyes widened. "Urk!"

Tonio's body shuddered.

"Grab an axe, Melegal!" Venir said, wrapping his arms around the monster, holding him to the ground.

Melegal hopped over towards the axe. "And do what?"

"Chop his head off!"

Melegal caught something in the corner of his eye.

I have a better idea.

Tonio slung Venir off and ripped the knife from his chest. "You already killed me! I'll make you sorry!"

Venir, huffing for breath, was too slow.

Tonio closed in, stabbing at him.

Melegal! What are you doing!

The thief was fooling with the underling on the blood-sucking floor.

Venir tried to dodge. Tried to block.

Glitch!

His own hunting knife caught him in the leg.

Twisting away, Tonio ripped a hunk out of Venir's back.

Slash!

Getting cut to pieces but still standing on his feet, Venir watched Tonio's final blow start down.

The monster's split face had a cruel smile on it. "Time to die, Vee-Man."

Tonio stopped, not moving a muscle, the bloody blade no longer coming down, a surprised look on his face.

"Venir," Melegal yelled, "catch!" The thief tossed him Mood's axe. "Be quick about it!"

Venir snatched it out of the air and whirled full force into Tonio's neck.

Slice!

Tonio's head bounced off the floor and rolled. His big body collapsed on the ground.

Venir collapsed as well. He snorted for air. Tried to shake the spots from his eyes. He reached over and pulled his knife from Tonio's grip.

"I knew I should have killed that Royal brat in the first place."

Pinching his nose, Melegal adjusted the dark cap on his head with the other hand, admiring Tonio's' corpse. He wiped the blood that dripped from his nose. *That was close.*

On the floor, Venir looked as bad as he'd ever seen him. It tugged at his heart a little. *Big lout.*

He helped Venir back to his feet.

"You know, you should have listened to me —"

"Don't start, Me."

CHAPTER 75

"**S**O WE ALL AGREE THEN," Boon said, standing in the alcove, eyeing the Keys on the pegs.

They were all there except one, which Melegal believed Jarla had.

Fogle didn't care much either way. The only thing that mattered was that the underlings didn't have the Keys. He looked back over at the Stone Wall he'd produced. It was still holding. Behind it were—he had no idea how many underlings.

The party all knew now that despite their victory today, the underlings were penetrating the City. The battle for Bone had just begun.

"Shouldn't we destroy the Keys and the chamber?" Fogle suggested.

Boon rubbed his brow. "That's up to you, Fogle. Take a Key and do with it what you like, but remember, it always leads back here. And as I understand it, the room is here now, but it might be elsewhere later."

"You mean it moves?" Melegal said, leaning against the wall, arms folded across his chest.

"That's how I understand it. But, I could be wrong. It might just stay here forever."

"And the big Key," Melegal said, eyeing the Key on the center peg, "who gets that? Does it work all the doors? Or just one?"

"I don't think we have time for that now," Boon said, twisting his beard. "The goal is to get the Keys out of the chamber and away from the underlings. Once we are free of this, you can do what you wish. Keep them or destroy them."

"Will you destroy yours?" Melegal said.

"Well, er," Boon added, "that's my concern. I think it might come in handy if I get stuck back in the Under-Bish." He looked at Venir. "It could increase our chance of freeing Mood from down there."

Melegal had already told them what his Key did. It would take him wherever he wanted to go, but it always led back to the chamber, where he would have to start all over again. Certainly the underlings would soon have a heavy guard on the chamber. He looked at Venir.

"What do you think?"

"Let's take them to the furnace and destroy them." Venir nodded over at the bodies of Tonio, Catten and Verbard. The underlings were eyeless now. "Or," he said, eyeing the sack that hung over Creed's shoulder, "we can drop them in there?"

"Hmmm..." Boon rubbed his chin. "I have another idea. Creed, would you oblige me and open the sack?"

Creed, cowl down, tossed the sack over to Boon. "Open it yourself."

Boon's eyes widened.

So did Venir's.

"Fogle, let me have the staff."

Taking it out of his backpack, Fogle tossed the staff to Boon, who dropped it into the sack.

"What did you do that for?" Creed said.

Boon stuck his arm inside, down to the elbow, and withdrew nothing.

"Care to try?" Boon held the sack out to Venir.

He took a breath and a step forward. He longed to have the armament back, but he longed for his own freedom too. "I'll pass."

Boon handed the sack back to Creed. "Try not to get too used to it, whoever you are."

Creed couldn't keep his gaze off Venir. The big man looked like he'd been chewed up by a dragon and spit out, but was used to it. Still, the dark circles under the man's bright eyes concerned him. He had the look of a man who'd faced every horror and form of death hundreds of times. He was elemental. Forged in iron.

"So, you used to have this?" Creed said as the others squabbled over the Keys.

"Aye, but it was different, as different as you and me."

"You like women?" Creed said, his voice deep and rugged.

Venir eyed him.

"You like wine?"

"Grog."

"You like fighting?"

"You just described every soldier in Bish."

"We're not so different, you and I."

Venir turned and faced him. Looked him up and down.

"I don't think so."

Creed, bigger than most men, felt small in that moment.

"Maybe one day we'll share our tales together," Creed said, smiling at Lorda. "Chat with some ladies. Share some wine ... er ... grog."

"No doubt you'll be hearing tales about me," Venir looked down at him, patting his shoulder. "That much is certain." Venir coughed a laugh. "And you'll need more than a goblet of wine to deal with that mantle."

Creed nodded, extending his hand. Venir took it in his. Hard as a rock. Like a vice. Creed grimaced a little.

"We've come to a decision," Boon said, snagging the Keys from the pegs. Keeping the big one for himself, he handed Keys to Eethum, Melegal, Fogle, Venir, Creed and Lorda. "Just give us a few minutes."

Fogle sat down and started reading from the spellbook while Boon held the glowing Orb of Imbibing in his hand. It pulsated with mystic life.

Minutes later, Boon said, "We're ready."

Fogle said, "Melegal, lead the way."

"Where are we going, Me?" Venir said.

"The furnace."

Venir walked over and pulled Tonio's shriveled head up off the sucking floor. "Good idea. We better burn this."

Melegal opened the door with the Key he was accustomed to.

"Everybody inside," Boon said.

One by one they entered, leaving the throbbing orb behind.

"And what is that for?" Eethum asked, pulling the door closed.

"It should destroy the chamber," Fogle answered.

"And possibly the castle," Boon added.

Lorda gasped as the door closed.

The stone wall Fogle Bone had created finally evaporated, to the glee of a stairwell full of underlings. Each of them watched the orb spinning in the room, getting bigger and bigger and bigger. Spinning faster, it started to whine and crackle. The underlings' gem-speckled eyes flittered back and forth at one another, gaping in confusion.

Finally, one said in underling, "Flee!"

Lord Almen was tattooed with long bolts sticking out of his legs and chest by the dozen. He kissed his mystic ring. The assault on him had stopped, and he crawled over to the door on top of the keep. Shaking and bleeding, he pulled it open.

I'll live! I'll avenge!

KA-BOOM!

The entire keep shook and then collapsed. Lord Almen fell through the roof that opened up, landing at the bottom in time to watch the rest of the keep collapse on top of him.

One by one, they tossed their Keys into the furnaces that fired beneath the busy streets of Bone. Hot and fiery flames reflected all over their shadow-cast and oily faces.

Boon pitched two pair of underling eyes in as well. One pair silver, the other pair gold.

Venir took one last look at Tonio's face, his mind eating at him. Had one isolated incident been the start of it all? What would have happened if he never fought Tonio to begin with?

"You aren't thinking, are you?" Melegal said.

Tonio's grey eyes popped open.

"Vee-Man!"

Lorda jumped, but the others remained still. "Tonio," she said, extending her hand and touching her son's face. An odd silence fell.

"Mother," Tonio said, black eyes returning to normal.

"Good-bye, Son," she sobbed, turning to walk away.

"But Mother," he said. His eyes turned black. Brows buckled. Lips curled. "You can't kill me, Vee-Man."

Venir held Tonio's head out over the vat of fire. "Maybe you can't be killed, but I bet you'll burn, Brat." He pitched him over the rim.

"Noooooooooo!"

"The city holds for now," Corrin said, taking a good look at the present company. "The Royals finally got off their arses and stirred a fight. I think the collapse of Castle Almen lit a fire under them."

Lorda Almen was crying on the bench by the fountain.

Melegal caressed her head. The woman had lost her home. Her entire family. He felt bad.

"Where to now, Melegal?" Venir said, drinking from the fountain. "You want to stay and fight, or do you want to go? You should have left for the City of Three last time, you know."

"Just a moment," Melegal said in Lorda's ear, releasing her petal-soft hands.

He limped his way over to Venir.

"Itching to see your family are you, Vee?" he said, smiling.

Venir stopped drinking and said, "What family?"

Splash! Splash! Splash! "Help!" Lorda Almen sounded like she was drowning. "Detective!" *Splash!* "Help!"

Turning, he saw Haze had Lorda's head stuffed down in the water. He hobbled over. Pulled her away.

Haze ripped a long blade across Melegal's chest.

"Are you mad?" he exclaimed, twisting the dagger from her hand.

She slapped his face. "I'm a one-man woman, and you're a one-woman man. Got that?"

He snickered. "Absolutely, my Lorda."

"Good," Haze said, "and I want to go to the City of Three. You promised me."

"No, I did —"

She glared at him.

"I suppose I did."

Corrin then said, "You aren't going anywhere. The city's under siege out there."

"You ever been out of the city before, Corrin?"

"No."

"You want to leave?"

"No, I'm going to stay and fight."

Creed stepped alongside Corrin. "This is where I'll be, as well."

"This is where you're supposed to be," Venir said.

"And what about me?" Lorda said, slinging her dripping wet hair over her shoulder.

Creed put his arm around her. "You're coming with me. The Bloodhounds can always use another queen."

The wizards approached.

"Get all the gear you can handle, men," Boon said. And then he noticed Haze's glare, "and woman. The underlings aren't going to let us congregate here forever. I can teleport you miles from the city, but you're on your own after that."

"I said I would never leave Bone again," Melegal said, shaking his head. "And I'm still certain you're the root cause of all this, Venir."

Limping towards the black dimension doors, Venir said, "Well, at least you have someone to blame. And what family are you talking about?"

Somewhere far away, the Elga bugs came. Slim's body went.

Master Sinway waited on his throne. Catten, Verbard and Kierway never arrived. He petted one of the Cave Dogs at his side and said, "This isn't over. It's just begun."

EPILOGUE

BRAK'S OVERSIZED BODY HELD TIGHT on the reins of Quickster as they rode into the City of Three. The poison had passed. He lived, but was far from back to himself again yet.

"Don't worry, Brak. We're almost there. We can get you a bed, healing and a comfortable room. And the stew you'll eat! As soon as you smell it, your mouth will water," Georgio said.

Georgio had been nicer to him since he almost died. But that probably had more to do with the City of Three than actual concern.

He wiped from his face the mist that blew in from the massive waterfalls he could see in the distance.

"Isn't that beautiful, Brak!" Jubilee said. "I've never even imagined anything like it. Billip, can we go there?"

"Yes," Nikkel said, "can we go there?"

"Soon enough. But I'm getting a gullet full at the Magi Roost first!" Billip said, smiling underneath the grit and sand that covered his face.

"I'm filling both my gullets!" Georgio said.

"You don't even know what a gullet is," Nikkel said, laughing.

"I do too."

"What is it, then?" Jubilee said.

"Uh... it's your belly."

Jubilee and Nikkel looked at each other and laughed.

"Isn't it?"

Everyone's mood lightened when they saw the city. Even Brak, who still felt as feeble as a kitten, felt better for it. He looked once up and down at the tall towers whose spires seemed to reach the clouds, but he wasn't impressed. He just wanted to rest. He was wondering about his father, Venir. He hadn't had any dreams about him lately. *Maybe he's dead.*

"This is it," Billip said, stopping in front of a building where a sign hung that read in bright letters, **THE MAGI ROOST.** Billip started dusting himself off. "Joline will kill me for going in there like this."

Georgio took off his boots, poured the rocks out and banged them together. He took a deep draw through his nose. "I can taste the stew already." He sniffed again and made a funny face. "And something else."

One at a time, Billip leading the way, they entered.

"Welcome, Travelers," a tall husky woman said. "Have a seat, and I'll get you some help."

Brak saw Billip and Georgio's hands fall to their sword belts.

"Just who in Bish are you?" Billip said, "And what have you done to this tavern?"

The Magi Roost was darker and filled with a seedier sort of characters. All the long robes and noses were gone. The smell of cheap wine and ale was in the air.

"And how did such an unattractive woman get in here? Where's Kam?" Billip demanded.

"Oh," the woman leaned over Billip with her hands on her hips. "You're one of her friends, are you?"

"Billip!"

It was Joline. She ran up and threw her arms around him, tears streaming down her face. "You're alive. I'm so glad you're alive." She kissed his cheek, then whispered in his ear. "But you need to get out of here."

"Joline!" a man sitting the bar said in a warning tone.

Billip gawped at him. He'd never seen such presence in a man before. Handsome, refined, distinguished, with eyes as blue as water.

"Don't dally with Darlene's patrons. She's likes to welcome them."

"I'm hungry, Joline," Georgio said, patting Joline on the back.

She shook her head. "You've changed so much, Georgio. You're a full grown man."

"Ah, I haven't been gone that long. Where's Kam?"

"Just grab a table," Joline said, "I'll get her."

"Mercy!" Darlene bellowed, "Get these folks a table!"

Mercy scampered over, chin down, and led them to their table.

"How have you been, Mercy?" Georgio said, hitching his arm over his chair and smiling.

"Georgio?" She seemed to wake up from a daze. "Georgio!" She sat down on his lap and hugged him. "I thought you'd never come back!" She whispered in his ear. "Just stay away from them." Her eyes flittered towards the woman Darlene and the man at the bar.

"Who is that?" he said. "I can handle him."

"No, no," she said, grabbing him by the collar. "Just leave them be, and they'll leave you be." She hopped off his lap. "I'll get you stew, to start." She eyed all of them. "And a big bowl for you, Georgio." She saw Brak. "And one for your friend, too." She patted Billip on the head. "I'm so glad you're back. So glad!"

"There's something spooky going on here," Billip said. "I don't recognize any of these people."

"Seems alright to me," Jubilee said, looking around. "Say, who's the beautiful lady with only one hand up there? That's kinda sad."

"What? There's no one in here with one hand," Georgio said, looking around. "Kam!"

She stood on the balcony in a long green dress, sunken eyed and waving her one-handed arm.

"Do you know her?" Jubilee said.

Billip said in disbelief, "What in Bish is going on here?"

FROM THE AUTHOR

U NFORTUNATELY, THE ENDING IS NEVER as much fun as the journey. As for this first series, there is more, I decided to wrap it up with this 6th book. It was time. I think readers wanted some resolution. That's what made it so difficult. I had a bunch of characters spread out all over Bish. That said, I didn't want to end it. Originally, I wanted this to be an ongoing saga, but I spread myself too thin and my writing was suffering for it. This first segment of Venir's life ends. But it feels good for me, finishing a full-length fantasy series.

Fear not, Darkslayer fans, the adventures of The Darkslayer will continue in the *Bish and Bone* series. Venir and Melegal's escapades are not over, if anything, it's just beginning, so hang in there. But I'm not spoiling things.

Next. THANK YOU! It has been my pleasure writing for you! Your support is a dream come true to me. My goal is to improve and write even better stories for you, but don't hold me to that. That way you won't be disappointed. ;)

So, will Venir and Brool be reunited? What do you think? But there is only one way to know for sure. Check out the next series, *Bish and Bone*.

Again, check in with me at The Darkslayer Report by Craig on Facebook. I want to hear what you thought of this series. And if you have time, I'd appreciate a sincere review.

Fight or Die,
Craig Halloran

ABOUT THE AUTHOR

Craig Halloran resides with his family outside of his hometown of Charleston, West Virginia. When he isn't entertaining mankind, he is seeking adventure, working out, or watching sports. To learn more about him, go to: www.thedarkslayer.com

OTHER WORKS BY CRAIG HALLORAN

The Darkslayer Series 1

Wrath of the royals (Book 1)

Blades in the Night (Book 2)

Underling Revenge (Book 3)

Danger and the Druid (Book 4)

Outrage in the Outlands (Book 5)

Chaos at the Castle (Book 6)

The Darkslayer Series 2

Bish and Bone (Book 1)

Black Blood (Book 2)

Red Death (Book 3)

The Chronicles of Dragon Series

The Hero, The Sword and The Dragons (Book 1)

Dragon Bones and Tombstones (Book 2)

Terror at the Temple (Book 3)

Clutch of the Cleric (Book 4)

Hunt for the Hero (Book 5)

Siege at the Settlements (Book 6)

Strife in the Sky (Book 7)

Fight and the Fury (Book 8)

War in the Winds (Book 9)

Finale (Book 10)

Zombie Impact Series

Zombie Day Care: Book 1

Zombie Rehab: Book 2

Zombie Warfare: Book 3

The Supernatural Bounty Hunter Files
(Coming 2015)
Smoke Rising
I Smell Smoke
Where there's Smoke
Smoke and Mirrors
Smoke on the Water

CONNECT WITH HIM AT

Facebook: The Darkslayer Report by Craig
Twitter: Craig Halloran

Printed in Great Britain
by Amazon.co.uk, Ltd.,
Marston Gate.